Echo of Bells

by

Jill Todd

Echo of Bells

First published in September 2016 by Black Pear Press
www.blackpear.net

Copyright © Jill Todd 2016

ISBN 978-1-910322-28-4

Cover design by Jill Todd and Mark Todd.
Background image from a photograph of Clutter's Cave,
by Moggz.

Black Pear Press

For Pete and Mark, my fantastic husband and son, without whose support and encouragement I would never have finished this story; and for my equally amazing Mum, who has cheerfully read more drafts than should be inflicted on anyone.

Acknowledgements

My thanks go to all those who were so generous with their time and knowledge: my son Mark (again), for his computer expertise, and for finding time to read the final draft; Leigh Salkeld, chartered certified accountant; Dee Eggleton, RGN; Lynne Sykes; David Bray, paramedic; Grace Edwards of Borth Tourist Information; and, last but certainly not least, my editors, Rod Griffiths, Tony Judge and Polly Stretton, of Black Pear Press.

THE FAMILIES

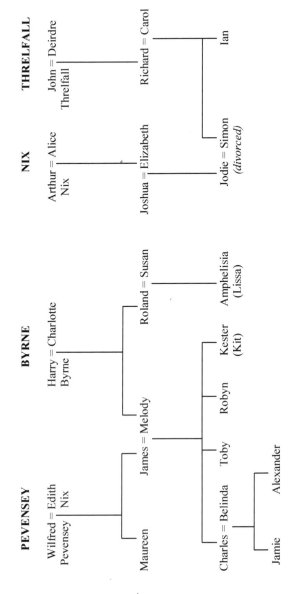

PEVENSEY

Wilfred = Edith
Pevensey Nix

Maureen   James = Melody

Charles = Belinda Toby Robyn Kester
                                  (Kit)

Jamie   Alexander

BYRNE

Harry = Charlotte
        Byrne

Roland = Susan

Amphelisia
(Lissa)

NIX

Arthur = Alice
         Nix

Joshua = Elizabeth

Jodie = Simon
    (divorced)

THRELFALL

John = Deirdre
       Threlfall

Richard = Carol

Ian

CHAPTER ONE

I shouldn't have left Grandad alone. I had phoned twice and left a voicemail, although I knew he would ignore any messages if he was working. Until four days ago— until the letter arrived—I wouldn't have bothered to call. But he had changed since then.

I glanced at the dashboard clock. Two-ten. In the hills dusk always fell early but today was different. Late November, louring clouds and a gale strong enough to bring down power lines. I could have waited and done the shopping tomorrow...

The first hailstones clattered on the roof. I turned on headlamps and wipers, battling to steer straight as my little Fiat shied at every gust. There were no lights anywhere. I had been right about the power.

In Little Malvern I took a left fork without slowing much, swung right at the Priory Church and up into Hereford Rise. Walkers never used this route on to the hills, and ours was the last house in the lane; it was safe to put my foot down. Still thinking about Grandad, I rounded the final bend.

Someone was there, walking straight towards me, too close to miss. With a yell I stamped on brake and clutch, and the car shrieked to a halt just as the man leaped aside and rolled into the ditch.

To my relief he stood up immediately, tapping his watch and brushing off his soaked and shabby overcoat. He looked about sixty and far from athletic, which made his fast reaction all the more surprising.

I opened the window and called out, 'I'm really sorry. Are you OK?'

Wind and hail rushed at me, stinging my face and whipping black coils of hair across my eyes. I scraped

1

back the tendrils and braced myself for some abuse—but with no more than a glance in my direction, the little man hurried off down the hill.

Closing the window again, I took several deep breaths and drove with exaggerated care up the slope towards home. I was still shaking when I turned in through the open gates of The Eyrie, parked outside the stables and snatched up my bags to make a dash for the house.

The kitchen door was unlocked as usual. As I went in, a gust slammed it behind me. Oh, well...I might have interrupted Grandad's train of thought, but at least he would have heard me come in. He would never admit to being slightly deaf.

Dumping my handbag along with the shopping, I shrugged out of my coat and called, 'Hi, Grandad. I'm back.'

No reply. I went through into the Tudor hall, the largest room in the house. The oak panelling and leaded windows gave it a permanent gloom, deepened now by the twilight. I flicked a light switch, without result.

Grandad's hat and coat hung on their customary peg. In the study I found his chair turned from the desk as if newly vacated, the desk itself strewn with papers. I cupped a hand around an abandoned mug of coffee, and the china struck cold.

It was then that the worries coalesced into fear. I ran back into the hall, calling again. The sound rang hollowly up into the stairwell, throwing back mutterings from the minstrels' gallery above. Just echoes...but the house didn't *feel* empty. I glanced over my shoulder at the massive chimneybreast, the only place where I had ever seen or imagined anything supernatural.

'Don't be so stupid,' I said aloud.

The door under the stairs was ajar. The cellar door. I opened it wide and looked down into blackness. The flight of stone steps was steep but there was a handrail, and the original, worn treads had been replaced a few years ago. In the light, no problem.

'Grandad?'

The answer came like a sigh, a soft exhalation that might even have held my name. 'Lissa...'

Fear snatched at my breath—and my eyes were getting used to the dark. I flew down the steps and with shaking horror knelt beside the still figure at their foot.

'Grandad!'

He said something, a formless whisper, unintelligible. I had been out for two hours; he could have been lying here for that long.

The big torch from the kitchen drawer lay close to his head. He must have fallen before he had time to turn it on. I snatched it up, and in my trembling hand the light danced over the blood matting his hair. The wound in his temple gleamed sickeningly and the flagstones under his head looked black. A dark puddle filled a dip in the floor. How do you measure a pool of blood? Was that a lot or just enough to scare me?

I spoke to him again and touched his face. He didn't know I was there. The glitter from beneath the half-closed lids was only reflected torchlight. His lips moved, the whisper just audible. 'Love...love.'

He never called me that.

'It's all right,' I said. Pointless words, and I was crying as well, but he couldn't hear me anyway.

'Loves...' he whispered. 'My fault. Told the truth...too late. Must tell Lissa.'

I clasped his cold hand. 'I'm here. It's all right.'

'Tell Lissa I'm sorry. We did it for the best. May God forgive us.'

My phone was upstairs in my handbag. 'Grandad, I'm going to ring for an ambulance. I'll be straight back. Can you hear me? I'll be very quick.'

When I left him, he was still murmuring, 'Tell her…we did it for the best.'

*

I travelled with Grandad in the ambulance, doing my best to answer his disjointed, meaningless phrases. The paramedics said there was a chance he could hear me, but there was no reassurance in that. When we finally made it to Accident and Emergency the doctors took charge and he was wheeled away at speed.

I walked on shaky legs to find a couple of free seats in the waiting area, hoping that Charles would arrive at any moment; but it was still only four-fifteen. If he was at the shop and dealing with customers, he wouldn't have picked up my text.

I heard the memory of Grandad's voice, half-joking, 'You may have the backbone of a jellyfish, girl, but try not to tremble in public. What would your dad think of you?'

But I had no way of knowing. Mum and Dad had died when I was three. As well as being a substitute father, Grandad was my employer, which gave me security but less independence than most twenty-five-year-olds took for granted. If he were to die…

I looked at my watch again. Four-seventeen. *Oh, Charles, how busy can an antique shop be?*

As if on cue, a shadow fell across me and a familiar voice said, 'God, Lissa, I'm sorry I took so long.'

I stood up with a sob of relief, and all six-foot-three of Charles Pevensey, my eldest cousin, enfolded me in a soggy embrace.

'What a night!' he said. 'Saturday traffic and a bloody monsoon. Have they told you anything yet?'

'No.'

'Thank God I picked up your message.' Letting me

go, he shivered and raked the dripping black curls off his forehead. 'Let's hunt down a drinks machine, eh?'

He bought us coffee and I told him everything, even about the letter.

'I don't know who it was from,' I said. 'Grandad told me it was none of my business. But he seemed to...to shrink somehow. As if he'd had really bad news.'

'Maybe he was still upset about old Mr Threlfall dying. They went back a long way.'

'I shouldn't have left him, should I?'

'That's nonsense.' He gave my shoulder a squeeze. 'Can you see his reaction if you'd started treating him like a geriatric case?'

I managed a faint smile. 'Yes. Oh, Charles, I'm so glad you're here.'

'Look, er...you'd better know, I rang Mum. She and Dad are on their way. Lissa, please don't look like that. You're not really afraid of her, are you?'

'Why shouldn't I be? You are. And she hates me.'

'She doesn't hate you. And *I'm* not scared of Mum. I keep the peace where I can, that's all.'

'I know it's Grandad's fault. The way he talks...You've heard him. "Thank God for Lissa. At least she's not a vulture like my daughter."'

Charles looked uncomfortable, but he'd had to make the call. With my father dead, Aunt Melody was Grandad's only surviving offspring.

'She'll b-blame me, won't she?' I said, the childish stammer catching at my words at the thought of Aunt Melody's wrath.

I was hoping her eldest son would deny it, but he didn't.

*

A doctor came to see us ten minutes later. I guessed at once, from the defeat in his face, even though some residue of hope made me wait with thumping heart and silent prayers.

He took us into a private room. 'I'm very sorry,' he said. 'Your grandfather had lost a great deal of blood, and his age was against him. I'm afraid he died without regaining consciousness.'

'May I—may we see him?'

He lay in the room where they had tried to save him. No longer attached to the tubes and monitors around the bed, he looked very peaceful. His face was clear of pain and strangely smooth, the lines of age, concentration and temper all less noticeable now.

Charles said quietly, 'If you'd like to be alone with him for a minute, I'll meet you back at Reception. Don't worry if you can't see me. I'll have nipped outside to ring Belinda.'

When he had gone I held Grandad's hand for a while, but he wasn't there. His proud, fierce spirit had gone to rest. If I had cried then, it would have been from self-pity.

A nurse took me back to Reception. Charles was there, along with his parents. They were flanked by two uniformed policemen.

I stopped dead. Uncle James ventured a sympathetic glance my way and then lowered his bulk on to a chair, removing himself from the action. Aunt Melody advanced across the tiled floor with menace in every tap of her heels. Her dyed-black hair was soaked and straggling to her shoulders, and her coat swung out. The effect was almost gothic.

One of the constables placed himself between us. 'Let's keep things civilised, shall we, Mrs Pevensey?'

'This is the one you need to talk to,' she informed him. 'His precious Lissa!'

The constable raised his eyebrows and turned to me.

'The hospital called us, Miss Byrne. It was felt that our presence might be beneficial.'

I could imagine what kind of scene had precipitated the phone call. Aunt Melody, however, was not ready to be pacified.

'This shrinking violet here,' she hissed. 'This oh-so-innocent, butter-wouldn't-melt, little Miss Byrne—'

'Mum, stop it,' Charles said, keeping his distance, assertiveness at war with the rules ingrained in him from childhood: *Don't upset your mother, you know how sensitive she is.*

Aunt Melody was not about to let me off the hook. Her dark eyes held mine with loathing. 'Dad was in good health and not in the least tottery,' she told the policemen. 'Do you think he couldn't walk down a flight of steps?'

'Mrs Pevensey, if you have any grounds for—'

'We all know she couldn't wait to get her hands on his estate.' Her voice shook, and she drew a steadying breath before putting in the clincher. 'My father didn't die by accident,' she said. 'His darling granddaughter killed him.'

CHAPTER TWO

I sat in the passenger seat of Charles's BMW as it purred through the wild night. The whirling leaves outside made me dizzy and I shut my eyes, letting the warmth from the heater waft across my face.

I hadn't been arrested. As Grandad's next of kin, Aunt Melody had been asked to deal with the formalities. I had been told that someone from CID would meet me at home in half an hour, a routine visit to examine the scene of the accident, and Charles had then whisked me out into the comparative peace of the rain-swept, gale-ravaged car park.

I stared down at my hands, which were clasped so tightly that the knuckles ached. 'I d-didn't push him, Charles.'

'I know that, you little idiot. And the police weren't fooled by Mum's play-acting, either.'

I glanced at his profile. In the fugitive light from oncoming cars the one visible eye glinted angrily.

'I don't think she was acting,' I said.

He snorted. 'Morticia Addams meets Cruella De Vil?'

'Well...she's always a bit melodramatic.'

'Only when she wants sympathy.'

I had never heard him so critical of his mother. 'I really...I am grateful to you, Charles. For everything.'

He shot me an aggrieved look. 'Did you expect me to take Mum's side? I'm not like the twins, you know, always ready to play the dutiful offspring and say the right thing just to keep her sweet.'

'They want to run the business when your dad retires, don't they?'

'I'm hoping the three of us will run it together. I've put as much into Beacon Antiques as Toby and Robyn

8

have.'

'You're too easy-going. If you keep quiet and go with the flow, they'll take your agreement for granted. And they'll walk all over you.'

This time his glance held both surprise and amusement. 'Brave words, little one.'

I felt myself blush. 'Sorry. I can't criticise, can I?'

'You mustn't worry.' He patted my hand. 'I'll be here for you.'

In practice, however, Toby would support their mother at an inquest, Robyn would stick by her twin, and Charles would either stay away or maintain a tactful silence. There remained the youngest of the Pevensey brood.

'We ought to tell Kit what's happened,' I said.

Charles's reply was a non-committal grunt.

'Do you think…' I began. 'I mean, will your mum…'

'Try to contact him? I doubt it. Don't forget, *he's* chosen to ignore *us*, not the other way around.'

I hadn't forgotten. I stared out of the side window, thinking of a past that was lost, as the car sped through the night towards home.

*

Detective Inspector Hughes turned out to be a Welshman with a chilly handshake but eyes like warm chocolate. He arrived seconds ahead of us, along with a younger, thinner colleague who introduced himself as Detective Sergeant Calder. I let them in by the back door, which was still unlocked, causing Hughes to raise his eyebrows.

I said, 'We used the f-front door, when the ambulance—'

'Take more care, in future.'

The words were accompanied by a twinkling smile, but since he undoubtedly knew all about Aunt Melody's performance, I was afraid to accept anything he said at face value. Fighting a wave of panic, I lit some candles while Charles went off with a torch to show the detectives the cellar. When they returned, Sergeant Calder commented, 'Not much wine down there.'

'Grandad sold the good vintages to pay the bills,' I said.

Hughes wanted to check the rest of the house for signs of a break-in, so I gave them a torchlit tour. Everything looked normal. Cluttered in places, but that was Grandad's way. Back in the candlelit kitchen we sat and drank tea, which Charles had made in our absence, and I wished I knew more about police procedure. No mention had been made of forensic evidence or dusting for fingerprints. Did that mean there would be no criminal investigation unless the post mortem suggested foul play?

At Hughes' request I fetched Grandad's wallet from his coat.

'I've read one of Professor Byrne's books,' the Inspector said, checking the wallet's compartments. 'About Sir Walter Raleigh, it was. Cracking adventure story…Now, what's this?'

He had found the mysterious letter. With a glance in my direction he read aloud,

'Dear Harry, I've just learned of the old tyrant's death and its consequences. It's vital that you and I meet to discuss what can or should be done. I'd suggest lunch in Aberystwyth, but there's no point asking Lissa to drive so far. Shall we say McCavity's, at 11am, a week on Tuesday? We can send the girl off on her own for an hour or two. Tell her we're old mates and want to catch up. She'll be safe enough.'

Hughes' voice tailed off as he squinted at the page. After a moment he handed the letter to me. 'Do you know who wrote this?'

The scrawled signature could have been anything. Charles, looking over my shoulder, did no better.

'Dated November twenty-second,' Hughes said. 'Last Sunday. McCavity's...a pub or café, perhaps?'

We couldn't help him. I felt that I had heard of the place, long ago, but the context eluded me.

'How about the "old tyrant"?' Hughes asked.

'I suppose...old Mr Threlfall,' I said. 'He died a couple of weeks ago. A stroke. I don't know of any worrying consequences.'

'John Threlfall?' Hughes' eyes showed a gleam of interest. John Threlfall and Arthur Nix, solicitors of Great Malvern, had been prominent in the local community for over half a century. These days the partnership was run by two of their respective grandchildren. Both old men had lived well into their eighties.

'Mr Threlfall and Grandad were friends for years,' I said. 'Old Mr Nix, too...and Charles's other grandfather, Wilfred Pevensey, who set up Beacon Antiques. Grandad was the only one left...'

My voice faded. John Threlfall, Arthur Nix, Wilfred Pevensey and Professor Harry Byrne. They were all gone now, the four patriarchs whose dreams and ambitions were still shaping the lives of their descendants.

Hughes replaced the letter in Grandad's wallet and handed it back to me. 'Moving on, then,' he said, 'do you feel able to tell us what happened this afternoon?'

Terror gripped me. 'Grandad had some w-work to do. He needed to c-concentrate. He said w-why didn't I do some Christmas shopping? We had lunch early and I w-went out...'

I bit my lip, willing myself to relax. Grandad had said, intending to be bracing rather than cruel, that I should try not to stammer in moments of stress, as it showed weakness and an inability to cope. I had seldom felt less able to cope than I did tonight.

'Take your time, Miss Byrne.' Hughes inclined his head towards the window. 'I'm in no rush to brave that weather for a while.'

I clenched my hands in my lap, breathed deeply, and started again. At my mention of the shabbily dressed man on the road below the house, Hughes looked pensive and asked for details of the incident, then let me continue without further comment.

When I began to describe how I had found Grandad, my stammer returned with a vengeance. Charles, seated protectively at my side, asked the Inspector, 'Can't this wait until tomorrow?' Hughes replied that no, regrettably it couldn't. I straightened my spine and finished the story, Sergeant Calder scribbling it all down.

'Grandad must have gone down to the cellar for a bottle of wine,' I said finally. 'One of us often does, at weekends.'

Hughes tapped his fingernail against his teeth. 'Do you see much of the neighbours? I only ask, because of what the Professor said in the ambulance.' He took out his own notebook and read aloud. '*Lissa, I took John's letter. Melody. Edgar. It's not lost, it's won. Neighbours won. Won five hundred. The others lost.* There was a break after that, and then, *We hid John's…*something inaudible. *We did it for the best. We didn't know. May God forgive us.*' He closed the book. 'The medic jotted it all down afterwards, but he can't be sure he heard everything correctly. Seems there was a lot more, but nothing clear.'

I had heard some of what was written, but for much of the journey the paramedic had been closer to Grandad than I was.

'Melody is Charles's mother,' I said. 'I suppose you

knew that. Edgar...I'm sorry, I can't think...'

Charles interrupted, 'Edgar Byrne was our great-great-grandfather. He bought this house in the 1890s.'

'John must be old Mr Threlfall again,' I said. 'I don't know about any letter from him. And our nearest neighbours are at the bottom of the lane. We hardly ever see them.'

Hughes nodded, then gave me that engaging smile again. 'This is all routine, you know. I'll have your statement typed up at the station, and you can call in and sign it next time you're in town.'

'There'll be an inquest, w-won't there? Can my aunt give evidence?'

'Of course not!' Charles exclaimed. 'She's not a witness.'

Hughes looked apologetic. 'I'm afraid that's not a deciding factor, sir. Hearsay, opinion, what you will, are admissible in a coroner's court. It's not a trial, you see.'

We stared at him.

'Don't worry,' he said. 'If the pathologist finds nothing to suggest foul play, the coroner is most unlikely to give any weight to, er...emotive outbursts.' He stood up and shook our hands. 'Thank you for being so helpful, Miss Byrne, Mr Pevensey.'

I managed to murmur something polite, and Charles showed them out. He returned to find me washing up.

'Leave that, Lissa,' he said. 'I'll finish here while you pack a bag. We want you to stay with us for a few days. Better than being here on your own.'

That was debatable. The Withies was a large house and Charles and Belinda would make me welcome; but their two boys, aged four and two, were going through what their parents called a 'difficult phase'. I was very fond of Jamie and Alex, but at that moment the thought of a house resounding with tantrums was too much to face.

'It's really kind of you,' I said, 'and thank Belinda for me, but I'd honestly rather be here. It's easier, because of the horses.'

'Then I'll stay, too.'

'You will not,' I said, trying for lightness. 'Whatever would Belinda say?'

Charles grimaced; his wife was jealous of all females under sixty.

'Ring us, then, if you change your mind,' he said. 'I'll call in at Mum and Dad's on the way home. It might...well, I'll try to smooth things over.'

Poor Charles. If he was no match for either Belinda or his mother, I couldn't hold that against him. He had done his best.

I thanked him and stood on tiptoe to kiss his cheek. 'Good luck.'

When he had left, I locked the back door and stood listening to the sound of his engine until it was lost amid the roar and whine of the wind. For the first time in my life, I was truly alone. The simple lack of human companionship gaped like a pit; another facet of that insidious soul-destroyer, self-pity.

Nor could I forget the hatred in Aunt Melody's face. If she were to persist in telling Hughes, or the coroner, that I must have pushed Grandad down the steps, there was no one I could depend on to contradict her. The twins had their own mercenary agenda, but I wished Charles and Uncle James were stronger characters. Kit would have stood up for me; defended me to hell and back.

The kitchen light suddenly came on. I almost wept again with relief. I went through all the downstairs rooms, flicking every light switch and closing the curtains. Unbelievably, it was still only ten past eight.

I came to the living room last, and couldn't help glancing at the DVD rack, at the blue spines of two series of *Age of Gold*. The illusion of company might be better than none. I could see the first programme's opening sequence in my mind's eye. Kester Pevensey— my cousin, Kit—striding through an olive grove, spinning a tale of gods and heroes, his voice skilfully modulated to enthral even the most casual viewer...

Bloody Kit; he was too much in my thoughts tonight. He had left the Malverns five-and-a-half years ago and yet here I was, pining for a glimpse of him on screen as an antidote to loneliness and grief. Pathetic. The night he had dumped his married girlfriend and left the area for good, I had found a note on our doormat, the words nearly illegible, scrawled in evident haste: *'Liss. I'm leaving. Going to hell, for all I care. Don't try to contact me. I'm finished with the lot of you. Kit.'*

I whispered, with new grief twisting the knife in the old, unhealed wound, 'What happened, Kit? Why did you do it?'

And knew, with tears, that I would never be told the answer.

*

I needed to do something constructive, and the horses would appreciate being brought in for the night. Tempest was pretty hardy but Smoky liked her comfort.

Picking my way from the back gate to the field by the meagre light of a pocket torch, I regretted not bringing the larger torch, which was still on the kitchen table. I hated black, overcast nights like this. The wind had dropped, and there was no sound but the rain dripping from the trees beside the track.

A twig cracked, somewhere in the woods to my right. I started to jog, clomping along in my wellingtons, throwing panicky glances over my shoulder. Reaching the stile, I scrambled over it fast; but the horses were already ambling towards me. I patted the neck of the first warm, snorting shape and immediately felt secure, which was absurd. If anyone had come after me, both animals would have fled.

They wore head collars in the field, and tonight even the volatile Tempest seemed content to be caught, walking peaceably beside me down the track. His eye-rolling alarm at the sight of my car was only a token protest, and none of us was spooked by any more night noises. At the stables, I dawdled over filling feed buckets and hay nets, unwilling to leave the horses' company. Smoky was mine but I loved them both, as much as I had ever loved a human being. Except one.

I thrust the memories aside; and my time with the horses was therapeutic in the end. By the time I let myself back into the house I was calmer, less afraid. The kitchen felt comfortingly warm after the chill outside. I hung up my coat and filled the kettle, glancing at the table to check that no mugs had been left unwashed.

There was nothing on the table. Not even the torch that I'd left there.

In breathless slow motion, I put the kettle down. My heart was bumping against my ribs, instinct leaping ahead of sluggish thought. Someone had moved the torch while I was with the horses.

I scuttled outside and squelched a few paces across the lawn, hugging myself and taking great gulps of cold air. What to do next? My car keys and phone were indoors.

Run to a neighbour's house and call the police.

But...could I be sure who had had the torch last? Charles had probably used it to show the police out, in which case I needn't stand coatless and shivering in the garden any longer.

Advancing to the back door, I picked up the cast-iron boot scraper, and re-entered the kitchen feeling idiotic but less defenceless. I locked up yet again, left my boots by the door and padded across the room, clutching my chosen weapon. Of course, no one was there. Still...

I tiptoed into the hall, moving into deep shadow as I headed for the light switch beside the front door.

Straddling the nearest window-sill was a man. The shock took my breath away. Petrified, I flattened myself against the wall. If I moved, he'd see me. What if he was armed?

At least I had the scraper. I fought to suppress an hysterical urge to giggle. It was like a game of Cluedo. Miss Byrne, in the hall, with the boot scraper. Except that I was no murderer. I was just a thoroughly frightened woman who really should have called the police five minutes ago.

The man sat motionless, a blacker silhouette against the dark window. The hall clock ticked more slowly than my heart. He was listening. He knew I was there—and he had the torch. At any moment he would turn it on. I had to move. *Now.*

I bolted for the kitchen, heard his whispered curse, felt rather than saw him scramble off the sill and leap forward. He was too quick. There was no escape. No choice.

In despair and terror I whirled, shrieking like a banshee, and swung the boot scraper in a vengeful arc.

CHAPTER THREE

His reactions were lightning fast. He ducked and flung up his right arm to shield his head, and the scraper slashed his forearm. He cursed and dropped the torch. It came on, and rolled in a half circle, sending our shadows writhing up the wall.

I aimed another blow and missed, the weapon's momentum nearly pulling me over. The man swore again. He grabbed my wrist, twisted the arm behind me and shoved me against the front door.

I screamed, 'Kit! Charles! Toby! *Help!*'

My attacker said, *'Christ!'* and dropped my wrist as if I had bitten him.

I turned, the scraper feeling like a ton weight now as I hefted it again, still yelling my cousins' names as if they were all within earshot.

The man had given up any attempt to fight back. He was retreating out of range and shouting to make himself heard. It took me a few seconds to realise what he was saying.

'Liss, it's me! Liss! *Shut up!*'

I rocked back on my heels. 'K-Kit?'

He leaned against the banisters to catch his breath, the fallen torch lighting his face eerily from below. He hadn't shaved, his hair was uncombed, and the sleeve of his sweatshirt was torn and bloody. Two interlaced scarlet streams were running down his right hand and dripping from his finger ends. A genuine armed robber could scarcely have appeared more disreputable, or more dangerous.

'What the hell are you doing here?' he said.

'I live here! You're the one who broke in and started attacking people!'

'*Me?* For your information—' He broke off with a grimace and flexed his arm, tweaking at the sleeve to see the damage. 'Jesus! Turn the light on, will you?'

I didn't care for his tone, but I was standing next to the switch. I thumped it with the palm of my hand and squinted mutinously at him. He had changed. His hair was lighter, no doubt from working overseas so much, and tonight the grey eyes were shadowed and bloodshot, as if he hadn't slept.

He looked at his arm and then at me, pressing his hand over the cut. 'What the fuck did you hit me with?'

'Only this—and stop swearing at me!'

He stared at the scraper, aghast. 'You aimed at my *head* with that?'

I had often wondered how I would feel, in the unlikely event of my ever coming face to face with Kit Pevensey again. Now I knew.

'You bastard!' I was trembling all over, partly with reaction but mainly with rage. 'You write that you're finished with the lot of us, stay away for five-and-a-half years without a word, and then climb in through a window in the dark and blame *me* for thinking the worst?'

He met my eyes without flinching, but the blazing anger died, if only to an unforgiving simmer. 'Great,' he said. 'So I asked for it. Thanks a lot.'

'You're welcome.'

He drew a deep breath, apparently striving for calm. 'I've seen Belinda. She told me what happened. I'm sorry, Liss.'

'I don't need your sympathy. I want you to leave.'

'You'd better know, it was Grandad who asked me to come back.'

I caught my breath. 'You're lying. He wouldn't have done that.'

19

'He posted a letter to my office on Wednesday, but I was in New York, so—'

'Liar!'

'OK, have it your own way.' He headed for the kitchen, nursing his arm. 'I'm going to clean this up.'

I didn't follow him. I was too exhausted and sick at heart to argue any more. I set the torch and scraper down and started up the stairs, anger draining away with the tears that ran down my cheeks.

He walked slowly back into the hall. I could see him on the periphery of vision but didn't look round, didn't stop.

'I'm so sorry, Liss,' he said. 'I shouldn't have lost my temper. The last thing I wanted was to make things worse for you.'

I turned to face him. 'Don't you dare do that!' I said.

'Do what?'

'Act so bloody kind.'

He winced slightly, looking up at me with a degree of compassion that made me wish I could truly hate him. Without speaking to him again I went on up the stairs. I was tired almost beyond thought, and thinking in any case brought only grief. When at last I crawled into my antique four-poster I pulled the duvet over my head, as if with that childish action I could hide from past and present alike.

*

I was sitting on the edge of the bed, naked and warm, eyes closed to concentrate on the senses of touch and smell. The air was scented with a musky, exotic fragrance. He had given me the perfume three weeks ago, for my sixteenth birthday.

He knelt behind me, brushing my hair from crown to shoulder blades, his other hand smoothing downward, following each stroke of the brush. The pressure of his inner thighs against my hips shifted in time with the movement of his arms. I was totally relaxed, luxuriating in the feel of the brushstrokes and his hand on my hair.

He set down the brush and wrapped both arms around me, resting his chin on my shoulder. I opened my eyes. We had drawn the red curtains to shut out the glare of a spring heat wave, and the cherry-coloured dusk cocooned us in warmth and privacy. I looked at him over my shoulder. In that light his skin appeared flushed, and the fair hair had a chestnut gleam.

'What is it?' I asked, amused by his quizzical expression.

'You were smiling. What were you thinking about?'

'That I'm a woman of the world, now.'

He grinned and hugged me more tightly, pressing his warmth against my back. 'It takes more than three weeks to turn a girl into a woman. She has to keeping working at it.'

'I'll need coaching, then.'

He kissed my hair and I turned within the circle of his arms, drawing my legs up so that we both toppled sideways, laughing. He rolled to lie full length on top of me, supporting himself on his elbows as his mouth found mine. The kiss, gentle at first, deepened until I twined my legs around his hips, rubbing myself against him so that he groaned and broke free of the kiss. 'God, Liss…'

'I want you inside me,' I whispered. 'Now.'

'Got a train to catch?'

I bit his shoulder gently. Unable to see his expression, I felt a quiver go through him—of laughter or passion; it was hard to tell.

'If you prefer it like this,' he said, 'I've got five minutes free next Wednesday. I'm sure we could fit in a quick—Ouch!'

21

I lay back on the pillow, smiling up at him.

He glanced down at the tooth marks on his shoulder, and grinned wickedly, grey eyes shining in the dusk. 'Well, as you've asked so nicely...'

It was a different experience this time. Wilder. No finesse. My body answered his and I dug my fingers into his back, arching against him as the waves of pleasure broke through me, in affirmation of love and shared delight and the certainty that this man was mine; my past, present and miraculous future...

At last we sank down together into the softness of the feather mattress, still entwined. He rolled on to his side, taking me with him.

'I love you, Amphelisia Byrne,' he said.

'I love you too, Kester Pevensey.' I stroked his back, feeling...nothing. My hand met only my own body, my own skin. Knowing I had lost him I screamed his name, and sat bolt upright in the cold darkness.

The bedroom door opened. He flicked the light on, crossed the room and sat on the bed, his hand warm on my shoulder through the thin nightdress.

'It's all right,' he said. 'You're awake, it was only a dream.'

I pushed a lock of sweat-damp hair back from my face and struggled to gather a few wits, blinking at the man who had been my best friend for the first twenty years of my life, and my lover for just five months, when I was sixteen. He was wearing only a pair of boxer shorts, and the memories conjured by the dream were disturbingly clear. I flinched from his touch and he dropped his hand, looking sheepish.

'You were yelling my name,' he said.

'Did I wake you up?'

'No such luck. It's just after midnight. Seven o'clock in New York. My body clock's still shot away.' He paused, fixing me with a level gaze which made me feel distinctly uncomfortable. I wondered whether I had cried out anything more incriminating than his name.

'What's the matter?' I said.

'Want to parley?'

It was the antique phrase we had used as children—borrowed from an old book, no doubt. In those days it had been easy to make up after a quarrel; we had been natural allies. A lot of cold and stinging water had passed under the bridge since then.

As I hesitated, he said, 'I really am sorry about Grandad.' He glanced down at his forearm, where two strips of plaster were doing their best to close a seeping gash. 'Maybe I did ask for this, a bit.'

Imagining verbal revenge occasionally was a long way from seeing actual bodily harm at close quarters. My stomach lurched.

'Does it hurt much?' I asked grudgingly.

Silly question. He responded with a shrug and a crooked smile. 'Might get it stitched in the morning. What's tomorrow? Sunday?' He ran a weary hand through his hair, which flopped down again to form an untidy fringe, as it had been doing since he was a child. 'Bloody jet-lag. My brain's scrambled.'

I looked away, smothering the surge of tenderness which had almost made me forget how much I despised him. I traced with my finger one of the flowers on the duvet cover. 'Did Grandad really write to you? An actual letter?'

'Yeah. Our production secretary opened it, ignoring the "private and confidential", and she emailed me a scan. The director was flying out, so he brought the original with him. I got the first available flight and was here by four o'clock.'

'We'd gone to the hospital by then.'

'And left the back door unlocked. The place felt like the Mary Celeste. I drove round to The Withies and found Belinda in. She'd just had a call from Charles, to tell her the bad news. She said she'd invited you to stay.'

'I just…wanted to be at home.'

I was aware that it sounded feeble, but he nodded.

'Belinda offered to put me up as well,' he said. 'To be honest, I was tempted. Didn't sleep much last night, and with the flight thrown in…but in the end I had a bite to eat with her and the kids and drove back here. Thought I'd crash in my old room.'

Strange to hear him call it that. He hadn't slept in that room for fifteen years; not since the Pevenseys had moved out of The Eyrie and into a house of their own.

'Have the police been here yet?' he asked.

'Yes. Inspector Hughes and a sergeant…'

'And they were, um…satisfied, were they?'

My careful composure disintegrated. 'You don't…you can't think…I wasn't even here when he fell!'

'Christ, they don't think *you* pushed him?'

'They didn't say so…but your mum told them I did.'

He swore under his breath, but said with certainty, 'If they didn't treat it as a crime scene, they're thinking it was an accident. Maybe Hughes came in person because of what Mum said, but they'd only have been following procedure. Still…' He hesitated. 'Could Grandad—I've got to ask, Liss—could he have been pushed by someone else?'

'No! Why would you even think such a thing? He hadn't been himself for days, and then, with the power cut…'

'Oh, Liss.' He stretched out a hand, then recollected himself with a start. 'Sorry. Old habits.'

I dashed a hand across my eyes as silence fell and lengthened between us. When it had become intolerable

24

I said, 'You had no right to break in. The kitchen light was on.'

'Thought you'd been home to pack and left it on for security. We could have passed each other between here and The Withies. I didn't want to leave this place empty overnight, so I found a window that responded to some coaxing. But then...' He slid me a doubtful look, as if to see how I would take it. 'Someone shut the back gate.'

'Me, I expect.'

'No.' An embarrassed smile tugged at the corners of his mouth. 'I crept along by the house, using the shadows. Felt like a right prat. Think I caught a glimpse of him, though. Just a shadow crossing the track.'

I swallowed, recalling my fear of an unseen watcher. 'It's a public footpath,' I said.

'Doesn't make it safe. I went as far as the field, but either he was hiding or he'd legged it. The light on my phone was running the battery down, so I came back here to find a torch before trying the woods. Thought it'd serve as a weapon, too, if needed.'

'Why didn't you turn it on, then? And why not put all the lights on indoors? Once he realised the house was occupied and someone was on to him, he'd probably have run a mile.'

'Probably.'

The amusement in his voice made me stare at him in disbelief. 'You *wanted* to catch him!'

'Well...yeah.'

'That's insane. He could have attacked you.'

'Give me some credit, Liss, I can handle myself in a ruck.' He glanced wryly down at his arm. 'Usually. Anyway, I had a look round indoors, just in case. Then...well, I hadn't come across the keys to the mortise locks, so I went to exit through the window.' Another rueful grin. 'And met a screeching homicidal maniac,

25

swinging what felt like an axe.'

I didn't smile. He was being evasive; and however tongue-tied I might be with some people, I had never had that problem with Kit.

'You came here expecting trouble,' I said. 'Grandad's letter cost you a night's sleep and brought you haring across the Atlantic, after you'd sworn never to see any of us again. And you decided to guard this house and arrest any prowlers personally. What the hell did he say?'

Kit subjected me to a long look, then stood up and left the room. With a muttered oath I scrambled out of bed, but before I was half way to the door he came striding back and handed me a sheet of paper.

'That's it, for what it's worth.'

The letter was handwritten, but however poignant I might have found that, its content drove any such thought from my mind.

'Kit, a serious problem has arisen. I'd hoped it would simply go away, but an old acquaintance has contacted me to voice his own concern. I'm afraid he's right. The situation is too dangerous to ignore and I can't risk involving the police. That could well make things worse. What I need is a temporary bodyguard for myself and, more importantly, for Lissa. Someone I can trust to protect my granddaughter while I resolve the problem. I believe you're the only possible choice. I'll brief you when you arrive, on the condition that you say nothing whatsoever to Lissa about why you're here. No sense in alarming the girl unnecessarily.'

He had signed it with a flourish: *'Grandad Byrne.'*

Long before I reached the end, bewilderment had given way to apprehension. 'I know what made him write this,' I said, and told Kit about the letter which had arrived last Tuesday, one day before the letter in my hand had been written. 'It's still in his wallet. In the kitchen.'

Kit came downstairs with me, for which I was grateful, though I wouldn't have told him so. The hall always developed a peculiarly penetrating chill at around midnight.

'Do you remember,' I asked, to break the silence, 'the time I came down in the night for some water, and saw a ghost by that fireplace?'

'Yeah. You'd have been…what? Nine?'

'He had fair hair, and holey jeans. I thought he was a guest. You know how much coming and going there was in those days. But then he just vanished, in a blink.'

'Scary stuff.'

'He was a bit like your dad, only slim—Oh!' I stared at Kit, goosebumps rising on my bare arms. 'He looked more like you. Like you do now.'

He grinned. 'So I'm a look-alike for a dead bloke. That's jet-lag for you.'

We went into the kitchen, which as usual proved less icy than the hall, and Kit sat at the table to dissect the letter from Wales.

'Aberystwyth,' he said, frowning at the spiky script. 'Sounds like this guy either lives or works there. Any ideas?'

'None.' I leaned against the sink, hugging myself for warmth.

'And sending a letter…' he said. 'Who does that any more? Apart from the old man.'

'I filter Grandad's emails for junk, and he doesn't— didn't—text. Maybe a letter seemed more secure. It was marked as private.'

Kit tilted his chair back, studying the enigmatic note with what I recognised as a historian's curiosity. 'McCavity's…that's a bookshop in Hay-on-Wye. Grandad took us in there once or twice, when we were kids. You'd have been too young to remember. I

27

wonder…Grandad and John Threlfall lost their only sons off the coast near Aberystwyth. They could have made a friend there afterwards and kept in touch.'

Their only sons. Roland Byrne—my father—and his friend Richard Threlfall, who had drowned along with their wives in a sailing accident twenty-two years ago.

The cold was striking up through the soles of my bare feet. I wriggled my toes, and clasped the thin nightdress more tightly around me.

'I still can't see why old Mr Threlfall dying would put anyone in danger,' I said.

'No. So we'll go to McCavity's on Tuesday. Have to hope this guy doesn't see Grandad's obituary in the meantime, and stay at home.' Kit raised his eyes to mine. 'The old man only wanted me as a minder. Whatever the problem was, he meant to solve it himself. Odds are, it still needs solving. I'd be inclined to get the police involved regardless, but it might be an idea to talk to this Welsh character first.'

'Providing he'll talk to *us*. You're right, though. About the police.'

'So you'll let me look after you? Shadow your every move?'

'I suppose so. Although why Grandad picked you, when he had Charles and Toby, and even Simon Threlfall, on his doorstep, I can't think. They're all about six-foot-three, for a start. What are you? Five-eleven?'

I only said it to goad him, but he cocked an amused eyebrow at me and answered the serious question behind the gibe. 'Maybe he wanted to keep it in the family. Charles isn't the boldest guy in the world. As for Toby, he's so screwed up, he'd need a month to work out whose side he was on—and the odds are, it wouldn't be yours.'

I couldn't deny it. Privately, though, I believed Kit

had been chosen because he had been my self-appointed protector throughout our childhood. Rightly or wrongly, Grandad had trusted in the strength of the old alliance, to override everything that had come between us since.

Kit said, seeing me shiver, 'Enough for tonight. Come on.'

We went upstairs together, but when he said goodnight I replied off-handedly, being deliberately cold. My bodyguard he might be; my friend he was not.

He got the message. I watched him open the door to his old room, and something in the movement, a nuance of body language, suggested defeat as well as tiredness.

On impulse I said, 'Kit!'

He turned, eyebrows raised in enquiry.

It was the last thing I had meant to ask, but I had to give him a chance to set things right. 'Why did you leave like that? If you just wanted to break with Jodie and make a fresh start, why cut the whole family out of your life? Why change your phone number, and block us all from contacting you online? You can tell me now, can't you?'

He hesitated, just for a second. Then his face went blank, like a shutter coming down. 'Goodnight, Liss,' he said, and went into the bedroom, closing the door quietly behind him.

CHAPTER FOUR

I sat on the stile beside the five-barred gate, watching the horses. Tempest's dark coat gleamed in the sun and he looked thoroughly pleased with life, prancing up and down with head up and tail held high, while Smoky munched the long grass near the hedge.

There were things I should have been doing, such as sorting out Grandad's papers, but my head ached from lack of sleep and it all seemed too much to face. Besides, the field was so beautiful, with the hills looming behind the winter woods, and the flatter land towards Welland glowing green and gold. The trickle of the stream was just audible. I turned my face up to the sun and shut my eyes.

'Hi, Liss.' His voice was so close that I jumped. He vaulted up to sit on top of the gate. 'Thought I'd find you here.'

He had on a decent pair of jeans, a clean tee-shirt and a leather jacket, and had clearly discovered our new power-shower. The scalding water had left his skin flushed under the tan, and despite last night's jet-lag and armed assault he looked fit for pretty well anything.

'Ian Threlfall just called in,' he said. 'Wants to see you at his office at nine-fifteen.'

'On a Sunday?'

'He's Grandad's executor. He asked for the old man's bank statements and so on, and he knew where they were, so I let him take them. Hope that was OK?'

'Yes…but then…why does he want to see me?'

'To read you the will.'

Unless I was the only beneficiary, Aunt Melody and perhaps even Charles and the twins would be there too. Another ordeal I didn't want to face.

'Are you invited?' I asked him.

'Nope. I'll try and get Old Southbrook to stitch my arm. He might even know something useful. That's if he's still around?'

'Alive and practising medicine, do you mean? Yes, he is. But Grandad hasn't seen him in weeks.'

'Worth a try, though. I asked Ian about his own grandad's will. His gran's provided for, and the house belongs to her now. Simon and Ian get a couple of grand each, but that's about it. Seems a lot had gone to charity, over the years.'

'If there's nothing odd about Mr Threlfall's will,' I said, 'what other consequences could his death have had?'

'Nothing illegal, that's for sure. He was too worried about the eternal flames.' Kit stared at the horizon, and I suspected him of trying not to laugh. 'Told me I'd go to hell once for giving him a mouthful of cheek. I was bloody careful crossing the road for at least a fortnight.' His stomach gave a loud rumble and he grinned and shrugged. 'Want to come back for breakfast? I can't leave you up here on your own.'

We walked down the track together. At the gate into the back garden, he paused with a frown, eyeing both it and the low wooden fence.

'This is an open invitation,' he said. 'You need an alarm system and security lights. And *always* lock the back door. Not just when you go out, but whenever you're alone in the house, day or night.'

The advice was sensible but sounded expensive. Back at the house, while he was tucking into a bowl of muesli, I re-read his letter from Grandad, as well as that of the man from Aberystwyth.

'By the way,' Kit said, with his mouth full, 'I had to clean up my blood in the hall, so I, er...did the cellar.'

'Oh. Thank you.'

Not that I wanted to depend on him for anything else, except a few days' bodyguard duty. It was irrelevant that for the first twenty years of my life he had stood up for me, fought for me and, our brief love affair aside, been my closest friend. Those days were gone.

'You shouldn't go to the field on your own,' he said. 'I know it all seems crazy in broad daylight, but I didn't imagine your trespasser. And the old man wasn't senile, or neurotic.'

I smiled thinly. 'You'd be in a position to know, would you?'

'Am I wrong?'

'No. So thanks, I'll bear it in mind.'

'And we'll swap mobile numbers,' he said.

'OK, but don't depend on mine. It's been temperamental ever since it fell in Smoky's water bucket.'

Kit looked about to make some comment, then apparently thought better of it. While I unpacked yesterday's shopping, he dealt with the phone numbers and then made me some toast. I nibbled at this without appetite, and he offered to come with me to Ian's office, for moral support. I told him to go and see Dr Southbrook as planned.

'I don't need a minder with blood poisoning,' I said. I still felt a bit shocked at my own barbarism, self-defence or not, but I wasn't soft enough to tell him so. He drove off in the silver Mercedes convertible which he had parked behind the stables last night.

Twenty minutes later, wearing my only smart suit and enough make-up to disguise my pallor, I was trying to persuade my own car to start. Perhaps, I thought with a brief rush of hope, fate had taken a hand. Ian and the Pevenseys would have to go ahead without me.

The engine fired at the fourth attempt, causing my

stomach to lurch with disappointment and a wave of renewed apprehension. Fate was not on my side after all.

*

The offices of Threlfall and Nix occupied the ground floor of a converted Victorian house in Great Malvern. Today, Ian Threlfall's car was the only one on the forecourt.

As I drew up, he bounced out of the premises like an anxious Jack-in-the-box, ginger hair sticking up in spikes. He wore a rather tight sweater adorned with penguins, which accentuated his rounded physique and removed any possibility of legal *gravitas*.

'Thanks for coming at such short notice, Lissa.' He took the requested documents, kissed my cheek and ushered me into his office. 'Robyn and I were so sorry to hear…well, she's quite cut up, as you can imagine. Much worse for you, of course. She's not coming, before you ask. None of the Pevenseys are. Take a seat. The coffee's on.'

I sat down, my initial relief at Ian's news fading as I watched him fiddling nervously with the percolator. He had never been close to Grandad. Something else was upsetting him.

Maybe Robyn had given him Aunt Melody's slant on events at the hospital. Ian and Robyn had been living together for six years and talked of marriage, but I didn't envy Ian his prospective in-laws and knew that he wouldn't relish being embroiled in a family row.

He sat down to face me across the desk, taking time to adjust the coasters, place the coffees down carefully, and remove his glasses to wipe them with the hem of his sweater. My sense of foreboding deepened.

'Bit of a surprise,' he said, 'Kit popping up again.'

'Yes. Ian, what—'

'Sorry about the mess.' With an almost furtive glance

in my direction, he tidied a stack of papers, slid them into a drawer and locked it.

'Was that Grandad's will?' I asked.

'What? No. Another client…' He picked up a pencil abstractedly and started doodling on a notepad—tiny arrows, all pointing in different directions—then shook his head as if to clear it and flung the pencil down. 'You're right,' he said, though I hadn't spoken. 'I'd better tell you straight. You're the Professor's sole beneficiary.'

So he had actually done it. Cut out the Pevenseys completely. To my shame, what I felt most strongly was relief. With no mortgage to worry about, I would be able to keep things ticking over.

'I'll need a job,' I said. 'I'll sign up with an agency tomorrow.'

'So…you were your grandad's secretary? I thought what you did for him was more in the line of historical research.'

'A bit of both, really.' I regarded him with unease. He was prevaricating; plainly he doubted my ability to deal with whatever obstacle lay in my path. 'What's wrong, Ian? Has my aunt said she'll contest the will?'

'She's considering it. That's not your biggest problem. How much did your grandad tell you about his finances?'

'I see the bills.'

Ian sighed deeply. 'He changed his will a couple of years ago. He invited me round, remember? That's when he left everything to you. He told me he was in a lot of debt. I asked if he'd thought of selling The Eyrie, but he said it was your inheritance. Joked that he'd have to live another ten years to pay everyone off. That's why I picked up his bank statements this morning. I've found seven creditors so far. His life assurance will help, but…I'm afraid you'll have to sell up.'

I think he went on talking for several seconds. I didn't

hear what he said because my ears were ringing. I put a hand to my lips; they were going numb, and the room was filled with a swimming brightness…

'Lissa!'

My freezing hands were clasped in Ian's warm ones, and I discovered that I was sitting on the carpet. The ringing in my ears had stopped but the floor was still rocking like the deck of a ship.

'I shouldn't have blurted it out like that.' His words came from very far away. 'Put your head down for a minute.'

I rested my forehead on my raised knees, shut my eyes and waited for the ship to stop rolling. 'I never faint,' I muttered. 'Should have eaten more breakfast.'

Ian patted my shoulder. 'Shock,' he said. 'Not surprising.'

A few seconds later I heard the clink of a teaspoon on china, and lifted my head carefully. He stooped to hand me another coffee. I took an obedient sip, and choked on something stronger than caffeine.

'How much brandy is in this?' I asked hoarsely.

'Only a teaspoonful.'

Ian's teaspoon must have been the size of a soup ladle. I slowly got up and sat on the chair again, while he fussed over me.

'You're sure you'll be OK? If you'd rather I drove you home…'

'No, I'm fine. I just don't understand. Why did Grandad keep paying me a salary, if he couldn't afford it?'

'I don't know, Lissa. All I've got is the paper trail.'

'Is there any chance that his debts will be written off, now—now that he's gone?'

Ian shook his head and leaned one hip on the desk, probably staying within reach in case I keeled over again.

'If you sell up, there might be enough left for a little flat.'

'I'll lose the horses.' Hearing the break in my voice, I looked anywhere but at Ian. Bad enough to have fainted in his office; it would hardly be fair to cry on his shoulder as well.

'I'm sorry,' he said. 'Will you tell me something honestly?'

I looked at him in surprise. 'If I can.'

'Kit says he'll be staying around for a while. Some nonsense about you being in danger. It sounded nuts, but...well, is there any chance he could be right?'

'I'm not sure. Grandad believed it.'

'The thing is...' Ian cleared his throat. 'Jodie and I work well together, but she's my brother's ex-wife, after all, and you know how Simon adored her. If she and Kit had just had a fling...if he hadn't actually proposed...and then to dump her like that and ride off into the blue, the same night she left Simon for him...Robyn kept saying we didn't know the full story, but—'

'Robbie said that?' I asked, incredulously. From what I had seen, all of her sympathies appeared to lie with Simon.

Ian shrugged. 'Kit's her baby brother, after all. She was very fond of him. I know she didn't always show it. But then we started hearing the details, and Jodie had her breakdown...I'm sorry if it sounds selfish, but I'm a bit worried about this dinner.'

'What dinner?'

'Tomorrow night. Didn't Kit tell you? He wants Robyn and me to host it, inviting the whole family...or at least, everyone of our generation. Not Jodie as well, obviously. It's short notice, and a weekday's not ideal, but they've all agreed.'

Even without Jodie Nix, the guest list was alarming.

'He's mad,' I said. 'There'll be a fight.'

'There'd better not be. We've just redecorated. He needs to ask us about the past, he said. Shall I call it off?'

'No...if we can keep things civilised, it might be productive,' I said hesitantly; but with the arrangements already made, I'd have been a fool to cancel.

'OK.' Ian sighed. 'I've always liked Kit, you know? He had the guts to do all the things that I couldn't, like standing up to the twins.'

I was unwillingly amused. 'You've found enough guts for that, since the old days.'

'Huh. Toby still frightens me to death. He's never got used to me being with Robyn. Bit of an unhealthy attitude, if you get my drift.'

'Seriously? But Toby's gay.'

'Toby's a lot of things. Good thing Robyn keeps him in line, mostly.'

I couldn't argue with that, and Toby had often seemed jealous of his twin's friends. I had just been too naïve to suspect a sexual motive.

'Strange, isn't it?' I said, with a sigh, 'how we've all stayed linked, somehow. My cousins, you and Simon, Jodie, me...all of us who used to play together at The Eyrie.'

'Maybe not that strange. Your parents and ours dying together...that's quite a bond. And of course Jodie's dad had run off.'

'I suppose. I never thought about it like that.'

We agreed that he would come to the house one day soon, to sort out the rest of the paperwork and discuss the house sale. I asked for a couple of days' grace— partly, although I didn't tell him so, because on Tuesday I would be in Hay-on-Wye.

'Don't worry, we'll arrange a date next week,' he said. 'That'll give you a breathing space. By the way, can you meet Simon for coffee at the Happy Rambler this morning? He'll wait for your text.'

I thanked him for passing on the message.

'See you tomorrow night, then,' he said. 'Eight for eight-thirty. And, er…I'm sure you don't need telling, but tread carefully with Simon. About Kit, I mean.'

He was right. I hadn't needed telling.

CHAPTER FIVE

The Happy Rambler café, as its name suggested, marked a junction of several hill paths. Popular both with locals and tourists, today it was packed with walkers taking refuge from the biting wind.

I had never liked entering pubs or cafés alone. I hurried through to the conservatory, where Simon and I often met, and was relieved to spot his auburn mane. He stood up to welcome me, and gave me a hug that lasted slightly too long.

'Charles rang me last night,' he said. 'I'm so sorry, Lissa. You didn't mind coming up here today?'

I shook my head. His eyes seemed an even deeper blue than usual. He had been wearing tinted lenses for a couple of years now, and sometimes he would change the shade.

I looked at the view over the valley, a panorama of fields and nestling villages. Far away in the west, there was snow on the Welsh mountains.

'This place always reminds me,' I said, 'how m-much I love living here.'

He reached for my hand across the table, obliging me to look at him. 'How are you, honestly?' he said.

Drowning, I thought. Being sucked down into a whirlpool of emotions that I couldn't begin to deal with.

'All right,' I said.

'You need a strong coffee and a bite to eat.'

It seemed a good idea. His brother's alleged teaspoonful of brandy was making me feel a bit light-headed. I let him order coffee and teacakes for us both and wondered, as often before, why I continued to keep Simon Threlfall at a distance. He was thirty-three, and sometimes the age gap between us seemed wide, but many women found him attractive. He was as tall as Charles and Toby, with the physique of a gym fanatic. Maybe it was the lenses, or the way he tossed his hair, as if to draw attention to the flowing locks that had once been pale ginger.

'I've missed you,' he was saying. 'Didn't you get my texts?'

'I'm sorry. Grandad was a bit off-colour. I didn't like to take an evening out. We could have gone riding one lunchtime but I didn't think you'd want to.'

He made a wry face. 'Too right. In case you've forgotten, that brute Tempest broke my collar bone and my ankle in one afternoon.'

'Oh, Simon! That was years ago, and in case *you've* forgotten, I'd offered you Smoky. You chose Tempest.'

'Kit dared me,' he countered, a hint of sulkiness in the line of his mouth. 'Besides, Smoky bucked me off into a cowpat once. You won't get me near one of those beasts again.'

In fact he had slid off docile Smoky while she was making a turn. I decided it was time to change the subject, and asked how his job was going.

He grimaced. 'I used to love history, before I had to teach it. I need a career change, Lissa. Something more lucrative. Your grandad thought I was bright enough for anything. Remember how I used to turn up at your house with my homework?'

'You got on well with him.'

'He let me call him Harry. I can't believe he's gone...' Simon regarded me with frowning concern. 'You could have rung me instead of Charles, you know. From the hospital. Why didn't you?'

'Charles is family.'

'And I'm only a friend.' His mouth twisted. 'So you keep reminding me. I'm not slagging Charles off, he's a

40

good mate, but all the Pevenseys are trouble for you, Lissa. Their mother's brainwashed them, hasn't she? Telling them you'll pinch their inheritance, just because she couldn't get along with your grandad.'

'Charles has never believed her. Nor has Kit.'

He waved a hand as if swatting at a gnat. 'Kit's irrelevant, and Charles will toe the party line. The thing is…' He frowned down at my hand, stroking it gently. 'You know how old-fashioned your grandad was, about passing everything down through the male bloodline.'

'But he couldn't, could he? Dad was his only son.'

'Which makes Charles the next in line. Your aunt's been pinning her hopes on that. I bet Harry set aside his principles and left you the lot.'

'Yes. The debts as well as the house. I'll have to sell.'

'Sell The Eyrie?' He looked really upset on my behalf. 'I'm sure it won't come to that. Harry may not have had much cash, but the furniture might be worth a bit. Remember how you little ones got fired up about the myth of the Byrne treasure, when we were kids? Probably you'd overheard Harry discussing contents insurance.'

'We've got some nice pieces, I suppose. They'd fetch a few thousand, but it won't be nearly enough.'

'You might be surprised. Just don't let your aunt in, or the twins. You never know what they might do.'

My heart jumped. 'What are you saying? Simon, if you've heard something…if one of the Pevenseys is really out to harm me—'

'*Harm* you? You don't mean physically?'

'I know it sounds bizarre, and I don't for a moment think…but Grandad was worried about me, this past week, and wouldn't say why.'

'But…no, Lissa, that's crazy. I meant verbal bullying, or taking valuables before you'd made an inventory. No one would hurt you.'

'You're right.' I withdrew my hand from his to fumble in my bag for a tissue. 'I'm sorry, I shouldn't burden you with all this.'

'Don't be silly. I know one thing, you're in no state to be living up there on your own. I'd offer you a bed at my place, if I thought you'd take it.'

'You've only got one bed.'

'Big enough to share.' He leaned forward, those cornflower-blue eyes seeming almost luminous. 'Lissa, we can't keep this up forever. Me doing all the chasing, you stringing me along.'

'I'm not! I haven't.'

'Is it because I'm divorced?'

'No,' I lied, feeling myself blush. Simon's tendency to rant about his ex-wife during dates had scared off more resilient women than me. 'Please, Simon, don't do this now.'

He must have heard the desperation in my voice. At any rate, he sighed and sat back. 'You're right,' he said. 'Bad timing. Friends, then?'

'Of course.' I drew a breath for courage. 'And you don't need to worry about me being alone. Kit turned up last night.'

His whole body stilled. '*What?*'

'To protect me. At Grandad's request.'

'You've got to be kidding!'

'I've seen the letter.'

'Don't trust him, Lissa! He's the worst of the lot, and he's always dragged you into trouble.'

I should have changed the subject again, or made some pacifying comment, anything except try to set the record straight. Why should I have bothered, after all? But anyone can be wise after the event.

'I do have a mind of my own,' I said. 'Kit's never

dragged me into anything.'

Simon's mouth was distorted by a bitter sneer. 'Not even into his bed when you were only a child?'

'I was sixteen—and it wasn't like that.'

'Wasn't it? He went off to Cambridge and left you behind.'

'I was just starting my A-levels. And it's none of your—'

'Kept you as his loyal little pen friend, though, didn't he? Hedging his bets, while he worked his way through every pretty girl in the faculty. Saving you to brighten up his holi—'

Simon reared back in the chair, one hand pressed to the cheek I had slapped, his eyes wide with disbelief. I could hardly believe it myself. I had stood up without being aware of it. My palm was tingling. I had never hit anyone before...except last night's 'burglar'.

I opened my mouth to apologise, and shut it again. I wasn't sorry. He had deserved it. Turning away from his flushed, astounded face, I bent to pick up my handbag, and straightened to find that we had the attention of everyone in the place. Blushing as hotly as Simon, I stalked out of the café without a backward glance.

I didn't expect him to follow me. At the sound of his running footsteps I whipped round, and he stopped at once. My finger marks were clear on his cheek, and his expression was still incredulous, although now for a different reason.

'Don't look at me like that,' he said. 'You don't think I'd hit you back, do you?'

I relaxed slightly. 'Of course not.'

'I could never hurt you. I love you.'

'You had no right to say those things. They weren't even true.'

'OK, so I lost my rag, but Kit has treated everyone

like dirt and you won't hear a word against him.' Simon sighed and stepped closer. 'Look, I'm sorry, all right?'

I could see in his face the certainty that I was not myself; that I would fall for his charms in the end. It was impatience that he fought to suppress, not despair.

'Call me,' he said, 'whenever you like. For any reason at all.'

I gave him a muttered goodbye, got into the car and slammed the door, the action as symbolic as he cared to think it. Damn him, I thought—and damn Kit Pevensey! It was all his bloody fault.

For a wonder, the engine started first time. I drove away from the Happy Rambler without looking back, and broke all the speed limits to get home.

CHAPTER SIX

Incredibly, Kit shrugged off the debt problem as of no account. 'If you don't want to sell, get a job and a mortgage. Take in lodgers, maybe. You've got six bedrooms.'

He was sitting at his ease on the window seat, with a steaming mug of coffee and not a financial care in the world.

'Fine,' I said sarcastically, sinking into an armchair and kicking off my shoes. 'You've set my mind at rest.'

'I'll buy a share in the old place, if you like.'

'I don't need handouts, thank you.'

He gave me a twisted smile. 'It'd be an investment, not charity.'

I felt a twinge of shame; but there was no way that I would accept such an offer from him.

'Did you see Old Southbrook?' I asked.

'Yeah. He stuck on a few steri-strips and called me a pain in the arse for disturbing him on a Sunday.'

'Dear old grouch.'

'He's pretty fond of you, too. Not that he told me anything, except that Grandad was never ill.' Kit hesitated, regarding me with anxious appraisal. 'I should have come with you, this morning. Would you like a hot drink?'

'No, thanks.'

He headed for the kitchen anyway, returning after a couple of minutes with a mug of coffee. 'There's whisky in it,' he said.

Grudgingly, I took a sip. There seemed to be rather more whisky than coffee. I was in danger of getting drunk on laced beverages.

I didn't thank him. He sat down again on the window

seat, leaned back into the bay and sipped his own drink.

'Has Ian arranged dinner for tomorrow?' he asked.

'You know he has. Why didn't you tell me? I felt like an idiot.'

'He didn't promise anything. I'm glad he's up for it. If we can get the Eyrie Gang together—'

'Except Jodie, but I suppose that can't be helped.'

He ignored the barb. 'They might well remember something we don't. No need to mention our man from Aberystwyth. We'll just say Grandad was concerned for your safety and we want to find out why.'

'They won't cooperate. Not with you.'

'I'll have to see that they do, for your sake.' He breathed in deeply, preparing himself for battle. 'Liss, you might not believe it, but I would have come back this Christmas, without the old man's letter.'

'You're right, I don't believe it.'

'So while I'm here, I want to set a few things straight on my own account. Like making peace with my family, for a start.'

'Good luck with that.'

'The thing is, I won't be going to Ian and Robbie's looking for trouble, but the shit is bound to hit the fan…' He was watching me steadily. 'I could do with an ally, Liss.'

Allies. Yes, we had been that and a lot more. Once upon a time.

'Then tell me why you left me that horrible note,' I said.

He drew a slow breath. After a moment he said, as if choosing his words with care, 'I'm sorry. It was a crap thing to do. I was raging at everything. Life. You got caught in the backlash. I wish I could explain. I just can't.'

I let out a bitter laugh. 'No surprise. Well, all right.

46

We can't be friends—friends confide in each other—but we're still blood brothers, and an oath is an oath. Whatever I think of you, I've never said it to one of your family. I'm not likely to start now.'

He hung his head, staring down at the palm of his right hand. I knew he had a small scar beneath the middle finger, where his penknife had once sliced too enthusiastically. I bore a similar memento. We had pressed our palms together, mingled our blood, and sworn an oath of eternal fellowship. I had been eight years old; he had been ten.

He said, with a crack in his voice, 'You're an exceptional lady, Amphelisia Byrne.'

If he chose to think so, who was I to disillusion him?

'When you want lunch,' I said, 'you know where the cooker is.'

He made beans on toast for both of us, and we ate from trays on our laps in the study, while surveying from armchair level the chaos on the floor. He had been turning out the contents of Grandad's desk.

'I don't suppose,' he said with his mouth full, waving a fork at the desk, 'that thing has any secret compartments?'

I set down my tray, crossed the obstacle course, and reached into the back of the bottom drawer to press a catch. A small drawer above it, which had looked like part of the framework, popped open.

Excitement ignited in Kit like a flame. He sprang to join me as I placed a bundle of old letters in his hand.

'All from publishers,' I said. 'Nothing exciting.'

He sat down to unfold the top one. A second later he muttered, 'What the...' And then, sounding breathless, 'Look at this!'

The letter was printed on headed paper; but, oddly, it was addressed to Mr John Threlfall, and the letterhead was that of Wilfred Pevensey, Kit's other grandfather and founder of Beacon Antiques. It was dated sixteen years ago.

'Dear John,' Wilfred had written,

'I fully appreciate your concern. My own grandchildren are currently as obsessed as yours by the myth of buried treasure at The Eyrie. Heaven knows how the story started. The important thing is to scotch it, before the persistent rumours tempt an opportunistic burglar.

'As regards your question: I would hesitate to guess at the value of the item you describe. If it exists—and I seriously doubt the veracity of your source—I can scarcely credit that Harry is fool enough to keep it hidden. If he were to sell, the rewards might run well into seven figures. You have more influence with him than I do. See if you can persuade him to see sense.'

The letter closed with the antiques dealer congratulating John Threlfall on his eldest grandson Simon's success in his A-levels, and expressing satisfaction that his own grandson, Charles, two months younger but in the same school year, had done even better.

'That letter wasn't there a week ago,' I said. 'I've never seen it before—Oh!' I met Kit's eyes with startled comprehension. 'Grandad said, *I took John's letter.*'

'Maybe he wanted it out of circulation. Forgotten about fast.' Kit surged to his feet, oblivious of the other documents, which slid off his lap to join the mess on the floor. 'Suppose this came to light after old Threlfall died?' Unable to keep still, he tried to pace the floor, found his path blocked, and whirled back to me. 'Could it have been what our Mr Aberystwyth meant, about the consequences of old Threlfall's death?'

'I don't see how—'

'If Grandad knew someone had read the letter and

48

believed that the Byrne treasure exists, whether there's really any treasure or not, maybe he was worried about a possible break-in.'

'Stop saying "treasure"! You sound like a ten-year-old.'

'Sixteen years ago...' he said. 'I remember that treasure hunt, don't you? I'd heard Mum and Dad talking, about how they'd looked for it as kids.'

'Never mind how it started. It ended with Grandad giving you a beating that could have landed him in jail, and probably should have.'

Too late I realised my mistake. In mentioning the punishment, I had reminded him of the reason for it. He opened his mouth to speak, and I retreated, holding up my hands to stave off what I knew was coming.

'Oh, no,' I said. 'If there was anything in the dungeon, we would have found it long ago.'

He laughed. 'Now who's talking like a kid? It was never a dungeon till the twins made it one.'

'You won't get me down through that trapdoor, Kit Pevensey, and that's final!'

He put his head on one side, and said just three words. 'I dare you.'

*

We stood in the stables' tack room, looking down at the trapdoor.

'This is pointless,' I said.

Ignoring me, Kit lifted the brass ring and pulled. The hinged trap opened with a creak. Stooping to peer into the blackness he put out a hand, palm up, and gave the order, 'Torch, Liss,' much as a surgeon might say, 'Scalpel, nurse.'

Compressing my lips, I obeyed. He shone the light on a rope ladder, then let himself down, calling a few seconds later, 'Coming?'

49

I went down, ashamed to feel my breath shorten and my palms grow sweaty. When I stood beside Kit, he gave me a tap on the shoulder.

'I won't let Old Trog eat you,' he said.

'Our resident troll only chews the tender, juicy flesh of little children, remember? Toby and Robyn were very specific.'

Kit was watching my face. 'You're not really scared, are you?'

'Not of Old Trog, idiot. But I was never afraid of the dark till the twins started locking us down here for hours.'

'I always held your hand, didn't I? Told you stories? And you were pretty eager to come down with me the last time, when we were going to clear the roof fall and find the treasure.'

'Doesn't mean I liked it.'

He snorted. 'Wasn't so keen myself, after the twins split on us. Never seen the old man so angry. Christ, I still remember the feel of that belt. Mum didn't stop him, either.'

'She said we could have been buried alive,' I muttered, shivering; but I followed him deeper into the cellar. The flagstones were thick with dust and strewn with wisps of hay and straw from the tack room above. In alcoves to right and left, there were old demijohns and a tricycle hung with cobwebs. Nothing had been stored here since the subsidence began.

The tunnel, perhaps originally a priest's escape route, was at the end of the dungeon nearest the house. Half a dozen worn steps led down to it. This was the site of the roof fall. Earth, stones, tree roots and broken timbers blocked the entrance from floor to ceiling, but we knew the tunnel must lead to the house. Its route under the back lawn was clear from the sunken ground above it.

'Even if Grandad did own something worth a fortune—and I know he didn't,' I said, 'there's no way he could have put it behind all that.'

'He didn't. Sixteen years ago, judging from the letter, he still had access to whatever he'd hidden, but this mess was already here. If he used the tunnel, he got in from the other end.' Kit took a step sideways, to shine the torch on the blocked doorway from a different angle. 'I hate to say it, but our elders and betters were right. We could bring the whole lot down if we try to shift this lot.' He paused, brow furrowed in concentration.

'What is it?' I said.

'Even after your parents died, there was you, Grandad and all of us Pevenseys living at The Eyrie, plus friends coming and going. When could the old man have used the tunnel? One of us was always wandering down in the night, for a drink or whatever.' His voice died away, and he gave me a wide smile of boyish delight, the torchlight gleaming on his teeth and in the depths of his eyes. 'You did exactly that. And saw a ghost, as you thought, standing in front of the old fireplace.'

'He wasn't *Grandad*. He was *young*.'

'And he vanished. What if he stepped into the tunnel?'

'But—'

'So who was he? Our friend from Aberystwyth?'

'I suppose it's possible.' I shook my head, throwing out the fantasy. 'No, it's not. How have you dreamed up all this, just by looking at a pile of rubble?'

'This is the dungeon, haunt of trolls, gateway to secret passages and hidden gold. Here, Liss, we can dream up anything.'

'That doesn't make it true!'

'No,' he said, more matter-of-factly. 'But if it might pay off some of your debts, it's worth investigating.'

We went back to the house and stood in front of the great stone chimneypiece. This was carved at the upper corners with a leaping stag but was otherwise plain, with a panelled surround. Kit pressed as many panels as he could reach, and prodded various parts of the stags' anatomy. Nothing happened. He stepped into the fireplace and peered into the cavernous sides and up the chimney, then set his foot on a jutting brick and began to climb.

'A lot of legends grow from a germ of solid fact,' he said, his voice echoing as his feet disappeared from view. 'Or what are my programmes about?'

After a minute or two he dropped into the fireplace and ducked back into the hall. There was a black streak down his face and his shirt was filthy. 'No germ,' he said. 'We ought to try the wine cellar. Something might be obvious that we didn't see as kids. Would you rather not come?'

'I don't think I can face it just yet.'

'OK.' He patted my shoulder. 'See you in a bit.'

Left alone, I found the hall's silence oppressive. I went outside and stood on the sunlit lawn. Kit found me a few minutes later, and his dejected shrug told its own story.

'No buttons, catches or moving walls,' he said. 'I guess it was always a longshot.'

'A fiction, more like.' I looked up at the hills, not wanting him to see the tears on my face. 'Grandad wouldn't have got himself into debt, would he, if he had a fortune stashed away?'

I heard him sigh. After a moment he said gently, 'Things will get better, Liss. Believe me, they will.'

I nodded, frowning at the tree-clad slopes.

'Let's bring some old boxes down from the attic,' he said.

Sorting through unlabelled boxes took all afternoon. The search turned up old papers and outdated history books, plus some third-rate etchings, a jumble of toys and several photo albums. We flicked through the albums and set them aside for later study, having seen no shots of anywhere that might be Aberystwyth. Nor were there any clues to hidden wealth.

We mucked out the stables together that night, and Kit mentioned guiltily that he might be called back to the studios in a week or two. One of the big guns of an American TV network had talked about flying over, partly as a result of the New York trip, to discuss a future series of *Age of Gold*, based on the discovery and settlement of America.

In a way I was relieved. Two weeks of his enforced company sounded like more than enough. If nothing was resolved by then, I could stay with Charles and Belinda. Even their children's tantrums would be better than this self-inflicted torture.

If only Kit had behaved like the rat that he was, it wouldn't have been so bad. Perhaps his kindness towards me was part of his mission to persuade us to forgive and forget. Well, I had given him two chances to confide in me, and he had turned me down flat. If I thought him beneath contempt, he had only himself to blame.

*

Next morning I drove to Worcester police station, as my statement was typed and ready to sign. By good luck I saw DI Hughes and managed to secure a copy of what Grandad had said in the ambulance. My request left Hughes looking thoughtful, but if he suspected my motives there was little I could do about it.

I arrived home to find that Kit had once again made havoc of my tidied piles of documents. Like Grandad, he seemed to work best when surrounded by muddle.

'Oh, wonderful,' I murmured.

Not having heard, he flashed me a smile. 'I've stocked up the freezer. Oh, and I've bought you a Christmas present. You'd better have it early.'

He picked his way across the littered floor to hand me an unwrapped box. I was the owner of a new phone.

'The contract's sorted,' he said. 'And my number's in there.'

Any bodyguard worth his salt would have had the same idea, and after all he could afford it. That, however, was the trouble; he was treating me like a charity case. It was the same with the freezer and the fridge, both now full of the best ready-meals and frozen vegetables on the market. Lunch proved to be salmon mornay with a glass of Chablis.

I thanked him with neither gratitude nor grace; but he couldn't have known that lately I had come to enjoy cooking. The fact that I was ashamed of my childishness made me scorn him all the more, as if he were to blame for bringing out the worst in me.

Over the meal, he studied the copy of Grandad's last words. '*Lissa, I took John's letter.* That's solved. *Melody.* Maybe he took it from Mum, though why she'd have had it…' He shook his head, and went on reading. '*Edgar.* Edgar Byrne? Brought the house back into the family around 1890, right? A high-value item might have come down from him. *It's not lost, it's won. Neighbours won. Won five hundred, the others lost. We hid John's…* That could be the letter again. *We did it for the best. We didn't know. May God forgive us.*'

He seemed to suppress a shudder as he put the paper down. 'That bit about the neighbours winning…the medic must have got that wrong. Those last sentences, though…And he says 'we'. Mr Aberystwyth, do you think? What had the old man done, Liss, to put you in

54

danger and make him beg forgiveness of a God he hardly believed in?'

I wished I knew. Now, at last, I allowed myself to remember Grandad; not the sharp-witted, acid-tongued giant who had raised me with as much affection as criticism, but an old, frail, broken man, whose final moments had been made wretched by pain and remorse.

Kit said quietly, 'I'm sorry.'

'I loved him.'

'I know.'

'He shouldn't have died like that.' Fighting for some measure of self-control, I sat upright and said, hiccupping, 'Sorry.'

'It's not wrong to cry for him, Liss. Even the old man himself wouldn't think so.'

I half laughed. 'Oh, no?'

Kit muttered something that I didn't quite hear, but I had an impression that the words had been savage and not aimed at me.

Aloud he said, 'How d'you feel about a ride on the hills?'

*

We found the horses standing together in the sun. Kit informed me that he would take Tempest.

'Why?' I said. 'Because he's had you off so many times, and you can't bear for him to have the last word?'

Undeterred, Kit began stroking him, then leaped back as Tempest tried simultaneously to bite his arm and stamp on his foot.

'He's forgotten you,' I said. 'You'd better ride Smoky.'

Kit conceded the point, probably to avoid irritating me; but he promised the horse, 'Next time we'll come to terms, you grumpy sod.'

Tempest behaved immaculately for me throughout the ride. We took the path up through the woods

55

towards British Camp, the ancient fort whose grassy ramparts crowned the Herefordshire Beacon. It was only two-fifteen but the lower slopes lay in shadow already, whilst high above the tree line an expanse of dead bracken flamed in sunlight. We came out above the reservoir to cross Swinyard Hill, and at Kit's suggestion made a detour via Clutter's Cave.

This was an oddity. In an area devoid of natural caverns it was as small as a boxroom and had to be man-made, but its origin was unknown, though it was said that a hermit had lived there once. The entrance faced westward and was approached by a path winding along the side of the hill. We had made love there, one summer evening; a memory that I didn't want to revisit. I held the horses while Kit wandered around the arm of the hill for a look. He was soon back.

'Spartan as ever,' he said. 'Bleak place, even for a hermit.'

'Perhaps he was doing penance for his sins.'

'Poor bugger. Can't have been much fun up here on a winter's night, with the wind howling through the entrance and the snow blowing in.'

If Kit cherished any memories of his own, he gave no sign. I set a faster pace on the way home, and behind us Clutter's Cave kept its lonely vigil over the distant hills of the west.

CHAPTER SEVEN

Kit knocked on my bedroom door five minutes before we were due to leave for Ian's house, and came in wearing a stylish suit over a blue tee-shirt.

'Oh, is that look back in again?' I said.

He grinned. 'My last clean shirt. You look fantastic.'

I had bought the short black dress in last summer's sales; the only item of designer clothing in my wardrobe.

'Thank you.' I sat down at the dressing table to brush my hair, watching him in the mirror. 'Why don't you borrow one of Grandad's shirts?'

The grin vanished. 'No, thanks.'

I had only asked the question to unnerve him. Even as a student, he had been squeamish about second-hand clothes. Maybe it stemmed from his talent for bringing the past so vividly to life; maybe the dead felt closer than he cared to admit.

'As you didn't want Jodie at this dinner party,' I said, breezily changing the subject, 'how will we find out about *her* memories? Or aren't they the kind you'd want to hear about?'

He leaned a shoulder against the wardrobe, arms folded. 'Give it a rest, eh, Liss?'

'Poor Jodie hasn't had much luck with her men, has she? First her father running off, then you, then Simon divorcing her.'

'The divorce was her first decent break. And as Simon will be there tonight, we couldn't invite Jodie. You can catch up with her some other time. You're right about her dad, though.'

I didn't remember Jodie's father and had never seen a photograph. He had walked out on his wife and daughter a few weeks before my parents died.

'What was he like?' I asked. 'Mr Nix.'

'Don't know, really. Why?'

'Just that I've heard a lot about Mum and Dad, and Simon's and Ian's parents. Mr Nix, though...even Jodie's never talked about him much. She did say once that he sent them money, right up until she finished at university. I just thought...if you remember anything that might help...'

Kit's reflection gazed at me solemnly. 'He laughed a lot. Used to kick a ball around with us now and then. He made us a go-cart once.'

'He sounds nice.'

'Nice enough, I expect. Want me to drive tonight?'

Evidently the subject was closed. No doubt any reference to Jodie pricked his conscience.

'I don't mind driving,' I said, 'as long as we take my car.'

Once again the Fiat started only at the fourth attempt, and even then was running roughly. We decided to use Kit's car for the trip to Hay-on-Wye in the morning.

Ian and Robyn lived in nearby Welland. As we pulled up on the drive, I recognised Charles's and Belinda's BMW, Toby's huge motorbike and Simon Threlfall's ramshackle MG sports car. Maybe the car was his incentive for changing career; it would take a serious injection of cash to restore it to glory.

Ian opened the door and welcomed us nervously into the hall. 'Are you ready to face the music?' he asked.

Kit gave him a glinting smile and clapped him on the back. 'So long as I'm calling the tune.'

A hubbub of conversation was emanating from the dining room, and my stomach tightened with apprehension as we went in. At the table, five heads turned, and five pairs of eyes widened in disbelief. Apparently, even Robyn had not been told to expect both of us. No wonder Ian was anxious. The table was laid for seven, not eight.

'Hi,' Kit said.

Toby leaped to his feet. 'Who the hell invited *you*?' he asked with a fierce look at Ian, assuming his guilt, exonerating Robyn without knowing the facts.

'I invited myself,' Kit said. 'Sorry to spring this on you, Robbie. Can the meal stretch to include one more?'

'Do I have a choice?' she asked dryly.

Toby advanced on us with aggression in every long-limbed stride, and my heart missed a beat. As he towered over us, I saw the fury in his dark eyes and shrank back, a scared little girl again. Just like old times.

He gave Kit a hard push in the chest. 'Get out!' he said.

Kit stood his ground. 'If Ian and Robbie ask me to leave, I will.' He slid Robyn a questioning look. 'I'd rather stay.'

Toby turned to his sister. 'Shall we throw him out?'

He must have meant Simon, Charles and himself, and possibly Ian as well. He was out of luck. Simon looked taken aback and Charles was avoiding his brother's eye. Ian had never raised a hand in anger in his life. He stopped hovering, though, and stood next to Robyn's chair, draping an arm around her shoulders.

'Tonight is for Lissa,' he said. 'Kit asked me to explain to Robyn, but I, er…felt he'd do it better.' Smiling at his guests as if unaware of the bristling tensions, he added, 'Shall we get dinner underway?'

I expected Robyn to protest, but she merely gave Ian a dark, baffled look and shook her head at her twin, who with obvious reluctance shoved his way back to his seat.

My place was set next to Charles and Belinda. Ian laid a place at the head of the table for Kit and made sure that we all had wine or a soft drink. No one seemed willing to break the silence until Simon suggested through his teeth, 'If you've got something to say, Kit, why not say it and go?'

'Good idea.' Kit raised his glass. 'To Harry Byrne. A man who lived by his principles and to hell with the consequences.'

The faces of his audience showed their distaste. I was mildly shocked myself; but Kit and Grandad had always been at odds, their relationship at best a respectful truce.

I raised my glass. 'To Grandad. May he rest in peace.'

Ian, Charles and Belinda followed my lead, if with less conviction. Robyn looked mutinous and glared at Ian, but she did take a sip. Simon sat as if frozen. Toby scowled. Neither touched his glass.

'The old man wrote me a letter last week,' Kit said. 'He wanted me here to protect him, and especially Lissa, from some unnamed threat.'

Toby burst out, 'That's crap! Show us the letter, then!'

'I haven't got it with me.'

'It's a figment of your imagination. That's the only thing you were ever any good at—bloody myths!'

Kit rolled his eyes in irritation. 'Never mind what you all think of me. None of us would want to see Lissa injured, or worse.'

Several voices rose in protest; mainly, I gathered, at what they considered his sensationalising of a non-existent risk.

'If you're so worried,' Charles said, 'why not go to the police?'

'Grandad was against it. He thought it might put Lissa at greater risk. We will talk to Hughes, but it would be nice to go armed with a few facts, or at least plausible theories.' He glanced around the table. 'Especially if the post mortem throws up any unanswered questions. If Mum intends to accuse Lissa in court, we might need to prove to the coroner *and* the police that Grandad was afraid *for* Lissa, not *of* her.'

'You're a bloody loose cannon,' Toby said, 'and you're out of your fucking mind!'

'Let's hope so. But if we go to the police now, and something happens to Lissa as a result, it'll be a bit late then to regret it.'

Belinda asked, getting straight to the point in her quiet way, 'Yes, but *why*, Kit? Who'd have wanted to harm the Professor? And Lissa can't have any enemies.'

'No? How about my mother? And no,' he raised his voice to quell an outburst of indignation from the other Pevenseys, 'I do *not* mean Grandad was afraid of Mum. I'm just pointing out that anyone can inspire hatred. By being born in certain circumstances, for example, or by having one stroke of luck more than someone else.'

'Or,' Toby muttered, 'by being an egocentric bastard who enjoys slagging off his own mother behind her back.'

Simon smirked, but the others paid little attention. They were casting covert glances at me and looking disturbed and increasingly thoughtful.

After a moment Robyn said, 'What do you want from us, Kit?'

'Your memories. Some of us lived at The Eyrie for years as kids—and Simon and Ian, you spent a lot of time there. Did any of you hear of someone who disliked the old man and might have harboured a grudge?'

'I don't quite see,' Charles said, 'why this has to be a problem from years ago. Why not someone he fell out with three weeks ago, or some crank who's taken exception to Lissa riding past his gate too early on a Sunday morning?'

'Because then Lissa would probably know about it. We need to cover the years that we don't remember as clearly as you do. If you think of something, however insignificant it seems, then please, *please* tell Lissa or me. If the information is sensitive, you can depend on our discretion.'

'Quite a claim, coming from a journalist,' Toby said.

'Is that right?' Kit said coolly. 'When have I ever been a snitch?'

Silence. Kit looked at his sister, and she averted her eyes with a frown. The twins had broken two of his fingers once, during a game of 'torturing prisoners'. He had told Aunt Melody that he had fallen out of a tree. I wondered if Robyn ever felt ashamed of the child she had been, or of the man that her twin had become.

'While we're on the subject,' Kit said, 'this needs to stay between ourselves. The last thing we need is the tabloids on our backs.'

'The *tabloids?*' Toby laughed. 'You think they'd care about the accidental death of an eighty-year-old academic, who may have been a touch paranoid?'

'No,' Kit said, 'but if the press discovers that I'm playing minder to my young, female...' He gave me a faint smile. '...beautiful cousin, and that I believe her life is threatened and intend to find out why, then I may as well forget it. Because Lissa and I, and maybe some of you, will be followed and photographed. Anyone with useful information could be scared off.' He glanced at me again, and I knew he was thinking of Mr Aberystwyth.

'This is laughable,' Toby said, laughing again to prove it. 'Who the hell cares what some fucking presenter of a history series gets up to?'

Kit shrugged. 'It's a crazy world.'

I decided it was time to put the old blood-brothers vow into operation.

'W-when the last series of *Age of Gold* started,' I said,

'Kit was on two chat shows and three magazine covers, and the *Radio Times* did a feature...' I felt hot colour rising in my face, and studied my wine glass with concentration. 'He's made history sexy.'

I dared to look up. Simon gave me a rueful smile. Even Toby appeared to be giving the matter consideration, despite his scowl. I looked at Kit, and his eyes sparkled back at me.

'That's more or less it,' he said. 'Sorry, Robbie and Ian, I've held up the meal longer than I meant to. Want me to leave now?'

To everyone's astonishment, Robyn said, 'No. Please stay.'

Toby and Simon turned on her identical looks of outrage, and she said gently, 'Toby, I know you're thinking of Mum, and you're right, Kit has caused a lot of heartache all round.' A glance at Simon. 'But the least we can do is sit down to one meal with him, as a gesture of goodwill.'

'Goodwill?' Toby spluttered.

'To Lissa.' Robyn rose, her figure-hugging dress and short black curls accentuating her height and commanding presence. 'Ian, could you open another bottle of wine? I'm going to bring in the soup.'

*

As dinner parties went, it was not a roaring success. Kit's attempts at conversation alternated with long, chilly silences, and I was glad when Belinda reminded Charles that they had to get home by ten-thirty for the babysitter. Simon took this as his own cue to leave, murmuring an apology to Robyn and an affectionate goodbye to me. Robyn went to wave them all off, leaving Ian, Toby, Kit and me at the table.

As soon as his sister was out of earshot, Toby snarled at Kit, 'So much for a friendly get-together. I hope you're satisfied.'

Ian said, yawning, 'Shut up, Toby, will you? We all know your views. You don't have to keep ramming them down our throats.'

Toby could not have looked more astounded if the china cat on the hearth had sprung to life and mauled him, and Robyn chose that moment to walk back into the room. Her twin stood up, putting on a martyred expression.

'I'd offer to help clear up,' he said, 'but I think I've outstayed my welcome.'

Kit said, 'We'll stay, Robbie. Call it returning a favour. It was good of you not to turn me away.'

Toby was more enraged by this than by anything else his brother had said. 'You sodding creep!' he hissed, and strode from the room without saying goodnight even to his twin. The front door slammed behind him with a force that shuddered through the house.

'Well,' Robyn commented, 'I'll say one thing for you, little brother, life is never dull when you're around.' But her tone held none of the humour the words implied. She added, to Ian, 'And as for you...'

'I wanted to tell you I'd invited him. I just...'

'You thought I'd say no. You were right.' Her cool gaze rested on me. 'Lissa, do *you* believe you're in danger?'

'I don't want to, but Grandad really wasn't senile, or paranoid.'

'No, he wasn't.' She sighed at the improbability of it all, and we helped her and Ian clear the table and fill the dishwasher. When we had finished, she thanked me with a smile before turning solemn eyes on Kit. 'I should thank you, too, I suppose. But you're still a self-seeking bastard. Please don't come here again.'

It took him by surprise, after her near-friendliness

during the past fifteen minutes.

'Robbie, we don't have to fall out,' he said. 'OK, I made a bad decision.'

'Is that what you call it?'

'I'm only saying that if you'd keep an open mind—'

'About what? The trail of destruction you left behind you? Or the fact that, in all these years, you've never cared enough about us to pick up a phone? You're despicable and shouldn't be forgiven.'

I saw him gasp, and he said shakily, 'Don't talk as if you hate me, Robbie.'

'I don't hate you. You're not worth anyone's emotion or anyone's trouble—and if you were in danger instead of Lissa, I wouldn't lift a finger to help.'

Ian exclaimed in horror, *'Robyn!'*

'It's all right,' Kit said. 'It doesn't matter.'

'Honestly, she didn't—I mean, we don't—'

'Skip it. Ready, Liss?'

I picked up my handbag and turned with him to the front door. As we walked to the car, Kit thrust his hands into his pockets, saying nothing.

'She didn't mean it,' I said.

'She did, but don't take it to heart.'

We drove home in silence, and turned in through The Eyrie's open gates. I pulled up beside Kit's Mercedes, glanced across at the house—and froze.

'There's a light,' I said. 'Moving, like a torch.'

We sat still, watching the windows, which were now so dark that I could have imagined the torchlight. But I knew I hadn't. We had left a light on in the study, to convince any prospective burglar that the house was occupied. All the lights in the house were now off.

The torchlight showed again, a shifting gleam behind the curtains downstairs. Kit released his seat belt and started to get out of the car.

I gripped his arm, whispering, 'Don't be an idiot! We must ring the police.'

'Wait here,' he hissed back, 'and don't ring anybody.'

'What?'

He snatched my phone off the dashboard and shoved it into his jacket pocket. 'Lock yourself in. Promise?'

'No! This is crazy. Kit, for God's sake—'

He had gone. I saw him cross the lawn to avoid the noisy gravel path. He let himself in by the back door, which was evidently unlocked, and vanished from sight.

I sat there for another five seconds, biting my lip in indecision. Then I got out of the car and followed him.

CHAPTER EIGHT

Kit had left the back door open, but there was no sign of him or anyone else. I reached for the boot scraper before stepping into the dark kitchen and trying the light switch. Nothing, and this time I couldn't blame the weather. Heart thumping, I set down my handbag, slipped off my shoes and padded across to the hall doorway.

A pair of dark figures, locked in a terrifying struggle, reeled towards me and crashed into the wall. One of them grunted and swore and I recognised Kit's voice. His taller assailant must have seen or sensed me there. He whipped round, and I looked up into the eye-sockets of a Hallowe'en skull mask.

I shrieked, then gathered sufficient wits to swing the scraper. His gloved hand shot out and grabbed my wrist, fingers digging in brutally. The scraper dropped from my hand.

Kit shouted, hanging on to his other arm, 'Liss, go! Run!'

The man shoved me aside. My stockinged feet slipped on the polished floor and I came down hard but didn't feel it. Moonlight was filtering through the curtained window; enough to show skull-face lashing out with savage accuracy while my cousin just tried to block the punches.

It was unbelievable. Kit wasn't fighting back. He was getting ruthlessly hammered, by someone whose priority was damage rather than escape. Even more incredibly, he was saying between the blows, 'We can talk—don't do this—you bloody idiot—'

I wasn't going to bet our lives on the man stopping for a chat. Shaking numbed fingers I cast about for my lost weapon, then scrambled back to avoid being trodden on, just as the man grabbed Kit's hair and slammed his head against the cellar door frame. Kit swore again and tried to rip off the ghoulish mask.

He didn't succeed. His attacker drove a fist into his stomach and kneed him in the groin, then seized his right wrist and twisted the arm behind him, keeping him from falling as his knees buckled.

I didn't guess what he meant to do, but perhaps Kit did. Regaining his feet he scraped a heel down the man's leg and elbowed him in the ribs. He received in answer a couple of wicked kidney punches.

I gave up on the boot scraper and threw myself down flat, lunging for the man's ankle, trying to tug him off balance—and he kicked backwards and trod down, grinding his heel into my forearm.

Whatever sound I made had a radical effect on Kit. He turned fast within the intruder's grip and started to fight in earnest, kicking and punching with speed and fury but far too late. Skull-face forced him round again and jerked the twisted arm upward. Kit cried out, clutching his shoulder, and the man whispered with blood-chilling venom, *'You're fucked!'* He kicked the cellar door open and hurled Kit through the doorway. I heard a sickening impact, and then a thudding, tumbling fall.

The same fall which had killed Grandad.

I flung myself on the boot scraper and closed my left hand around it, just as the man turned and found me in his path. He hissed, 'Out of the way, bitch!' and kicked my shin, and in an access of mindless rage I swung the scraper at floor level.

It slammed into his ankle and very nearly felled him. While he cursed I took another swipe at his legs. He avoided that one and leaped past me, blundering across the kitchen to the open back door. Next second he was gone into the night.

I scrambled up and ran to the top of the steps, shouting Kit's name into the darkness.

No answer.

Check the power. I stood on tiptoe, found the fuse box and the main isolator switch, then felt lower for the cellar light switch itself.

Instant illumination. He was sitting on the bottom step, hugging himself as if winded, or as if hurt beyond speech or breath. I ran down the steps and stooped in front of him. His head stayed bowed, face invisible.

I touched his arm. 'Kit?'

He looked up. There was blood in his hair and running down his face, but he was fully conscious. It was his expression that scared me.

'You should've gone.' His voice was unrecognisable. 'That fucker hurt you, didn't he? I heard—'

'Kit! Shall I call an ambulance?'

'What? No.' He sat up straighter. I saw the pain shudder through him and he squeezed his eyes shut, left hand gripping the edge of the step.

'Oh, God,' I said. 'Did he break your shoulder?'

'It's OK. Give me a minute.'

Nothing was OK. 'Why didn't you defend yourself?' I asked in despair.

'Thought, if it was Toby...he'd stop.'

'*Toby?* But he couldn't—he wouldn't have—'

'Tall enough. If it was Simon...should've let you ring the cops.'

'Whoever it was, I got him with the scraper. I hope it bloody hurt!'

Kit shot me a glimmering look, then saw the angry-looking mark on my forearm. 'Shit! Fucking bastard!'

'I'm fine. It's nothing. Did you hear what he said to you?'

'Yeah. Let's prove him wrong.'

He grabbed the handrail, summoning resolve, and hauled himself to his feet. I looked at his face and moaned. He started to limp up the steps and I put my arm around him, then dropped it as he winced from my touch.

It took a couple of very long minutes to reach the kitchen, and I hurried to secure the back door. The lock was intact; not only had our burglar known where to find the fuse box, he had also had a door key.

Echoing my thoughts, Kit said, 'Who else has a key to this house?'

'Only Charles. If I go away, Grandad often stays— stayed—with Dr Southbrook or old Mr Threlfall. Charles looks after the horses.'

'And you didn't see fit to tell me that?'

'No…well, it's only Charles. And you didn't ask.'

Muttering what sounded like, 'Give me strength,' he slid his arms out of the once-smart jacket and dropped it on the table before sitting down slowly, supporting his right elbow. His face was ashen.

'Let me drive you to the hospital,' I said.

'No. Stop fretting.' He nodded towards his abandoned jacket. 'How's your phone?'

I retrieved it without hope, but miraculously it still worked.

'Can you help me get this tee-shirt off?' he said. 'Please?'

I tried to be careful, but despite his denials it was obvious how much I was hurting him. I resorted to using scissors.

The shirt had afforded little protection. As well as the fist-sized blotches on his arms and torso, his lower back was scraped raw, the grazes filthy with dust. A long welt crossed his ribs on the right side, presumably from that initial, crashing fall on to the edge of a step.

I didn't know whether it was anger or reaction making my hands tremble. Either way, it wouldn't do. I gave myself an inward pep-talk, equipped myself with a flannel and a bowl of water, and returned to my patient with at least the appearance of taking such events in my stride.

'Who'd have had access to Charles's key?' he asked, while I was cleaning the cut along his hairline.

'The family,' I said. 'Simon, maybe. But Simon wouldn't hurt me.'

'He wore blue contacts at dinner. Did you see? Vain git.'

'What does that prove? Hold still.'

Luckily the cut was not deep. The abrasions on his back took longer to deal with, but his ribs worried me more. I touched the bruised area gently—and something grated under my fingers.

Kit gasped, '*Christ!*'

'I'm sorry.' I was gasping a bit myself. 'That settles it. You must go to hospital.'

'They'd ask questions. Goodbye discretion.'

'But you could have internal bleeding or...or anything.'

'Not very likely.'

'Oh, and what makes you such an expert?'

He rolled his eyes. 'Liss, I'm not dying, OK?'

I regarded him in seething silence, weighing alternatives. 'I'm going to ring Old Southbrook,' I said.

'Don't be daft. He'll be in bed.'

'Tough.'

The doctor answered eventually. Judging from his voice he had been asleep, and my apology served to irritate rather than appease. Nor was he impressed by the news that my cousin had broken a rib but didn't want to go to A and E.

'What are you calling me for?' he said. 'Make the decision for him.'

'I can't. We don't want....' I paused to compose myself, afraid he would think me hysterical. 'We can't even call the police.'

'What're you talking about, girl?' I heard a mattress creak, as if he had sat up fast. 'Is this connected with Harry? With what happened to your grandad?'

'I...we don't know.'

'Give me ten minutes.'

He arrived promptly, with three staccato jabs at the doorbell. His opening gambit of, 'Now, what's all this cloak-and-dagger nonsense?' seemed unpromising; but before I could reply, he slung his coat over an empty peg and asked where the patient was.

Kit had stayed in the kitchen. It was the warmest room. Naked from the waist up, he was shivering from more than the onset of shock.

'Sorry to drag you out of bed,' he said as the elderly doctor gusted in. 'Lissa's panicking over nothing.'

'I'll be the judge of that. And meanwhile, you can tell me what's been going on.'

Kit insisted that the doctor look at my arm first, but he confirmed there was no serious damage. While he was examining Kit and dressing the deepest grazes, we explained about the break-in and our suspicions regarding the culprit. The doctor appeared more shocked than surprised.

'If you think he threw you down those steps because Harry died that way,' he said, 'we're talking attempted murder.'

Kit shook his head miserably. 'I can't believe that.'

'No? You've got three fractured ribs, torn ligaments in your shoulder—possibly another fracture there—plus some minor damage around your right knee, and more contusions and abrasions than I've time or energy to count. Bruising over the kidneys, too. Not passing blood, are you?'

'Er...not yet.'

'Fingers crossed, then. Is that the lot?'

Kit raised a feeble grin. 'Apart from my nuts. It's OK, I think they'll live.'

Dr Southbrook clicked his teeth in exasperation. 'Anything stolen?'

'We haven't checked.'

'Don't check tonight! And Lissa, if his condition deteriorates in any way—rapid breathing, nausea, dizziness, *anything*—call an ambulance! I'll give you a sling, lad—'

'No, don't. Thanks anyway. Not a good look for a minder.'

The doctor grew still, fixing his patient with a penetrating stare. 'If you're afraid this man will come back, you must notify the police.'

'And if my brother ends up in jail? I want to put things right with my family, not turn them against me forever.'

'They're not worth it, lad. I'm Jodie Nix's GP, don't forget.'

Kit gave him a narrow look, but I couldn't read whatever message passed between them.

'Yes, well,' Dr Southbrook said, 'I won't strap your ribs. Not recommended these days. But stay out of trouble! And get that shoulder X-rayed.'

Kit smiled slightly and made no promises.

The doctor took a triangular bandage from his bag and thumped it down on the table. 'Use this as a sling whenever you're off duty. I'll leave you a prescription for codeine and enough pills to last overnight. And while I'm here,' he added, 'you mentioned yesterday that Harry had written to you. Can I see the letter?'

I fetched it, along with a blanket to stop Kit's shivers, and for good measure brought the letter from Mr Aberystwyth as well.

'Didn't know Harry had a friend there,' the doctor said, reading with concentration. 'If he *is* a friend. It might have been this character who was here tonight.'

'If it was,' Kit said, wrapping the blanket around himself, 'he's the same height as my brothers and Simon Threlfall.'

'Let's not rule him out. What's McCavity's?'

Kit explained, adding defensively, 'Liss and I are going to keep the appointment. Liss can drive.'

'Nonsense! The last thing you'll want tomorrow will be a long car ride and a hike through Hay-on-Wye. We can't send the girl off on her own, obviously, but *I* can go with her.'

'No,' Kit said, before I could speak. 'It's very good of you, but—'

'I'm too old, is that it?'

'Not at all, sir. I'd just rather no one knew we'd confided in you. For your own safety.'

The doctor glowered at him. 'Harry confided in me himself. I should have told you yesterday. An ethical dilemma. He came to see me last Wednesday.'

As far as I knew, Grandad had only gone for a walk that day.

'What was wrong with him?' I asked.

'Nothing. He wanted me to salve his conscience.' Dr Southbrook sighed as if, even now, he had difficulty believing it. 'Asked if I thought a pre-emptive strike could ever be justified, to ensure your safety. I pressed him to explain. He wouldn't.'

I said faintly, 'A pre-emptive strike?'

The doctor's eyes met mine, and his craggy face

softened. 'My dear girl, he was talking about premeditated murder.'

We more or less gaped at him.

'Grandad wouldn't plan to k-kill someone,' I said.

'He'd have done that and more for your sake. He thought the world of you, my girl. Never doubt it.'

I had doubted it all my life. I put a hand to my mouth, swallowing tears, willing myself not to cry. Kit gave my arm a gentle squeeze.

'But,' I said, 'he'd asked Kit to come back and protect me. Why do that, if he meant to—to resolve things on Saturday?'

'Maybe he hadn't made a plan,' Kit said. 'What if his intended victim turned up here, and the daft old bugger saw his opportunity, but then…'

'I suggested he seek police protection,' Dr Southbrook interrupted. 'He claimed that he couldn't. I should have gone to the police myself.'

'No,' I said. 'I mean that's not how…It was an accident.'

The doctor cleared his throat. 'Yes, well, I'm sure the post mortem will confirm that. Even so, I'll have to tell Tom Hughes that Harry was afraid for his life. Harry's intentions can remain private, so long as you come clean with Hughes about tonight.'

'We can't do that,' Kit said. 'Not yet.'

'So you'll risk this girl's life, just to smooth things over with your wretched clan?'

'No! It's for Lissa's sake more than mine that we've kept quiet.'

'What rubbish! Be honest with yourself! Whose interests are you serving here?'

'Not my own, apparently,' Kit flared back, 'or I wouldn't be needing your services.'

Old Southbrook drew breath, struggling to find

words to express his outrage. His patient slowly stood up, gripping the edge of the table, and faced him eye to eye.

'Like your friend...' Kit hissed the words through his teeth. 'Like Harry, I may be stubborn, I may be misguided. You could say it's cost me dear enough tonight. But like Harry, I would do anything to keep his granddaughter safe. So don't you *ever* accuse me of putting my interests before hers!'

As a declaration of commitment, it went pretty far. Kit seemed to realise this himself. He sat down, taking care not to meet my eyes.

'I only meant, I won't let her be hurt again,' he said.

In Dr Southbrook, all the righteous fury had gone. He clamped a hand on Kit's good shoulder and said gruffly, 'I spoke out of turn. I apologise. Not at my best at this hour.'

Kit shot him a reluctant grin. 'Who is?'

'Hmph. You might bear in mind, Harry didn't ask you to play detective. You're not honour bound to go stirring up a hornet's nest.'

'The nest is stirred up already. If we want to avoid getting stung again, we need information. McCavity's is our best hope.'

Dr Southbrook sighed. 'Well, I've said my piece. Ring me tomorrow morning if you want me to step into the breach.'

I went with him to the back door, and he laid a kindly hand on my arm. 'Look after each other,' he said, with an ominous glance back at Kit. 'See that lad of yours takes things easy.'

He wasn't my lad any more, but I nodded, lacking the energy to challenge the doctor's assumptions. As he stomped off to his car I locked the door again, and turned to meet Kit's eyes. He had virtually pledged to give his life for me if necessary. Barely knowing what to say, I ventured, 'Things just keep getting worse, don't they?'

He grimaced with contrition. 'I'm so sorry.'

'Oh, don't. I wasn't sniping. If I'd stayed in the car—'

'I *promise* you, Liss, I'll have that bastard for the way he hurt you, and I won't need to put him in the dock to do it.'

I shook my head; there had been enough violence already.

'Let's go to bed,' I said; and then, seeing him blink, 'You know what I mean. Do you want any help?'

'No. Look after yourself for a change.'

I dawdled over tidying the kitchen, knowing he would appreciate a clear field. When I did pass his bedroom, he softly called my name. I put my head around the door.

'I was wondering,' he said, 'if you've got an old shirt you don't care about? I don't want to get blood on the sheets.'

'My shirts wouldn't fit you. I'll fetch one of Grandad's.'

'No. I don't—'

'He really wouldn't mind,' I said crisply, and shut the door before he could argue.

I hadn't been in Grandad's room since the night he died. Now, as I turned the light on and crossed to the wardrobe, I resolutely thought only of the job in hand. I snatched the first clean shirt and shut the wardrobe door.

From the small, sombre-toned portrait above the bed, the hooded eyes of my namesake watched me unemotionally. Amphelisia Byrne, 1592. The picture had come with the house. Edgar Byrne, my great-great-grandfather, had bought The Eyrie after establishing that Amphelisia was a direct ancestress.

Edgar had been a romantic, spending several years

trying to prove that Amphelisia was Shakespeare's lover, the elusive 'Dark Lady' of the sonnets. He had failed. So had Grandad, sifting through the same meagre evidence. The only sure fact was that a Mistress Byrne of Malvern had known Shakespeare's patron, the Earl of Southampton.

We had had her portrait valued; an indifferently executed work by an unknown artist. Certainly not treasure. A pity. Grandad would have liked to think of his 'Dark Lady' coming to my rescue.

I took Kit the shirt and, mindful of Dr Southbrook's warning, reminded him to wake me if he felt ill. We set our alarms for eight-thirty. In the event I rose before eight, stamina at a low ebb after hours of nightmare-ridden catnaps. My bruised arm was predictably stiff. Had this been any other day, I would not have driven a car from choice.

After a hot shower, which failed to act as a cure-all, I dressed with shivering speed, went down to make some tea and took Kit's up to his room. I found him sitting on the bed, completing the nasty job of unsticking the shirt from his back. He brightened a good deal on seeing what I carried.

'Manna from heaven,' he said. 'Sleep all right?'

'No. You?'

He made a wry face, eased off his shirt and stood up to take the mug. Half way to his feet he froze, clutching at the bedside table and looking so agonised and sick that my own stomach contracted. I set the tea down and put out a hand to help him, and he raised some semblance of a grin.

'Ouch,' he said.

'For pity's sake, sit down for a minute.'

'Better to move around, I should think.' He straightened up by inches, groaning in spite of himself and almost laughing with embarrassment.

'Oh, Kit,' I said, 'you can't want to come to Hay.'

'We're not dragging Old Southbrook into this.'

'He's an adult. He can make his own decisions.'

'Liss, I'm going to McCavity's.' A sideways glance, faintly sparkling. 'Piece of cake.'

'Don't be ridiculous!'

'All I need is a hot bath and a couple of pills. Then you'll have your minder back.'

I wasn't going to win. Muttering under my breath I turned away, and he said accusingly, 'What?'

'Men!' I repeated, and left him to it.

CHAPTER NINE

When the doorbell rang, it was still only nine o'clock. I thought it might be a special delivery—Grandad did sometimes order books online—until I went downstairs and saw the outline of a tall, dark-haired figure through the frosted glass in the front door.

I took a step back, calling over my shoulder, 'Kit!'

The letterbox opened, and a pair of brown eyes much like my own peered through it. 'Lissa, it's me. Charles.'

'What do you want? *Kit!*'

'Please let me in. There's no one with me. Lissa, please.'

I still hesitated; but I couldn't accept that Charles was our villain.

As soon as I opened the door, he surged past me, then rocked to a halt as if afraid to go further without permission. He swung round, running a hand distractedly through his hair. The curls were already tousled; he must have done the same thing several times since combing them. This alone, from the usually neat and dapper Charles, seemed sufficient evidence of a guilty conscience. He was not a violent man; but complicit? Yes, that I could believe.

'Where's Kit?' he said. 'Is he all right?'

'He's not in the mortuary. Do you care about the finer points?'

Charles gasped. 'Lissa, I didn't want…Oh hell, this is—'

'Well, what a surprise,' Kit said, from the landing.

Charles looked up and stood like stone, watching his brother descend the stairs. Kit was dressed, and the cut along his hairline was barely noticeable, but he was nearly as white as his borrowed shirt and he couldn't hide the pain that jolted through him at every step.

I had enough sense not to offer him a hand in front of Charles. He gave his appalled brother a glare that would have seared through steel.

'Would you believe,' he said, 'we disturbed a burglar last night?'

Charles's Adam's apple bobbed convulsively. 'You should never do that. Never try to tackle a burglar yourself.'

'You don't say.'

'But you must be all right? I mean—'

'Yeah. Anyone tries a stunt like that again, he'll get more than he fucking bargained for. Tell your friends!'

In the circumstances this should have sounded ludicrous, but he did in fact look so angry and so startlingly dangerous that I almost believed him myself.

Charles groaned. 'That's not what I meant.'

'I should bloody well hope not!'

'Did you see...could you tell...'

'Who he was?' Kit reached the foot of the stairs and paused there, holding on to the newel post. 'Slim build. Strong. Tall. A bit like you.'

The silence fizzed with shock. Charles opened his mouth and shut it again.

'Or Toby,' Kit said. 'Or even Simon. Any other ideas?'

Charles found his voice. 'I can't—'

'Course not. Just like the old days, eh? The rest of the Eyrie Gang against the two youngest recruits. Or is it the Pevenseys closing ranks against their black sheep?'

'It's not like that. Not for me.'

'So you weren't sent to check I was out of action, and you haven't come to gloat. Just why the hell *are* you here?'

'Why do you *think*? You're my brother!'

Kit hadn't expected that. I thought it affected him

81

more than he wanted Charles to see; but he said, with undiminished wrath, 'Then maybe we should be on the same team. Whoever was here last night, he went for Liss as well.'

'No.' Charles slowly shook his head. 'No.'

'Didn't brag about that, did he? Face up to it, Charles! The man you're protecting doesn't care who he hurts. Was it Toby? Simon? Did we just disturb him, or was he waiting for us?'

'No! My God, no. Surely...' He was struggling to convince himself as well as us. 'Have the police been here?'

'Not yet.'

Charles exhaled with relief, and one trembling hand raked through his hair again. 'We can keep them out of it, can't we? All we—all he wanted was the letter, and he got it, so—'

'Which letter?' Kit flashed back at him.

'Oh...this'll sound crazy. It was about the Byrne treasure. Grandpa Pevensey wrote it to old Mr Threlfall, years ago.'

'We've seen that.'

'You found it?' Charles looked shattered. 'What Grandpa said...he was talking hypothetically. The rumour was always nonsense.'

'Then what the fuck is all this about?'

'It doesn't *matter*! Not any more. Kit...' Charles's eyes were beseeching; but I saw more hope in them than dread. In spite of everything he trusted us to be loyal, not just to him but also to the family, or the Eyrie Gang. 'Please don't report this,' he said. 'You can't begin to guess what harm you could do. An—an innocent party could be hurt.'

This was more than I could take. 'How dare you try to shift that bastard's guilt on to us!' I said. 'We've every right to report anything we like. Whoever attacked us wanted your brother crippled or dead, but of course you don't give a damn that he's been in *agony* all night—'

'*Liss!*' Kit protested furiously.

'—just because someone you'd rather not offend wanted some stupid letter! Well, if you stood by and let it happen, Charles, I hope you do feel guilty. You bloody well deserve to!'

My final words echoed through the hall and around the gallery above. Charles's despairing gaze flicked from one of us to the other, but there was nothing he could say. He turned and stumbled out through the doorway and down the path to his car as if unable to see clearly.

I closed the door, shutting him out. He could have been our ally, but instead he had chosen the easier option, the quiet life.

'Great!' Kit said. 'So much for convincing him I'm still a viable bodyguard.'

'I think he stayed convinced.'

'No thanks to you.'

Although his churlishness may have been a macho reflex, as my speech had undoubtedly embarrassed him, he was right. I had gained us nothing; and whatever I had told Charles, talking to Inspector Hughes was still out of the question, at least until this afternoon.

In the meantime, we had an appointment to keep.

*

The silver Mercedes was a thing of beauty. The thought of its likely worth did nothing for my nerves, as I slid into the leather driving seat and found myself surrounded by an interior in showroom condition.

Never an over-confident driver, I had become increasingly jittery during the past four years, since Grandad's deteriorating eyesight had cost him his licence. As my reluctant passenger, he had pointed out all of my inadequacies behind the wheel. However, unless I could drive this awesome machine the fifty miles or so to Hay-on-Wye, we would not be in McCavity's bookshop for eleven o'clock.

Kit edged in beside me, clicked the door gently shut and leaned back, holding his breath.

'You can still change your mind about coming,' I said.

'So can you.' He fastened the seat belt awkwardly with his left hand. 'If your arm's sore, we'll take a taxi.'

'A *taxi*? To *Hay*?'

'It wouldn't break the bank.'

'No, well, we're not doing it. I'm perfectly fit to drive, thank you.'

'It always amazed me,' he said, 'when the others used to call you Mouse.'

Whether or not this was a compliment, I could think of no reply.

After a moment he said, 'Liss, why did you go for Charles like that?'

'Do you need to ask? You heard him!'

'Yeah. Just wondered why you were so incensed on *my* account.'

'Obviously, because you're the one suffering most.'

'Why,' he asked, 'would you care?'

Startled, I met his searching gaze. Something passed between us, almost like a flash of recognition, and he gave me the smile I had known when we were lovers. My stomach swooped as if with panic, and Kit seemed equally disconcerted. He cleared his throat.

'Want to go over the controls?' he asked.

He explained just about every button and gadget, but only the heated seats held any appeal. I cast a meaningful glance at my watch and reminded him that we should pick up his codeine before leaving Malvern. Two minutes later, we were on our way.

Being an automatic, the car was easy to drive; but the sense of latent power was a physical thrill—the difference between riding the docile Smoky at leisure along a hilltop ridge, and guiding Tempest along the same route on a tight rein with my heart in my mouth.

After a stop at a chemist, Kit rang the production secretary on *Age of Gold*, holding his phone to let me hear both sides of the conversation.

'Kester!' The voice was young and huskily female. 'Didn't you get my messages? How are things in the backwoods?'

'Never a dull moment.'

'Is everything all right? You sound knackered.'

'My grandad died.'

'*Kester!* He was scared, wasn't he? What happened?'

I recalled then that she had opened Kit's 'private and confidential' letter, and found myself resenting the fact that this unknown woman should know our business.

'He fell down some steps,' Kit said dryly. 'No story there.'

We heard her gasp. 'You sod, you know that's not—'

'Skip it, Rusty. Will you do me a favour and keep your ear to the ground this week? There'll be some power-play and I might need to know the outcome.'

'All right.' A pause. 'Don't stay away too long.'

The command sounded more personal than professional. Not that his private life was any concern of mine.

As he disconnected, he said, 'We came down this road on the motorbike, Liss. Remember? Before I went to uni. We stopped for lunch, and I asked you to come and live with me.'

I remembered all of that delicious spring and summer. 'We were kids,' I said.

'Would the old man have given his blessing, do you

think, if you'd asked him?'

'I'm not sure. But we'd have been crazy to do it.'

He was quiet for a while. At last he said, 'Follow signs to Hereford, Liss. Want the sat-nav to talk you through it?'

But I knew the road. We were soon through the weekday traffic and out in the country again. I was starting to feel less intimidated by the Mercedes and in other circumstances might have enjoyed the experience, but today I wanted only to reach Hay safely and on time. My arm ached, and I was aware of Kit's far worse discomfort, despite—or because of—his mostly silent concentration on the passing scenery. I turned the radio on, but neither music nor a lively debate raised my spirits. Even the weather was dismal. One way and another, I regretted the economising instinct which had made the taxi idea seem immoral.

We left the main road at last, and crossed an ancient toll bridge over the River Wye. Ahead of us the rain-swept hills, bereft of any sign of the modern world, shone briefly emerald in a shaft of sun.

'We're crossing into the past,' Kit murmured. 'Ghosts and shadows and distant voices. No guarantee they'll like us disturbing their rest.'

Of course it was nonsense, but all the same I shivered a little. Kit's imagination may have advanced his career, but I could have done without it today.

'We are going,' I said, 'to meet an ordinary, unghostly friend of Grandad's.'

'Or,' Kit said, 'a man with something to hide, who won't like the fact we've read his letter, won't want to talk, and might just conceivably have attacked us or put someone else up to it.'

His anxiety was infectious. We had been assuming that our search for the truth the route to safety. I began to wonder now whether knowledge would prove more dangerous than ignorance.

If so, we were travelling not just into the past, but towards a precipice from which there might be no turning back.

CHAPTER TEN

Hay-on-Wye is a small Welsh border town, graced by a castle and a view of the river and the Black Mountains. It is also a bookworm's Mecca, with a welter of new and second-hand bookshops specialising in every subject imaginable.

I parked with ease in the nearly empty car park, and scrambled out of the Mercedes with half an eye on the time. As I walked around the bonnet, Kit levered himself out of the passenger seat.

Heated seats notwithstanding, at that moment he didn't look like anyone's idea of an assault deterrent. He caught my eye and grinned weakly, pushing himself upright.

Following Google Maps on my phone, we headed for the town centre and McCavity's Antiquarian Books. Although the weather seemed to have put off most would-be visitors, there were some pedestrians, and Kit attracted several double takes and a couple of lengthy stares. He returned these in passing with a smile and a casual 'Hi,' turning on the charm without apparent effort.

I should have expected it. He was, according to the media, a thinking woman's hunk, and in Hay the tourists were likely to be intellectuals.

'Quite an ego-trip,' I murmured.

'What do I say to that? Yes, so you can despise me, or no, so you can call me a liar?'

My remark had been a straight observation; I hadn't meant to kick him when he was down. I said quietly, 'Is that what you think of me?'

'Must deserve it, mustn't I? You can't all be wrong.'

'You didn't deserve last night.'

He sent me a fleeting smile and stopped to rest,

88

propping his good shoulder against a lamp post. 'It's not always convenient, being recognised,' he said, 'but it's a buzz. And if I'm nice to people, the ratings go up. Great. Medway renews my contract.'

I must have looked cynical.

'All right,' he said, grinning. 'With or without the fan club, it's the best job I can imagine. I'd do it for half what they pay me—and don't tell that to the accountant!'

'You always were a romantic,' I said.

'Maybe. Why not? But I like the money, too.'

We went on down the street, in my case with growing trepidation; but McCavity's, when we finally stood outside it, didn't look like a gateway to danger. It was merely a tall, half-timbered shop-front, sandwiched between others similar.

Kit caught my hand and we stepped over the threshold, in my case with a sense of taking a momentous and irreversible step; and the mustiness of old books closed around us, as though we were indeed in the embrace of ghosts.

*

The ground floor turned out to be a maze of ceiling-high bookshelves, and there were several solitary male customers. None of them appeared to be looking out for a friend's arrival.

A guide to the shop's layout showed three storeys, accessible by stairs and a lift. We decided to search one floor at a time, Kit using the lift while I took the stairs, on the grounds that I hardly needed a minder in such a public place.

Walking through the rooms, I allowed my gaze to linger on a couple of likely customers, but one looked away and the other buried his face in a book. On the second floor, having almost given up, I found Kit cornered by two teenage girls.

'We're doing Classical Civilisation for GCSE,' the taller girl was saying in a soft Welsh lilt. 'We always watch your programme. Can we take a selfie with you?' She already had her phone out.

'Not right now,' he said. 'So you're bunking off school?'

She exchanged glances with her friend, and shrugged.

He let it go. 'What's your name?'

'Eve. This is Bronwen.'

Eve was a thin, long-legged blonde. Her friend was small and dark. Both girls wore black coats and trousers and would have been suitably inconspicuous for a day's truanting, if not for Eve's shimmering, waist-length hair.

'You can have an autograph, if you like,' Kit said.

The girls rummaged in their bags and came up with a folded envelope and a school diary. Kit took out a pen and signed with a left-handed flourish. If the result was different from his usual signature, they were not to know.

'Off you go, then,' he said.

'We thought you might tell us about the next series,' Eve said.

'Look, I don't want to be rude, but I've got an appointment and—'

'In a bookshop?' Eve said, with a nervous giggle, as if aware that she had overstepped the mark.

I spoke from behind them. 'Kit, we have to go.'

The girls looked far from pleased to see me.

'Lissa and I work together,' Kit said. 'Go back to school, OK?'

They grimaced at each other, but little Bronwen said, 'Bye, Kester,' and they walked off, whispering, glancing back a couple of times as if still unable to believe their luck.

Kit put his hand on my arm, commanding my

attention. He was staring at something behind me. I turned around.

The man stood quite close, watching us, hands thrust in his pockets and legs braced apart. Mid-fifties, neatly trimmed hair and beard, weathered complexion. He was as tall as our burglar, and his stance reminded me of a gunfighter's in some old Western, as if he were waiting for one of us to move, so that he could shoot us dead.

'Steady, girl,' Kit muttered. 'Just a friend of Grandad's, remember?'

The man took his right hand out of his pocket, causing my heart to leap wildly, but he only wanted to shake hands. If he found Kit's grip at all feeble, he didn't remark on it.

'Well, well,' he said. 'Kester Pevensey, man of the moment. And...Lissa, is it? Roland and Susie's little girl?' He was English, not Welsh.

'You knew my parents?' I asked.

His face softened briefly, allowing me a glimpse of...what? Sorrow? Guilt?

'I don't understand why you two are here,' he said. 'Is Harry ill?'

'He died three days ago,' Kit said.

The man looked so stricken that I wished we had broken the news more gently.

'*Died?*' he whispered. 'How?'

'An accident, at home,' I said. 'He f-fell down some steps. Were you a friend of his? You haven't said.'

'An accident?' He shook his head as if to clear it. 'My God...can we talk somewhere more...there's a pub just down the road. I need a drink.'

He had long legs and a fast, loping stride. We didn't try to keep up, and after a few seconds he slowed down for us. In the pub he bought a round and led us into an unoccupied alcove. We edged around the table to sit opposite him, a manoeuvre that he watched in a glazed fashion; then abruptly the dark eyes snapped into focus.

'Surely,' he said to Kit, 'you haven't had an accident as well?'

'Fell off a horse.'

'Oh.' He glanced from one of us to the other. 'I'd better introduce myself. Or does either of you recognise me?'

Neither of us did. Nonetheless there was something familiar about him. I thought perhaps we had met, long ago.

He leaned forward, elbows on the table, and pressed the tips of his index fingers together in front of his lips; a pensive, secretive gesture which seemed to characterise the man.

'Perhaps you were too small when I left,' he said. 'I doubt you'll have seen a photo. I'm not remembered with affection in the Malverns.'

I regarded him with new eyes and racing thoughts. 'Are you Jodie's father? Mr Nix?'

'Please, call me Joshua.'

I became aware of Kit's stillness, and glanced at him. The colour had drained from his face; I had rarely seen him so angry. Perhaps he knew more than I did, about how this man had treated his wife and daughter before he left them.

I gave his arm a warning squeeze, and told Joshua, 'Last week Grandad asked Kit to come home and protect us. We don't know why, but we think you do. After he died, you see, we found your letter.'

A kind of spasm crossed Joshua's face, and he looked at Kit as if trying to draw his soul out through his eyes. '*Was* it a horse?' he asked.

'I've said so.'

Joshua sat back, perhaps trying to appear relaxed. If

so, the effort was wasted. He was nearly as strung up as Kit. 'Harry and I had private business,' he said. 'I can't share the details with you.'

Even through his leather sleeve I felt Kit's muscles shift and tense. I was so aware of his battle for self-control that my own body trembled.

'If you knew the old man,' he said, 'you know he'd beg you to tell us, rather than see Lissa get hurt.'

'Harry's dead.' Joshua leaned on his elbows again, bringing his face so close to mine that I recoiled from those dark, tormented eyes. 'If you keep the police out of it, I'll be responsible for keeping you safe.'

'You?' Kit muttered. 'Your idea of responsibility to your daughter was to disappear and throw money at the problem.'

'That's my business, and none of yours.'

'With your track record, why should we believe you'd keep your word?'

'Stop it, Kit,' I said.

Joshua said quietly, 'Then believe this. If you talk about me, to anyone at all, you may live to regret it.'

Kit said roughly, 'And if that's a threat—'

'It's nothing of the sort! If a police investigation leads them to me, then Harry's name and mine will be dragged through the dirt. I don't mean some sordid little scandal. I mean that your grandfather will be remembered, not with liking or respect, but with a shudder of revulsion.'

If his intention was to shock, he succeeded, at least where I was concerned. Not with respect but with a shudder. Dear God.

It was Kit who asked, 'What in hell did the pair of you do?'

Joshua's mouth twisted. 'What we thought was best.'

'We did it for the best,' Grandad had said. 'May God forgive us.'

93

I found my voice. 'Was that why you left?'

The haunted eyes narrowed. 'I'm not warning you away from the police so that you can go off on some half-baked crusade. You need to leave Harry's past, and mine, well alone.'

'We can't forget what we already know,' I said.

'What does that amount to? That Harry and I had a mutual concern, which I'll now have to resolve without his help?'

'What it amounts to,' Kit said, 'is an old man just happening to fall to his death, three days after writing that he was afraid for his own life and his granddaughter's. It amounts to Harry Byrne begging God to forgive him as he was dying, for whatever you and he did twenty-odd years ago, and you sitting there quaking at the thought we might go to the police.'

Joshua shook his head, and when he spoke it was hardly above a whisper. 'Bring the past to light now, and it would be like calling out at the foot of a mountain and starting an avalanche. I'd hate to see Harry's memory reviled, but he can't be hurt any more. It's the people you care about, not to mention you yourselves, who'd be the ones to suffer.'

We regarded him in silence. I feared that his words had the ring of truth, but he clearly had his own reasons for wanting us warned off.

Kit said, with more control now, 'Whatever you did, was it connected to the Byrne treasure? Is there something hidden in the tunnel?'

Joshua caught his breath. 'You haven't been listening to those old tales?'

'The thing is,' I put in, 'it's not just about the money. I'm wondering about the house foundations, because of the subsidence under the lawn. I really ought to know...is there a way into the tunnel, from the house?'

94

'Your guess is as good as mine. We wasted a lot of hours looking for that entrance as kids. We were all mates then—your dad, Richard Threlfall and me. But the whole tunnel must have caved in decades before we were even born.' He drained his glass and stood up. 'I'm afraid there's nothing else I can tell you.'

I wondered nervously how Kit would react; but he took out his wallet and a pen, wrote some numbers on the back of a business card and scooted it across the table. 'If you want to contact us, phone any time,' he said.

Joshua pocketed the card with a nod, and the three of us left the pub together, if not exactly in accord. As we emerged into the drizzle, I asked why he had chosen McCavity's for the rendezvous. His face twisted, and he looked up at the shop sign above our heads.

'If not for this place,' he said, as though to himself, 'if not for McCavity's Antiquarian Books…'

'What about it, Joshua?' I asked.

He looked down at me, and said with brisk dismissal, 'Go home, both of you. Sit tight, bury your curiosity, and forget I exist.'

Fat chance. As we watched him lope away, I opened my mouth to make some comment—and it stayed open. I spluttered, 'That's—look! That's him. The same man.'

'What man?' Kit said.

'Following Joshua! The man I nearly ran over on Saturday.'

Kit frowned at the small figure bustling along the street after Joshua Nix. Then he grabbed my hand and started to hobble after them, almost running.

We had no chance of narrowing the gap. I protested loudly and dragged at Kit's hand, but after a short distance he stopped of his own accord, holding his ribs and apparently trying not to breathe.

'Don't faint!' I said, clutching at him.

'No.' He shut his eyes.

'Stay here,' I said. 'I'll follow them.'

His eyes flew open. 'You won't! I don't trust that bastard.'

Beside me, a soft Welsh voice said, 'Kester?'

Eve and Bronwen stood there, regarding their idol with puzzlement and concern.

Kit was a long way past considering the ratings. He glared at them. 'I told you to go back to school.'

They shuffled their feet, cheeks flushed from more than the cold air.

'We sort of waited around,' Eve said. 'Are you OK?'

'I'm fine.'

'You look awful. And you were limping. Have you been in an accident?'

'No. Eve—'

'Whatever. I don't know why you can't send Lissa after that man you were with, unless he's a stalker or something. But we'll see where he goes, if you like.'

Kit sent me an incredulous look, which thanked God for the country's thinking women.

'There's another man, following our friend,' he told the girls. 'Short, overweight, going bald. Brown overcoat. Stay well back and—'

'Kit, no!' I said. 'If Joshua sees them, he'll know we put them up to it. You said yourself we shouldn't trust him.'

But the damage was already done.

'We're going,' Eve said. 'You can't stop us.'

And they went.

∗

'Your friend drives a dark blue Audi,' Eve said. 'Quite tidy, but we didn't get close enough to see the number plate. Sorry.'

It was some twenty minutes later. Kit had decided to hear their story in the comfort of a nearby tearoom, where he had bought hot chocolate and toasted sandwiches all round.

'What are you apologising for? You've done brilliantly,' he said. 'Anything else to report?'

Eve nodded as she chewed and swallowed a mouthful of toast. 'We followed them to the car park. The little man's car is an old Ford, dark red, Y362 something. They drove off towards Brecon.'

'They might join the road to Builth Wells, and go on to Aberystwyth,' Kit said, addressing me rather than the girls.

'That's miles,' Eve said. 'Is that where the tall man lives?'

'We're not sure. Look, will you promise me something?'

Silly question. They would have promised him the earth.

'Lissa and I are researching a story,' he said. 'I can't explain, but it's vital that you don't talk to the press about today, or mention it online.'

Eve frowned. 'Why?'

'Best that you don't know,' he said, adding flippantly, 'Life or death, and all that.'

'You're joking, right?' She studied his face, seeing no doubt the ravages of the past twelve hours; and she said, aghast, 'Did someone hurt you? Was it the stalker?'

'He's not a…. Look, Eve, all I need is a promise.'

'We promise, then.' She glanced at Bronwen. 'Of course we do.'

'Thank you. You've done wonders. We couldn't have managed without you.'

They glowed, and I felt a pang of guilt. Plainly they didn't care that they had been used, but all the same…

Kit was saying, 'You will go back to school this afternoon?'

'I suppose so.' Eve wrinkled her nose. 'We're bored with it now. We don't want to go to college full-time. We'd rather do an apprenticeship. Something interesting, you know? Travel, maybe.'

Bronwen added, 'We want some excitement, see?'

'Get the best GCSE grades you can, then,' Kit said. 'There's a lot of competition out there.'

They nodded, and Eve said, 'We'll never know what all this is about, will we?'

'Nope. Life's a bitch. Lend me your phones a minute.'

Eve blinked. 'What for?'

He extended a hand across the table, palm upwards. 'Please?'

After some hesitation, they complied.

'Are you giving us your number?' Eve asked, incredulously.

'I'm deleting the videos you took of those two men, and the shots of Lissa and me with our friend, and the one of me in the bookshop. Wouldn't want to find ourselves on YouTube.'

'Shit,' Eve muttered. 'We wouldn't have…'

'I know. I'm just removing the temptation.'

They would be texting, of course, about three seconds after leaving us.

We parted from them outside the teashop and they went off happy enough. Lucky girls. This had been an isolated incident for them, spiced with intrigue but unconnected with real life.

For us, the past still beckoned, luring us towards a safe haven or the brink of the precipice. And unlike Eve and Bronwen, we couldn't turn our backs and walk away.

CHAPTER ELEVEN

Travelling home at prudent speed through a veil of rain, we speculated endlessly about the whole conundrum. What shudder-inducing crime could be committed for the best of motives—in the perpetrator's view, at least? Only, perhaps, the murder of someone intent on causing harm. Had Grandad considered a 'pre-emptive strike' for my sake, because he and Joshua had done something similar once before?

In the absence of either knowledge or evidence, I baulked at telling Hughes anything in case it precipitated some catastrophe, whilst Kit was set against trusting Joshua to 'keep us safe' while we did nothing at all.

'Whatever you think of him,' I said, 'he didn't know about last night. Or if he did, he deserves an Oscar. Besides, I whacked that man's ankle pretty hard, and Joshua wasn't limping.'

'Guess it was Simon, then,' Kit said, adding with a sigh, 'Or Toby.'

'You're not thinking of confronting them about it?'

'Not today, Liss. And if what happened twenty-odd years ago is the key to all this, maybe we should talk to the older generation.'

'You mean old Mrs Threlfall?'

'I meant my dad...but yeah, whatever.' He sounded very tired. 'No use asking Auntie Maureen. She wasn't even in the country.'

Maureen was his dad's sister, who had married and emigrated to Canada about forty years ago.

The torrential rain was making driving difficult. I switched the wipers to high speed. 'The man who was following Joshua...' I said, peering through the downpour. 'If he lives near Malvern, which is possible, he'll drive back along the Hereford road.'

'Let's wait for him, then. If Eve was right about the age of his car, he might not stay on Nix's tail for long.'

We pulled into a lay-by, where an alternative route from Builth Wells joined the road from Hay. It was a long wait, and the rain was unrelenting. Every time a lorry charged past, the car rocked and a deluge hit the side windows. The minutes dragged.

'There!' Kit almost shouted it, making me jump.

I fumbled to start the engine. A red car from the Builth Wells road was cruising away from us. I lurched out of the lay-by and put my foot down, reaching behind me for the seat belt.

The last time I had felt acceleration like that, I had been on the back of Kit's motorbike, doing a ton down the M5.

'Sure it's him?' I gasped.

'Registration Y362. Liss, take it easy!'

I glanced at the speedometer and stopped breathing. We were doing a hundred and ten. Through water streaming up the windscreen I could see us gaining on the red Ford at a startling rate. I braked firmly.

The deceleration was just as dramatic. I felt my own seat belt tighten and didn't dare look at Kit.

'Sorry,' I said.

'Flash him. Keep doing it till he stops.'

'I didn't know we were going to—'

'Just do it!'

I flashed the driver three times before he pulled over. We stopped behind him, and got out of the car.

He opened his door and stood behind it, squinting and wiping a finger across his glasses. As we approached him he said, with quavering dignity, 'Stay back, Mr Pevensey!' He waved his phone in our direction. 'Or I'll call the police. What do you want?'

We stopped, not so much from fear of the threat as—in my case, anyway—from complete astonishment.

Kit said, blinking rain out of his eyes, 'We just want to talk.'

'Hardly the place, if I may say so.'

'You obviously know us. Who are you?'

The man groped in his pocket and drew out a business card, which he held at arm's length for our inspection. 'Daniel Chubb,' he said. 'Private investigator.'

Fooled by years of screen stereotypes, I had imagined such people as down-at-heel mavericks, with a tendency towards chain-smoking and alcoholism. Mr Chubb looked more like an amiable vicar. I ventured a little closer to read the soggy business card. He lived in Ledbury, only a few miles from Malvern.

A car sped past, giving us all a dousing from the flooded gutter. I gasped, and Mr Chubb flinched behind his car door. Kit swore so savagely that the detective, who didn't know he had anything else to curse about, raised his eyebrows in a way that reinforced the impression of a virtuous cleric.

'You're right,' Kit said, with sour humour. 'This is not the best place. Can you come to Miss Byrne's house? Now?'

'If you insist,' Mr Chubb said, pocketing his card. 'I know the way. But be assured,' he added, 'I'll tell someone where I'll be.'

*

Since we got away from the lay-by more quickly, we reached home well ahead of Mr Chubb and had time to change into dry clothes. I fetched Kit another of Grandad's shirts.

'I'll do a wash tonight,' I said, walking back to his room with it. 'If you want your stuff to go in with mine...'

He stood with closed eyes, forehead resting on his hand against the door frame. As my voice registered, he looked up with a start, as if I had caught him in some kind of wrongdoing. How he could feel like that was beyond me.

'Is it really bad?' I said.

He shook his head and visibly pulled himself together. 'How's your arm?' he asked.

'A bit stiff. It's nothing. Kit, please don't be so hard on yourself. I don't expect Superman.'

'Just as well.' He shrugged out of the wet jacket, dropped it over a chair and began fumbling with his shirt buttons. 'Haven't done a great job of looking after you so far, have I? The old man wouldn't be raising any cheers.'

True enough; but I wasn't obliged to share Grandad's view.

'Come here,' I said gently. 'Let me do that.'

I helped him out of one shirt and into the other, though I was half afraid to touch him. Quite apart from the black weal across his ribs, the injured shoulder was swollen and discoloured, and all the bruises looked worse than ever.

'You ought to get this shoulder X-rayed,' I said. 'Tell them what you told Joshua—that you fell off a horse.'

'What's the point? If it's cracked, it'll mend.'

'And hurt like hell in the meantime.'

His eyes lit with wry amusement. 'Is that rhetorical, or do I have to answer?'

'Oh, you're hopeless,' I said, but I was possessed by an almost maternal desire to put my arms around him and comfort him; an urge so strong that I stepped back, putting physical distance between us.

'What's up?' he said.

'There's…something I have to know.'

His expression grew wary.

'Five-and-a-half years ago,' I said, 'when you came down from Cambridge, straight into Jodie's bed...If I'd made a fight of it then...if I'd tried...would you have come back to me?'

'Oh, Liss, what difference can it—'

'*Would* you?'

He rubbed a hand over his face in utter weariness, and perhaps from sheer lack of energy said, 'Yeah, probably. Happy now?'

It was like a punch in the solar plexus. I went on, with difficulty, 'And if you had, would the rest still have happened? Would you still have gone? Cut yourself off from everyone?'

'Does it matter?'

'Yes, it does. Because if you were a coward, so was I. I could have fought for you, but I was...well, too proud, I suppose. And too hurt to believe I could win.'

His face softened. 'I told you, Liss. None of it was your fault.'

'Was it yours?'

'Mostly, yes.' The wariness was back. 'Look, we've been through all this. I can't confide in you, you can't forgive me.'

'I can. It took last night, and Charles this morning, to make me understand. If you can't talk to me, that's because I haven't earned it.'

He groaned, 'That's nonsense.'

'No, Kit. You don't have to make allowances.' This was much harder than I had anticipated. I took a deep breath, hugging my arms around me. 'I've been a bitch to you and I was wrong. Seeing how the others treat you, and what they've done...I hate it. I know we can't go back. But from now on, if you need a friend...you've got one. That's all.'

Whatever reaction I was expecting, it wasn't what I

got. He laughed; not out loud but silently, turning away as if in shame, pressing his forehead and the palm of his hand against the wall.

I said shakily, 'Kit?'

He turned very slowly to face me, and he wasn't laughing any more. His eyes were bright with tears. I hadn't seen him cry since he was about eight years old.

'What did I ever do to deserve you?' he said.

I don't know what might have happened then; but at that moment, through the silence between us, jarred the sound of the doorbell.

*

Mr Daniel Chubb sat in the living room drinking tea and crunching chocolate digestives, his coat drying on the fireguard and his glasses reflecting the newly kindled fire. Kit stood by the mantelpiece, sipping whisky and eyeing the detective, his expression grim enough to have unnerved a far bolder man. I pressed Mr Chubb to accept a third biscuit, before explaining that we had gone to Hay to keep a business appointment and asking why *he* had been there.

'My dear Miss Byrne, I followed you,' he said.

We had told no one except Dr Southbrook our reason for going.

'Why?' I asked.

'I've been hired to trace Joshua Nix,' he said. 'My client rang early this morning, to let me know that you're investigating your family's past. He felt we might help each other. But I decided to be discreet. In Hay, I heard you say goodbye to your friend, and you called him Joshua.' Daniel Chubb looked down at his biscuit, cheeks turning pink. 'I found that interesting. I followed him until he turned on to the Builth Wells road, but he was driving like a madman. I couldn't keep up.' Sighing, he shrugged off the failure. 'However, I'm afraid he's not

Nix.'

'Are you sure?' Kit said.

'No resemblance at all. I've seen a photo. Nix in his youth had fair hair, grey eyes, and was around five-feet-ten or -eleven.'

'But...' I didn't feel like admitting that he had just described my ghost, and substituted, 'That sounds more like Kit.'

'Yes, indeed. The Nixes and Pevenseys are distantly related.'

'Granny Pevensey was born a Nix,' Kit agreed, refilling his glass.

'I can't see why this man in Hay would claim to be Joshua,' I said. 'What if we'd remembered the real Joshua, or seen a photo?'

'He must have thought the gamble worthwhile,' Mr Chubb said.

'So where does that get us?' Kit downed his second drink at a gulp. 'Who's your client, Mr Chubb? Why is he looking for Nix? And what were you doing near this house, last Saturday afternoon?'

Mr Chubb, who had been studying his teacup as if hoping to read his fortune in the dregs, looked up sharply. 'I had an appointment with Professor Byrne. He wanted my advice concerning a threat to his granddaughter. That's all he would say on the phone. If I might ask, Mr Pevensey, is that why *you* are here? To look after Miss Byrne?'

Kit sidestepped the question. 'I'm staying for the funeral. Did you keep your appointment?'

'I'm afraid not. The Professor had asked me to arrive discreetly, so I parked further down the road. I rang the doorbell several times. There was no reply, so I left.' Mr Chubb took off his glasses and began polishing them with a tissue. 'Obviously, I can't name my client. But I swear to you, I had nothing to do with the Professor's accident.'

His distress seemed genuine, which was no proof of innocence, but instinctively I liked him and was tempted to trust his word.

'Even if you can't reveal your client's name,' I said, 'can you tell us why he, or she, wants to find Joshua?'

'I don't know why. If you have the address of the man in Hay, that might be a start.'

'We don't,' I said. 'Although…he was in Aberystwyth last week.'

At this point Kit interrupted, following his own line of thought, 'Why were you scared of us, in the lay-by?'

'Ah.' The little man made a business of removing the last smear from his glasses and replacing them on his nose. 'Because someone wants to sabotage my investigation. I don't know who.' He regarded Kit with a smile. 'And the way you looked, Mr Pevensey, as you came towards me…what I mean to say is, if I were intending to harm Miss Byrne, I would consider you a person to be reckoned with.'

Kit smiled back with irony and rested an elbow on the mantelpiece.

I asked, 'What do you mean by sabotage, Mr Chubb?'

'Anonymous texts.' He pushed his glasses higher up the bridge of his nose. 'At first, they advised me to drop the case, referring to my client by his surname. Then one said, *Do you live alone?* I do, as it happens. The last one was, *So little time. Don't waste it.*'

'That's horrible,' I said. 'Have you told the police?'

'I will, if the threats continue. But I'd like to crack this one, if I can. The thing is,' he added, with an endearing blend of modesty and satisfaction, 'I may not have found Nix, but I've uncovered a lot of information. More, perhaps, than my client intended. And I'm hooked.'

The contrast between his nervousness and the bravery of his words was striking, and he was close to the heart of the mystery. If he could get there, so could we.

Mr Chubb glanced at his watch, and rose at once to retrieve his coat from the fireguard. 'My, my. Nearly five o'clock. I'm usually home before dark, these days. Thank you for the tea. I'm afraid I'm rather a glutton for digestive biscuits.'

I stood up myself, and placed a detaining hand on his arm. 'Mr Chubb, my aunt is saying I pushed Grandad down the steps.'

It seemed impossible, now, that the scene at the hospital had been only three days ago. So much had happened since, that I felt only a minor flutter of nerves at the prospect of Aunt Melody repeating her accusations at the inquest.

'You saw what time I came home,' I said. 'If you would testify...'

He nodded several times. 'I must, of course, although I don't relish the prospect. Once my texting friend knows I was in contact with the Professor, he or she might assume that I was in his confidence. On the other hand...' His eyes twinkled. 'If I gave you no alibi, could I live with myself? Somehow I doubt it.'

In his own perception at least, he was risking his life for my sake. On impulse I gave him a hug and kissed his cheek.

'You're welcome,' he said, blushing.

'Don't forget,' Kit said, 'you're not the only one under threat. Refusing to name your client could increase the risk for all of us. Can you live with *that*?'

Mr Chubb pondered the matter, head cocked to one side like a pensive robin. Finally he sighed. 'He's Mr Threlfall. The solicitor.'

I said blankly, 'Ian? What possible reason—'

'My dear Miss Byrne, I only know that he seems desperate for me to succeed, and will pay me for as long as it takes.'

The revelation served only to deepen the mystery, but he refused to part with any more information. We gave him our phone numbers and I showed him to the front door, encouraging him to contact us at once if he changed his mind.

On the way back I paused to retrieve my post from the hall table, where it had lain unopened since our return. There were sympathy cards from Jodie Nix and old Mrs Threlfall, and a letter from the coroner's office, notifying me that the inquest would be on Thursday.

Kit followed me into the hall. 'What d'you think?' he asked. 'Next stop, Ian and Robbie's house?'

He was right, in principle. In practice, however, he'd had far more than enough for one day and was never going to say so.

'I'm so tired,' I said truthfully. 'Can we leave it for tomorrow?'

He was easily convinced. I made a quick freezer-to-oven supper, for which neither of us had much appetite. Kit made no reference to what had passed between us before Daniel Chubb's arrival, so I let him off on that score also, and we sat down to look through the old photo albums.

The earliest was one that neither of us had seen before. Despite a number of gaps, where only the photo corners remained, it was a poignant and fascinating memento. The first pictures must have been fifty years old, their colours faded to unnatural tones of pink.

'Is that Grandad?' I said. 'Wasn't he the image of Charles?'

'Liss,' Kit said, 'if I give you the keys to my flat, will

you go and stay there for a while?'

'Look, that's our grandmother. *Charlotte*, it says. Grandad took down the photos of her. I don't think they were very happy together.'

'Put that down and pay attention. I can see to the horses for you.'

'I'm not going, so you may as well shut up about it. Old Southbrook told us to look out for each other, in case you'd forgotten.'

'He didn't mean you to risk your life, and you know it.'

'If you can be stubborn,' I said, 'so can I. Blame the genes.'

He rolled his eyes to the ceiling. 'Why would you want to be here, when you could be safe in Kent?'

If I knew the answer to that, I was not about to share it with him.

'Let's look at the photos,' I said.

The album contained several shots of 'Roland and Melody' as children. In two or three, Dad was laughing, with his sister looking at him askance, possibly jealous even then. Another picture showed a group of children.

'Look at this little boy,' I said, pointing. 'He's very like you were, at that age. You don't think…if the man we met wasn't Joshua…'

'This could be?' He frowned at the old, blurred shot. 'So where *is* Nix? It'd be safe to use his name, wouldn't it, if you knew he couldn't turn up and contradict you?'

I felt the colour drain from my face. 'You're not suggesting that he and Grandad may have killed *Joshua*?'

'Not impossible, is it?'

'But he was Jodie's father. How could they think it was for the best?'

'OK, so my imagination's in overdrive. Forget it, Liss.'

He turned another page, to discover a shot of Dad

floating off a sandy beach, laughing up at Mum as she prepared to dive from a rock. They looked carefree. Happy. I wished I could remember them.

I had kept a secret, though, since earliest childhood. Sometimes, half asleep, I would seem to feel Mum's arms around me, or catch a waft of her perfume, or hear a memory of Dad's voice singing lullabies in the dark. Precious dreams, too private to share.

'Wonder why so many are missing,' Kit said, indicating the gaps on that page. 'D'you think someone has been deleted from family history?'

'Perhaps.' I tried to turn over again. 'Oh, that's the end. No, wait…no, it's not.'

The last two pages had been stuck together by a twisted photo corner, and perhaps the photo thus hidden had been missed when the others were removed. It was an informal shot of a bride and groom. The girl was a Caribbean beauty, the groom fair-haired and smiling, with a roguish sparkle. It was not his looks, though, that caught my breath, nor even his startling resemblance to both Kit and my ghost. His bride was Elizabeth Nix, and someone had written a caption: *Lizzie and Josh.*

On the lawn behind the young couple, a few wedding guests stood drinking and chatting. I recognised only one. He was young and smiling, but although the years since then had turned his dark hair grey and lined his face with sadness, he was undoubtedly the man we had met in Hay-on-Wye.

Mr Chubb had been right. Whoever Mr Aberystwyth might be, he was not and never had been Joshua Nix.

CHAPTER TWELVE

I would have risked bringing the horses down from the field alone, but Kit refused to allow it. I let him lead Smoky and he managed pretty well, but we were not indoors again until nine-thirty. He said apologetically that he would turn in now, if I didn't mind.

'How could I mind?' I said. 'You've been marvellous.'

He smiled faintly, turning away—and the doorbell rang again. Kit motioned to me not to answer it before going to the door himself.

'Who is it?' he called.

'Ian. Don't mess about, I'm freezing.'

Kit shot me a despairing look, but he did unlock the door. Once inside, Ian stood chafing his hands and looking both nervous and shifty.

'Sorry,' he said. 'I know it's late. Robyn's out with the girls, so...well, to be honest, she doesn't know I'm here. Can we have a quick chat?'

Resignedly, we made him welcome. I cooked him beans on toast because he hadn't bothered with dinner. Kit sank into an armchair, while I perched on the edge of the sofa and tried to conceal my impatience.

Ian said finally, through the last mouthful of beans, 'You might have realised why I'm here. Daniel Chubb phoned. He told me you'd met.'

'You don't say,' Kit murmured.

Ian frowned. 'Is this a bad time? I just thought—'

'Can you skip the excuses and get to the point?'

Ian began to fiddle with his knife and fork. 'If you're upset with me, because of what Robyn said—'

'We're not,' I said, with an imploring glance at Kit. 'It's been a long day, that's all. We really do want to hear...whatever you came to say.'

What Ian had to say, however, at first seemed hardly worth it. While sorting through his late grandfather's effects, he had discovered personal documents left in old Mr Threlfall's care by Joshua Nix. He had therefore hired Mr Chubb to trace their owner.

'So,' I said, 'when Mr Chubb rang you today—'

'He mentioned the man you met in Hay-on-Wye. That's the main reason I'm here. I know who he is, you see.'

Even Kit paid attention.

'His name's Hywel Price,' Ian said. 'He's another of Grandpa Threlfall's old clients. I've only met him since Grandpa died.'

'Why would he pretend to be Nix?' Kit said.

'He wouldn't. That is…you couldn't have misunderstood?'

We assured him that no, we couldn't.

Ian's bewilderment looked genuine. 'It makes no sense.'

'Where does he live?' I asked.

'He didn't say. We've met once, in Rhayader, but he was only there on business.'

'Surely,' Kit said, 'as his solicitor, you'd have his address on file?'

'Grandpa did, I imagine, but it's been mislaid.' Ian grew strangely reluctant to look either of us in the face. 'I didn't realise, when I saw Price, or I'd have asked him then.'

Kit regarded him with raised eyebrows, but all he said was, 'Did he mention Builth Wells? Or Aberystwyth?'

Ian's fair skin turned pink, which seemed to confirm that he was not telling us the whole truth. 'No,' he said.

'Chubb said he was heading that way.'

'Perhaps he was, then.' Ian set his plate aside and stood up. 'Well, I won't keep you any longer. I'm, er…very sorry you had such a rough time last night, Kit. Charles is quite cut up about it.'

Into a stunned silence, Kit said, 'He *told* you?'

Ian looked puzzled. 'He didn't have to, did he? I already knew.'

'*What?*' Impelled by outrage, Kit pushed himself out of the armchair; not a brilliant move in the circumstances. He winced and sat down again, hunched and breathless, watching Ian fiercely through narrowed eyes. 'What the fuck are you talking about?'

'Don't swear at me!' Ian said, but the response was automatic. He was staring at Kit. 'God, you look…what's the matter?'

'You know everything. You tell me!'

'How can I know…?' Ian began; then his mouth fell open, and he blinked rapidly behind the round lenses. 'Charles popped in today, after work,' he said. 'Robyn was…well, talking about you, and he actually stood up for you. He said you'd been hurt enough. I thought he was having a dig at her, for the awful things she said last night. My God, what have they done?'

We gave him an edited but pretty accurate account of the break-in, omitting Old Southbrook's story but including our subsequent conversation with Charles.

'You're saying Charles knew *in advance*?' Ian paced the carpet, flexing his fingers as if missing his doodling pencil. 'How could he have? Even if it was one of the gang, they couldn't have guessed you'd stay to help clear up.'

'He didn't need many minutes' head start,' Kit said, gingerly relaxing back against the cushions. 'And they all left before us. If it hadn't happened that way, or if we hadn't turned up for dinner, I guess he'd have waited till we were asleep.'

'But they couldn't *all* have been in on it. Not my

Robyn.'

It was a plea for reassurance, which we were in no position to offer.

'I can't believe it.' Ian said. 'If the gang is behind this—'

'Don't get carried away,' Kit said. 'I doubt if anyone planned to give me such a hammering except the one who did it. Besides, I destroyed your brother's marriage and drove your business partner to a nervous breakdown. Isn't that how the story goes?'

'Who says so? Simon? Your mum? I'm not dancing to that tune.' Ian sounded, for once, astonishingly aggressive. 'Jodie's never slagged you off, which has always made me wonder. And this isn't just about you, is it? To think...to *think* that sodding coward went for *Lissa!*'

'Yeah,' Kit said; and seeing the look that flashed between them gave me a glow of primitive and wholly non-feminist satisfaction.

'Well, this has gone far enough,' Ian said. 'The others can think what they like, including Robyn. From now on, I'm on your side.' He regarded us with crusading fervour, and drew himself up to his full five-feet-six. 'So, I'd better put my money where my mouth is, hadn't I?'

Kit lifted his eyebrows. 'Meaning?'

'Robyn and I came across some old diaries, when we went through Grandpa Threlfall's effects. I read them. I wanted—' He spread his hands, pale blue eyes seeking mine. 'You understand, don't you, Lissa? I was looking for stuff about Mum and Dad.'

Yes, I was familiar with that species of yearning curiosity. Ian had been nine when his parents died.

'It was mainly appointments,' he said. 'But there was something else.' He sat down again with a sigh. 'The day after Joshua left...a few weeks before Mum and Dad died...Grandpa wrote, *Joshua has gone. I don't believe it. It feels wrong.* And then, the next day, *They all know but they won't tell me.'* Ian swallowed. 'Those words...I can't forget them. He was hard, you know that. Even Gran used to keep things from him. The next entry was, *Oh God, I think I guess.* And two days later, one final sentence. He'd nearly gouged through the paper.'

Ian lowered his voice to a whisper, as though the shade of old Mr Threlfall might be listening, ready to berate his grandson for breaking a confidence. 'The words were in capitals. He'd written, *SWEET JESUS CHRIST, WHAT AM I TO DO?'*

I let my mind conjure John Threlfall, that harshly moralistic man, filled with doubts and suspicions that he couldn't bring himself to express even in writing; and I shuddered in the warm room.

Ian said quietly, 'If Grandpa believed Joshua was dead, he wasn't thinking of natural causes. And he wouldn't have been so...well, upset, unless someone he cared about was involved. He wasn't that close to Joshua.'

'Was there anything else?' I asked. 'Later that year?'

'Nothing. No other personal notes at all.'

'Not even at Easter? He had nothing to say about his son and daughter-in-law drowning? Or about taking you and Simon in?'

'Not a thing. So I hired Daniel Chubb, to find out whether Joshua was still alive.' Another sigh. 'I'm starting to think I've wasted my money.'

'He's found out something,' Kit said. 'Not necessarily about Nix.'

Ian stared. 'He hasn't said that to me.'

'You might have a word with him, then, don't you think?'

'Yes. First thing tomorrow. Look, I shouldn't keep

you up any longer. I wouldn't have come if I'd known...Just take care, both of you.'

We saw him out, and for the second time closed the door on the freezing night. I felt drained to exhaustion. If Grandad had killed Joshua...

I couldn't think about it. Kit put his good arm around me and held me close, not moving, not speaking a word, offering comfort as naturally as he would have done in the old days. Finally I raised my head and stepped back a little.

'I'm hurting you,' I said.

'Not really.'

'Liar.'

He rolled his eyes, half-smiling. 'Don't worry about it. If we're talking about dishonesty, though, Ian's changed a bit. He didn't used to be secretive. He was nervous tonight, too. Couldn't keep his hands still.'

'I know...but he's been like that for ages, on and off. Almost since you left, I think. And he wouldn't be much of a solicitor if he hadn't learned to be discreet.'

'Forget discretion, Liss, he was lying in his teeth.'

'About Price, you mean? I suppose Ian must know where he lives.'

'And they've spoken recently. Today, I should think. How else did he know the man in Hay *was* Price?'

'Mr Chubb told him.'

'Yes, that we'd met a tall, grey-haired man called Joshua. Ian met Price in Rhayader, not Hay. Why would he make the connection?'

It was a fair point, but I couldn't analyse the implications. Not tonight.

'One thing's for sure,' Kit said. 'Next time Ian goes to Wales, we'll be behind him.'

I didn't ask how he would arrange it. I was too weary to care. We went to our separate beds, and I didn't tell him that I had my own agenda for the morning. There was someone I needed to see alone. Someone who would know a good deal about Joshua, but who also, according to her business partner, had never had a bad word to say about Kit.

Jodie Nix.

CHAPTER THIRTEEN

Jodie stepped out of the offices of Threlfall and Nix the minute I drew up on the forecourt. A yellow coat swung out from her shoulders, enhancing the golden-brown skin tones inherited from her Jamaican mother. She looked like a flash of tropical sunshine, and much younger than her thirty-one years.

I had rarely seen her since the divorce. Even without the complication of my friendship with Simon, his presence at most of the gang's social functions had meant that his ex-wife had been excluded, despite her being Ian's business partner.

She slid now into the Mercedes, greeted me with a kiss and made some kind remark about Grandad. I thanked her for the card.

'You look worn out,' she said.

'I suppose I am, a bit. I've b-been to three agencies this morning. No one needs a researcher who can speak Italian and Greek. I'll apply for something secretarial but it w-won't pay enough.'

'You poor thing.' She gave my hand a squeeze. 'I'm so glad you rang. Let's go for a walk on the hills. It'll do you the world of good. We'll park by the Happy Rambler.'

As we drove out of town, she added, 'I must say, I adore this car. My Neil is still wildly in love with his old Porsche, or I might be able to nag him into buying one of these.'

Despite everything I had to suppress a smile. Image and its trappings meant a lot to Jodie. If Simon's MG had been in its present state when he proposed, she might not have married him.

'I assume this belongs to Kit?' she added. 'Ian told me he was back.'

I sent her a quick glance. Her face showed only serenity; but she had very dark eyes, the irises nearly as black as the pupils. I could never read them.

'My car's not running well,' I said.

'How *is* Kit?' It was a straight question, no apparent undertones. 'I gather he's still getting outrageously suntanned for a living.'

I said he was fine. In fact he had been in bed when I left, his acknowledgement of my job-hunting mission a grunt from under the duvet, followed by a reminder to leave my phone switched on.

'How are you?' I asked Jodie.

'Great. I'm pregnant. Did Ian tell you? Neil is over the moon.'

'That's wonderful. Congratulations.'

We parked across the road from the Happy Rambler café and set off along a lonely ridge, the wind whipping at our hair. I could imagine how Kit would have reacted to the choice of venue.

'I've heard all about the dinner party from Ian,' Jodie said. 'You'll be wanting *my* memories now, will you?'

'If you don't mind,' I said diffidently. 'Especially anything about your dad. You've never talked about him much.'

'No.' She frowned, as if analysing her reasons for the first time. 'I think I was ashamed. Not long after Dad walked out, your parents and the Threlfalls died in that awful accident. They were victims, but Dad had *chosen* to go. Then, as I got older, and he kept sending money but nothing else, not even a text, I didn't *want* to talk about him.'

'And now?'

She shrugged good-naturedly. 'I don't see why not. Let's see…he left school at sixteen and got a job with a local builder. No interest in being a solicitor like his dad.

Our garage was full of bits and pieces that he could turn into just about anything.' She sighed with regret for the past. 'He and Mum were married at eighteen. Far too young. He was a lovely dad, though. Unfortunately, he was also lovely to any pretty woman he met.'

'Do you think that's why he left? For another woman?'

'Maybe. One Saturday in February he went out to buy some car spares, or so he said. We never saw him again. A couple of days later, he sent Mum a cheque. There was a note with it, addressed to me. It said...I'll always remember...*Goodbye, my little Jodie. I'm so sorry, I just can't stay any longer. Be happy. Love always, Dad.* He must have been drunk when he wrote it. It was his handwriting, but the words sloped uphill and ended with a wobbly kiss.'

Jodie had quickened her pace as if to leave the old grief behind. I was half running to keep up with her.

'Mum received standing orders after that,' she said. 'I got a cheque on my eighteenth birthday, though. And my twenty-first. There was no card.'

'So the last payment was ten years ago?'

'Oh, no. They're smaller these days, but Mum still gets them every month. Why do you think she's never filed for divorce? A court settlement would give her less than Dad sends her, and she and her boyfriend are quite happy without a marriage certificate.'

Jodie fell silent, deep in her own thoughts, and I faced a few demons of my own. Was Joshua Nix alive and well? Or had Grandad and Price killed him after the note was written, and felt so guilty that they had used his bank account to send payments to Elizabeth and Jodie, even forging his signature on cheques? Was that how Grandad had sunk into debt?

Jodie stopped walking. 'I gave him a neck-chain for his birthday, once,' she said. 'It had a chunk of gold-coloured metal hanging from it, with the word 'DAD' stamped into it. He always wore it under his shirt, even though it was horribly cheap and used to make a green stain on his chest. I never imagined he'd leave us. Not like that. So final.' She gave me a disconcertingly shrewd stare. 'Are you looking for him?'

'N-no,' I stammered, taken off guard. 'We're questioning everyone, about everything.'

The dark eyes lingered on my face, but then, apparently satisfied, she turned towards the west. I followed her gaze, recognising the hills I had seen at close quarters yesterday, from Hay-on-Wye. The foothills of the Black Mountains.

'I'm not bitter about him any more,' she said. 'Some men are just unreliable. That's life.'

'You've been unlucky,' I said.

'Only with Dad and Simon. My Neil is the most reliable person I've ever met. And of course...' She sighed. 'Kit never let me down.'

'Jodie! How can you say that?'

She turned slowly to face me, the black eyes shadowed, a veil for thoughts and motives alike. 'I've known for ages,' she said, 'that what I did to Kit was very wrong.'

'What *you* did?'

'After he went away, I kept quiet while everyone else dug in the knife. Later I was ill, but that's no excuse.'

My heart was thumping, but I asked without emphasis, afraid of pushing her too hard and losing her confidence, 'Kept quiet about what?'

'He really didn't tell you? And yet he's staying in your house, and you talk as if you're a team. A couple. I think you still love him.'

This time I was the one who looked away. 'I'd be a fool if I did, wouldn't I?'

Jodie slid her arm through mine and started walking again, more slowly now, up the path to the summit of the Worcestershire Beacon.

'He told me once,' she said, 'that you'd given him up for his own good, before he went to Cambridge, because he wasn't ready to settle down. He said he'd been too young and heartless to see it.'

I stared. 'Kit said that?'

'You stayed friends, though, didn't you?'

'We had no reason to fall out.'

'So you say. I couldn't have done that, in your place, feeling the way you did. The way you still do.' She gave me what could only be called a look of admiration. 'I wish I had half your steel, Lissa.'

The compliment was so bizarre that I laughed. 'I haven't got any steel. I don't know how you can think it.'

She stopped and faced me, hands on hips. 'Toby flogged you once with bramble stems. Three lashes. Simon wasn't there, or he'd have stopped it. I'll say that for my ex; he didn't like to see you little ones get hurt. Charles was useless, and Ian and I were always terrified of the twins. I think Kit was in bed with flu.'

'He got back at Toby, a couple of days later.'

She smiled. 'I remember. Bless him. He fought like fury, all skinny arms and legs. Toby had a lovely black eye before he knew what was happening. I thought he was going to kill Kit for that.'

'Good thing Simon and Robbie pulled them apart,' I said.

'Robbie was a bully, but she's not a sadist. Seriously, though, the things we let the twins do to you and Kit…you were both so little. It makes me ashamed. And you never cried, did you?'

'Not in front of them. As soon as I was on my own with Kit, I used to bawl my eyes out. Especially in the dungeon. No steel at all.'

Her eyebrows quirked. 'Whatever you say, Lissa.' She shivered in the wind and wrapped her arms around her, gazing at the distant Welsh mountains. 'Kit never loved me, you know. He was sorry for me and I adored him. If we'd got married, we'd both have regretted it.' She faced me again, with determination. 'Ask him what drove him away.'

'I have. He won't tell me.'

'I made him promise…but I won't hold him to it any more. Dr Southbrook knows what happened. I had to tell someone. And I'm not the wreck I was, five years ago.'

'Why can't *you* tell me?'

'Because it should come from him. And…' She bit her lip. 'Will you say, I'm so sorry I was such a coward? His mother and Toby, and Simon—even my mum, at first—they sowed poison in everyone's minds, and I let them.' Jodie was crying now, tears sliding down her cheeks and dripping on the yellow coat. 'I don't expect either of you to forgive me, but if Kit would like us to meet…if it would help…I'd love to see him.'

'I'll tell him,' I said. 'Please don't be upset. It can't have been all your fault.'

'You don't understand,' she said.

I hugged her, and we clung together for a long moment, while many of those involved in our linked and separate lives went about their business far below, complacent and oblivious.

I drove her back to work in time to meet her first client of the afternoon. As I said goodbye she gave me a wan smile, clearly believing that once I knew the truth, I would never want to see her again.

Unlikely as this seemed, it was now up to me to find out.

*

When I got home, the Fiat had a man underneath it. I avoided running over his blue-overalled legs, and he slid the rest of his body into view and stood up, beaming. He was Martin, the young mechanic from the local garage.

'Mr Pevensey called me out,' he said, wiping his hands on his overalls. 'I've put a new battery in. Just changing the oil now. Not much wrong with the poor old girl. All she needed was a bit of TLC.'

I thanked him, and entered the house prepared to do battle.

Kit was sitting along the living room sofa, wearing Dr Southbrook's sling and typing left-handed on his laptop. He was whistling tunelessly under his breath, frowning as though concentration was an effort. I swallowed my intended protest and asked instead how he was feeling.

He sat back, rubbing his neck muscles and giving the laptop a disgusted grimace. 'I'm doing a book about the Americas,' he said. 'Companion to the new series. It'll need to be in print by next autumn, if we get the funding and the series goes ahead.'

'Can't it wait a day or two?'

'Have to, I think. Nothing I've written today would stand criticism. How can a couple of hours' typing be so bloody uncomfortable?' He caught my look of sympathy then and sat up straighter, making a fair attempt to appear more cheerful. 'Should've fought from the start, shouldn't I? Gone in hard, fast and dirty.'

'So what exactly did you study at Cambridge? Practical scrapping?'

'I've had my moments.'

'Ever considered anger management classes?'

'Ah. Wise words from the Boot Scraper Kid.'

I laughed shortly, and decided that a change of subject was in order. I didn't feel quite ready to analyse the difference between self-defence and the visceral pleasure I had experienced on Monday night, feeling the scraper connect with an enemy who richly deserved it.

'I saw Martin,' I said, walking around behind him to untie the sling. 'The garage will charge extra for calling someone out. If you'd waited, I could have driven it to them.'

'You'd have put it off, though. What're you doing?'

'You need a massage. I'll be very careful of your shoulder, but say if I'm making things worse.'

He snorted with reluctant humour, supporting his elbow as I removed the sling. 'Not sure that you could, much.'

I set to work, with a lot more on my mind than the job in hand, but after a few minutes the knotted muscles in his neck and upper back started to relax. He groaned softly with relief.

'That feels incredible. Bit of an expert, aren't you?'

'A farrier taught me.'

'Did he?' Laughter rippled through his voice. 'Before or after shoeing the horses?'

'Whichever.'

He didn't enquire further.

'Your mechanic recommended an electrician,' he said. 'I gave him a call. He's going to fix up security lights tomorrow afternoon. Another guy's coming round to quote for an alarm system. I guess he could include a price for lights, but I don't want to waste any more time, so—'

As my hands stopped moving he broke off, tilting his head back to look up at me.

'What's the matter?' he asked. 'You do need better security.'

'But I don't need you to pay for it. Oh, Kit, please don't think I'm ungrateful, but you keep buying me things all the time. I wish you wouldn't. I know you're trying to be kind but I don't want charity.'

'Course you don't. Call them late birthday presents.'

He had missed five of my birthdays. I had longed to know why, yet now that the truth was within my grasp I was afraid to hear it. Afraid that it might prove harder to deal with than the lies.

As I hesitated, he asked how I had fared with the agencies.

'A nightmare,' I said. 'I…met Jodie afterwards.'

'Yeah? To ask about her dad?'

'Partly.' I moved to stand in front of him. It was now or never. 'She wants you to know that she's sorry, and that you can tell me…whatever you couldn't before.'

He was very still, hardly seeming to breathe.

'Will you?' I said. 'Please?'

He didn't reply at once. All he did was to shut down the laptop and lay it aside, and through the silence between us I was aware of the clock on the mantelpiece ticking; a sombre rhythm, mourning wasted time.

CHAPTER FOURTEEN

'Guess I should start with Simon,' he said, pouring two glasses of wine on the grounds that we might both need it. We were sitting at opposite ends of the sofa, half facing each other. Symbolic, perhaps.

'Simon gave Jodie a hell of a time,' he said. 'Before they were married, sweetness and light. After the wedding, a different story. He was snide, contemptuous, always putting her down. None of you found out, did you? He didn't like Jodie mixing with the old gang.'

'But Simon's not like that. You don't think she might have been playing you, a bit?'

'I did wonder. So when I came home after graduating, I took her out to lunch to get at the truth.'

Jodie's appearance had shocked him. She had lost a stone since the Easter break and was nervous and edgy, unable to keep her hands still.

'She didn't know why Simon had changed,' he said. 'When she suggested marriage guidance, he hit the roof, but she was still looking for a way to turn things around. They'd only been married two years.'

'Poor Jodie,' I said. 'And poor Simon. Don't forget you've only heard her side of it.'

He compressed his mouth, and plainly thought Simon's angle not worth hearing.

'You didn't tell me any of this at the time,' I said. 'Not even when I knew you were sleeping with her.'

'How could I? She'd talked to me in confidence. She started coming to the flat—you remember I rented that place in Worcester?—and things developed from there. Then, one evening, she turned up in a dreadful state. Shaking, white as a sheet. Simon had guessed, about us. They'd had a row, and he'd chucked a pan of boiling water at her.'

I gasped. '*Simon?* No...I'm sorry, Kit, but I can't accept that. Did you see any burns?'

'She was lucky. He missed.'

'Convenient.'

'Whatever. I believed her. I left her at the flat and rode up to their house. You'll have heard Simon's version of the next bit.'

'You hit him.'

The corner of his mouth twitched with remembered satisfaction. 'Floored the bastard. I went upstairs and threw some of Jodie's things into a case. Simon came up after me, yelling and so on, but too concussed to do much. Then, when I got home...' He shook his head, bemused even in recollection. 'Jodie had our future mapped out. It was crazy. We hadn't discussed marriage, but there she was, all set to trade one husband for another.'

'She needed a trophy. She wanted to be able to say, "this is what I've thrown away, but see what I've got instead!"'

Kit lifted his eyebrows and obviously thought me catty. 'Or,' he said, 'she just needed to feel she wasn't a total failure.' Which was a kinder analysis than mine, and probably just as true.

'Did you turn her down?' I asked.

'Didn't get the chance.' He was watching me over the rim of his glass. 'Mum phoned. Simon had rung Charles as soon as I left him.'

'And your mother wasn't exactly over the moon?'

'She was virtually incoherent. Said I had to go and see her right then, straight away. She was still trembling when I got there. Dad was out, working late. Mum poured me a drink, and sank into a chair as if she'd lost the strength to stand up. Then she told me.'

He was silent for so long that I said, 'Kit! Told you what?'

His jaw clenched briefly. 'When Charles and the twins were small, Mum and Dad went through a bad patch. Nix was on hand. Charming, kind, a shoulder for Mum to cry on. Also married, with a three-year-old daughter, but he didn't let that cramp his style. I'm the result.'

'Joshua's your *father*?' Then the other thing hit me, and I went cold all over. 'Oh, God.'

'Yeah. Jodie's my half-sister, and I had to go home and tell her. Mum wanted it kept dark, but I was in no mood to humour her.' He broke off, sipping the wine. After a few seconds he continued with grim resolution, 'Jodie was shattered. She made me promise not to tell a soul. Ever. She left there and then, and went back to her mother's. Couldn't bear to be anywhere near me.'

He paused for another gulp of wine, avoiding my eyes. I was afraid that whatever I said would sound inadequate, so I kept silent.

'I wasn't keen on staying around either,' he said. 'I packed a bag, wrote you that bloody note, and rode straight down to London.' He was still frowning into the glass. 'I guess Mum's version of events was pretty damning.'

'She said you'd proposed to Jodie but couldn't go through with it. She said—I swear, Kit, I never believed this for an instant—she said you'd told her you couldn't be saddled with a conniving little slut who was second-hand goods anyway.'

As soon as the words were out, I wished them unsaid. His head jerked up, eyes narrowing painfully.

'I'm sure that was *Mum's* opinion of her,' he said. 'It explains a few things, though, doesn't it? Such as the way they all looked at me on Monday night. What was it Robbie said? *"You're not worth anyone's affection or anyone's trouble. You're despicable and shouldn't be forgiven."* I can see now why she thinks that way.'

I grimaced, not at the words so much as the fact that he had recalled them with such accuracy.

'I'd have thought your mum would want to make it up to you,' I said, 'instead of turning everyone against you.'

He almost laughed. 'Someone else always has to carry the can for Mum's mistakes. That night, she ended up screaming that it was my fault for sleeping with a married woman, and how could she have known I'd do that to Simon? Fair point, I guess. But then she started blaming her father, saying it was his fault she'd slept with Joshua.'

'She blamed Grandad? How did she work that one out?'

'Search me.' He shifted position to ease the aches, and I passed him another cushion as he continued, 'I asked Mum why she hadn't had an abortion. She was shocked. Wouldn't have considered it. My good luck.'

'She didn't treat you like the family's baby,' I said, remembering. 'If anything, she spoiled Charles and Toby, not you.'

'Nor Robbie. Mum always preferred boys. Legitimate ones.'

'Does your dad know?'

'Oh, yes. They sorted their marriage out somehow. Dad's always treated me the same as the others, I'll give him that.'

'I'd never have guessed you weren't his,' I said thoughtfully. 'You may be the image of Joshua, but you're like Uncle James, too.'

'I've got Granny Pevensey, née Nix, to thank for that little quirk of fate.' He raised a bitter smile. 'You're right, Mum didn't treat me like the others, but that did me a good turn. Grew up bloody-minded, didn't I? Set out to prove her wrong *and* show I didn't give a toss for her opinion.'

He had succeeded, too. In spite of the wild streak which had earned him two brief exclusions from school, he had achieved awesome grades at A-level, a place at Cambridge, fame and fortune at twenty-seven. Nonetheless, I recalled his trembling rage when he had met the man we thought was Joshua Nix.

'You could have told me,' I said. 'I know you promised Jodie, but—'

'When you and I were together, Toby always ribbed me a bit, about keeping it in the family.'

'Oh, like the way he treats Robbie is normal! Anyway, it's not illegal between cousins.'

'No. But that night, I kept thinking...first you, then Jodie. There'd been girls at Cambridge, but nothing like...' He swallowed convulsively. 'I was afraid that...maybe there was something wrong with me. And I had to get away, to start afresh.' He bowed his head, saying with aching remorse, 'Forgive me, Liss, that's all I could think about.'

He sat with bent head, unable to meet my eyes. I don't know what he expected from me. Condemnation? Anger? Disgust? I stood up and took his glass, setting it down beside the laptop. Then I stooped in front of him and clasped his hand between both of mine.

'Look at me,' I said.

He smiled slightly at the tone of command, but he did obey.

'We're blood-brothers,' I said. 'That's the deal. And if it means anything to you, I think you did the best thing.'

A breath of agonised laughter escaped him. 'Christ, Liss! The best thing? Adultery, incest, desertion, cowardice...'

'Yes,' I said. 'You ran away. Have you thought how

131

much worse it would have been if you'd stayed? When Simon and Jodie were divorced, there was no mention of adultery. Jodie's mother persuaded him to make things easy for her, because of her breakdown. Do you think he would have agreed to that, if you'd still been around? And think how you've felt, these past few days, with the family treating you the way they do. How would you have dealt with that five years ago, on top of everything else?' I gave his hand a little shake. 'If it comes to that, you might not be the success you are now, if you hadn't gone south and landed a job at Medway. So on the whole—I know it sounds heartless—you should thank your stars that things turned out the way they did.'

He was gazing at me in wonder, as if he had never seen me before, or as if seeing me clearly for the first time.

'I should thank my stars for you,' he said.

I half-laughed, squeezed his hand and let it go. 'Don't be silly. I just don't think you should—'

'Liss,' he said. 'When you were sixteen, I asked you to move to Cambridge with me and you turned me down flat. Have you ever regretted it?'

I blinked, wishing I could read the thoughts behind his eyes, wishing I could answer truthfully without putting our new closeness at risk; wishing most desperately for an ounce of the steel that Jodie claimed to see in me. But he had been honest with me at last; I owed him honesty in return. Whatever the consequences.

I stood up and bent over him, and kissed his forehead. 'Every day,' I said, and walked out of the room without looking back.

*

I went upstairs and started tidying my wardrobe, which didn't especially need it. I would have to face him again soon enough, but not quite yet, not until I felt able to talk to him straightforwardly and without tears.

Why had I been such a fool? I could have sidestepped the awkward moment with some flippant, unrevealing comment. Why, *why* hadn't I been careful to take things slowly? If I had lost him now...

When the knock came on my bedroom door I gulped, fighting for any degree of composure.

'Can I come in?' he asked.

I didn't answer, but turned from the wardrobe and started adjusting the position of the clock on the bedside table. He opened the door anyway. On the edge of vision I could see him watching me.

'Did you mean it?' he said.

There was no point in denying it now. I put the clock down and faced him squarely.

'You know I did.'

We looked at one another for a stretched space of time.

He stepped forward at the same instant as I; and then we were together, clinging tight, his mouth seeking mine with hunger and tenderness and, it seemed to me, a fair measure of gratitude. I tangled my fingers in his hair and tasted wine on his lips, and was conscious both of a sense of terrifying risk and joyous homecoming.

I suppose I more or less undressed us both. When we were naked we sat on the bed together and I tentatively took charge, pushing gently at his chest, encouraging him to lie back on the duvet.

'Relax,' I said.

His eyes laughed up at me; but after a short while, having discovered that I knew a little more than he had taught me, and also that I remembered the things he liked best, he let me do very much as I pleased. When, finally, I lowered myself on to him he groaned—though not with pain—and I rode him at first with small, finely calculated movements and teasing relish, and then with bolder strokes, taking as intense a delight in his responses as in my own.

When we lay separate again but still companionably touching, he said, with a beatific smile, 'Just goes to show, the consensus was right all along. I really am a selfish bastard.'

I propped myself up on one elbow to see him better. 'If you think all that was just for your benefit, you flatter yourself.'

'What I think,' he said, 'is that you haven't been living like a nun.'

'Lucky you, then.'

The smile widened. 'Couldn't agree more.'

'If you must know,' I said, 'I went out with an Italian student for six weeks, not long after you left, and then the farrier for nearly three years. And I bet your list of conquests is a good deal longer than that.'

'Three years is impressive,' he said.

He didn't ask what had gone wrong, but the question hung in the air between us. I didn't think I would confess that the farrier had been adorable in many ways, except for the fact that he hadn't been Kit Pevensey.

I drew a finger over the scattering of bruises on Kit's chest and stomach; a testament, in their way, to the strength of his commitment to me. After Monday night, he could have despatched me to, for instance, Charles's house, and gone home to recuperate. Even if he didn't yet know what he wanted from our relationship, he had earned my patience.

'What do you do for fun, these days?' I asked, tracing the hard swell of muscle in his upper arm. 'Apart from the obvious.'

'Play a bit of squash. Tennis sometimes. Skiing in the

winter. I'll teach you to ski.'

That suggested a future. It would do well enough, for the time being.

'Will you be honest with me, now?' I asked. 'That secretary, at Medway. Rusty, was it? Are you and she—'

'Not any more. Her real name is Lucinda. I cooled things down when she started dropping hints about moving in.'

'You're a love-rat,' I said.

'If that's what you call having a healthy survival instinct. Rusty Cullingham would have eaten me whole and spat out the bones. Do you, um…fancy a shower?'

I leaned over him, looking down into his mischievous eyes. I could see the flecks of dark blue in the clear grey irises, and his lashes were thick and tipped with gold. I loved him so much, I was afraid he would see it.

'A shower together?' I asked.

'Is there any other way?'

'Are you up to it?'

His mouth curved deliciously. 'Part of me is. Not so sure about the rest.' He pinched my bottom. 'Might be fun finding out.'

We made love again under the hot spray. As he couldn't lift me, I stood on a home-made and precarious wooden step meant for reaching high cupboards, and held on to a variety of fixtures and fittings. The shower curtain got ripped and a little shelf came away from the wall, bringing down assorted plastic bottles of shampoo and shower gel, and all in all there was as much laughter as passion, but neither of us was complaining.

In spite of Grandad and all the crowding problems, I had never felt so brimming with happiness, nor so deeply fulfilled. I should have had more than a twinge of guilt, but my conscience seemed to have taken a back seat, at least for this hour of this glorious, unbelievable day.

'It's better,' I said, gazing up at him, seeing every minute detail, down to a tiny scar at the corner of his left eyebrow, and the water droplets beading his lashes. 'Even better than I remember.'

'We were kids, then.'

'We're still cousins. Do you mind, Kit?'

A frown creased his brows, so that my breath caught in my throat. With sudden panic I wished I had kept quiet, swallowed my doubts.

'If I minded,' he said, 'I'd still be a kid. And I wouldn't be here.'

He reached for a towel and wrapped it around us, holding me close enough to feel his heartbeat; and it was only then that I reared my head back with a gasp.

'We've forgotten Martin!'

His eyebrows shot up. 'You wanted to invite a friend?'

'No, idiot. The mechanic. I didn't even lock the door. What if he comes looking for us?'

'We'll pay him,' Kit said, wrapping us up again; and in that warm cocoon of safety I could fool myself into believing that nothing, not even the past, could hurt us any more.

CHAPTER FIFTEEN

The inquest was held at Worcester Magistrates' Court. I had envisaged it as something like a trial: formal, frightening and highly public. In fact, aside from a reporter from the local paper, the only people there were either involved in the proceedings, or were members of the family.

I felt sick with fear, as I sat watching the dark heads of my aunt and her three eldest offspring bent close together in whispered consultation, while Uncle James sat bemusedly aloof. Aunt Melody had dressed in lavender and cream rather than her preferred black, and her hair hung in loose curls to frame her face. She looked pale, vulnerable, and not at all intimidating.

Ian edged out of the family's orbit and came to find us. His rounded cheeks were flushed, but a recent haircut made him look more professional and less like an anxious hedgehog.

'Try not to worry,' he said, pressing my hand as he darted a frosty look at his future in-laws. 'Remember, you're not on trial—' He broke off, frowning at someone behind us.

I turned my head. The man who had just shuffled into court appeared much more nerve-racked than when I had last seen him. He took a seat at the back, mopping his forehead with a tissue. Mr Chubb was going to make good his promise.

'I must catch him before he leaves,' Ian said. 'His phone always goes straight to voicemail. Goodness knows what he's been up to.'

'Hiding, I should think,' Kit said, which earned him a startled glance from Ian.

The only other person to approach us was Dr

Southbrook. He sat next to me, leaning forward to glare at Kit, on my other side. 'Went to Hay, did you?' he asked, not loudly but not whispering.

'As planned,' Kit said.

'Worth the effort?'

'I'd say so.'

The doctor scowled. 'Be aware, lad, you've had enough codeine. Don't buy more over the counter. It's an opiate. Highly addictive.'

Kit nodded. 'Thanks for the advice.'

'I don't appreciate being excluded, you know. I've known these families a long time, and I'll help in any way I can.'

'That's very good of you, sir. We'll keep it in mind.'

'Stubborn, blasted…you're as bad as Harry ever was. I'll keep pestering. Never doubt it.' Old Southbrook subsided into his seat, but not before he had caught my eye and winked.

The hearing began promptly, putting an end to further clandestine conversations. The courtroom was silent as the coroner, a woman with gaunt features and an air of inexhaustible patience, explained—to my surprise and cautious relief—that it was not a function of the hearing to apportion blame to any individual for Professor Harold Byrne's death, but simply to establish when, where and how he had died.

She then went on to summarise the pathologist's report. 'Professor Byrne died of shock occasioned by severe blood loss, as a direct result of a head wound consistent with his fall. Stone dust found in the wound corroborated this. Contusions on the limbs and trunk were also consistent with such a fall. No evidence was found of other injuries, nor was there any sign of a struggle having taken place.'

The coroner shuffled another sheet of paper to the

top of her pile of documents, before continuing.

'Professor Byrne was admitted to hospital at fifteen-fifty on Saturday, twenty-eighth November. The surgeon who attended him has estimated that he received his injuries approximately two hours prior to admission, and certainly after the power failed. Therefore I need to feel confident that he was alone in the house, at or around thirteen-fifty.'

She glanced up from the reports, and said mildly, 'Miss Amphelisia Byrne, would you take the witness stand, please?'

She tried to make it easy for me. She was courteous throughout my faltering account, and waited until I had finished before asking whether Grandad had been able to speak to me, before the ambulance arrived.

'A few words,' I said, 'but they didn't make sense. He hardly knew I was there.'

'Had anything struck you as odd or out of place when you first entered the house?'

'No. Everything seemed normal...apart from the power cut.'

She thanked me, and that was that. I walked on unsteady legs back to my seat, where Kit linked his fingers through mine and murmured that he was proud of me.

Detective Inspector Hughes was the next to give evidence. 'Our enquiries have revealed the Professor to be a strong-minded man,' he said. 'I doubt he'd have allowed a power failure to prevent him from visiting the cellar. I believe his death to have been an accident. Having said that...' He glanced in Aunt Melody's direction. 'I should touch on a suggested motive for murder.'

He dealt summarily with the rumours of Grandad's hidden wealth, stating that the Professor and Miss Byrne were known to have lived very austerely, and that Mr Ian Threlfall, the executor of Professor Byrne's estate, knew of no such fortune; nor was it mentioned in the will.

'Miss Byrne will inherit Professor Byrne's whole estate,' he added. 'However, having spoken with Dr Geoffrey Southbrook, I understand the Professor was concerned about some unnamed individual seeking to harm his granddaughter or himself. Whatever we choose to make of this, the Professor was clearly not afraid of Miss Byrne. Nor was she in the house at the time of his fall, as Mr Daniel Chubb will confirm.'

Mr Chubb, having been duly called, showed his customary mix of twitchiness and bravado. He stated that the time had been two-twelve when I had nearly run him down. He had checked his watch, making sure it was still functional after his tumble into the ditch. If anyone else had visited The Eyrie, they had either been on foot, like himself, or had parked behind the stables. There had been no vehicle on the drive when he had rung the bell at two o'clock. If *I* had left the house shortly before that, I would have driven past him; and he knew the car.

'As to why Professor Byrne wanted to meet me,' he said, with regret, 'I'm afraid I've no idea.'

'There's one point I'd like to clear up, Mr Chubb,' the coroner said. 'A man in your profession would surely keep abreast of local news. It puzzles me that you waited until yesterday to come forward.'

'I'd been away for a few days,' he said, with a wan smile. 'A cottage in Somerset. I deliberately left my laptop at home and chose not to buy a paper. The phone signal was poor. I found the seclusion relaxing.'

It sounded plausible, but I wondered why he hadn't mentioned the text messages, and whether he had received any more. I resolved to speak to him after the hearing.

For the moment, he was scuttling back to his seat. The coroner, with the relaxed air of one old acquaintance to another, called Dr Geoffrey Southbrook.

Old Southbrook was as good as his word. He told the court that Harry Byrne, his patient and close friend for three decades, had visited him on the Wednesday prior to his death, to speak of his conviction that his granddaughter's life was in danger.

'And you felt his worries were real,' the coroner asked, 'rather than having some basis in a medical or psychological problem?'

'Harry's faculties were acute. And he certainly didn't suffer from paranoid delusions.'

'He was a man of strong opinions. Might he have overreacted, after some kind of altercation in which idle threats were exchanged?'

'He might have.'

'Do you believe that his fall was accidental?'

Old Southbrook paused. 'I've seen the pathologist's report,' he said finally. 'Harry was strong and fit, for a man of his age. If he'd been attacked, I'd have expected evidence of a struggle. I think he was worried and preoccupied, and missed his footing. But...' A swift glance my way. 'That's not to say his worries were unfounded. If I were Miss Byrne, I'd watch my back. And if I were Tom Hughes...' A challenging stare for the Inspector. 'I'd do my best to watch it for her.'

'Thank you, Dr Southbrook,' the coroner said, with a quelling look. 'You may step down.'

As the doctor walked past Hughes, the policeman gave his old friend a tolerant smile which revealed nothing of his thoughts.

I dared not meet Aunt Melody's eyes as she was called to speak. After Mr Chubb's and Dr Southbrook's testimony, she could hardly go on insisting I was a murderess. Instead she adopted a pained, defiant tone.

'There's something priceless hidden in that house, and my niece knows where it is. Of course she'll deny it, so that she gets to keep it if I contest the will. There won't be much else, once my father's debts are paid off. And even if she didn't push him—'

'We've established that she did not.' The coroner's patience was not inexhaustible after all. 'And as far as I can gather, there's no evidence that any priceless item exists.'

'Of course it exists. We've always known it.'

The coroner sighed. 'Mrs Pevensey, do you have reason to believe that your father died at the hands of a person or persons unknown, *other than your niece?*'

Aunt Melody went white, her plum-coloured lipstick standing out starkly. 'Certainly not!'

'Thank you, Mrs Pevensey. That will be all.'

As she stepped down, Kit loosened his vice-like grip on my hand and whispered an apology.

The coroner glanced around the court. 'Having heard the evidence,' she said, 'I'm satisfied that Professor Byrne fell while descending his cellar steps by torchlight. Whilst the concerns he expressed to Dr Southbrook do raise the possibility of foul play, there's no evidence to suggest this occurred. I therefore record a verdict of Accidental Death. The inquest into the death of Professor Harold Byrne is now closed.'

*

Kit and I wanted to thank Daniel Chubb, but Ian, having finished his own brief talk with the detective, bounded to intercept us.

'You did really well, Lissa,' he said, pumping my hand. 'I'll let you both know the date of the funeral, in case no one else does. You may have gathered, I've told Melody she wouldn't gain much by contesting the will.' He looked searchingly at Kit. 'How are things?'

'Investigations? Pretty much at a standstill.'

'I meant the bones.'

'Oh, bugger the bones.'

Ian smothered a laugh. 'Macho git, aren't you?'

Their eyes met in fellowship and mutual amused respect, just as Robyn glided to Ian's side amid a waft of Chanel. She linked her arm though his.

'What are you two muttering about?' she asked. 'Nothing to hide, I hope?'

'Not a thing,' Kit said. 'Had any thoughts?'

'About the past? I'm not sure. How about the burglary at Ian's grandparents' house? Could that be significant?'

Before we could react, Ian said sharply, 'That was nothing. A storm in a teacup.'

'Really?' Robyn said. 'The thief took three thousand, one hundred and forty-eight pounds. We heard your grandpa telling Grandad Byrne.'

'How can you possibly remember the amount?' Ian said.

She shrugged, looking both annoyed and surprised at his reaction. 'I don't know. Children remember weird things.'

'Just a second,' Kit said. 'This was a break-in at old Mr Threlfall's place, right? How long ago?'

'The year everyone either walked out or died,' she said. 'It was a week or two after Jodie's dad left. And I remember *that*, Ian, because most people thought he'd sneaked back and done the job.'

'Not "most people",' Ian said, glancing at the doorway through which everyone else was now leaving. 'Only Granny Threlfall. And I wouldn't bother asking her about it, if I were you. She's incredibly anti-social these days. Sorry, have to make sure Robyn's mum is OK...'

He virtually dragged an indignant Robyn away, and Kit and I made our way thoughtfully back to the car.

'Why would Ian be so defensive about the burglary?' I said.

'Maybe he knows who did it. Maybe *he* did it.'

'For heaven's sake! He was only nine!'

'Simon, then. Or the two of them, egging each other on. Or their mum and dad. Ian wouldn't want *their* good names trashed, would he?'

'In any case,' I said, unconvinced, 'I can't believe it was Joshua. He'd been gone for at least a week when it happened. And if Ian thought Joshua had done it, I think he'd tell us.'

I had chosen to drive the Mercedes today, despite the Fiat being back in working order. Once in the privacy of the car, I put the rest of my thoughts reluctantly into words.

'Kit, what if this whole thing is a fantasy? Grandad was worried about me, but he died by accident. Joshua walked out on his wife. It's not exactly unheard of. Even what happened on Monday night…well, you've stirred up some strong feelings, but they're nothing to do with Grandad's past.'

'And Hywel Price, making out he was Nix? And John Threlfall's diary? And Grandad begging God for forgiveness?'

'I didn't say I had all the answers. I just—'

'Joshua's letter to Jodie. She thinks he was drunk, right? Let's say he wasn't. Let's say his hand shook because he was writing it under threat.'

My mouth went dry. Talk about big jumps. Not just murder, now, but calculated malevolence, persuading a man to say goodbye to his daughter under threat of death, and then killing him anyway.

'No,' I said. 'That's enough. We don't even have a

144

motive. And whatever happened, it wouldn't have been premeditated. Not like that.'

I agreed, nonetheless, that talking to Mrs Threlfall would be a sound idea. We rang her landline from the car, but either she was out or she didn't choose to pick it up. We tried Daniel Chubb next, but his phone went straight to voicemail. I left a message.

'What time's the electrician coming?' I asked Kit, looking over my shoulder to reverse out of the parking space.

'Half-one. I'm seeing the burglar alarm rep at two. So...' His hand inched up my thigh. 'Just enough time for you to drive me home, ply me with good food and wine, and seduce me on your satin sheets.'

'Cotton sheets.'

'Cotton,' he said, 'will do fine.'

CHAPTER SIXTEEN

'You do realise,' Kit said, an hour or so later, 'this house is a long way from Maidstone?'

We were lying on my double bed, the cool air of the room chilling our sweat-damp skin, raising goosebumps. I shivered and pulled the duvet up to our waists.

'You've got an efficient car,' I said.

'A four-hour commute is a bit much for anyone. And what I don't have is a nine-to-five job.' He sighed, stroking my hair. 'Sometimes, like now, I can take time off at short notice. Between series I get long breaks, but while we're filming my feet hardly touch the ground for three months. I'll never get to see you. If you sell this house and I sell the flat, we could buy a place in Kent with stabling for the horses.'

I raised myself to one elbow, feeling light-headed with the sudden surge of hope and using flippancy to hide it. 'Is that a romantic proposition?'

He grinned. 'It's a lecherous proposition from a bloke who can't keep his hands off you.' He slapped my bottom. 'What d'you think? Would you like a fresh start down south?'

'I…I don't know.'

'Think it over. No rush.' He regarded me all the same with solemn eyes.

'What is it?' I said.

'What would the old man have done, if you'd ever decided to leave?'

'Managed, I'm sure. But I preferred to stay.'

'Why, though? Why choose to work for a grumpy old bugger who paid you a pittance?'

'He wasn't grumpy all the time. Anyway, why not? I've never been much of an extravert, and I'm not particularly bright. All I know is history, and how to find out about it.'

'Yes, those sound like authentic Harry Byrne quotes.'

'That's unfair!' Shocked, I sat up, glaring down at his unsmiling face. 'No one else would have given me that level of responsibility—' I broke off, uneasily aware that this time I was indeed quoting Grandad.

Kit sat up beside me. 'Didn't you ever wonder—don't you wonder now—how many of his values and opinions were worth anything at all?'

'No! That's a dreadful thing to say.'

'What he did to you was pretty dreadful. His son was dead and his daughter hated him, and he was terrified of losing you as well. He convinced you that you were too inadequate to survive without him.'

'I'm not going to listen to this.' Throwing aside the duvet I scrambled out of bed and grabbed my clothes. I stood with my back to him, dressing myself fast, conscious all the time of his eyes on me.

'I know you loved him,' he said, 'but when did he last praise you for something—even for being good at your job?'

It was too near the truth. I snatched up his own bundled clothes and threw them at him. 'Don't you dare talk about him like that! He loved me and took care of me and he's dead!'

'You're alive. You drove the Merc to Hay and back. You did fine. An unfamiliar car, roads you didn't know, heavy rain and a high speed chase. Didn't that prove something to you?'

'It proved I can drive a hundred miles. Where is that going to get me?'

'Anywhere you like.'

I faced him with anger fuelled by a sense of betrayal. 'All this, because it would be more convenient for you if

I lived in Kent!'

The hurt in his eyes told me I was wrong, though he might have cringed to know it.

'If that's your opinion of me,' he snapped, 'there's not much hope for us, is there?'

The question hung in the sizzling air between us. I was afraid to breathe, afraid that the euphoria of the past twenty-four hours could after all be destroyed by a word or a look.

Whatever showed in my face, his own expression changed. He swung his feet over the edge of the bed and crossed the room, taking my hands.

'Listen to me,' he said. 'You're a great girl. Not thick, not incompetent, not a coward. The old man wasted your talents, wasted *you*, and if I'm not careful you'll end up no better off with me than you were with him. Shut away in this old tomb of a house while I breeze off round the world. You're worth more than that.'

'You're wrong. About Grandad, and about me. I'm not a high flyer. Whatever you say about him, you can't change that.'

'No, but you can. Believe in yourself, Liss. That's all it'll take.' His eyes searched my face, and I glimpsed the birth of a thought. 'I didn't want to upset you,' he said, much more gently. 'I'm very sorry.'

'You meant what you said.'

'Maybe some of it. You know I didn't see eye to eye with the old man. I won't be a hypocrite and pretend otherwise.' He dared a rueful smile. 'You'll have to take me as I am or not at all.'

'You're bloody arrogant.'

'Only as a last resort. Will you come to the office Christmas party with me? It's on the twelfth.'

'At Medway? No, I won't.'

I was envisaging a horde of cynical, hard-drinking

men and their chic female counterparts, the latter all looking down their noses at me and making eyes at Kit. Also I could hardly believe he had the nerve to ask, after he had been so foul about Grandad.

'Please, Liss.' He drew me closer, and kissed my lips with lingering tenderness, his naked body warm through my clothes, scented with body spray and the sharper tang of sex and fresh sweat. 'Please.'

I should have resisted, shown him that he couldn't win me around just like that. But of course I didn't.

'I wouldn't know anyone,' I said at last. 'What would I talk to them about?'

'You'd be lucky to get a word in. There aren't many shy types in our business. If they start that way, they don't stay shy for long.'

'Are you really that keen to go?' I asked.

'Only if you'll be with me,' he said, and kissed me again, knowing he had won.

*

The electrician installed three exterior lights to illuminate the back garden, front lawn and stable yard, their sensors activated by body-heat. The man selling alarm systems gave a price which took my breath away. Kit said that we'd let him know, then phoned two other companies, making appointments for tomorrow afternoon.

We saw the horses fed and watered, and Kit went upstairs for a shower while I curled up in an armchair in the living room, to think. Finances aside, I had sometimes longed to live in a house with warm, bright rooms and no ghosts; but The Eyrie and the Malverns were home. If Kit expected me to trust the strength of his feelings and move to Kent with him, I wished he would confess to feeling more than lust and a gallant urge to protect me.

Maybe in a few days things would be clearer in my

mind.

We went to bed early, and settled finally to sleep curled close together; and perhaps it was the uncertainties chasing each other through my head which made me dream. I was buried alive, not in a coffin but in something resembling a crypt. Stone walls started to crumble around and over me, choking me with dust. I tore at them, ripping my nails, searching for the way out that had to be there, if I could only find it...

Someone was with me. His hands scrabbled at the wall as frenziedly as mine, and a beam of light turned his hair to gold and gleamed in the grey eyes as he sent me a desperate grimace.

'Get us out!' His voice was a croak. 'Get me out!'

'I can't,' I said.

His skin was thinning, falling away from the bones. He beat on the wall in a paroxysm of rage and despair. 'How much longer? Oh, God...' He dropped to his knees, arms hanging limp, and looked into my eyes. His hopelessness tore at my heart. 'Help me.'

'I can't get us out,' I whispered. 'I don't know how.'

His mouth opened, lips drawing back from his teeth in an agonised rictus, shrivelling in decay as the skin cracked and darkened. His eyelids fell away, but he stared up at me still in dreadful appeal...

I woke screaming for Kit, but his arms were already around me, turning me to face him, holding me tightly so that I could feel his reassuring solidity. 'It's all right, Liss, I'm here. You were dreaming, that's all. You're all right now.'

The horror was slow to leave me, but gradually I stopped shuddering.

'Do you want to tell me about it?' he asked.

I didn't, but he cajoled me into it.

'My poor girl,' he said. 'Even if Nix is dead, it was

150

only a dream. You don't really believe in ghosts, do you?'

'But I saw him, didn't I? By the fireplace that time. The treasure-hunting summer. We'd been all round the house, knocking on panels and prising up floorboards. Don't they say ghosts can be disturbed by that kind of thing?'

'Hush.' He touched his lips to mine. 'You've seen too many movies. As for dreaming about being buried yourself...' He kissed me again, soothing me with lips and gentle hands. 'Nothing will happen to you while I'm around.'

I didn't say any more. I didn't want him to think the subject was preying on my mind. But the truth was, he would soon be recalled to Medway and probably sent abroad again, whether the mysteries had been solved or not. I had indeed begun to feel safe while he was around; but he wouldn't be around forever.

CHAPTER SEVENTEEN

Ian Threlfall and Jodie Nix shared a secretary, a forty-something paragon named Sandra, whose wardrobe must have rivalled Jodie's for brilliance of colour. When we walked into the outer office on Friday morning it was a day for turquoise polka dots. She gave us both a welcoming smile, which changed to one of speculation as she studied Kit.

'I know you, don't I?' she said. 'Are you an actor?'

He introduced himself, to Sandra's delight. Robyn, it seemed, had never mentioned her connection to Kester Pevensey.

'Is Jodie about?' he asked.

'I'm afraid she's with a client. She shouldn't be more than five or ten minutes. If you wouldn't mind waiting...'

No problem, he assured her, sitting down and stroking a leaf of the nearby rubber plant with an idle finger. Even I would not have guessed how nervous he was, had I not seen him, less than an hour ago, push away a perfectly appetizing cooked breakfast.

'Shall I stay?' I asked quietly.

'Liss,' he murmured, with amused reproach, 'I'm not a five-year-old visiting the dentist.'

As our eyes met, I felt a quiver deep inside me, a sensual echo of our last encounter, or simply impatience for the next. I had a vision of the look on Sandra's face, if I were to take him right here, on the carpet in front of her desk.

With inappropriate laughter bubbling up, I bent and kissed his mouth. 'I'll be back in an hour,' I said.

I left the car on the forecourt and walked into the centre of town, wondering what Christmas present I could buy, for a man who presumably had everything he needed. I hurried past Beacon Antiques' impressive shop-front. That was one place where I wouldn't be seeking ideas.

In the end I bought a card that pleased me—tastefully lustful but not emotionally over-the-top—but still no present, and went back to Threlfall and Nix. I found Kit once again in the outer office, flirting shamelessly with Sandra, and I began to have an inkling of how he meant to discover when Ian was next off to Wales.

There was no sign of Jodie, but he said they had had a long chat, and he seemed light-hearted, younger, as though a physical burden had dropped away. I was glad for his sake but also unreasonably jealous, because Jodie Nix had done for him what all our lovemaking had not.

With an effort I swallowed my petty resentments. It would have been cruel to tarnish the bright morning for him. In the car, I alerted him to a smudge of Jodie's lipstick on his cheek, saying with determination, 'I'm glad it went well.'

'So am I.' He took my hand and kissed the ends of my fingers. 'Let's go home to bed.'

*

That afternoon, while Kit was seeing burglar alarm reps and working out his New York expenses, I summoned the courage to go through Grandad's room. Having sorted his clothes from the wardrobe into bags for recycling and charity, I started on the dressing-table drawers.

Here, I discovered my first school report, and a drawing of a blue, monstrous creature surprisingly captioned, 'Grandad'. Also a home-made birthday card, which I had given him before I learned to spell. Courage in tatters, I sat on the floor with the pathetic items on my lap. Grandad's treasure.

I didn't realise Kit was there, until he stooped beside me and dropped a kiss on my hair.

'Enough for today, eh?' he said.

'Why did he keep all this? He wasn't sentimental.'

'I guess he was proud of you.'

'Then why couldn't he say so? Why could he never say?'

'Come on, Liss. Come and help me with these bloody receipts. You were always better at maths than me.'

The bookkeeping was done in ten minutes. Kit wanted to visit Toby that evening, to confirm our intruder's identity and stop the same disturbing questions from going round in his head day after day. A phone call to Ian confirmed that the twins called in at their parents' house most weekdays, at around six. It seemed wiser to meet Toby there than at his own home. More witnesses.

'You know what'll happen, though,' Ian told him. 'There'll be an almighty row and you'll be no further forward. Even if Toby's innocent, he'd rather hate you than play Happy Families. Helps him justify the way he bullied you as a kid.'

Kit grimaced at the truth of it. 'I still need to have it out with him.'

'Yes, well…be careful.'

We had a couple of hours to spare before six. While Kit went on with his manuscript, I invited a friend to come and help me school Tempest, feeling guilty that I had not yet told her my new phone number. Gaby and I spent a companionable half-hour at the field, and I suffered her advice on life and decision-making ('God, if he was mine, I'd never let him out of bed, let alone out of my sight!') but I mentioned none of the mysteries.

When she had gone, I nerved myself to return to Grandad's room, fortified by the spell in the open air. This time I searched every drawer thoroughly. I found only two other items of interest. One was a leather-bound journal, with the owner's initials written on the inside cover in a copperplate hand: *EB, 1904.*

EB must be Edgar Byrne, my great-great-grandfather. I glanced up at the portrait of Amphelisia. Perhaps Grandad's efforts to identify her as Shakespeare's Dark Lady had been fired by Edgar's journal. He had never told me; I had only been eight or nine when he had finally given up on Amphelisia. I resolved to study the book when I had more time.

The other item was Grandad's gold pocket-watch. It was only when I turned it over and saw the inscription that I felt a frisson of shock.

'Darling H, love always. A.'

My grandmother, Charlotte, had died before I was born. Grandad might well have had a girlfriend and seen no reason to tell me about her, especially if she was married.

I was suddenly conscious of a prickling sensation at the back of my neck, and a coldness as if someone had opened a refrigerator door behind me. I turned quickly, with a panicky leap of the heart; and my movement seemed to stir the air, so that the chill felt like what it surely was—a perfectly normal draught.

Shaking my head at my own idiocy, I slipped the pocket-watch back into the drawer, and went downstairs to remind Kit that it was time to make a move.

CHAPTER EIGHTEEN

The Pevensey family home was an attractive Edwardian house, set into the hillside on the outskirts of Great Malvern. We walked up the steps between shrubs and water features, our way illuminated by solar lights. The garden was Uncle James's pride and perhaps a refuge from marital pressures. Gardening bored my aunt.

It was Uncle James who opened the door to us, and he made no effort to hide his dismay. 'What do you want?' he asked, with a glance over his shoulder. 'You shouldn't have come here. Either of you.'

'How're you doing, Dad?' Kit said.

'You can't come in,' he muttered. 'You've caused enough upset.'

'Is Toby here?'

Before Uncle James could reply, Toby erupted into the hall, pushed past his father and employed the same form of greeting as at Ian's dinner party. He gave Kit a hard shove, this time aimed with accuracy and spite at his bad shoulder. I cried out with shock, and Kit recoiled with a hiss of pain.

'What does it take for you to get the message?' Toby said.

But adrenaline is a powerful anaesthetic, and Toby's words had removed any doubt that he was our culprit. Kit straightened up and delivered an impressive left hook.

It caught Toby on the bridge of the nose. He fell back, almost knocking Uncle James over, blood pouring from his nose; and Kit grated, 'That was for Lissa. We're quits. Let us in or I call the police!'

Toby staggered upright, dark eyes flashing with the promise of mayhem; but at that moment Robyn darted out of the lounge, took in the situation with one glance and threw a slender arm across her twin's chest, stopping him in mid-lunge.

'That's enough!' she said. 'Both of you, enough! Come inside and shut the door!'

We did so, Kit staying in front of me. Robyn's arm across Toby was only a psychological barrier, and he looked about as controllable as a wounded bull. Blood from his nose was smeared across his cheek and one sleeve, where he had tried to dash it away, and there were scarlet blotches down his white shirt front.

Robyn glared at the pair of them. 'This is our parents' *home*, in case you'd forgotten.'

'The Eyrie is Lissa's home,' Kit said through his teeth. 'Do you know what he did to her there?'

For the first time Robyn looked unsure of herself. She glanced up at her twin. 'What's he talking about?'

'Nothing,' Toby snarled. 'Bloody nothing.'

'Yeah, right,' Kit said.

'Is this about Monday night?' Robyn queried sharply.

Toby's eyes flickered and he shouted, at last on the defensive, 'She nearly broke my fucking ankle!'

'Good!' I yelled back at him. 'You could have broken Kit's fucking neck!'

All of them, including Kit, stared at me with open mouths and staggered expressions; and it was not the accusation which had silenced them, but hearing me swear at Toby for the first time in my life.

Uncle James, whose presence I had forgotten, cleared his throat. 'Coffee, anyone?'

Robyn inhaled deeply, squared her shoulders and stood back from the action. 'What a great idea, Dad. Toby, go and clean yourself up. Lissa, Kit, come into the lounge. Let's see if we can sort this out like civilised people, shall we?'

I was sure Toby would refuse, but Robyn stared him down. He turned and flounced off upstairs, his body language shouting that this was a temporary ceasefire, not a truce. Kit and I likewise did as we were told, without the amateur dramatics, and Uncle James went off to make coffees to order.

The lounge was comfortable but minimalist. My aunt had modern tastes, and Uncle James had chosen not to indulge his own preference for antiques. Aunt Melody was ensconced in an armchair of mushroom-coloured leather.

Kit said awkwardly, 'Hi, Mum,' and dropped a kiss on her hair in passing. 'How have you been?'

'As if you care,' she said.

He sat next to me on the sofa. Robyn switched off the television. She asked Kit if he wanted to wait for Toby, and he nodded.

Silence descended. The atmosphere was intolerable. When Uncle James brought in the tray of coffees, his hands shaking, the rattle of the mugs was a relief. He mopped the tray with a tissue before trying to work out which drink was whose, which at least forced us all to speak, however inane the subject.

Into this scene walked Toby. He still wore the gruesome shirt but his nosebleed had stopped, and the smirk hovering around the corners of his mouth suggested that he had calmed down a bit and started thinking.

Robyn subjected him to a high-wattage glare that dared him to misbehave. She pointed to an unoccupied chair, and he sat in it.

'So.' She surveyed the company with folded arms. 'As we all now know, Toby went to The Eyrie on Monday night.'

'Robyn!' my aunt said. 'You promised.'

158

'To keep quiet? So I did. Maybe I shouldn't have.'

Aunt Melody turned to Toby. 'Darling—'

'Mum!' Robyn said. 'Stop playing for sympathy. Kit, Lissa, Toby didn't break in, Charles lent him a key. I know you thought you'd disturbed a burglar. I haven't heard the details and I don't want to.' She arched her brows at Toby. 'Kit says you're even, now. Happy with that?'

Toby's smirk became a full-blown sneer. 'Fine by me.'

I supposed he was entitled to his amusement. One sore ankle and a nosebleed, against what he had done to me, and Kit would overlook everything else. If Toby thought his brother a fool, I could scarcely blame him.

'There's one condition,' Kit said.

Toby's complacency remained intact, but my aunt regarded her youngest son with haunted eyes.

Robyn flared her nostrils like an animal scenting danger. 'Which is?'

'That you explain why Toby, or all of you, needed to steal a sixteen-year-old letter from Grandpa Pevensey to John Threlfall, suggesting that the Byrne treasure might just possibly exist.'

Aunt Melody moaned and pressed a hand to her mouth. Toby sat on the arm of her chair and patted her shoulder.

'What will you do, if we refuse?' he said. 'Try to press charges? Hughes would think Lissa was just getting back at Mum. He'd ask why you didn't report the break-in straight away. You'd be had up for wasting police time.'

Kit said quietly, 'Why should Hughes think that naming you as our burglar would be a way to get back at Mum?'

For one glorious moment I saw Toby lost for words. I was aware, in peripheral vision, that Uncle James had retreated to the kitchen doorway, torn no doubt between curiosity and reluctance to get involved.

Aunt Melody answered for him. 'Isn't it obvious? How would any mother feel, at the thought of seeing her son in the dock?'

'I'm your son, too. I'm surprised you could forget.'

She must have feared that he would tell the twins everything. She swallowed, eyes filling with tears; then she dropped her head in her hands and began to cry.

Toby hugged her into his side. 'Are you satisfied now?' he asked us.

Aunt Melody looked up at Kit. 'I wanted Charles to go instead,' she said brokenly, 'but he wouldn't do it. I knew Toby might lose his temper. I told him I wouldn't forgive him if he scarred you. And he didn't, did he?'

Kit slowly stood up. 'You knew Toby would hurt me if he could. Did you even *try* to warn me?'

She hiccupped plaintively. 'How could I?'

'How could you *not*?'

She had no answer. All she could do was cry. I regrettably felt no sympathy for her at all.

Robyn, wide-eyed at what she was hearing, crossed the room and laid a hand on Kit's arm, but whatever she said was drowned out by Toby's violent protest.

'Keep away from my sister!'

Anyone would have thought Kit, not Robyn, had made the overture.

'*Our* sister,' Kit said.

'And I'm not your property,' Robyn snapped at her twin. 'Will you explain about the letter, or shall I?'

Aunt Melody moaned.

'Oh, Mum,' Robyn said, 'you're not helping. Pull yourself together! Toby?'

He showed no sign of wanting to explain, but gave Kit another hot stare and then carried on patting his mother's shoulder, murmuring words of reassurance with more gentleness than I had ever seen in him before.

Robyn, disenchanted, drew a long breath. 'Ian's grandad was a real squirrel,' she said, addressing Kit and me as if no one else in the room mattered. 'He'd kept paperwork going back sixty years. After he died, Ian and I went through it all. When I found the letter to him from Grandpa Pevensey, I showed it to Mum.'

Kit groaned, raising his eyes to the ceiling.

'Yes, all right,' Robyn said. 'I just felt she'd be interested. Haven't you ever got it wrong and screwed things up?'

Kit was silenced.

'Mum thought,' Robyn went on, 'that if she went to The Eyrie and faced Grandad Byrne with the letter, he might be shamed into telling her what, and where, this wretched heirloom is. And yes, she hoped to persuade him to let her have it.'

My aunt burst out, 'He had no right to hide it away, keeping it for his precious Lissa. I was his only daughter. Charles was his eldest grandson. He should have given us *something*.'

She had used the wrong approach all her life, I thought. With fewer loudly aired grievances, she might indeed have won a share in The Eyrie for Charles— though not, admittedly, any non-existent treasure.

'Dad snatched the letter,' she said. 'He claimed it was rubbish. Old men's gossip. He told me to leave. But later in the afternoon...' She pushed a strand of long hair out of her eyes, her lower lip trembling. 'Charles rang us and said...said...'

'He told her Grandad was in hospital,' Toby interrupted. 'Do we have to spell it out? She'd been with him, probably minutes before he fell. They'd quarrelled. Robbie and Ian knew she'd gone there. What if Ian had told Simon, or their gran, or Jodie? Mum was scared to death. Why else was she desperate to get the letter back? It could have been used as evidence.'

'But...' Words momentarily failed Kit. He turned to his mother. 'I know you wouldn't have hurt the old man. I'd have *given* you the bloody letter, if you were that worried about it.'

'Oh, sure,' Toby said. 'We'd have been likely to ask, wouldn't we? You'd have gone straight to the law, rather than see your precious Lissa accused.'

'Don't talk such crap! I wouldn't point the finger at Mum. What the hell do you take me for?'

Toby opened his mouth, but Robyn halted him with a fierce, 'Don't you dare!'

'So,' Kit said, looking down at Toby, 'you made sure that if anyone got the blame, it wouldn't be Mum.'

Toby stood up in his turn, regaining the psychological advantage of height. 'Nothing I did incriminated Lissa. All I did was to set Mum's mind at rest.'

'You could have taken the letter and gone. You had enough of a head start on us. Why didn't you?'

'Bet you wish I had.' Toby was stoking himself up into a rage. Robyn said something, but he was past paying her any attention. He bent over me and jabbed my breastbone with a vicious forefinger. 'And as for you, little Miss Mouse. Creeping round the old man all these years, making sure of your inheritance.'

'Let her alone!' Kit said, grabbing his arm.

Toby made a brief attempt to shake him off, and then ignored him. 'You're still not telling, are you?' Another jab, painful even through the cushioning layers of shirt and sweater. 'Something worth a fortune. And now it's yours and you're hiding it, just like the old man did.'

'I said, let her alone!' Kit dragged his brother round and shoved him away from me.

Toby staggered against a one-legged table, which

crashed over, sending a cup of coffee rolling on to the white carpet. The spreading stain appeared to unhinge his mother, but he recovered his balance and, to the accompaniment of her shrieks, launched himself at Kit.

Several things seemed to happen at once. Kit stepped back, Robyn lunged in front of her twin to intervene, and Uncle James made some verbal protest which deflected Toby's attention for a split second.

He hit Robyn instead of Kit; a glancing blow but hard enough. She fell back, more or less into Kit's arms, and since he couldn't support her they both ended on the floor.

From the rest of us, even Toby, there was a moment of utter stillness, during which Kit disentangled himself from an ungainly sprawl of limbs and helped his sister to sit up.

'You OK?' he said.

'Yes.' Her voice was unsteady, and she put a hand to her mouth. Her lower lip was bleeding where a tooth had cut it. She looked up at her twin.

Toby shook his head, denying the unspoken accusation. 'It was an accident,' he said. 'You know it was.'

With Kit's help she got to her feet, dabbing at the blood with a tissue as she scanned us all with savage condemnation. 'Is this what we've come to?' she said. 'We're a *family*. Is this the best we can do?'

None of us spoke; but I glanced at Toby, and with trepidation saw that his guilt was being translated into a blaze of rekindled anger. He needed to lash out at someone; and Kit had in any case been the intended target.

'If he hadn't come back,' he said, pointing an accusing finger, 'none of this would have happened.'

'He's one of us,' Robyn said.

It was all Toby needed, to goad him into speaking his mind with no regard for anyone's opinion. 'You really want to know why?' he demanded of Kit, voice rising as though a part of him had longed for just such a moment. 'Why I waited for you? Why I wrecked your shoulder and chucked you down those steps?'

'Yes. I really do.'

'Because the chance was there and it was *sweet*. Waiting for you in that house, hearing the car drive up...you've no idea. And then the bonus, that you guessed who I was, and wouldn't even make a proper fight of it. So...' He leaned forward slightly, eyes alight as he spaced the final words with gloating malice. 'I— made—you—suffer.'

If he hoped to shock us, he succeeded. Uncle James was looking as sick as I felt, and Robyn was staring at her twin in disbelief. To my aunt's credit, she had forgotten all about the stained carpet. Kit's face was as blank as a wall.

'Toby,' my aunt said. 'Darling, that wasn't why—'

'Yes, it was.' He gave Kit a chilling smile. 'You won't shop me, though. Not now that the inquest is over, and you know I'm not a threat to Lissa. You're a stupid bastard, aren't you, when all's said and done?'

'Your fault, then,' Kit said bitterly. 'You made me swear an oath of loyalty to the Eyrie Gang, when I was too small to realise it was only a game.'

'It's *all* a game, little brother. The trick is to enjoy scoring the points.'

Toby was enjoying himself now, that much was certain. Whatever his parents and sister thought of him, I loathed him so deeply it turned my stomach. There was no point in telling him the truth about Kit's parentage. As Ian had said, he needed Kit to be the guilty one. If Toby was placed squarely in the wrong...No, he would never forgive his brother for that.

Kit glanced down at their mother, and on impulse stepped forward to take her hand; but she snatched it back. He turned and walked out of the room, and I rose and followed him.

Robyn caught up with us in the hall. 'Kit, don't go like this,' she said.

'Not much to stay for, is there?'

'I know you saw Jodie this morning. She and Ian had a long talk afterwards, and...we don't keep secrets from one another.'

'Do you keep them from Toby?'

'I never used to. Do you want me to keep this one?'

'Your choice.'

'I will, then.' She ducked her head, as if ashamed to meet his eyes; and shame was not an emotion I would have associated with Robyn Pevensey. 'I owe you that,' she said.

'Oh, Robbie, you don't owe me anything.'

'I was so angry with you, after you cut us all off like that. Mum was upset, and that wound Toby up. Simon was distraught. Jodie was ill. You caused a mess, and left Ian and me to deal with it.'

'I'm sorry. It was unforgivable.'

She flinched. 'Don't say that,' she whispered. 'What I said on Monday evening...You know me, don't you? I say stupid things, when I'm angry. Please don't hate me.'

'Robbie, I don't. I never would.'

'Oh...*you!*' She gave a hiccupping laugh, dashing at the tears on her cheeks. 'You're such a *bugger*. I never cry.'

He smiled ruefully. 'Mates, then?'

For answer she hugged him, which can't have done the fractures any good, but I guessed that such an antidote to Toby's poison was worth a few twinges. I felt like an interloper, but at the same time I was so glad for

165

Kit's sake that my own throat constricted.

After a minute Robyn disengaged herself, looking searchingly into his eyes. 'What did Toby mean? He only told me that you'd both thrown a few punches and Lissa had whacked him with something. Did he hurt you?'

'Not much. I'm sorry. I should've had the sense to let it go.'

She tried a grin, wincing as it hurt her mouth. 'No one would think you were the youngest.'

He cocked his head, puzzled, and she said in exasperation, 'You're not responsible for our mistakes.'

Kit acknowledged her perception with a grimace. 'Better listen to your own advice, then. You and Toby are not two halves of the same person.'

'Try telling him that.'

He kissed her cheek. 'Bless you, Robbie. I'm glad you were here tonight.'

'You wanted more, though, didn't you? I'm a poor consolation prize.'

'Yes, I did. And no, you're not.'

'I'll sort it out. Toby's a drama queen, that's all.'

'You can't sort this.'

She managed half a smile. 'I'll try, at least.'

He kissed her again, and she stood on the steps and waved us off into the rain-filled night, as if this was any normal leave-taking at the end of any family visit; and in silence we drove away from the house that Kit had once thought of as home.

CHAPTER NINETEEN

The Medway Christmas party was held in the function suite of a riverside hotel. As Kit's flat was miles away, Rusty Cullingham had booked him a room. I had no idea whether she hoped to share it.

Driving the Mercedes south down the M5, I grew increasingly nervous about entering Kit's world, an alien place whose inhabitants would have no interest in a shy provincial nobody.

'Why the frown, Liss?' Kit asked. 'Not worried about the party, are you?

'Of course not.' I flashed him a smile. 'It'll be fun.'

He was undeceived. 'At least it gets us out of Malvern for a day or two. I'm starting to think we're banging our heads against a brick wall.'

I understood his frustration. Jodie's mum had flown to Jamaica for Christmas and turned her phone off, Daniel Chubb had failed to respond to our messages, and Ian's gran had hung up on me twice.

On the other hand, since the row at his parents' house we had enjoyed what amounted to an eight-day honeymoon. Although I knew that I needed time to grieve for Grandad, I had spent most of every day and night feeling ecstatically, guiltily happy. Or as my friend Gaby put it, 'totally loved up'.

'Did you mean what you told Ian yesterday,' Kit asked, 'about putting the house on the market after Christmas?'

'Of course. I've no choice.'

'Didn't hear you mention moving to Kent.'

'You said there was no rush to decide.'

'So I did.' He turned his head to look out of the side window, and I could neither see his expression nor guess at his thoughts.

The journey to Maidstone turned out to be easy, despite the minor irritation of the M25. I suspected that Kit had only asked me to drive to build my confidence, but perhaps that was no bad thing.

Having made good time to the hotel, we had two hours to while away before the party. We dealt with the first hour to our mutual satisfaction, and while Kit was in the shower I unpacked my bag, including Edgar Byrne's journal.

I had read the first thirty pages or so; mostly domestic trivia, but still fascinating. It seemed odd that Grandad had never mentioned the journal. Any information I had gleaned about the Edwardian Byrnes had been by roundabout routes.

I sat naked on the bed to continue reading.

Sunday, 3rd January, 1904. *Mary has been safely delivered of a healthy boy weighing over seven pounds. Our son and heir! We have named him Frederick John, after my father.*

Thursday, 28th January. *Little Freddie continues to grow and thrive. His sisters have already started to spoil him. I have been playing the proud father, but the financial problems hang about me like a fog. Mary is so blissfully happy, I cannot bring myself to burden her.*

Thursday, 11th February. *Where are your secrets hidden, Amphelisia? What a culmination to a career! 'Edgar Byrne, the well known (and debt-ridden) Shakespeare scholar, has proven that Mistress Amphelisia Byrne of Malvern was the Bard's beloved Dark Lady, whose identity has been shrouded in mystery for three hundred years.'*

Oh yes, Amphelisia, you could save me. Did the great man give you nothing to remember him by? Some precious gift, which you might have secreted somewhere in this house?

What of that ring on the fourth finger of your right hand? Was it engraved with a message of love from the Bard himself?

No, I daresay not. More likely a gift from your husband. Do not mock me with those dark eyes, Amphelisia! I have to joke to stop myself from weeping.

Poor Edgar. Was that how it had begun, the myth of the Byrne treasure? Had Grandad, reading his journal, been fired by the same dream? Had he spoken of that dream, with such passion that someone had believed the story was true?

Kit stepped out of the shower, towelling himself abstractedly, his eyes first on me and then on the journal. 'What does old Edgar have to say?' he asked, trying to read over my shoulder.

'That he was broke and desperate,' I said. 'How many children did he have? Seven, wasn't it?'

'Five girls, then a boy. I looked it up yesterday, while you were busy with Ian.' His voice was muffled inside the towel as he scrubbed at his hair. 'I can guess how the journal ends.'

'How, then?'

'He paid off his debts.' Kit emerged from the towel and tossed it over a chair. 'His aunt died and left them a packet.'

'So it wasn't the Dark Lady who made him rich,' I said.

'Nope. Just common or garden probate.' He dropped to one knee on the bed, and swept my hair aside to kiss my neck. 'Don't sound so disappointed. You didn't believe in the Byrne treasure anyway.'

Which was true, but my parents has gone so far as to name me after Amphelisia. If anyone was entitled to wonder about her life and loves, I had a better right than most.

169

I wriggled away from Kit, who was nibbling my ear. 'Don't do that. You know I hate it.'

'How about this, then?'

With a shriek, I scrambled to the far side of the bed and swung my feet to the floor, stuffing the journal into my handbag.

'If we're going to this party,' I said, 'at least let's be on time.'

'And leave early? Sounds good to me.'

I stood up, naked in front of the mirror, and started to experiment with my hair. I always put it up when I needed to feel more confident. Not that taming the curls would help me control any situation whatsoever.

'Leave it down,' Kit said.

'No, I don't think so.'

'It wants to curl,' he persisted, half smiling. 'Besides...' He stroked the damp waves. 'I love the way it ripples over your shoulders like this.'

I lifted quizzical eyebrows at his reflection, and his eyes met mine in the mirror. He left my hair alone and slid his hand around in front of me, pulling me back against him. His skin was warm and still wet, and he smelled of shower gel.

'No one gets to parties on time,' he said.

*

The function suite was large enough to have been a ballroom, in the days when the building had been a private country retreat. Chandeliers still hung from the domed ceiling, though now lit by electricity, and the cream and dusky-pink decor suited the Georgian splendour.

Walking through the doorway, I clung to Kit's arm. My knees were threatening to buckle with terror. Everyone there seemed to be talking at once, raising their voices to be heard over the noise of the live band, which was already tuning up.

I should have worn something else. My long, ice blue dress, which had looked all right in the fitting-room mirror, now seemed scarily low-cut. I shouldn't have allowed Kit to buy it for me, especially after lecturing him for treating me like a charity case, but temptation had beaten pride hands down. I had never owned a dress so expensive, nor so beautiful.

A short, blonde girl in pink detached herself from a group near the door with a whoop of delight. 'Kester! I've been trying to reach you for days! Nice suit! Is it new? And who's this?' She gave me a smile that showed off large, very white teeth. 'That dress is *gorgeous*.'

She was introduced to me as Fran Dexter, the editor's PA.

'Rusty told me about your grandad,' she said. 'I'm so sorry.'

Kit steered her away from the subject, and before long she had launched into a tipsy account of how someone called Nick had been an absolute *bastard* all bloody *week*, and she'd have told him to bugger off, but she was afraid of *never* working on the programme *ever again*. We all headed for the buffet together.

'Fran's my best mate here,' Kit said, squeezing her shoulder. 'Nick Darwin's our boss. He's the editor on *Gold*. Did I tell you that?'

'Er…' I said, feeling slightly bemused by the number of people and the snatches of half-heard conversations. Somewhere to my left a man was saying, 'So there we were, lumbered with all the gear plus three suitcases and a live bloody monkey, and we couldn't get Nick to answer the sodding phone!'

In the next huddle of people a woman squawked, amid much laughter, 'But of course it turned out she was a hooker, who remembered him from Reykjavik, of all

171

places.'

'Liss,' Kit said, grinning at my expression, 'come and meet Rusty.'

Fran made her excuses and drifted away, and I prepared myself to face Lucinda spit-out-the-bones Cullingham. But there was nothing obviously scary about her. In fact she was beautiful, with flame-coloured hair and huge eyes with dilated pupils, which suggested she might be high on more than Christmas spirit. I hated her on sight.

She greeted Kit with a lingering kiss on the lips, ignoring his embarrassed attempt to pull away.

'And you must be Kester's little cousin,' she said, smiling at me. 'Lissa, isn't it? How sweet.'

I managed a polite smile.

'I was so sorry to hear about your grandad,' she said. 'Kester's such a dark horse, I had no idea he was related to Professor Harry Byrne until that letter arrived.' She widened her eyes as if the association impressed her, which I was sure it didn't. 'I'm afraid you're going to be hopelessly bored tonight, Lissa. All we ever do is talk shop.'

She turned her back on me as if I had ceased to exist, and linked her arm through Kit's. 'There's someone you simply have to meet,' she said.

He detached himself with firmness. 'Thanks for booking Lissa and me a room,' he said.

She slanted me a look of swift reappraisal. 'A *pair* of dark horses. Kester, darling, I didn't know incest was one of your vices.'

I managed not to wince, but the muscles along Kit's jaw clenched, and he said coldly, 'That's enough, OK?'

Rusty read the danger signals and wisely changed the subject.

'I'm starving,' she said. 'Let's eat.'

The buffet was superb, and I was glad to see Kit pile his plate shamelessly high. Making up for lost time. Between one thing and another, he seemed to have spent the past week-and-a-half living almost exclusively on alcohol, painkillers and sex.

Rusty remained attached to us, or rather to Kit, stroking his arm while regaling him with an improbable-sounding tale involving herself, a lecherous Oxford don, a wrongly booked flight and the ancient Celts. He laughed a good deal, though the humour of the story eluded me. I ate salmon quiche without appetite, and wondered how early we could leave.

A man beside me, who had been in conversation with someone else, suddenly gave me his full attention.

'You must be Lissa,' he said. 'Delighted to meet you.'

He was middle-aged and nearly bald, with a lopsided mouth that made him seem permanently amused. I wished that Kit had taken time to introduce us before Rusty began spinning her sticky web.

'Nick Darwin,' my neighbour enlightened me. 'Glad you and Kester could make it. Does that mean your family problems are sorted? I'd like him to get Turkey out of the way before Christmas.' He broke off, hearing what he had said, and chuckled deep in his throat. 'No pun intended. Kester wanted to make the trip in the New Year, but it looks as if we can squeeze it in beforehand, if he flies out no later than the twenty-first.'

I could barely conceal my dismay. We had nine days left, to solve the mysteries and feel assured that no lurking danger remained. Perhaps Nick would agree to postpone the trip if necessary. Despite Fran's complaints about him, he seemed the understanding type.

'Kester rang me on Thursday,' he was saying. 'He told me all about you. So you worked as a historical researcher for Professor Byrne? Also as his PA?'

'Yes,' I said, cheeks burning as I wondered what else Kit had said.

'You're a talented lady.' Nick's small, shrewd eyes narrowed. 'Are you looking for new employment in the same line?'

Before I could reply, he exclaimed in consternation, 'Your glass is empty! Can't have that. Red or white?'

'White. Thank you.'

He refilled it, saying, 'Kester may have mentioned, we've attracted US sponsorship for a new series of *Gold*, about the settlement of the New World. We've also been talking to Jack Janssen, from a channel owned by one of the big US networks—the guy Kester met in New York. The series won't air until late next autumn, but we've got a UK network slot in April-May for seven programmes, so we're going ahead with another European series to fit into that.' He smiled, assuming my comprehension of the logistics. 'As you'll appreciate, with two series in preparation at once, we'll need two extra researchers.'

'I see,' I said, seeing all too clearly.

'They'll be on three-month contracts, but one thing leads to another. Get a toe in the door, make a few contacts. I imagine you've some useful names in your diary.'

'A few. Mainly dons who specialise in English history during the sixteenth and seventeenth centuries, plus a couple of archaeologists, and...well, experts in various fields.'

'In England?'

'Not all of them. There's Mr Bissias in Corfu, and Angelo Castileone in Venice.'

'Really? So you've had to travel, for your job?'

'Oh, no. We exchange emails, and talk on the phone.'

'In English? Italian? Greek?'

'Whichever. I learned Italian at school, and took a

174

refresher course a couple of years ago. And I can get by in Greek. Grandad taught me that at home. It's useful with Mr Bissias. His English isn't good.'

Nick Darwin's brows were half way up his forehead. 'Is that all? No other languages at your fingertips?'

'I did GCSE French, but I'm hopelessly rusty.' I blinked in surprise at my glass, which Nick had refilled again.

'Speaking of Rusty,' he said, 'there's a little matter that she and I need to settle. Will you excuse me for a second?'

Without waiting for an answer, he broke into Rusty's animated discussion with Kit and drew her away. Kit turned to me, looking sheepish. Rusty had monopolised him for at least twenty minutes.

'How are you and Nick getting along?' he asked.

'You planned this whole thing. You set me up!'

'I opened a door, that's all.'

'Without asking me first! What have you told Nick about me?'

'The truth. That you're clever and talented, with bags of experience in historical research.'

'You shouldn't have exaggerated.'

'I didn't.'

'What if he offers me a contract?'

'Sign it.'

I glared at him. 'Shouldn't you be letting Rusty know where she stands?'

'She knows. She's just flirting.'

I was neither appeased nor reassured; but within an hour, Nick Darwin had succeeded in banishing Rusty from my mind, along with every other coherent thought. Seeking me out once again, and seeming deliberately to choose a moment when Kit had been cornered by someone else, he said casually, 'What do you think, then,

Lissa? How would you feel about working on *Age of Gold* for three months?'

The sixty-four thousand dollar question. How *would* I feel, apart from terrified, inadequate, uprooted, hopelessly at sea...

As I hesitated, he said, 'You'd be a junior researcher among four others, three of them highly experienced. Plus you'll have plenty of opportunity to travel. It's usual to send someone on ahead. After Turkey, we'll be looking at Sicily, Malta, Tunisia...'

'In the wake of Odysseus?' I guessed, with a swift inner vision of Kit, aged eight or nine, holding my hand in the dungeon, whispering old stories in the dark.

Nick beamed. 'Kester was right about you,' he said.

'I'd—I'd have to move down here,' I said. 'To Kent.'

'Would that be a problem?'

'No. At least...'

He patted my hand in a fatherly manner. 'Talk it over with Kester, and let me know in a week or two.'

He drifted off, and with a sudden longing to breathe fresh air I headed for the French doors, slightly hampered by four-inch heels and too much wine.

The freezing air caught at my breath. It was reassuring to think of Charles taking care of the horses for me. He was so familiar with them that even Tempest rarely gave him any trouble.

Hugging my bare arms around me, I wandered down to where a distributary of the River Medway ran beneath tall trees. I leaned against a trunk, shivering, and watched the dark current.

Footsteps crunched towards me over the frost, and Kit ducked under a branch and stood beside me. I didn't look at him, though on the edge of vision I could see his breath misting on the air, just like mine.

'You shouldn't have done it,' I said.

'Shouldn't I?' He took off his jacket and draped it around my shoulders. 'Want to tell me what he said?'

I relayed the gist of our conversation, and at some point Kit decided he could draw me into his side without provoking an abusive reaction.

'I'd let you down,' I said finally. 'I'd be a pathetic, stammering wreck. You'd be ashamed of me, and people like Rusty would giggle in corners.'

'Not in my hearing, they wouldn't!' He turned me to face him. 'And I'd never be ashamed of you. Liss, get it into your head that you'd be an asset to the programme, not a liability.'

'I'm not like Rusty.'

'No, thank God! How could you let any of us down? You'd be doing what you're good at.'

But I knew he was wrong.

'Come back inside,' he said. 'You're freezing.' He gave an elaborately staged shiver. 'And so am I!'

In a haze of despair only partly induced by alcohol, I let him lead me in.

*

It was not a bad party, in the end. Nick went out of his way to charm, making no mention of our private conversation, and Fran Dexter turned out to be amusing, likeable and piercingly intelligent. Other colleagues of Kit's came and went, not all of them from the *Age of Gold* team. Medway Television, though not one of the regional giants, had several other programmes on air or in the pipeline.

Brimming with Dutch courage, I felt I acquitted myself fairly well, even with Rusty. She invited us to her New Year's Eve party, but I declined without consulting Kit. It was a relief when, shortly afterwards, he slid me a covert grin of approval.

It must have been three o'clock when we went to bed.

The next thing I knew was sunlight searing through my eyelids. I groaned and rolled over, hiding under the duvet.

'Are you alive?' Kit asked from somewhere above me.

'No! Close the curtains!'

'They're serving breakfast.'

'Oh, don't.'

'Is there anything I can do,' he said, drawing nearer, 'to take your mind off your hangover?'

'If you bounce me about, I'll be sick.'

He chuckled heartlessly and dragged the duvet off. 'Get up, then. I'll make you a nice black coffee.'

By the time we got downstairs it was nine-thirty, which earned us a disenchanted look from the waitress. Nick Darwin and Rusty were sharing a table, and something in their manner suggested they had shared more than that during the night. If so, they had my blessing.

We chose a table to ourselves. Kit ate a fried breakfast while I drank more black coffee and nibbled dry toast. Nick and Rusty finished before us, and stopped at our table on their way out.

'A good do, wasn't it?' Nick said, his arm around Rusty's waist.

'Sure,' Kit said. 'How's Olivia?'

'Bastard,' his boss retorted, grinning.

'Takes one to know one.'

Nick laughed, and patted me on the head. 'When you've made up your mind, Lissa, let me know.'

When they had gone, I asked Kit who Olivia was.

'Nick's third wife,' he said. 'She's about your age. They've got two little girls.'

I resolved not to be taken in by the editor's twinkling bonhomie. His personal life aside, Fran found him difficult and demanding to work for, and she was in a position to know.

*

Kit drove home, as I was so hung over. We made a detour via his flat, to pick up his post and some clothes, and called in at a service station for lunch. It was mid-afternoon when we arrived back at The Eyrie.

A blue hatchback was parked outside. As we stopped beside it, the door opened and Inspector Hughes and Sergeant Calder emerged.

'Inspector,' I said, trying not to sound as breathless as I felt. 'How can we help you?'

'Good afternoon, Miss Byrne, Mr Pevensey. I wonder if you'd like to tell me where you've been for the past...' He checked his watch, '...twenty-seven hours? Or are your neighbours down the lane mistaken about when you left?'

'We went to Maidstone,' Kit said. 'Office Christmas party.'

Hughes eyed him cynically. 'Well, isn't that lucky? A perfect alibi.'

'What for?' Kit asked.

'Is either of you acquainted with Daniel Chubb? He was at the inquest.'

I nodded, with growing apprehension; and Kit said, 'We've met. Why?'

'He's been murdered, Mr Pevensey.' Hughes paused, for thought or dramatic effect, before adding the rest of it. 'We found a photograph of you in his wallet.'

CHAPTER TWENTY

Kit said, for the second time, 'That's not me.'

We had all migrated to the relative warmth of the kitchen, but both Hughes and Calder had refused my offer of tea. The Inspector's attitude was less sympathetic than on the evening of Grandad's death, and the chocolate-brown eyes were no longer gentle.

He now returned Kit's neutral gaze with disfavour, tapping the photo which lay on the table—a copy of the snap found in Mr Chubb's wallet.

'If this is Joshua Nix,' he said, 'he looks, or looked, enough like you to be your brother, wouldn't you say? Or your father, given the gap in time?'

'We're cousins,' Kit said, 'a few times removed.'

Hughes looked unconvinced. 'Had Chubb been hired to trace Nix?'

'Yes. That's why he came to see Lissa and me. To ask if we knew where Nix was.'

'Which you didn't?'

'No. Can you tell us how Chubb was killed?'

It seemed that Hughes could reveal, however grudgingly, the details that would be made public. Mr Chubb's body had been discovered by his niece, who had found the curtains drawn and the front door ajar. Daniel Chubb, lying fully clothed in an empty bath, had been strangled with a piece of twine; the sort one could buy at any garden centre. The time of death was believed to have been between nine and eleven o'clock yesterday evening, although a full post mortem had yet to confirm this.

'Poor Mr Chubb,' I said. 'Poor little man.'

Hughes' thick brows twitched upward at the inner corners; a trick more reminiscent of a begging puppy than an interrogator, though I didn't think he would be pleased to know it.

'Neither of you has shown much surprise,' he said.

'Chubb had received anonymous texts,' Kit said, 'warning him to drop the Nix investigation.'

Sergeant Calder scribbled in his notebook. Hughes continued to eye us with shrewd appraisal.

'Geoff Southbrook is worried about you two,' he said. 'He asked me out for a beer last night. Told me that you were intent on putting yourselves at risk, and that I should be watching you like a hawk. He wouldn't be more specific. Became very coy, he did, when I pressed him to explain. Now what do you make of that?'

'Dr Southbrook is an old family friend,' Kit said. 'Maybe Grandad told him about the letter from Wales. The one you found in his wallet.'

Hughes frowned, and gave us up as a lost cause. I could feel the last vestiges of goodwill evaporate.

'Mr Pevensey, please don't treat me like an idiot,' he said. 'I've wondered many times what was on the Professor's mind, the day he died. He'd been anxious to talk to Chubb, but didn't live long enough to keep the appointment. Do you know who hired Chubb to trace Nix?'

'Chubb didn't want to tell us.'

Whether or not Hughes heard the evasion, he turned to me. 'Miss Byrne?'

I shook my head.

There was a charged pause before Hughes said, 'Chubb's house had been ransacked. According to his niece, however, nothing of value was missing.'

'She may not know if case notes had been stolen,' Kit said. 'Nor if computer files had been copied or deleted.'

'No, Mr Pevensey. She may not.'

'And if there's a connection with the Nix case, why

181

would the killer leave Nix's photo in Chubb's wallet, for you to find?'

'Ever considered a career in the police, sir?' The sarcasm was biting. 'The victim's wallet had fallen behind the washbasin, perhaps during a struggle. We think the killer missed it.'

'So, *are* you assuming a connection with Nix?'

'I'm not assuming anything, sir. Not even your innocence.' His glance lighted on me. 'Nor yours, Miss Byrne. I wouldn't like to think either of you was withholding evidence.'

Kit shot me a troubled look, from which I gathered he felt much as I did. To have blurted out Ian's name would have seemed like telling tales. The old rules of the Eyrie Gang were deeply ingrained in us both. And of course, we knew Ian couldn't be guilty.

In an attempt to redeem ourselves in Hughes' eyes, we gave him Nick Darwin's contact details and the name of the hotel in Maidstone. He and the sergeant departed with dour looks and reluctant thanks.

I rang Ian at once. His initial shock was overlaid by bewilderment that we hadn't given Hughes his name.

'We wanted to talk to you first,' I said. 'We thought you'd want to ring Hughes yourself.'

'I'd better, hadn't I? Oh God.' He sounded nervous to distraction, as well as upset about Chubb. 'What if he was killed because I hired him?'

'Even if he was, you're not to blame.'

'Maybe not, but...God, what a bloody awful thing to happen.'

After he had rung off, we changed into old clothes and, at my suggestion, armed ourselves with a flask of hot soup, mucked out the stables, and led Smoky and Tempest up the track. The field, always my refuge in times of trouble, now seemed the only place to go.

As often in our teenage years, we sat on the stile and watched the horses cavorting in the late afternoon sunshine, their lengthening shadows reaching towards us across the grass. Ian was not the only one with cause to feel guilty. Neither of us could shake off the suspicion that, if we had ignored Price's warning and come clean with Hughes two weeks ago, Daniel Chubb might still be alive.

The temperature plummeted as the sun went down; there would be another frost tonight. Sunk in gloom, we walked the horses back to the stables, Kit saying without enthusiasm, 'Janssen's flying over from New York, to meet Nick and the team. The meeting's not confirmed for tomorrow, but it's likely. I'll have to be there. Want to come?'

I didn't need time to think about it. I was no more keen to spend the day alone at The Eyrie than he was willing to let me.

Late that evening Rusty telephoned, to confirm that the meeting with *Gold's* potential sponsor was tomorrow at two o'clock. We decided to set out at nine-thirty, to reach Maidstone in time for lunch.

In the morning Kit's phone rang again, twenty minutes before we were due to leave. I went on clearing away the breakfast things, assuming it was another call from Medway, until I heard him say, 'When?...That's great. You're a wonderful woman...No, if Ian didn't say it was confidential...besides, I can't tell you how important...Thanks, Sandra. I won't forget this.' He disconnected, snatched up his leather jacket and headed for the door, informing me over his shoulder, 'Ian's off to see a client in Rhayader. Leaving in half an hour or less.'

'Is it Hywel Price?'

'According to Sandra. What's more, we were right.'

He slanted me a brilliant look; one that I had seen before, both on and off screen, when his digging into the past had broken open the sweet kernel of a mystery. 'Ian didn't meet Price for the first time after his grandad died. They've met in Rhayader more times than Sandra can remember.'

By the time I had grabbed my handbag and a coat, and had locked up the house, Kit was sitting in the passenger seat of the Mercedes. I hurriedly brushed bits of straw off my waxed jacket and scrambled in beside him, fastening the belt as I pulled away.

'D'you mind driving again?' he asked.

'Why should I?' Feeling cautiously confident, I flashed him a grin. 'You're the one who says I can do anything.'

He quirked an amused eyebrow. 'That's my girl.'

'What about your meeting, though?'

'What about it?' But he reached for his phone to tap in the office number.

I heard a familiar, grainy voice. 'Medway Television, *Age of Gold*.'

'Rusty, can you put me on to Nick?'

'And a good morning to you too, darling. How would you like to take me out to lunch?'

'I can't make the meeting.'

She gave a long whistle. 'My, oh my, *aren't* we living dangerously! Can't your sweet little cousin do without you?'

'Stop bitching and put me through.'

We heard her draw a startled breath; and she said as if through her teeth, 'Yes, *sir*.'

Once Nick Darwin came on the line, Rusty's sulks faded to insignificance. 'For Christ's sake!' he shouted. 'Janssen is flying in specially.'

'We got along fine in New York. He won't chuck the whole deal if I miss one meeting.'

'What the hell am I meant to tell him? That you're too busy shagging your cousin in sodding Malvern?'

So much for benign paternalism. My mouth fell open. Kit counted to five under his breath before saying, with icy calm, 'Apologise for that.'

'Don't even think about giving me orders!'

'Then don't talk about Lissa in those terms!'

'Oh, for—' Nick Darwin paused to rethink his tactics, and ground out, 'I apologise, but you're an arrogant sod and you're on thin fucking ice!'

'Yeah, well, someone I knew was murdered on Saturday night. I told the police you could give us an alibi.'

'Jesus Christ!' The rise in decibels made us both wince. 'How the fuck am I going to keep this out of the papers?'

'Bye, Nick. I'll be in touch,' Kit said, and cut him off.

'Can he sack you?' I asked. 'Terminate your contract, or anything?'

'He won't try. It'll blow over. And this,' he nodded at the road ahead, 'could be more important.'

We parked on double yellow lines, where we could see Ian's office forecourt without much risk of being spotted. He emerged five minutes later and drove off without a glance in our direction. I edged into the Monday morning traffic and followed his lovingly polished red Citroen.

It seemed too easy, and it was. Before we were out of Malvern, I lost him. Caught by traffic lights, I sat biting my lip, while Kit drummed his fingers on his knee in an accelerating beat that made me want to scream.

When the lights changed, I put my foot down. The Mercedes had its uses. I caught up with Ian after three or four miles, glimpsing the Citroen while there was still a car between us. I kept a discreet distance through

Leominster, dropping back further when the road opened out through the sheep-dotted hills of mid-Wales. Ian drove at an unhurried fifty miles an hour and patently hadn't seen us.

We came gradually into a bleak winter landscape. At first there was only a rime of frost, lying on the hills and trees like snow. But as we approached Rhayader, we were seeing the real thing; the road was clear but there were drifts along the verges. The hills were shrouded, luminous under a leaden sky.

'Should have checked the forecast,' Kit said. 'Looks like there's more to come.'

The snow was still holding off when we reached Rhayader. Neither of us was surprised when Ian continued through the town without stopping.

By lunchtime we were nearing Aberystwyth; but Ian took an unexpected exit at a roundabout and, according to the sat-nav, led us roughly north-west. There was hardly any traffic on the winding road and I let him draw well ahead, afraid he would see us in his mirror.

For several miles I had been watching Ian's car rather than following road signs, but now an odd feeling crept over me. We were heading towards the coast, north of Aberystwyth, which could only mean...

'Is this the road to Borth?' I asked.

'And Ynyslas,' Kit said.

Ynyslas, at the mouth of the River Dyfi, where Ian's parents and mine had drowned. I had never visited the place, but of course I knew the names.

At the end of the lane we found no red Citroen; just the sea and the village of Borth. In summer it must have been a cheery place, but today the coastline was white and windswept. The cafés and souvenir shops had a desolate air, and the few intrepid shoppers bowed their heads against the wind. Snow flurries splattered on our windscreen.

No telling which way Ian had gone. We tried a road that took us parallel with the coast and, at last, straight on to a deserted beach. And there, where the estuary ran into the sea…

Instead of turning the car around, I switched off the engine and got out. Seconds later, Kit was at my side.

'Sorry,' I said, 'I know we should be looking for Ian.'

'As we're here, Liss, we'll pay our respects. Two minutes' silence, in remembrance.'

I had known him all my life and he could still surprise me. I stood on tiptoe to kiss his nose. Then, hand in hand, we made our way down to the shoreline. Ynyslas beach was in sombre mood, the waters of sea and estuary reflecting the menace of the clouds. A fitting scene for a long overdue tribute.

My foot sank in wet sand, burying my leg to the knee. Icy sea-water gushed into my shoe. I shrieked, and Kit dragged me out, but next moment his own foot disappeared and he yelled in his turn.

We clambered on to a firm island of sand, surrounded by tidal pools, and gazed out across the choppy waters of the Dyfi estuary. On the other side, a short way upstream, was the fishing village of Aberdyfi.

'D'you know the folk song?' Kit asked. '*The bells of Aberdyfi?* There's a tale about this place, too, older than the song.'

'What sort of tale?'

'My sort. A legend, with maybe a grain of truth at the root of it.' He turned his face towards the sea. 'Long, long ago, a fertile land is said to have lain out there. Cantre'r Gwaelod, the Lowland Hundred.'

A born storyteller, he gave the words rhythm and resonance. I shivered in the wind.

'A man called Seithennin,' he went on, 'looked after

187

the sluices and embankments keeping back the sea. One night, Seithennin got drunk and forgot to shut the sluices. The people of Cantre'r Gwaelod, and all of its sixteen cities, were lost under the waves forever.'

'It couldn't be true, though,' I murmured. 'Could it?'

'It's true the sea level has risen. A few thousand years ago, there was a forest out in the bay. Not so sure about the cities.' He reached for my hand, twining his fingers through mine. 'Close your eyes.'

'Whatever for?'

He kissed my hair. 'Just for a minute.'

I did as I was told, and he spoke next to my ear, his soft voice seeming to fill all my senses. 'They say that when the air is hushed, and the dusk draws down, the bells of those drowned cities can still be heard. The current stirs them, down there in the dark, and sets them swinging in their forgotten steeples...'

He paused on a catch of breath as if listening. Perhaps he was. Our Byrne ancestors had been Irish, way back, and the blood of Celtic warrior-poets flowed more strongly in Kit than in the rest of us.

'The bells toll out their ghostly knell,' he murmured, 'keeping the memory of all that was lost, and of all the souls who perished. In the quiet even-time...' His voice faded. Even the wind seemed silenced; a lull between the wild gusts.

Two minutes, in remembrance.

CHAPTER TWENTY-ONE

I opened my eyes and looked again at the estuary, wondering what other echoes might sound here. Simon's and Ian's grandparents had been as reticent as Grandad, but we had been told the bare facts.

The two couples—Roland and Susie Byrne, Richard and Carol Threlfall—had come here for a spring break, and on Easter Saturday had chartered a yacht. On Sunday they had sailed downriver from Aberdyfi and been caught in a squall. The Threlfalls had been competent sailors and the harbourmaster would have advised them of the shifting sandbar, but a gust must have blown them on to it. The boat had capsized, and they had drowned.

I had no reason to doubt what we had been told, but now that I saw the place, it seemed almost incredible that they had died like that, so close to the beach. Even if they had neglected to wear lifejackets, at least two of them could swim. I remembered the photo in Grandad's old album: Mum diving off a rock, while Dad laughed up at her. Novice sailors or not, they had been completely at home in the water.

Kit tightened his arm around me. 'OK, Liss?' he asked.

I nodded. 'If Price lives near here, it's an odd coincidence.'

'Is it? He knew your parents and Ian's. Maybe they'd planned to meet him, the weekend they died. All the same, what we're stirring up…'

I shivered. 'You said it before, didn't you? Ghosts and shadows and distant voices?'

'Stories are one thing.' He indicated the estuary. 'No harm in listening for bells. Hauling them to the surface, though…who knows what else you might drag up?'

'Evidence of what really happened,' I murmured.

'If you want to change your mind, Liss, we don't have to find Ian's car. We can still go back.'

'We can't,' I said sadly, thinking of Mr Chubb. 'Not any more.'

We retraced our route as far as Borth, but found no sign of the Citroen. Dejectedly, I turned on to a minor road signposted to Aberystwyth, slowing down now and then to check the occasional farm track.

At the end of one such rutted byway stood a cottage, its walls as white as the snow-covered roof. Thin curls of smoke rose from the chimney, to be blown horizontally and lost on the wind. The name on the gate had faded to illegibility.

Ian's Citroen was parked by the front door. With a sharp exclamation I braked, and Kit thumped a triumphant fist on the dashboard.

'*Yes!* Right, stay here. If I'm not back in twenty minutes—'

'No!' I grabbed his arm and hung on. 'Don't you dare do this to me again!'

'Oh, Liss! Whatever Price is guilty of, he's not likely to murder me in front of Ian.'

'What if he killed Mr Chubb, and Ian guessed and came here to confront him? He'll have to kill Ian as well.'

'Get a grip, girl!' To my fury, Kit was nearly laughing. 'Can you see Ian, of all people, haring off for a showdown with a killer? And you said at the beach—'

'I don't care! I am not going to sit here *worrying* for twenty minutes!'

Before he could reply, the cottage door opened. The woman who emerged was tiny, silver strands of hair escaping from the hood of an over-sized coat. She had only come out to put a bag of rubbish in the bin, but in my opinion her presence settled the matter. Price would hardly kill anyone with his elderly relative as a witness.

'You're right,' I said. 'It'll be fine.'

I drove right up to the cottage, ignoring Kit's infuriated protests. There was no way he could *make* me sit and wait for him, short of tying me to the seat. I pointed this out. He gave me a look in which humour vied with annoyance and won by a narrow margin.

'Don't tempt me,' he said.

We got out of the car. As we approached the swathed figure, she turned towards us, her faded blue eyes squinting to see us through the snow.

'Joshua?' she quavered.

My heart leaped with shock. Kit said, hand politely extended, 'I'm Kit Pevensey, Joshua's cousin. This is Lissa Byrne. We're sorry to trouble you, but we need to speak to Ian Threlfall.'

'He's gone out with Hywel.'

She hadn't shaken Kit's hand. Instead she retreated into the porch, and I realised what she was seeing. A fair-haired, grey-eyed stranger, appearing out of the swirling whiteness, like the ghost of the man she had known.

'You *are* Joshua.' Fear trembled in her voice.

'No,' he said gently. 'I'm Kit, and I'm as real as you are.'

'Oh!' She blinked, and even raised a smile. 'In that case, you'd better come in.'

We followed her through a narrow hall, into a sitting room where the wood burning stove and much of the furniture looked pre-war, in contrast to the new suite, flat-screen TV and expensive music system. The air smelled of festive potpourri. Amateur seascapes adorned the walls, and above the mantelpiece hung a photo of a little boy with a mop of dark hair.

As our hostess ushered us to the sofa, I said, 'I'm

sorry, we don't know your name.'

'Miss Price, but you must call me Angharad. Do sit down.' She peered at Kit. 'Pevensey, you say? Wilfred and Edith's boy?'

'They were my grandparents.'

'Of course. You're so young.' She turned to me. 'And you're Lissa. Amphelisia. Roland's little girl.'

She knew so much about our families that I was possessed by a morbid desire to find out what Grandad had never told me; all the details of the accident. But first things first.

'Can you tell us,' I asked, 'how long Hywel and Ian might be gone?'

She shook her head. 'My nephew does as he pleases. I'll make some tea, shall I?'

Tea was served in bone china mugs decorated with rosebuds, and Angharad talked freely, needing no prompting. 'I knew them all, of course. Deirdre Threlfall was a great friend. Her husband died last month. What a prig he was! And Wilfred and Edith Pevensey, so *very* respectable. And Harry.' Her eyes were drawn to Kit again in fascination. 'You're so like poor Joshua.'

'Why *poor* Joshua?' he asked.

'He was a lovely young man. One for the ladies, though. I heard he was very clever in bed.' She smiled at me. 'I've often wondered, and I'm sure you're in a position to know…does that talent run in families?'

Kit spluttered into his tea. I passed him a napkin, not daring to meet his eyes, and drew a careful breath to suppress my own rising giggles.

'Angharad,' I said, 'have you seen Joshua since he left the Malverns?'

I think she started to reply; but at that moment Hywel Price and Ian walked in.

Kit and I both stood up, as much from survival

instinct as courtesy. While Ian stopped in the doorway, looking thoroughly disconcerted, Price strode into the centre of the room and glowered down at us.

'Pevensey!' He spat out the name like a curse. 'This is how you get your stories, is it? By forcing your way into people's homes and intimidating old women?'

Kit countered peaceably, 'I'm a historian, not a reporter, and I don't think your aunt feels intimidated. Why don't you ask her?'

Her nephew had no need to do that. She stepped between him and us, a striped tea-cosy clasped to her breast like a shield.

'We've been having a chat, Hywel,' she said. 'Don't you dare spoil it!'

Price made an explosive sound that might have been a laugh, but there was little mirth in it. He transferred from Kit to me a stare that was both fearful and blazingly angry. 'I thought you'd have had more sense. Didn't what I said count for anything?'

Ian stepped forward. 'Come on, Hywel, you need to calm down. It's not the end of the world.'

'Isn't it?' Price was obviously making an effort at self-control. After a second or two he sighed, and cast a meaningful look at his aunt. 'All right. Do the honours, will you, Ian?'

To my incredulous dismay, Ian placed a hand firmly under Angharad's elbow. 'We'll leave them to it, shall we?' he said. 'Didn't you promise to show me your postcard collection?'

As the door shut behind them, I edged closer to Kit, who drew me into his side. Price watched this manoeuvre with a twisted smile.

'You've decided I killed Chubb, is that it?' he said.

I caught my breath. 'N-no,' I stammered.

'Did you?' Kit said.

'No,' Price said, 'I did not.'

'But you know who did.'

My stomach dropped through the floor. Kit was pushing him too far. Ian would hardly turn a blind eye while his client committed double murder, but as to whether he could prevent it...

Price said, heading for the sideboard, 'I need a drink. Will either of you join me?'

'No, thanks,' Kit said.

'At least sit down.' Price's hand shook a little as he poured himself a brandy. 'I can't think with you two hovering there like avenging angels.'

Restoring his mental agility was not a priority. We remained standing.

'That scared, eh?' he enquired nastily.

About me, he was dead right. Kit returned his stare with a glint of humour, and looked obstinate rather than intimidated.

'Why did you tell us you were Nix?' he asked.

'I was expecting Harry. I had to think on my feet.'

'Because of the crime you and Harry committed?'

Price's expression froze. 'What crime? All I said was that digging up the past could lead you into danger and ruin Harry's reputation.'

'To the extent that he'd be remembered with a shudder.' The last trace of amusement had gone from Kit's voice. 'Chubb is dead. Lissa could be next. I'd say we're within our rights to ask a question or two.'

Price unexpectedly sank into an armchair, crossing his long legs in an unconvincing pretence at relaxation. Despite his next words, I didn't believe he had relented so easily.

'I spent a lot of time with Aunt Angharad as a child,' he said. 'As well as being a friend of the Threlfalls and Byrnes, she was a teacher, so our holidays coincided.

Whenever she visited the Malverns, she took me with her. I really did know your parents as kids. Josh was a mate until the day he chose to vanish. He'd laugh, if he knew I'd used his name in an emergency.'

'Fair enough. Why was meeting us an emergency?'

'I've made a life here. I've got a girlfriend, and a decent job—not very lucrative in the winter, admittedly—with a local boat delivery firm. Check that out, if you like. What happened in Malvern was another life. I don't want it raked up again. I was afraid you'd trace me if I gave my own name.'

'Then why—'

'I had to convince you that I knew your families.' He looked down at his brandy, swirling it around the glass. 'The warning still stands.'

'Have you solved the problem, whatever it is?' Kit said.

'Not yet.'

'*Can* you?'

Price lifted his chin. 'You entered this house under false pretences. You're on very uncertain ground.'

My innards performed another somersault, but Kit was still giving back stare for challenging stare.

'How deeply is Ian involved?' he asked.

'He's my solicitor.'

'He's told a few lies for your sake. He might like to be in on this discussion. Shall I call him?'

A bristling silence. Kit walked casually towards the door.

'No!' Price hadn't moved from the chair. I wondered what he was planning now. Another lie, or something worse? He looked sufficiently harmless at the moment, sitting there among the floral-printed cushions, sipping brandy.

'You're right.' He was still addressing Kit rather than

me. 'There are things I'd prefer Ian didn't find out. He doesn't know what I said to you in Hay, nor what I'm about to tell you now. Harry and I had a...an acquaintance with a score to settle. We used to think time would mellow him, but we were wrong. We felt that Lissa, and Harry himself, might have become a target. You too, perhaps, now that you're back in the Malverns, although Harry seemed to think you could look after yourself.'

'Why us?' I put in.

'The reasons are irrelevant.'

'Really?' Kit snapped. 'DI Hughes might disagree.'

Price rose slowly and set down his glass. Kit stood his ground, which obliged me to do the same, as he held my hand tightly. In every other way I might not have been there. The men faced each other, brown eyes meeting grey with equal ferocity.

'Go to Hughes, then!' Price said. 'By the time he gets here, I'll be gone. And you won't have saved Lissa.'

'Then give us a name! Let Hughes stop this fucking nonsense once and for all!'

'*I* will stop it. Not Hughes, and not you.'

'And if you can't?'

'I'll deserve any punishment the law can devise.'

'No,' Kit said, scarcely above a whisper. 'If Lissa comes to harm, you'll wish the law had got to you first.'

Price drew a sharp breath. Seeing his fist clench I cringed against Kit, but he only pivoted on his heel, strode to the hall door and threw it wide.

'You've had your pound of flesh, Pevensey,' he grated. 'Get out of my life!'

CHAPTER TWENTY-TWO

We left without argument. Price watched us all the way down the track and into the lane, but at Kit's suggestion we stopped in the first lay-by with a screen of winter foliage.

'I'll have to go back,' he said.

I had known he wouldn't give up; had seen it in the stubborn set of his jaw, and in the covert look he had given Price in the hallway. He had gone willingly only because I was there too.

I clasped his hand. It was warm and steady; not chilled by fear like mine.

'There's another way,' I said. 'If we go home now, we can tackle Ian tomorrow, and—'

'Hush,' he said, smiling. 'It's Angharad I want to talk to. She may be a bit senile, but she knows "poor Joshua" is dead. Maybe that's why Price was so furious. He was terrified of what she might have given away already.'

'But Price could be there when you go back. He said he doesn't get much work in the winter. Even if we watch the place until he goes out, he could come back unexpectedly, just like today.'

'Liss!' He was laughing. 'Don't fret so.'

'Don't *fret*? Hywel Price probably killed Joshua *and* Mr Chubb, and God knows what hold he's got over Ian.'

'Ian doesn't seem *afraid* of Price. Besides, Ian will go home tonight. We'll stay in a little B and B, if we can find one open. I'll make sure Price doesn't cause us a problem.' He kissed me briefly, daring me not to believe in him. 'Tomorrow, he'll be miles away.'

*

Charles was surprised to receive a phone call from me, and astonished by the news that we were snowbound in

Wales. 'I didn't realise the weather had been so bad,' he said. 'Where are you?'

'The Brecon Beacons,' I lied, looking out of the café window at the falling snow, which obscured our view of Borth seafront. 'We planned to have a day out, to get right away from...well, everything.'

'Ah.' A pause, as Charles chose his next words with care. 'Meaning the altercation with the family, I assume. Robbie did mention it.'

'I was thinking of Daniel Chubb,' I said, with a touch of acid. 'Did you hear what happened to him?'

'Hughes came to see us. God knows why. Belinda and I had never heard of Chubb until the inquest.'

Not sure how best to answer this, I made an effort to bring the conversation back on track. 'The thing is, Charles, we'll have to stay here tonight. I'm sure the main roads will be clear by tomorrow, but if you wouldn't mind looking after Smoky and Tempest again...'

Charles didn't mind. On the contrary, he sounded grateful for the chance to do us a favour. I thanked him, and felt no remorse for the lies. By my reckoning he had deserved them.

We bought a few toiletries and started hunting for somewhere to stay. As the tourist office was closed, this took a little time. We eventually struck gold with a guesthouse a mile outside of Borth, where the owners welcomed us like friends and insisted that it would be no trouble to cook us an evening meal.

That afternoon we worked out a plan of campaign. An internet search showed only one local firm specialising in boat delivery; the next nearest was forty miles away in Barmouth. As for the Prices' landline number; among numerous Prices in the online phone book, the only entry which ticked all the boxes was A Price, Llanberis Cottage, Borth.

In the privacy of our en-suite room, Kit's first phone call was to Fran Dexter. He trusted Fran, he said; Rusty Cullingham had hidden agendas.

'It's you!' Fran exclaimed with relief at hearing his voice. 'Where have you been? Nick's been getting your voicemail all day—'

'I need a favour, Fran. Strictly off the record. Got a pen?'

He asked her to buy a cheap pay-as-you-go phone and ring Price at ten-thirty the next morning. The story was that her employer, a Mr Dexter, wanted a boat sailed from Barmouth to Fowey, Cornwall, on Boxing Day. Mr Dexter's usual skipper couldn't work over Christmas and Price came recommended.

'Bill me for the phone,' Kit added. 'If Price asks about the boat, say it's a big Moody. Plead ignorance of the details; he'll have to ask Mr Dexter. Stress he'll be well paid, cash in hand, but he'll need to go to Barmouth *now*. Mr Dexter wants to meet him personally. Give him a real address for his sat-nav. That's it, Fran. Think you can carry it off?'

'Are you kidding? I once played Juliet at school. But why—'

'Thanks, you're amazing. Just don't say anything to Nick.'

Before she could persist with awkward questions, he rang off. Instead of exhibiting satisfaction at a job well done, however, he sat staring down at the phone, brows drawn together in concentration.

'Are you afraid she'll let us down?' I asked.

'I'm wondering if we've let *her* down. How do we know Price sails yachts up and down the country? He could have invented that, to throw us off some other scent.'

'Surely not.' Frowning, I conjured Hywel Price in my

mind's eye. 'He's strong, isn't he? Muscular. I can see him doing a physical job.'

'Doesn't make him a sailor. He could be a roofer. Or a grave-digger.'

'Don't say that. Not even as a joke.'

He patted my arm comfortingly, but his thoughts were miles away.

'Fancy a walk into Borth?' he said.

'In a blizzard? Can't we wait till it eases up?'

'Nope. People keep telling me I'm a journalist. Time I acted like one.'

*

The premises of Owen and Son, specialists in boat delivery anywhere in the UK, any day of the year, were tucked away behind a shop selling beachwear. We knocked and went in, to find the office occupied by a young woman of eighteen or so. She was reading a magazine—understandably, as the telephone was silent, her in-tray was empty and there was not a customer in sight.

She didn't appear to recognise Kit, but her eyes lit up at the sight of him. 'Can I help you?' she asked.

'I hope so,' he said. 'I've got a yacht over at Barmouth. A thirty-footer, nothing grand. I need her sailed up to Scotland next week. Oban, west coast. A mate of mine recommended one of your skippers, a guy called Hywel Price.'

The girl looked blank. 'He's not one of ours.'

I grimaced at Kit, saying under my breath, 'Next stop, Barmouth.'

'But our skippers are both very experienced,' the girl added quickly. 'Kyle Owen, he's the boss's son.' She consulted a computer screen. 'Yes, he's free.'

'We'll think about it,' Kit said.

She bit her lip, and hurried to provide a second

200

option. 'If you're wanting someone older, there's Joshua.'

Coincidence, I thought; but Joshua was a reasonably common name. I asked, 'Is that Joshua, um…'

'Nix,' she said. 'Do you know him?'

While I struggled to reassemble some wits, Kit enquired casually, 'He's about six-three, right? Grey hair, short beard, eyes that look straight through you?'

The girl nodded, not quite smiling at the description. 'Has he done a job for you before?'

'Not exactly. Thanks for your help. We'll be in touch.'

'Don't you want to make a booking? I'm sure Joshua—'

'See you later, maybe.'

We left the girl to her mystified disappointment.

'I can't believe it,' I said, as we trudged back to our lodgings through the driving snow. 'Why would he play Nix at work and Price at home?'

'Search me. He's making his life bloody complicated, and he could be laying himself open to a murder charge.'

'You think so? I mean, if there's no body…'

'It's legally possible. Hard to prove, I should think. But if he's being paid as Nix, the odds are he's using his identity for banking, credit cards, tax forms…you name it. That'd look pretty incriminating.'

'I wonder if his aunt knows.'

'Mail for Nix must land on her doormat. Makes it vital to speak to her again. But as soon as we get home, we'll have go to Hughes with all this. Price can drop all the dark hints he likes, but if we keep quiet now, we could be in real trouble for withholding evidence.'

He was right, of course.

'You do realise,' I said, 'that we're going back to Llanberis Cottage together or not at all?'

'Might as well, if Price swallows the bait and heads for Barmouth.'

201

Back at the guesthouse, we were served a huge roast dinner, followed by a steamed pudding which defeated even Kit; and throughout the meal our hosts were rarely out of earshot for longer than a minute or two, making any discussion about tomorrow impossible.

Afterwards, having retreated to our room, I sat in bed and watched Kit undress. This was a much more pleasurable pastime, now that he no longer moved as if every inch of his body hurt. Even the bruise over his ribs had faded to a yellow smudge.

He must have sensed my eyes on him. He glanced up, lifting an eyebrow in amusement. 'Enjoying yourself?'

'How are the cracks? And don't make some stupid joke.'

His mouth twitched at my bossy tone. 'The ribs are OK. Catch me a bit, sometimes. Shoulder's still a nuisance. Why the inquisition?'

'It's hardly that.'

'Not nervous about tomorrow, are you? Giving the bodyguard a quick medical?'

'No!' But, to my shame, he was at least half right.

'Don't feel guilty about it,' he said.

I threw a pillow at his head and he caught it, grinning.

'Just keep reminding yourself,' he said, 'if there was any danger, I wouldn't be letting you come. How are you getting on with Edgar's journal?'

The book had been in my handbag since the Medway trip. Glad to change the subject I started leafing through it, then let the pages fall open at random. I read aloud:

'**Wednesday, 10th August.** *George continues to prattle about our collaborating to create LLW. The scheme has a certain mad appeal. If the project were to fail, of course, we could both be looking at a lengthy stay at His Majesty's pleasure.*'

Before I had finished this narrative, Kit had

scrambled on to the bed beside me and was avidly scanning the handwritten text.

'What scheme's this?' he asked. 'What's LLW?'

'I've no idea. I've missed out a huge chunk.'

We flicked back through the closely written pages. There was no earlier mention of LLW, but we did discover that George Livesey-Byrne was Edgar's cousin and closest friend, a young novelist and playwright struggling to establish his reputation in Edwardian society.

'Let's go forward, then,' Kit said. 'What comes next?'

What came next only served to deepen the mystery.

Wednesday, 17th August. *George visited again this evening. He has started LLW! He handed me three pages for review. I could not resist making some changes to give it the ring of authenticity, greatly to George's delight, but I do feel that I am being asked to don the cap and bells against my better judgement.*

'The cap and bells,' I murmured. 'The sign of a professional jester. Were they writing comedy, do you think?'

We persevered in search of answers. There were no more entries of relevance for nearly two months, when George again arrived laden with what was evidently, by this time, a sizeable manuscript.

Sunday, 2nd October. *I will say one thing for George, he works like a Trojan when the mood takes him. At his insistence and purely as an intellectual exercise, I have promised to revise the first draft.*

Monday, 10th October. *To my own surprise, LLW has taken hold of my imagination, although I still refuse to countenance George's wild plans for profit. He has invested in a machine at second hand; but despite the temptation, our imprisonment would be of little financial benefit to our families.*

The final mention of the project was the last entry before those dealing solely with Christmas festivities:

Wednesday, 14th December. *Aunt Eliza has passed away; a happy release. The great surprise is that she has bequeathed to me an extraordinarily generous sum, hardly less than young George is to receive. To my relief he approached me yesterday, to suggest that we consign LLW to a safe place, where it will remain as insurance against any future monetary crisis. I have placed it beneath a loose floorboard under the bed, where no one is likely to find it by chance.*

Kit and I looked at one another, and I could practically see the possibilities rioting through his mind.

'*A machine at second hand...*An old printing press?' he said. 'They forged a book. One that would bring in a lot of cash if it could fool the experts. George had the imagination but he needed Edgar, the historian, the scholar, to make his work ring true.'

'Edgar was right,' I said. 'It would have been risky. Could it still be under that floorboard?'

'Interesting to check.'

'Edgar and Mary would have used the master bedroom. Grandad's room. Kit, what if the secret died with George and Edgar? What if Grandad was the first person to find the book again? If he hadn't read this journal by then...if it was lying forgotten somewhere...'

'He might have hoped LLW was the genuine article,' Kit finished for me.

'The Byrne treasure?'

'Why not? He could have told a few friends, maybe even one of the family. By the time he'd studied the book more closely, or had it valued by an expert, it may have been too late to scotch the rumours.'

'*I told the truth too late,*' I quoted softly. 'Grandad said that, when I found him.'

Kit reached for his jacket, paused to slide me an uncertain look, then drew a pen and a folded sheet of paper from an inside pocket.

'Hughes' transcript of Grandad's last words,' he said. 'Could be worth another look. Would you rather I did it alone?'

I hesitated only for a second. 'More sensible to tackle it together,' I said. 'I knew him better than you did.'

At the top of the page were the words Kit had pencilled in when I had relayed them to him; the words Grandad had spoken in my hearing alone, before the ambulance arrived.

'Love. Loves. My fault. Told the truth too late. Tell Lissa I'm sorry. We did it for the best. May God forgive us.'

Then the typescript:

'Lissa, I took John's letter. Melody. Edgar. It's not lost, it's won. Neighbours won. Won five hundred. The others lost. We hid John's...We did it for the best. We didn't know. May God forgive us.'

'We know about the letter he snatched from Mum, the day he died,' Kit said. 'We know Grandpa Pevensey wrote it to John Threlfall, about the alleged treasure. About LLW. *It's not lost, it's won.* Could that be the key? L for lost, W for won?'

'But why the second L?'

'Mm.' He sat back, tapping the pen against his teeth. '*Neighbours.* If the paramedic misheard that, what else could it be?' He scribbled words down the margin, saying them aloud. 'Cabers. Labours. Sabres. Tabors.'

'Sabres might win a battle,' I said. 'Labour's won? Maybe an old election...but he didn't care much about politics. If he'd said "Labour's Lost", at least that would have meant *something*, but—'

'Say that again,' Kit interrupted urgently. 'Labour's

Lost?'

'*Love's Labour's Lost.*' I raised my eyebrows mockingly at his stunned expression. 'Comedy by Shakespeare. Ever heard of it?'

'LLW.' He sounded bemused by his own thoughts. '*It's not Lost, it's Won. Labour's Won.* When he kept saying *love* and *loves*, he was trying to tell you the full title. *Love's Labour's Won.*'

'There's no such play.'

'I've heard of it.' He hesitated, doubting himself. 'Haven't I? Come on, Liss, you of all people should know.'

'The title was mentioned a couple of times, around 1600. It could have been a clerical error for *Love's Labour's Lost*, or just possibly a real play. Quartos of individual plays were often printed, nearly always without the writer's permission. But even if *Love's Labour's Won* existed, and was printed, no copies have ever turned up…' My voice died away. I said with awe, 'Oh!'

Kit beamed triumphantly. 'That's it, isn't it? A struggling playwright and a Shakespeare scholar, collaborating to forge…what? Not exactly a book, I guess. Maybe not even bound. Just a printed quarto of a "lost" play by the Bard himself. Could they have pulled it off? Would it have seemed credible, a single copy surviving unnoticed for three hundred years?'

'Perhaps. Forensic science wasn't so hot in those days, and Amphelisia *might* have been Shakespeare's mistress.'

'Good point. Where better than The Eyrie, for a lost quarto to turn up?'

'And all the real copies might well have been lost. As few as five hundred would have been printed—' I gasped, clutching his arm. 'It's not *Won five hundred, the others lost.* It's the other spelling. *ONE five hundred.*

No…*one OF five hundred, the others are lost.*'

'Jesus.' Looking as thrilled as if we had just stumbled upon Eldorado, he planted a kiss on the side of my head. 'You're a brilliant woman.'

'But we don't have a clue why Grandad spent his last moments trying to tell me about a fake. If it mattered so much, why had he never mentioned it before?'

'He wished he had,' Kit said slowly. '*Tell Lissa I'm sorry.*'

'But that was about Joshua…wasn't it? Could there be a connection?'

'Must be. He was talking about Joshua *and* the quarto. What if Nix tried to steal it, not realising it was a fake? Grandad and Price may have caught him in the act and killed him.'

'But why would they! How could they think that was for the best?'

Kit shook his head. '*We didn't know,*' he murmured.

'What could he have meant?' I said. 'What didn't they know?'

But that was a question neither of us could answer.

CHAPTER TWENTY-THREE

Kit rang Fran Dexter first thing in the morning to inform her that the man she wanted to talk to at Llanberis Cottage was Joshua Nix, not Hywel Price. Fran was understandably perplexed.

'So why…' she began, and then heaved an exasperated sigh. 'Never mind. The police were here yesterday. They insisted on interrupting the meeting with Jack Janssen. I thought Nick would explode.'

'Janssen went off happy, I trust?' Kit said, giving me the phone while he sat on the bed to pull his socks on.

'The deal's in the bag,' Fran said. 'That's my bet, anyway. And he was full of praise for you, so Nick has simmered down a bit. Oh—you don't know an Eve Temple, do you?'

'Met a girl called Eve a couple of weeks ago. Didn't get her surname. Why?'

'She rang yesterday, claiming to be a friend of yours and saying she'd lost your home address.'

'Christ. You didn't give it to her?'

'Give me a break! I offered to pass on a message, but she hung up. By the way, the Turkey trip's been brought forward. Your flight's booked for six on Friday evening, that's the eighteenth.'

Kit groaned, which she naturally misunderstood.

'Don't worry, you'll be back by the twenty-third, so no need to cancel Christmas! Bugger, I'll have to hang up. Nick's trying to buzz me. I'll email you the details.'

As he disconnected, I said uneasily, 'We've only got three days.'

'Mm. I'd ask Robbie and Ian to put you up, but I'm not so sure about Ian any more.'

'There's still Charles and Belinda. He's used to helping

out with the horses, which would be a plus.'

'Charles wouldn't stick his neck out for either of us, if it came to the crunch.'

'Simon, then?'

The suggestion was half-hearted; but the mere mention of Simon's name was inflammatory. Kit glowered at me.

'Don't even think about it!' he said.

'Aren't you overreacting just a bit? Whatever he might like to do to *you*, we both know he wouldn't harm *me*.'

'Wouldn't he? You're sleeping with the enemy. When he and Jodie fell out, he threw boiling water at her.'

'So Jodie says.'

'Oh, yes,' he countered snidely. 'I forgot. She's a liar.'

'Don't talk to me like that! She can't be impartial.'

'And you can? What the hell is it with you and Jodie? If it's because of me—'

'*You?* Of all the egotistical—'

'Call me what you like. You're not staying with Simon and that's flat!'

We glared at one another, neither of us prepared to be the first to break eye contact. The fact that I had not the smallest desire to stay with Simon was suddenly irrelevant.

'And why's that?' I asked, spitefully and straight from the heart. 'Because Simon loves me and isn't afraid to say so?'

I saw anger shudder through him like a breaking wave. He said, scarcely above a whisper, 'Don't you ever compare me to that *tosser!*'

Part of me longed to yell at him, 'Say it, then! If you love me, say it!' But the other part, the cowardly part, was afraid of hearing that I was just a pleasant interlude, an unexpectedly rekindled flame which he assumed would burn itself out within a month or two.

Before I could find any sort of answer, he stood up with his back to me, jerkily pulling on his trousers. 'If that's what...' He shook his head and tried again. 'If you can even *think*—'

'How can I know what to think?' I cried out, driven to recklessness. 'You won't tell me what you feel!'

With breathtaking speed he rounded on me and dragged me up into his arms, crushing my naked body against him.

'This is what I feel!' he said.

The kiss was hard and searching and not tender in the least, but I wasn't exactly unwilling. Finally he pushed me back on to the bed. We were both breathing heavily.

'I've got a lousy track record,' he gasped, 'but this is now, this is real. I want to make love to you and never stop. I'll take a chance on the future if you will. How much more do you want?'

I reached out and pulled him down to me.

'Nothing more,' I whispered; and my thought added, 'for now', but I didn't say it.

*

When we stopped outside Llanberis Cottage there was no sign of Price's car. Fran's acting ability, allied to Price's desperation for winter employment, must have won the day—and with all the snow, it would take him a good three hours to drive to Barmouth and back.

Angharad opened her door with an ingenuous smile and ushered us into the living room. 'I was afraid you wouldn't come back,' she said, 'after Hywel was so rude. He's had to go out, but I expect that's just as well.'

I occupied the sofa, while Kit lounged against the wall by the window to give himself a view of the gateway, just in case. Our hostess prodded the wood-burning stove with a poker, then settled herself next to me.

Since I wanted to ask about my parents, we had agreed that I should do this first, to gain the old lady's trust before raising any controversial topic.

I began tentatively, 'Angharad, you knew my parents, didn't you? Roland and Susie Byrne?'

She regarded me with smiling eyes. 'Roland was a sweet little boy. I used to visit Deirdre in those days. Deirdre Threlfall. Sometimes little Roland and Melody would be there. Three times a year I used to go, until her husband put a stop to it. The fact is...' She lowered her voice conspiratorially. 'John Threlfall always disapproved of me.'

'Surely not,' I said.

'I was a mistress, after all. John never blamed Harry.'

'Harry?' In staggered comprehension I saw again in my mind's eye the inscription on Grandad's pocket watch: *Darling H, love always. A.*

'Of course.' She bent close to my ear. 'Hywel isn't really my nephew. He's our son. Harry's firstborn son.'

I gasped, glancing at Kit, who looked equally astounded. I knew Grandad's marriage had been less than idyllic, but for him to have fathered another child, and never to have given the smallest hint of it...

'They came to see me, you know,' she added in the same hushed tone, as if sharing a guilty secret. 'On Easter Saturday. They'd crossed the river from Aberdyfi and walked all the way here from the beach. They went back to the yacht to sleep, of course. I hadn't enough beds for four visitors.'

'Was that the first time you'd seen my dad and Richard Threlfall, since they were children?'

'Richard?' She looked puzzled, then her face cleared and she nodded vigorously. 'Oh, yes. It was twenty years since John Threlfall had stopped me from visiting, you see. He was the one to blame. He didn't like...' She stopped with a gasp, and the faded blue eyes grew round, darting from one of us to the other. 'I haven't said anything that matters, have I?' She reached for my hand. Her own was trembling. 'Forgive me, little Lissa, I didn't know. I didn't know.'

'It's all right,' I said. Her small hand felt impossibly fragile, as if the bones might break from my slightest pressure. 'Truly, it's all right.'

Nonetheless, her words had struck a sinister echo. *'We didn't know,'* Grandad had whispered.

'Let's not talk about John Threlfall,' I said.

'It was a beautiful day.' A tear spilled down her seamed cheek.

'Do you mean…that Easter weekend? The Saturday?'

'It was Sunday when they died. The day after they came to see me. A lovely day. So sunny and warm.'

'But,' I prompted her, 'then there was a squall.'

'Oh, no. I went out to the gate, to wait for my visitors.'

She was confused, surely. Her four visitors had come and gone the day before.

'Which visitors, Angharad?'

'Hywel, of course. He'd phoned to say they were coming. He didn't live with me, in those days.' She squeezed my hand. 'And they both came. I was so pleased. But then we heard it. Sound carries, you see, and the windows were open.'

'Heard what?'

'I kept the cuttings. Hywel doesn't know, but it seemed only right…I think you should see them. Do you want to?'

My heart flipped over. Did she mean newspaper cuttings? Reports of the accident?

'Yes, please,' I said.

She was gone for a couple of minutes. I paced the

floor, hugging myself in impatience and growing dread. Kit left the window and put his arm around me.

'Why did she ask me to forgive her?' I said.

'She's old, she's probably confused.'

'She seems clear about—'

He raised a finger to his lips as Angharad shuffled back into the room. Wisps of her previously neat hair now waved about her head, as if she had been burrowing in a cupboard. She placed an envelope solemnly in my hand.

It contained two cuttings, brown with age and fragile along the creases. I took them to the window to see the text more clearly. Kit read over my shoulder. Neither article bore a date; Angharad had cut too close to the type. But they must have come from a local paper, and the subject matter pinpointed them in time.

TRAGEDY ON THE DYFI

Four holidaymakers are believed to have died yesterday, when their chartered yacht, Aberdyfi Belle, exploded at the mouth of the Dyfi estuary. The tragedy occurred at 10.15 am and no other vessel was involved. Two bodies were recovered by coastguards; a third has since been washed up at Aberdyfi. The fourth crew member is still missing.

A police spokesman said it was too early to be certain what had caused the explosion. The victims have not been named.

The second cutting gave more detail.

ABERDYFI BELLE—CHARTERERS BLAMELESS

The inquest into the deaths of Richard and Carol Threlfall, both aged 32, and their friends Roland Byrne

(31) and wife Susan (25), was concluded today. The four had been victims of Easter Sunday's tragedy on the River Dyfi, when the yacht Aberdyfi Belle exploded. A forensic expert found that the blast had probably been caused by gas in the bilges, which the crew may have failed to pump out as instructed. This gas could have been ignited by a spark, possibly when a match was struck to light the cooker.

The pathologist stated that Susan Byrne, who is thought to have been in the galley when the explosion occurred, had died instantly. The Threlfalls had been thrown clear of the boat. Although strong swimmers, they had suffered severe injuries and drowned before help arrived. The body of Roland Byrne has not been recovered. It is believed that he may have been in the galley with his wife at the time of the explosion.

The coroner recorded a verdict of Misadventure on all four victims, stating that the owners of Aberdyfi Belle were exonerated from blame, the yacht having recently passed stringent tests of seaworthiness.

Richard and Carol Threlfall leave two young sons, aged eleven and nine. Roland and Susan Byrne leave a three-year-old daughter. The children are being cared for by relatives.

I stared numbly at the sheets of faded newsprint. 'Roland Byrne…in the galley with his wife,' I murmured to Kit. 'He was blown to bits. I've laid flowers on his grave, but he's not there. And Mum…'

'Sit down,' Kit said, guiding me to the sofa. 'Angharad, can you make Lissa a cup of tea, please? With plenty of sugar.'

She must have gone into the kitchen. I had no eyes for anything except those cuttings.

'I wonder how much was left of Mum?' I said.

'Your mum and dad died instantly,' Kit said gently. 'Neither of them can have suffered.'

'You're right. It's more horrible, but q-quicker than drowning.' My voice caught on a sob, and I drew a steadying breath. 'Sorry,' I said. 'I can hardly even remember them. It's ridiculous to get upset.'

'Of course it's not. Liss, do you mind if I ask Angharad a few questions?'

'What's the point? The cuttings say it all, don't they?'

'I'm afraid they don't. Joshua vanished in February, and Hywel Price took his identity. Then...' He grimaced at the cuttings. 'This happened. Five people, in six weeks. Price was here when the boat blew up, and so was someone else.'

'I don't understand what you're getting at,' I said; but I did.

'Grandad never told you about this. He may just have been trying to shield you, but we need answers, Liss. Will you back me up?'

I shrugged helplessly. All at once I didn't want to know any more. Price's words in Hay were starting to make sense: 'Bring the past to light now, and it would be like calling out at the foot of a mountain and starting an avalanche.'

The old lady returned with a tray of tea, and Kit wasted no time on preliminaries.

'Who came here with Hywel, Angharad, that Easter Sunday?'

She froze, staring at him, the mugs clattering as she began to shake. Kit leaped up and rescued the tray. It was Angharad's turn to be steered to a chair, and she sank into it as if the strength had gone from her legs.

'I gave Lissa the cuttings,' she quavered. 'I can't do more.'

He took her trembling hand, kneeling in front of her. 'Why not?' he asked. 'Are you afraid of Hywel?'

'Hywel would never hurt me.' She looked both

215

indignant and astonished. 'I meant it would be wrong to tell you. Terribly wrong.'

'Did Hywel kill Joshua?'

She gasped, free hand flying to her mouth. 'No! He didn't do it!'

'Then who did?'

'Kit, stop it,' I said. 'You're frightening her.'

'I'm not,' he said grimly, standing up. 'It's what she knows that's frightening her. Angharad, the person Hywel brought here on Easter Sunday...had he or she murdered Joshua?'

She stared up at him blankly. At first I thought she hadn't understood. Then she struggled to her feet. Nearly a foot shorter than Kit, she had to tilt her head back to look into his eyes.

'I've told you all I can,' she said, with dignity.

'Maybe,' Kit persisted, 'it wasn't his fault.'

'Of course it wasn't! He didn't mean to kill them!'

'Them? Angharad, did Hywel's companion kill Joshua *and* blow up the *Aberdyfi Belle*?'

Her reaction was fast and astounding. She reached sideways and snatched up the poker. 'Get out!' she shrieked. 'Get out of my house!'

We retreated in haste, and I pushed the cuttings into my handbag. Angharad followed us into the hall, still brandishing the poker. The situation had become farcical; a breath of hysterical laughter escaped me. We scuttled out through the front door, shoes scrunching in a fresh fall of snow.

'And don't come back!' she shouted after us.

But her reaction had told us one thing for sure. However I might shy away from the knowledge, Angharad's unnamed visitor that Easter Sunday had murdered Joshua Nix, my parents, and Richard and Carol Threlfall.

Which made my feelings irrelevant. Kit and I were now right on the edge of the precipice. Even Daniel Chubb had not come so close to the truth, yet someone had seen him as a threat. And Daniel Chubb had died.

CHAPTER TWENTY-FOUR

Kit drove us home, insisting that I wasn't up to it. He was ready to tell Fran that the Turkey trip was off, but I assured him that I'd be fine with Charles and Belinda. I felt that he had pushed his luck far enough with Nick Darwin. Not even a thinking woman's hunk was indispensable.

During our lunch stop in Rhayader, Fran emailed to confirm the flight details. Having committed himself, Kit seemed resigned to going, but he grew increasingly silent as the miles passed.

'Ian's hiding something, isn't he?' he said finally, as we approached the Malverns in fog and fading light. 'If Hughes finds he's an accessory after the fact, he'll be finished. No career. Maybe a jail sentence. We'll have destroyed his life…and Robyn's.'

It sounded melodramatic, but he was right.

'I'm sorry,' I said.

'Yeah. Life's a bitch.'

*

We arrived home to find Charles in the tack room. He had settled Smoky and Tempest for the night, having led them up to the field that morning without my asking. I was touched by his thoughtfulness, and said so.

'I was glad to do it,' he said, and indicated the brass ring of the trapdoor. 'I don't suppose you remember Old Trog?'

'How could we forget?' I said lightly.

Charles looked sheepish. 'I invented him to scare the twins, to keep them out of the dungeon after Simon and I found it. When they got too old to be fooled, they used the story to scare the pants off you and Kit.'

'You found it?' I said. 'I didn't know it was ever lost.'

'Not exactly, little one.' He gave me an indulgent pat on the head. 'But the pallets and hay bales were right over the trapdoor. One day when the bales had got low, Simon and I saw the ring. The find of the century. We'd have been about twelve, I think.' Charles smiled at the memory of boyish delight. 'We used to keep it covered, remember? None of the adults guessed, or not until years later, when you two were caught down there. Grandad Byrne said the tunnel had caved in thirty years earlier and the whole place was unsafe.'

'I did gather that,' Kit said, 'while he was tanning my arse.'

Charles looked disapproving of such levity. 'The point I'm making,' he said, 'is that if the subsidence affected the foundations, this old place may be worth less that we think.' He glanced from one of us to the other, looking puzzled. 'Don't you care?'

I took a deep breath. 'We're a bit...we've got other things to worry about. Do you want to come in for coffee?'

Charles had no objection. I put the oven on to warm the kitchen, and we sat around the table.

'Do you remember,' I asked him, 'if any of the adults were away from home, the weekend of the sailing accident?'

He looked bemused. 'Why on earth?'

'Do you, Charles?'

He shrugged. 'Grandad Byrne and old Mrs Threlfall went to Wales to identify the bodies. Can't remember anyone else being away.'

'So,' Kit said, 'John Threlfall stayed to look after his grandsons? Bit out of character, I'd have thought.'

'You're right. According to Simon and Ian, the old tyrant wasn't a great source of comfort. When they were brought home, they both thought their gran would be there.'

'Brought home from where?' Kit said.

'Ian was at cub camp. Simon was on a school trip, canoeing on the Wye. I'd have gone myself, but Mum was worried about the risks.' He looked piercingly at me. 'What's this about?'

I showed Charles the clippings. Judging from his expression, we were not the only ones who had been given a sanitised version of the facts.

'I've never heard a whisper of this,' he said. 'Where did you get these?'

'From Angharad Price,' Kit said.

'Who?'

'Grandad Byrne's mistress.'

Charles blinked. 'You're joking.'

'She lives near Ynyslas,' Kit said. 'She had a son, Hywel, by the old man. They used to visit the Malverns, till John Threlfall stopped them coming. Don't suppose you've ever heard Mum or Dad mention him?'

Charles shook his head, dismissing the Prices. He frowned at the clippings. 'This is a ghastly story.'

'Yeah. Liss is pretty upset about it. And with everything else that's happened...Could she stay at The Withies, while I'm in Turkey?'

Charles assured me that I was always welcome. I was less sure of Belinda's reaction. She would not enjoy seeing Charles escort me home twice a day to attend to the horses; but that would have to remain their problem. I had enough of my own.

Charles had to see a client in Leominster on Friday morning, but he promised to be at The Eyrie by two o'clock. Kit would leave at two-thirty. Charles would help me muck out the stables, and I would then follow him home in the Fiat.

'You've got my number,' he reminded us. 'Any

changes, give me a call. Otherwise, I'll see you on Thursday, at Grandad's funeral.'

We had said nothing to Charles about *Love's Labour's Won*; but as soon as he had gone, we went up to Grandad's bedroom. The bed, or its predecessor, must have stood in its present position in Edgar's time. There was nowhere else it would fit. Under my namesake's hooded gaze, we dragged it out, shifted a chest of drawers and rolled back the carpet.

There was only one ill-fitting floorboard. We prised it up and peered into the space beneath. Dust, fluff and a couple of dead woodlice. No forged quarto.

Ridiculous to feel disappointed. There was no reason why Grandad should have returned it to Edgar's old hiding place; yet somehow the failure served as a fitting anticlimax to the whole depressing day. We replaced the board and tramped downstairs. I sat down to watch the news while Kit was in the kitchen making coffee.

When he hadn't returned five minutes later I went to find him. He was standing by the kettle, staring down unseeingly at the two empty mugs beside it. I slid an arm around him, and he jumped.

'Sorry,' he said, reaching for the coffee jar.

'Are you all right?'

'I keep seeing Robbie's face. The way she cried, that Friday night...' He sighed, and rummaged through the cutlery drawer for a teaspoon. 'Price had it right, didn't he? This thing is going to affect everyone we care about, and none of us can guess how it'll end.'

There was no denying it. Price had tried to warn us in Hay but we had chosen not to listen, and now it was too late.

*

Wednesday was fine and sunny, very different from the previous day in Borth. We arrived at Worcester Police

221

Station and asked for Inspector Hughes. He looked surprised to see us.

'I understand you've been on your travels again,' he said. 'Mr Charles Pevensey mentioned the Brecon Beacons.'

Kit assured him that we had been nowhere near Brecon, but that we had important information and would appreciate twenty minutes of his time. Hughes raised his eyebrows but guided us to an interview room, accompanied by a female PC with a reassuring smile. We confessed everything except about Toby's 'burglary', and the fact that Kit was Joshua's son. It couldn't matter to Hughes, Kit had said. I would have preferred to keep nothing back, but it had to be his decision.

The tale proved longer than anticipated. At the end of half an hour, Hughes tilted his chair back at a perilous angle and said, 'Well, that's all very interesting.'

'Will you follow it up?' Kit asked.

Hughes brought his chair down with a thud. 'Mr Pevensey,' he said, the rebuke softened by a smile, 'I'll do my job.'

'How about protection for Lissa?'

'I'm afraid we don't have the manpower. Miss Byrne hasn't actually been threatened.' He raised a hand to fend off Kit's reply. 'Please don't leap down my throat, sir. I understand your concern, and of course we can't rule out a connection with Daniel Chubb's murder. Let's begin with Nix's disappearance, and the matter of the *Aberdyfi Belle*. Who do you think was with Price at Llanberis Cottage, the day of the explosion?'

But as far as we knew, no one from the Malverns, except the four victims, had been anywhere near the place.

'We haven't spoken to my aunt yet,' Kit said. 'Maureen, my father's sister. She married and emigrated to Canada long before Joshua left, but she'll have known the Prices.'

A phone call to Belinda gave us Maureen's number. When Kit made the call to Canada, Hughes and I listened too. It was a while since Maureen had visited England, and I had forgotten how overwhelming her personality could be.

'Darling! How marvellous to hear from you! I hear you've done terribly well for yourself...'

The pleasantries continued for long enough to establish that we had been lucky to catch Maureen, as she often walked the dogs before breakfast. It was seven o'clock in Toronto.

'Nobody except dear Belinda ever tells me anything,' she continued at high volume, 'These petty family squabbles! I've no time for them. I hope you haven't rung to *involve* me.'

Kit hastened to reassure her, and put the relevant question when she next paused for breath.

'Angharad Price? Of course, darling,' she said at once. 'A great friend of Deirdre Threlfall's. She never brought a boy with her.'

'Yes, she did, Auntie,' Kit persisted. 'He used to hang around with you and the others, at The Eyrie.'

'If you say so, dear. He must have been appallingly dull. My memory is usually excellent. Why on earth does it matter now?'

Kit fielded that one by promising to write and tell her all about it.

'That's odd,' he said, disconnecting. 'She used to remember everything. I bet she still knows my exam grades better than I do. Why would she have forgotten Price?'

'People get old,' Hughes said.

At sixty-five, Kit's aunt was hardly ancient, but she

223

might be excused one minor lapse of memory. Back in the interview room, we searched our own memories for other elderly suspects, but drew a blank.

'Is it possible,' Hughes asked tentatively, 'that the Prices could be protecting someone younger? How old would your brother Charles have been, twenty-two years ago?'

'Eleven,' Kit said, sounding breathless. 'But—'

'And Simon Threlfall?'

'A couple of months older. For Christ's sake, I'm the last person to hold a brief for Simon, but—'

'Children do occasionally kill, sir. It's rare, but it does happen.'

We knew it, naturally. We just couldn't believe it of people we had grown up with. Into our silence, Hughes said, 'The rest of you were younger, is that right?'

'Under ten,' Kit said.

'Do you recall where you all were, that weekend?'

Kit relayed the information Charles had given us, about Simon's canoeing trip and Ian's camp. 'If either of them had gone AWOL,' he said, 'I think Charles would have heard. The rest of us were at home.'

Hughes shrugged. 'Well, thank you for all your help,' he said, standing up. 'If I need to check any details, Miss Byrne, I'll contact you at your cousin Charles's house. Don't forget,' he added, as we were leaving the interview room, 'this is a police matter now. Let it go.'

His concern was endearing, but police protection would have been of more help.

After lunch I left Kit busy on the telephone and drove back into Worcester. I was in no mood to think about Christmas, but its proximity had to be faced. Dispiritedly, I bought treats and toiletries, the usual cop-outs when imagination failed. I still had no idea what to buy for Kit.

When I arrived home, he had transformed the cluttered living room, fixed the bathroom shelf—which we had broken a week ago—tightened or replaced all the old window locks, and booked the company with the best quote to fit a burglar alarm on Monday, assuming Charles and I would be available to let them in. We had less than forty-eight hours to ensure that The Eyrie was a fortress, to which Charles and I could return every day without fear.

In the meantime, there was Grandad's funeral. Not until we entered the church on Thursday morning, did the significance of laying him to rest wake all the memories, tightening grief like a fist around my heart.

The service was well attended. I found myself greeting people, mainly academics, whom I hadn't seen in person for years. Most of our gang was there, too, except Jodie, who had stayed to man the office so that Ian could accompany Robyn and the other Pevenseys.

Simon and his grandmother had come to pay their respects, not in his MG but in the family hatchback that had been his grandfather's. Deirdre Threlfall had aged since her husband's death. I recalled the chilling words from John Threlfall's diary: *They all know but they won't tell me.* Did Mrs Threlfall know the killer's name?

She spoke to us briefly, shaking my hand and expressing condolences in her ice-cool way. I didn't question her; it was Hughes' case now.

My grandmother, Charlotte, a committed Christian, had reserved plots in the churchyard for her family. Next to Grandad's new grave, Mum and Dad lay together, sharing a stone. Or at least, Mum's remains were buried. As for Dad's...

I stood between Kit and Robyn, while cold drizzle soaked through my jacket. Tears ran down my face with the rain; and I didn't know if I was crying for Grandad or my lost Dad, or for Robyn and Ian's future, or only for myself.

When it was over, Kit intercepted Charles to finalise the arrangements for my visit. I gathered my courage and approached Simon, who despite the weather had taken off his suit jacket to peer under the bonnet of his grandmother's car. He straightened up when he saw me and tossed back his hair, wiping his hands on a tissue.

'Lissa,' he said, with a sigh. 'How are you?'

'All right.' To avoid looking into those impossibly blue eyes, I indicated the car. 'Problems?'

'Oh, that's Gran for you. One minute she can smell petrol, then she thinks the tracking is out. I doubt if she knows what tracking is. She wants Ian and me to buy her a new car. I keep telling her I'm broke.'

'Poor Simon,' I said, without irony.

'Yes, well, I expect I should be more tolerant.' He glanced around at the clusters of people, most of them now leaving. 'It went well, I thought. The service. The vicar was charitable, considering the old man hadn't been to church in twenty years.'

'Grandad liked him. They had some good debates.'

'I'm sure.' Simon frowned down at his blackened hands, giving them another fastidious wipe. 'I often think about the old days. I can't say Harry replaced my dad, but I loved the old bugger.' He flicked at a dripping lock of hair, and smiled at me. 'So you're back with Kit.'

'I came to tell you.'

'Don't look so sad, Lissa. We were just friends, isn't that what you always said? Pity, though. I'd have made you happier than he ever will.'

He was already thinking of me as an opportunity lost. Irrationally, I felt insulted, even though I had never wanted him to suffer for my sake.

On impulse I said, 'Simon, why were you so unhappy

226

with Jodie?'

He blinked, and didn't answer, his eyes unreadable.

I went on quickly, floundering, 'It's really none of my business.'

'Oh yes, it is,' he said, on a breath of mirthless laugher. 'I read her diary, the week after we were married. She wanted Kit, but she'd never managed to hook him. You were always in her way, and then he went off to Cambridge. I suppose she thought me a reasonable second best.' He laughed shortly. 'Story of my life.'

I bit my lip. 'Please say we can still be friends.'

A spasm of pain crossed his face. 'You'll always be special to me, Lissa.'

We kissed, as friends; and with a touch of nostalgia for our lost and shared past, I watched him walk back to his grandmother.

CHAPTER TWENTY-FIVE

Our investigations had put many mundane chores on hold. At eleven-ten on Friday morning, just over three hours before Kit was due to leave for Heathrow, he was ironing shirts in the living room while I sat on the floor writing Christmas cards.

A car drew up outside. Kit was nearer the front door and got there first. The visitor's low, rumbling voice was unfamiliar, but his words brought me instantly to my feet.

'Delivery for Mr Pevensey, from a Miss Cullingham.'

'From Rusty?' He sounded stunned. 'You've come from *Maidstone?*'

'Like I said, special delivery. My wife watches your programmes. As soon as I realised it was you, I knew the money wouldn't be an issue.'

I went into the hall. The taxi driver was looking pleased with his morning's work. Kit sent me a despairing grimace and threw his arms wide, for once completely at a loss.

I walked to his side and stared in disbelief at our delivery. There were two items, and they were not parcels. They were Eve and Bronwen, from Hay-on-Wye.

*

Kit wrote the driver a cheque and hustled the girls into the living room.

'Sit down,' he said, with deceptive calm, 'and start talking. You've run away, right?'

Eve reacted with a defiant lift of the chin; but both girls sat down.

'We've shown initiative,' Eve said. 'We couldn't get you on the phone, so we hitched to the studios.'

'Why, for God's sake?'

'We want to work for Medway. As we did you a good turn in Hay, we're hoping you'll be able to get us in.'

'To do what? Eve, you're not qualified to do *anything*.'

The girl's colour rose. 'If we could get an apprenticeship after our exams, that'd be amazing…but we'd be happy with work experience at Easter, or during the summer. When we told the man in Reception that you'd…well, that you'd invited us, Miss Cullingham came down to talk to us. She was really nice.'

'I bet she was.'

'She booked us into a hotel, and sorted out the taxi for this morning.' Eve met her hero's eyes boldly. 'It's not such a big thing, is it? I mean, you can claim it on expenses.'

Kit laughed out loud, very bitterly. 'Sure. I can just see the accountant's face if I tried that one.'

'Oh,' Eve said, and Bronwen looked on the verge of tears. I was suddenly sorry for them. However ill-judged and foolhardy their venture, it had taken courage.

I asked Kit, 'What shall we do?'

'The best we can.' He began pacing the floor, expending his frustration in jerky strides.

Eve stood up. 'Will you help us, then? We don't mind what we do. Filing. Making tea. Whatever.'

He swivelled to face her. 'Be your age! There are no apprenticeships. And to the best of my knowledge, Medway's never given students work experience. Even if they did, it'd be organised with a local school. What have you told your parents?'

'That I'm at Bron's. Bron told her mum she's with me.'

'And what do you think the papers will make of it, when that taxi driver—' Kit stopped on a catch of breath. 'How old are you?'

229

'Sixteen in January.'

'And you, Bronwen?'

She gulped. 'June.'

Words failed Kit. He sat down and dropped his head in his hands.

Eve was old enough to perceive the problem, but also young enough to blame her hero for being so easily frightened. 'Don't worry,' she said, with contempt, 'we'll make sure you're not accused of anything. You won't lose your job.'

He raised his head. 'My job? Christ, that'll be the least of it. I don't actually know the usual sentence for abducting two children—'

'We're not children! You're not being fair. We did you a huge favour that day—'

'So you want to put me on the sex offenders' register?'

'That's crap! You're a coward and an ungrateful pig!'

Kit inhaled through his nose and stood up, looking quite unlike his charming TV persona. Eve took an involuntary step back.

'Ring your parents,' he said. 'Tell them you'll be home in an hour-and-a-half.'

Neither girl moved.

'*Do it!* I've got to be at Heathrow by four o'clock and the last thing I needed was a trip to sodding Hay!'

As Eve started rummaging in her shoulder bag, he stalked out of the room. Bronwen looked as if she would like to shrink into the upholstery. I could guess that her resolve to go to Medway had never been strong; she had been carried along in her friend's wake and was profoundly regretting it.

I followed Kit up to his room, and found him folding clothes with practised speed and throwing them into his suitcase.

'Bloody kids!' he said.

'Let me take them home, then you can go straight to Heathrow.'

'Kind thought, Liss, but I'd rather speak to their parents myself. Nip any rumours in the bud.' He checked his watch. 'Half-eleven. Should just make it. I'll take your car, OK? The Merc isn't built for three.'

It was built for speed, however, which the Fiat was not.

'You'll have to drive like a lunatic,' I said. 'You'll kill yourself.'

'Never.' He gave me a fleeting kiss before bending over the case again. 'Charles is meeting you here at two o'clock, right? If you drive into Malvern now, sit in a café—'

'I haven't packed.'

'Pack, then. I can wait five minutes. We'll leave together.'

'I can't do it in five minutes. And I haven't mucked out the stables.'

He straightened abruptly. 'You're not to go down there on your own. Promise me, Liss! Charles can help you when he arrives.'

'Yes, all right.' I chewed at my lip. 'I'll stay here and pack, and wait for Charles.'

Kit regarded me for several seconds, then pulled out his phone and rang his brother. 'Change of plan, Charles,' he said. 'I need to leave now. Liss will explain. No chance you can get here earlier, is there?' A longish pause, then he sighed. 'Thanks, mate, I owe you one.'

He ended the call, scowling. 'Said he knows the client pretty well. He can skip lunch and be here for one o'clock. God, Liss, I wish I'd cancelled the bloody flight.'

'For heaven's sake! Listen to yourself! You're always telling *me* to stop fretting. I'll ring you, OK? As soon as I get to Charles's house.'

He was not reassured. He held me in a hard embrace, rocking me gently as if he couldn't bear to let me go. In the end I held him away from me.

'Finish your packing,' I said. 'I'll be downstairs.'

On the landing I came face to face with Eve. Her eyes were red, and there was a smudge of mascara across one cheek.

'Why is Kester scared to leave you alone?' she said.

'Oh…a friend of ours was killed. The police don't know who did it.'

Her eyes widened. 'And now he has to take us to Hay. But Miss Cullingham must have known about his flight.' She paused, and belatedly worked it out. 'She wanted to screw things up for him, because of you.'

'I'm afraid so.'

'What a bitch. We didn't mean to cause Kester any trouble. Or you,' she added as an afterthought.

'No, well, I'm sorry your hero turned out to be only human.'

She glanced towards the bedroom doorway. 'Human is cool.'

'In that case,' I retorted, flippantly but meaning it, 'you'll travel in the back, with Bronwen.'

*

They left a few minutes later. I waved them off, and felt utterly lost. Even the weather had turned gloomy, with low cloud on the hills, and rain in the wind. At least I wouldn't have to feel guilty about Smoky and Tempest missing their visit to the field.

I went upstairs and started packing.

It was the noise that alerted me. Tempest, neighing repeatedly. Despite his tendency to affect alarm outdoors, it was unlike him to make a fuss inside his box.

Kit's bedroom overlooked the stable block, so I went

to his window. I couldn't see the door of either box, but nothing was obviously amiss. No stray dogs or cats, no sign of a trespasser.

Tempest let out an urgent whinny. I couldn't just ignore him; and it was broad daylight. Nonetheless I dropped the phone in my pocket before venturing outside.

I made my way to the stables, glancing to right and left, even walking backwards for a few steps to check no one was following. Tempest was looking over his half door. I fondled his nose, calming him with soft words. He was quivering all over. I went into the box and checked him for cuts or other injuries, then kicked at the straw in case a rat had got in. Nothing.

'You're an old fraud,' I said.

He rolled a disapproving eye and failed to enlighten me. I went outside and bolted the half door, giving him a final pat on the nose—and something registered; an inconsistency, glimpsed on the edge of vision. I turned fast.

Not fast enough. An arm was clamped around me from behind, pulling me back against a man's hard chest. His strength pinned my arms to my sides. I screamed, thrashing and kicking, trying to twist around to see his face.

All I saw was a dark hoodie. I shrieked again, dug an elbow into his ribs and kicked his shins. The iron grip shifted. Smoky's stable blanket descended over my head, smelling of warm horse. It made a nonsense of my efforts to escape. The man wound it around me, lifted me and slung me over his shoulder in a classic fireman's lift.

We were still in the stable yard. I could hear his footsteps on the paving stones. In a moment we would reach the gravel path...heading for where? The back gate, with its track to the field and the hills beyond? Was I being kidnapped for ransom, by someone who believed *Love's Labour's Won* was genuine, or just being taken to a lonelier place to die?

He had stopped. No gravel. I heard a familiar creak. The tack room door. Now I understood. This was the old game, which had only ever ended one way.

'No!' My voice was muffled by the blanket, but I knew he could hear me. 'Toby, don't!' It had always been Toby, with Robyn looking on. But Robyn had grown up; it was her twin who still needed to crush people to boost his self-esteem.

If he was my captor now, he gave no sign. He merely swung me off his shoulder and dropped me. Visualising the open trapdoor, and the drop to the flagstones below, I clutched at him. One of my hands was still caught in the rug. The other found the edge of his hood. He whispered a curse, dragging at my hand. My feet flailed, treading air. My knee struck the edge of the open trap.

I shrieked, 'No! *No!*'

He wrenched his jacket from my grip; but my foot had found purchase. I wedged my heel against the edge of the hole and pushed upward. He kneed the back of my thigh. The leg buckled but I forced it straight, and he grabbed my upper arms and swung me round.

I knew I was lost. Knew, in one of those split-seconds before disaster, when time itself runs slow, that everything was over, that all our precautions had come to nothing. Then he let go; and I fell.

CHAPTER TWENTY-SIX

The impact was as hard as falling off a galloping horse. I had done that a few times, but at least then I had seen the ground coming. It was far more terrifying to hurtle through the air in blind darkness, to hit an unyielding surface with shattering force and no warning. I landed on my feet and one hand and slammed down on my left side. Could have been worse, I thought vaguely. My head hurt, and my arm was trapped underneath me. Everything else felt numb. The smell of horses was clogging my nose and throat. I wished the air would clear...

The real world came back with a jolt. There was something over my face. I couldn't breathe. Coughing and gagging I thrashed over, clawing at the folds of the horse blanket. It came off quite suddenly. I drew in a great, gasping breath. Above me, the trapdoor thudded into place. I was shut in the bloody dungeon, on my own, in the fucking *dark*!

I started to scramble up, intending to rush for the rope ladder, to batter the trap open before he could bolt it. As I put weight on my left hand, it gave way, pain searing through wrist and forearm. My shoulder hit the floor again and I closed my eyes, fighting a wave of nausea, clamping my mouth shut to keep from groaning. Sod Toby Pevensey! I wouldn't give him the pleasure.

In the old days, I would have heard his laughter. The sound I heard now was easy to identify and infinitely more frightening. He was dragging pallets across the tack room floor. If he wanted only to prevent my escape, he could simply have bolted the door. He was covering his tracks, concealing the trap from anyone who might come looking for me. No doubt he would pile up some hay bales to complete the camouflage. Perhaps this was indeed a kidnap…unless he had gone to dig a shallow grave…or unless he meant to leave me here, returning now and then to witness my gradual deterioration…

I found enough breath to yell, 'You bastard! Let me out!'

He was already leaving. I could hear his footsteps making for the door. He hesitated there, long enough for me to abandon the last shreds of dignity to cry out, *'Please!'*

Then he was gone. I was alone in the dark.

*

To some extent I was used to impenetrable blackness. It often lurked along the path leading up to the horses' field. There, I banished it with torchlight. Here, though, in this place where darkness had first become for me an instrument of torture, a weapon to break my spirit and reduce me to shuddering terror…here it was a rather different matter.

I sat up. My wrist was hot to the touch. I gingerly turned my hand to loosen my watch strap, which caused another sickening thrust of pain but no sensation of grating bones. Good news, as far as it went.

As for the rest: the numbness had worn off and my left hip and thigh were fiercely sore. Bruising, I thought, and maybe a pulled muscle from my efforts above the trapdoor. I could cope with any of it, if only I could *see*. Squinting upwards, I tried to make out the line of light where the trapdoor fitted badly. As a child I had hungered for that gleam, clung to the sight of it like a drowning man to a plank.

It wasn't there today. The pallets and hay bales had deprived me even of that small source of comfort. There was no light at all.

Thank God I had the phone. With shaking fingers I

dragged it out of my pocket, felt for the power button and tapped it. The screen lit up. Wonderful, beautiful little invention.

Two words appeared. 'No service.'

Of course there was no service. How could there be? No signal underground. I moaned, and tapped the 'assistive light' icon. The light came on, bright as a torch, sending the darkness leaping back into corners and crevices.

I still couldn't see, but only because my eyes were full of tears. I dashed them away, stifling a giggle of pure hysteria. I might be going to die in this bloody place, of dehydration or hypothermia or in some far more gruesome fashion; but at least, if I were careful with the battery, I wouldn't have to die in the dark.

I said aloud, hiccupping slightly, 'You're not going to die at all, you silly cow!'

Illogically, this made me feel a bit better. I swung the light upward, and received a severe blow to morale. The rope ladder had gone. My attacker had removed any chance of my hammering on the door to attract attention.

Well, all right. Stop panicking and *think*. There must be something else I could stand on.

I shone the light around my prison, illuminating the shallow alcoves beyond various low archways. The search revealed two dusty demijohns of home-made wine, a child's rusty tricycle, and a mildewed pair of curtains. I couldn't imagine how to make use of any of it, beyond a fleeting temptation to get extremely drunk.

It might be feasible, all the same, to drag some rocks or lengths of timber from the roof-fall, pile them up under the trapdoor and...

What if my assailant was still in the grounds? Whatever his plans, he might come back to silence me if

I started making a din. There was only one quiet option. Dig through the debris at the tunnel entrance, and follow the tunnel to the undiscovered exit in the house.

Oh, marvellous, I thought. Crush injuries and asphyxiation might provide a quicker death than some of the alternatives on offer, but the prospect hardly beckoned. Don't think about that. Essential to do *something.*

Slowly, cradling the sore wrist, I picked myself up. My hip protested sharply and the back of my thigh went into cramp. I used a few of Kit's oaths and added one or two of my own, trying to straighten my leg as I aimed the light at the tunnel entrance. The blockage looked as daunting as ever, but at least the doorway, built when the average person had been shorter than today, was barely my own height.

Best to start at the top. I hobbled down the steps and laid the phone high on the rubble. Then I slid my left hand inside my half-zipped coat to improvise a sling, and eased my way painfully up the mound of earth, roots and broken timber. Lying on top, I pulled at a tangle of roots wedged under the lintel, and felt a disproportionate sense of triumph when it came free almost at once.

Within a few minutes I was making quite good progress. The work was rough on the fingers, but the stones were small and all the root masses responded to a few good tugs. Not until there was a fair-sized gap between the debris and the lintel did I realise what I was seeing. The lintel itself, and the beams of the tunnel roof just beyond, were completely sound. Not sagging, not cracked. However genuine the subsidence further along might be, this mess had not fallen from above.

Someone had worked very hard to bring it here. Rather than brick up the collapsing tunnel or seal the trapdoor, he had created a fake roof-fall. A barrier that would raise no questions because it looked natural.

I shook my head, throwing out the implications that whispered into my mind like treacherous ghosts. I had no time to waste on the past. The here and now was too pressing. I needed a hole large enough to crawl through, and my way was blocked by a huge tree bole, the first major obstacle I had encountered.

In a frenzy of renewed effort I dragged at it, kneeling up and leaning back to get some leverage. 'Come on, you bugger!' I said aloud. 'Come *out*, you bloody...sodding...'

It lifted so suddenly that I fell backwards and tumbled down the slope. The tree stump bounced and slid after me, and crashed into my sore leg.

I managed to roll aside, groaning the most obscene words I knew. A minute or two passed before I was able to sit up, taking deep breaths and struggling to regain a degree of equilibrium. My thumb and forefinger were bleeding where the nails had torn, and the air around me was full of dust motes, stirred up by the tree and by my own fall. They swirled in the beam of light from my phone, still perched on the rubble.

I couldn't hide from the truth any longer. Realisation swamped me; a tide of horror that turned me cold. The chamber that would become a crypt. The rending nails. The dust-filled air. I had dreamed all this.

There was only one thing missing.

'Oh, no,' I whispered. 'Oh God, no.'

Futile, stupid words. Whatever lay behind the rubble had been there more than twenty years. No prayers would remove it.

I scrambled to my feet and lunged for the phone, stumbling back to the wall that flanked the steps, twitching the light from alcove to shadowed alcove, making certain that I saw into every corner, every possible hiding place.

No ghost. I was crying, though, in hard, racking sobs that hurt my chest.

'Kit!' I howled. 'Please come! *Please!*'

I didn't expect him to come. I knew he couldn't. He must be half way to Hay-on-Wye by now.

I dried my eyes on my sleeve and, still sniffing and hiccupping, went back to work. What else was there to do? I had to find the way out, unless I preferred to end up like...

'Shut up, you silly bitch!' I said aloud, with pathetically little conviction. Dragging out a length of rotten timber I threw it to the floor, working now with impassioned energy, drawing on reserves of strength that I hadn't known I possessed. I knew the light would run my phone battery down fast. I might have three or four hours, at best.

In less than twenty minutes the hole was large enough. I retrieved the phone and heaved myself up to peer into the tunnel beyond—to the authentic, naturally formed roof-fall that blocked the way only a couple of metres ahead.

It took me a moment to understand. To accept the unavoidable, disastrous fact. This was not the way to freedom. This was just an extension to the perfect tomb.

I dropped my head on my arm and wept.

*

A good deal more time passed before an observation permeated my despair. The cool air that issued from the tunnel was *moving*. If there was a draught, it must be coming from somewhere.

Galvanised, I wriggled through the hole on my stomach, slid down the other side, and directed the light on to the subsidence ahead. The tunnel roof sagged in front of it. Anyone trying to shift that lot would indeed risk being buried alive. Yet there was that draught. I shone the light at the floor around my feet—and screamed, backing against the rubble.

He lay tidily, legs straight, arms at his sides. Not dumped there anyhow, but *arranged*. His flesh had gone, and if he had been wearing clothes they had rotted long ago. All that remained was a pitiful collection of bones.

Having guessed what I might find took none of the horror from the discovery. The phone trembled in my hand, shadows shifting so that the skull's expression seemed to change...

With my own eyes tightly closed, I slid down against the rubble and put my head between my knees. Finally, the ringing in my ears stopped. Then I nerved myself to look again.

It was a skeleton. So what? A lifeless object. Not a man any more. Ludicrous to be afraid, to feel my breath shorten and my heart race...

'Get me out,' his voice cried in my head, the echo of a nightmare brought fearfully to life.

'Help me,' I whispered, breath shuddering between my teeth. 'Please help me.' And scarcely knew if I was pleading with God or Kit or the dead man himself.

There was something lying on the ribcage, so delicately balanced that the slightest touch would have dislodged it. A small, dark rectangle, attached to a length of black string.

No, not string. That would have rotted with the body, destroyed by the chemical process of decomposition. Very slowly, flinching from even the thought of touching him, I reached out, snatching my hand back the second it closed around the oblong of tarnished metal on its equally blackened chain.

'I gave him a neck-chain for his birthday. He always wore it, even though it was horribly cheap and used to make a green stain on his chest.'

241

It was still possible to trace the letters stamped out of the metal.

D-A-D.

My skin prickled with gooseflesh; but within the irrational fear was pity. He had died so young, and been so maligned ever since. I had been three years old when he disappeared. Perhaps on some unconscious level I had remembered him. That elusive memory may have conjured his shade, both in childhood and in recent nightmares.

And yet...

'Get me out,' the dream image had begged me.

'I can't,' I had said.

Not good enough. Hesitantly, swallowing bile, I laid his daughter's treasured gift across the disjointed finger bones, sealing the pact, making of it a vow not to be broken lightly.

'I will try, Joshua,' I said.

*

Dangerous as the true roof-fall looked, I had to break through it. Given the alternatives of returning to the dungeon, or sitting staring at Joshua Nix, the decision was easy.

I worked with much more care this time, but also with a compelling sense of urgency. My dwindling battery aside, it was now one-fifteen. Charles would be up there, somewhere, reluctant to leave without me because the Mercedes stood on the drive. Unless, of course, my attacker had had the foresight to remove it.

After three hours, I had cleared a hole nearly two metres long beneath what passed for the ceiling. It had taken a long while, because for every few handfuls of earth that I threw to the floor below, one would thud or trickle down from above.

This had become unnerving, partly because here the

beams which roofed the rest of the dungeon had long ago collapsed, but also because, as my makeshift tunnel had lengthened, I had been obliged to slither right inside it to continue the job. Only my feet were now outside. Luckily, my stubborn scraping and digging was not making the small landslides any more frequent.

I tilted the phone to look ahead. There was no sign, yet, of a breakthrough, but it was much too soon to give up hope. I reached forward, scraping away a little more earth, a few more stones, wincing at the pressure on cut and abraded fingers.

A trickle of earth fell in my hair. I shook it out. A stone bounced on my shoulder blade, and at the same instant, with a small *shushing* sound, the last hard-won centimetres of my tunnel succumbed to another miniature landslide.

Three tiny events, from three different directions, in as many seconds.

Get out.

I wriggled backwards, which brought down more earth, or else it was happening anyway, clumps of dirt and stones sliding down, settling around me.

Get out.

I turned sideways to move more quickly, glancing up at the mud ceiling just above me. It seemed to sigh; a faint susurration, not even a tremor.

I flung an arm up over my face as the roof came down.

*

Pointless to fight, to struggle against the depth of solid earth. But of course I tried, from instinct and panic and a strong disinclination to die. I kicked and punched and turned my head aside, spitting out soil as the earth pressed down.

My flailing fist struck upwards into nothing at all. I

243

felt cold air on my hand and forearm—and now, directly above me, there were stars. Three pinpricks of light in the blackness. I lay blinking up at them, and didn't believe they were real.

Tentatively, afraid of losing the mirage, I pushed up again with my good hand, and a clump of turf fell away. Above me now hung a cloud-ripped sky with a scatter of stars, a rising moon edging the clouds with light.

I had done it. However it had happened, the night sky meant escape. Freedom. Life would continue. Unless whoever had shut me in the dungeon was still here.

I shoved turves off my chest, rolled over and crawled on elbows and knees, out of my grave and over the lip of the sunken area, on to solid ground. Then I looked back at the remains of my little tunnel.

I hadn't been thinking straight, down there. No wonder I had felt a draught. Since the lawn had already subsided, filling the tunnel with earth from floor to ceiling, there could never have been more than a few centimetres between me and the night air. If I had had the sense to dig vertically, from the top of the genuine roof-fall, I would have been out in five minutes.

I clambered painfully to my feet. The back of the house was in darkness, which allowed the moonlight to throw many areas of the garden into shadow. A bar of blackness lay beneath the side fence, and a black pool under an apple tree could be concealing anything. Or anyone.

At least the tack room door, still frighteningly close, was clear in the moonlight and definitely shut. The stable yard was empty of menace. So was the driveway, or all of it that I could see.

The Mercedes had gone, but Charles's BMW was there. Did that mean I was safe? Or had my attacker driven Kit's car just far enough to hide it, returning on foot to make sure of my silence?

I started to limp towards the back door, breath coming in agonised gasps. After hours of lying virtually immobile in the cold, my abused muscles were so stiff that every movement was torture.

The spotlight facing the stable yard flared into life. I tried to shield my eyes, glancing sideways at shadows that were now blacker than before. I dared not look again. A breeze lifted my hair like an icy breath. The hairs rose on the back of my neck.

Gritting my teeth I hobbled faster. Only a few more steps. No distance…

Two metres or twenty, I couldn't do it. My leg was buckling with weakness, thigh muscles clenching in spasm. I couldn't walk, could barely stay on my feet, and if he was behind me…If he had seen me and was running silently, swiftly…

Hopping and stumbling I hurled myself against the door and wrenched at the handle.

It was locked. The bloody door was locked.

'Charles!' I rattled the handle, pounded on the glass, looking over my shoulder now in panic, expecting at any moment to see some figure of darkness emerge from the shadows. 'Charles! *Charles!*'

The kitchen light came on, and the door opened so fast that I fell into his arms.

'Liss!' He was crushing me against him, his voice shaking. 'I thought you were dead. Where have you…Oh, my little Lissa. My darling girl.'

It wasn't Charles. It was Kit.

CHAPTER TWENTY-SEVEN

Charles was there too, as it turned out. Having installed me on the sofa, my well-meaning saviours replaced my torn coat with a blanket, plied me with hot, sweet, brandy-laced tea, and asked the inevitable questions. I couldn't blame them. I was scratched, bleeding and covered in dirt, and it was more than five hours since I had gone to calm Tempest.

All the same I felt drained and shamefully close to tears, reaction setting in with a vengeance. My bruises ached. My wrist was throbbing. All I wanted was a bath and a soft bed.

I told them the beginning, at least. Charles stood staring down at me with a dazed expression, while Kit crouched at my side, motionless as an unexploded bomb. I wondered if they were assuming Toby's guilt, as I had. With hindsight, all I knew of my attacker was that he had been strong and ruthless, with a knowledge of how to access the dungeon.

'Did you get through into the tunnel?' Charles interrupted. 'Is the exit in the garden, then?'

I shifted my grip on the mug. The heat was stinging my sore fingers.

'No,' I said. 'The roof-fall wasn't…it wasn't…'

'Never mind,' Kit said. 'You got out, that's all that matters.'

Charles said, 'We must call the police.'

'Later.' Kit looked at my face and said decisively, 'I'll run you to A and E first.'

'I'd like…before that…to have a bath.'

'My darling.' He kissed my hair. 'Of course.'

I limped upstairs on Kit's arm, and he ran the bath and helped me to undress. Gratefully I lay back in the steaming water, while he sat on the closed toilet lid and told me what had happened in my absence. Charles, arriving to find both cars missing, had assumed that I would soon be back. When I failed to appear, he had rung Belinda, in case I had gone straight to The Withies. Later he had spoken to Toby and Robyn at work, Ian at his office, and Jodie and Simon on their respective mobiles.

An eventual call to the police, though not to Hughes in person, had elicited the response that I could not be classified as missing after only four hours, especially as I had taken the car.

'He rang half the sodding county and not me!' Kit said. 'I'd been trying to call you all the way to Hay, and then Charles was constantly engaged. By the time I got hold of Belinda, she was practically gibbering.'

He had driven straight from Hay to The Eyrie. I would have seen the Fiat, if I had fled to the front door instead of the back. He had found Charles ringing the hospitals.

'Said he hadn't seen any point in worrying me.' Kit span the toilet roll in frustration. 'Give me strength! As if I'd have got on the bloody plane without knowing you were safe!'

'Kit,' I said.

He left his seat to kneel by the bath, stroking my hair. 'I'm sorry. We won't talk about it any more tonight.' He dipped his hand in the water, frowned critically, and reached for the hot tap.

'Kit, I found Joshua,' I said.

His head snapped up. He knew at once what I meant. For an instant his face mirrored my distress, as if he would take it into himself and suffer in my stead. Then, seeing how I had begun to shake again, he scooped me up, wrapped me in a bathrobe and carried me to the soft bed that I had longed for.

I told him the rest of it, sitting huddled under the duvet, my hand resting in his. He sat on the side of the bed, very still, looking down at my damaged fingers. Only when I described my panic-stricken flight to the back door did he raise his eyes to mine.

'Thank God you took the risk!' he said. 'If you'd stayed outside...'

'What risk?'

'It might not have been Charles, or me, who let you in. If whoever attacked you had clobbered Charles as well, he could have been in the house.'

I had been incredibly stupid. My need for sanctuary had been so overwhelming that my brain had shut out the most terrifying scenario of all; and, as Kit said, thank God it had.

'There's something else,' I said. 'What Grandad said, in the ambulance. The paramedic thought it was *We hid John's*...and then something he couldn't catch, but I think...I think...'

'*We hid Josh in the tunnel.*' Kit rubbed a hand tiredly over his head. 'My sweet girl, don't think about it now.'

The afternoon's events had taken their toll on him, too. His expression was grim, lines of stress etched deeply from nose to mouth. I wondered if he would be able to make peace with Joshua's memory; but at this moment it was clear that his concern was all for me.

He found me some clean clothes and drove me to Accident and Emergency. Charles insisting on coming too, despite having to fold his long legs into the back of the Fiat. He seemed nearly as upset as Kit, which I found both unexpected and touching. A couple of hours later, I left the hospital with my left wrist strapped and supported by a sling but thankfully not encased in plaster. As I hadn't felt like explaining everything to the doctor as well as the police, I had told her the easy lie about falling off a horse.

We went straight home, with Charles still in attendance. Kit called the police, and despite the late hour Hughes arrived in person, along with DS Calder, several uniformed officers and a variety of experts. The tack room was cordoned off.

Hughes treated me with the same compassion which I had so distrusted the day Grandad died. I knew him a little better now, but still found making the statement an ordeal. By the end I was shaking so violently that my teeth chattered.

'No threats, I think you said?' Kit remarked to Hughes, as Calder finished scribbling. 'No need for police protection?'

Hughes had the grace to look mildly embarrassed, but also defensive. 'This was an opportunistic attack,' he said. 'Whoever carried it out couldn't have known you'd leave early.'

'Which means he was hanging around the place, waiting his chance. A police presence would have helped.'

'So would yours, sir.'

'Is that official? If you want a job done, do it yourself?'

Hughes bristled. 'Whatever this man planned to do with Miss Byrne, the only certainty at this stage is that he knew of the cellar under the tack room. We've no reason to think he knew about the remains in the tunnel. Of course, we may discover a connection with your family troubles, or with the Chubb case.'

'How reassuring,' Kit said, unpleasantly.

Hughes tapped a finger against his teeth. 'I'll ensure that a patrol car drives along the lane every evening after dark, but I'd recommend that you install an alarm system.'

'That's in hand.'

'Of course, if Miss Byrne had rung the station as soon as she suspected something was wrong, we wouldn't be having this conversation.'

'And you wouldn't have Nix's remains. Seems you got lucky.'

Hughes snorted. 'All right, I'll concede that one. If you're interested, the Prices have gone to ground. The cottage is shut up, and Price's employer hasn't heard from him in days. If you could help us produce an e-fit…'

'Sure. You won't need both of us, will you?'

'No, you'll do. Perhaps you could call in at the station tonight, then, sir?' Hughes quirked his lips. 'And you might give us the registration number of your car, if you'd like us to look for it.'

At Kit's request, Charles took me straight to The Withies. Kit promised to join me as soon as he could, and within half an hour I was installed in the guest bedroom, the two little boys mercifully fast asleep in their room along the landing.

I lost consciousness under a peach-coloured duvet and slept as though anaesthetised, with no dreams at all.

*

I was awoken by the sound of screaming.

The noise sent my heart into overdrive. I lay rigid in the bed, and realised only gradually that the shrieks were those of a child's tantrum.

Kit was not beside me. I wondered whether he had gone out early, or whether he hadn't come in last night. The lack of him was an instant dampener to my spirits, which were pretty low already.

Sighing, I eased out of bed and took twice as long as usual to shower and dress. Negotiating the stairs was depressingly painful, and having made the effort I nearly turned around and went back up again. The sound of raised voices issued from beyond the closed kitchen door.

I drew a long, slow breath, and opened it—to be met by Jamie and Alex, being shepherded out of the room by their mother. Belinda, usually so quietly spoken, was almost squeaking in agitation. 'Come into the playroom, come on. Didn't you say you wanted to put the tent up today? Oh, Lissa, will you be all right? I'll be straight back.'

I went into the kitchen. Ian and Robyn were there, plus Jodie and a blond surfer-type, who was presumably her boyfriend, Neil. They were all standing, and Robyn's expression was fierce, though it softened when she saw me.

'Lissa!' She stepped around the table and gave me a kiss. 'How are you feeling?'

'All right.' I glanced nervously at the others. Ian looked pale and preoccupied. Neil had his arm around Jodie, whose eyes were swollen from crying. She was dressed all in black.

Whatever the row had been about, tension still crackled in the air like static. I sat down gingerly on a hard chair and wished I had stayed in bed.

'W-why are you all here?' I asked.

'Ian and I called in to see how you were,' Robyn said, with a dark look over her shoulder at Jodie. 'Belinda rang us last night.'

'Lissa.' Jodie took a tentative step towards me. 'I had to come. I have to know—'

'That's enough!' Robyn said, sounding all at once exactly like Kit. 'You think *you're* upset? You just stop for a minute, and imagine what this has been like for Lissa! The last thing she needs is you bullying her into going

251

through it all again.'

Jodie's face crumpled. 'How can you lecture me about bullying?' she sobbed. 'You of all people!'

I said firmly, 'It's all right, Jodie. What did you want to ask?'

'Oh...' Still hesitant, she put out a hand to take mine, then saw the state of my fingers and froze. Her lips parted in shocked understanding. 'You dug...That's how you found him.'

'Yes.'

'Did he seem...peaceful?'

A man murdered in his twenties, vilified after death, howling into my dreams for release and redemption. Peaceful...dear God.

'I don't know how he died,' I said. 'But the keepsake, the one you bought him, was on his chest. Whoever put him there, they'd taken the time to do that, as if—I know it makes no sense—as if they cared.'

'I see. Thank you. That's really all I wanted to hear. If I have to think of him...and I can't help it...I'll think of him like that.'

She and Neil took a subdued leave of us all, including Belinda, who returned from the playroom to see them out. Only when the back door had closed behind them did Ian say, to no one in particular, 'I suppose it's cut and dried. The Professor killed him.'

I shook my head. 'I think he and Price hid the body, to protect someone else.'

If Ian had been pale before, he now went white. 'Price? *Hywel Price?*'

Robyn was aghast. 'Ian's...client?' She hesitated perceptibly over the description. Perhaps she hadn't wanted to say 'friend'.

'Kit did an e-fit picture of him last night, for the police.'

I was prepared for another outburst from Ian, but he simply frowned and hunched his shoulders, doodling with a finger on the wet draining board. Little arrows, all pointing in different directions.

'But,' Robyn said, 'who were they protecting?'

'If I knew that,' I said wearily, 'I might know who threw me in the dungeon.'

It was an unfortunate choice of words. I was aware of the twins' voices echoing down the years like the gleeful chant of a nursery rhyme. *'Throw them in, throw them in, throw them in the dungeon!'*

Robyn shook her head at the unspoken accusation. 'Not Toby. I'm not saying he wouldn't have hurt you.' She hugged herself as though feeling a chill wind. 'But I know he didn't kill Jodie's dad when he was nine years old!'

'Inspector Hughes doesn't seem to have ruled anyone out,' I said.

Robyn stared. 'Let's hope he's eliminated the under-fives, or you and Kit will be on the suspect list.'

She meant to be kind; she was fighting my corner. She didn't know that Kit and I had taken a decision that could ruin her life.

It was all suddenly too much to bear. I bowed my head, letting my hair fall forward to hide the tears. Robyn drew up a chair and put her arm around me, which made me feel worse than ever.

'Where *is* Kit?' I said, despising myself for the anguish I could hear in my voice.

'He went to The Eyrie with Charles an hour ago,' Belinda murmured. 'They wanted to see how, um…how things were progressing.'

No comfort. My body ached. I shifted position, and the abused thigh muscles knotted savagely.

'What is it?' Robyn said. 'Lissa, whatever's wrong?'

'Just cramp…Sorry…to be such a wimp. I'm fine, really.'

'Of course you're not. Who would be?' She stroked my hair back from my face. 'I couldn't sleep last night. I kept thinking, if what happened to you was somehow because of what Toby and I did, when you were little…'

'Oh, Robbie, don't! I don't deserve it. We told the police everything. We had to. And if Ian…if Ian…'

'If Ian what?' She realised then what I meant, and rolled her eyes, almost laughing. 'Lissa, even if Price did help to bury the body, Ian can't be struck off just for knowing the man!'

Her logic was persuasive. The only problem was, I was not convinced that Ian had taken her fully into his confidence. I slanted him a desperate look, but he was concentrating on his arrows, his sharp lawyer's brain no doubt working overtime.

Robyn said, with authority, 'We're leaving, all right? You're not to give all this another thought, or not until you've had some rest. Go back to bed, and stop *worrying!*'

Easy for her to say; but I went, mainly from lack of energy to do anything else. I woke again three hours later, feeling just as sore but less of an emotional wreck. The memory of my performance in the kitchen made me cringe.

This time when I inched downstairs every room was empty, but there was a note for me on the kitchen table, in Belinda's neat handwriting.

'Lissa, we're down by the stream. Come and join us.'

I ventured outside. Beyond the leafless trees, a climbing frame and swing were hung with spiders' webs. Hearing voices, I picked my way across the wet grass and around a giant rhododendron bush.

Beneath the willows from which The Withies took its name, Kit and the boys were crouching to inspect a battered yellow go-cart, while Charles and Belinda watched from a nearby garden bench.

'I'll make you a better one,' Kit was saying to Jamie. 'I knew a man once, when I was your age, who made us the best go-cart ever. Yours will be as good as that.'

'He was a kind, clever man,' I said. 'Just like Uncle Kit.'

Jamie and Alex came running, Jamie chattering as only a four-year-old can. 'Mum says you're staying for a couple of days. Is that till the day after *this* day? Will you stay until *Christmas* Day? Have you got us a present?'

Kit rescued me, fielding the questions with laughter and changing the subject to Christmas itself, and what the boys hoped to receive from Santa.

Much later, in private, I heard about his trip to The Eyrie with Charles. Although Joshua's remains had been taken away, the tack room was still out of bounds. All the coming and going was making Tempest jittery, so they had led both horses up to the field, broken up the ice in the trough and left them grazing on the long grass by the hedge.

There had been no sign, in or out of Tempest's box, of whatever had alarmed him yesterday; but even the flick of a brightly coloured scarf in the yard outside would have been enough to spook him, and most of my acquaintances knew it.

The continued police presence at The Eyrie gave me a good excuse to stay at The Withies, although no one else seemed to feel that an excuse was needed. I spent most of the day watching the pre-Christmas television fare, while everyone, including two-year-old Alex, pampered me with food, wine and cheerful company. Both Kit and Belinda were with me when the local news came on.

An attack on a young woman at her home yesterday

*has led to the discovery of human remains. Lissa Byrne, of
Little Malvern, found the remains after she was assaulted
by an intruder and thrown into a disused cellar beneath a
stable block. The remains have not yet been formally
identified, but a police spokesman stated that a connection
between the two crimes has not been ruled out. Miss Byrne,
who suffered minor injuries, is recuperating with friends.*

At least the reporter had not made the connection
with Kit, which would please Nick Darwin. The editor,
despite an enraged reaction to the news of Kit's missed
flight, had not tried to terminate his contract—yet.

The next day being Sunday, Charles and Belinda took
the boys into Worcester to see Santa, leaving
immediately after Kit had returned from tending the
horses. Kit spent the rest of the day at The Withies,
making a start on the promised go-cart. Robyn phoned,
as did Old Southbrook and my friend Gaby. Simon, who
had heard the basics from both Charles and Ian, rang for
reassurance that I was all right, and we had an amicable if
rather stilted conversation.

By Monday I felt a good deal more mobile. While Kit
was at The Eyrie supervising the fitting of a burglar
alarm, I helped Belinda to bake endless batches of mince
pies, which gave me time to think. I wondered whether
Dad had known that Hywel was his half-brother. If so,
had he been angry at his father's infidelity? Or jealous,
perhaps, of Grandad's older, firstborn son? And if not
for Hywel, would Mum and Dad have died? The
questions went round in my head interminably.

On Tuesday the twenty-second, Kit and I went back
to The Eyrie. The police and forensic team had long
since departed and we stood hand in hand on the drive,
in the winter sunshine, looking up at the old house that
had harboured the secrets of so many generations.

'All those years,' I murmured, 'Joshua was here. Do

256

you think he tried to tell me?'

'Liss, you know what I'll say to that.'

'And yet it's your job to bring the dead to life, and you cringed at having to wear Grandad's shirts.'

'Never said I don't have issues. Are you happy to stay here tonight?'

'As you're with me.' I looked up into his eyes. 'But I want to move away, to start afresh.'

He caught his breath. 'You mean in Kent? With me?'

'If we can rent somewhere for a year or two. My roots are here, though. I'd like to think we might come back, one day…maybe buy a place on the other side of the hills?'

He nodded slowly. 'If that's what you want. I won't be at Medway forever.'

Which was a declaration of commitment, if not of undying love. Enough progress, surely, to justify taking the risk.

For the next two days we lived in the expectation of news from the police, or even a media invasion, but all that happened was that the Mercedes was discovered in the car park at the Shrub Hill Worcester railway station. It was towed back to The Eyrie, with the ignition switch ripped out but no other damage.

'Ah, well,' Kit said, as he inspected the mangled wiring. 'We can't get it fixed before Christmas. At least the Fiat's in working order.'

'You're very philosophical.'

He straightened up and put his arms around me. 'She's a beautiful machine, Liss, but that's all. I thought you were dead, remember?'

I rewarded him with a kiss. 'That man…he wanted everyone to think I'd caught a train. What do you think he meant to do with me?'

'It doesn't matter. He failed, and he won't get a

chance to try again.'

Next time Robyn phoned, I asked if Ian had heard from Price.

'Not a word,' she said, sounding surprised that I had needed to ask. 'Don't you think I'd have called you, if there'd been any developments?'

I didn't know what to think. Now that the investigation was out of our hands, Kit and I seemed to be in limbo, oblivious to what might be going on behind the scenes. This alone was enough to make me feel nervous; and the house didn't help. Every hour of darkness brought some new creak or groan, or so it seemed to my over-sensitised ears. I had more nightmares than at The Withies; and it was not Joshua's ghost that haunted me, but a figure who stood just beyond the edge of the light, watching me, and waiting.

The days were better. By Wednesday I had abandoned the sling, and having the use of two hands more than compensated for the aches. As I could also now walk without anything seizing up, we went into Great Malvern and bought frivolous, hurriedly concealed gifts for each other, along with a fibre-optic tree which would fit on a window sill.

Perhaps it was crass to celebrate Christmas at all, but we both felt we had earned a little festive cheer. When we made love it was with the same sense of forbidden pleasure. For me, closing the bedroom door was symbolic; we were shutting out past, present and future. The old four-poster bed became a sanctuary, and the best escape of all.

Robyn and Ian had invited us to lunch on Christmas Day. They would visit Simon and old Mrs Threlfall for tea, Robyn said, and call in on Charles and Belinda before the children's bedtime. I gained the impression that she had no plans to see her parents or Toby.

Kit and I had decided to spend Christmas Eve by ourselves. It was a gloriously clear, bright day. Difficult to believe the forecast, which was promising snow by nightfall. The bookies were giving short odds on a white Christmas. Kit did some long-overdue work on his laptop before accompanying me to the field, where he brushed Tempest, tacked him up and galloped him around. While I was at The Withies, he had made a point of getting to know the horse again.

In the evening, as we sat back to back on the living room floor, giggling like children as we wrapped each other's stocking-fillers, Kit asked suddenly, 'Have you got a passport?'

'Of course.' I tore off a length of tape with my teeth. 'I went to Corfu last year, and Malta the year before that.'

'Ah. With the farrier.'

'Who else? Why?'

'Just think we deserve a holiday. D'you fancy the Canaries, or somewhere a bit more exotic? How about Saint Lucia?'

'It sounds wonderful, if we can wait a week or so.' I waved my bandaged wrist at him. 'I'd get an odd suntan if we went tomorrow.'

'We can book the first two weeks in January, if you like. I can put Turkey off till after that.'

I was still imagining spending a fortnight in paradise, when the landline rang. I picked it up, saying, 'Merry Christmas, whoever you are!'

'Lissa.' It was Ian. 'Can—can you come over? Now?'

The break in his voice caused my stomach to drop through the floor. 'What's wrong?' I said. 'What's happened?'

'The worst...' He couldn't go on; I was sure he was crying.

'Is it Robbie?' I said; and then, as he didn't answer,

'Ian! Has something happened to Robbie?'

Kit snatched the phone. 'For Christ's sake, man, talk to us! Is Robbie hurt?'

I watched his face, my hand pressed to my mouth. He lowered the handset and raised haunted eyes to mine.

'He rang off,' he said.

'Ring him back.'

'What's the point?' He crossed the room and grabbed his leather jacket off the sofa.

I scrambled up and followed him, snatching my own coat off the peg in passing.

'He'd have told us, if anything awful had happened,' I said, struggling to convince myself. 'Wouldn't he?'

'Not if he couldn't bring himself to say it.' Kit flashed me an agonised glance over his shoulder, and added the words I hadn't dared even to think. 'Not if she's dead.'

CHAPTER TWENTY-EIGHT

The house looked normal enough as we drew up. There was no police car, no ambulance. Just a friendly glow of lamplight through closed curtains. The first snowflakes were settling on shrubs and windowsills, and on the holly wreath above the porch.

Kit leaped out of the car. I caught up with him just as Ian opened the door.

'What's happened?' Kit said. 'Where's Robbie?'

Ian looked glazed. He was deathly white. 'She—she's inside.'

We ran past him. The hall was a mass of blue and silver tinsel. I was aware of the effect; didn't pause to admire the details. The lounge door was ajar. From beyond it came a soft footfall, and a sigh.

We catapulted ourselves into the room.

Robyn, wearing a festive red jumper, was clearing away the remains of the evening meal. As we rushed in, she said, 'Hi,' scooped up an armful of crockery and passed it through the hatch into the kitchen.

We might have been fooled, if not for the fact that her face was as pale as Ian's. The blusher along her cheekbones stood out like a doll's.

Kit groaned with relief. 'Thank God you're safe!' He rounded on Ian, who had slunk into the lounge behind us. 'You silly bugger, we thought something terrible had happened.'

'It has,' Robyn said. Her dark gaze slid past us to the hall doorway.

Footsteps descended the stairs and crossed the hall without a pause—and Hywel Price strode into the lounge as if he owned the place.

Kit exclaimed fiercely, 'You!'

Robyn stepped in front of her brother. 'Kit, don't! He didn't hurt Lissa. You must hear him out.'

'Why? What the hell are we all doing here?'

It was Price who answered. 'Finding out the truth. Isn't that what you've wanted all along?' He crossed to the table and poured himself a large brandy. 'There's no such person as Hywel Price. There never was.'

'Is that a fact? Who are you this time? The Ghost of Christmas Past?'

He smiled bitterly. 'You could say that. I'm Ian's dad. I'm Richard Threlfall.'

No one spoke. No one moved.

After an eternity I said blankly, 'You can't be,' at the same instant that Kit said, 'Prove it!'

Surprisingly, it was Ian who reacted to that. 'Come off it, Kit! Do you think I don't know my own father?'

'But...' I said.

'Yes,' Richard said. 'I'm dead. Body identified by grieving relatives. Inquest held. Case closed. What next? Rest in peace?' The haunted eyes regarded me steadily. 'There's no peace for the wicked, Lissa.'

'But they...they found your body. It was Dad who was missing...'

'Your grandad went to identify Roland's body, and told them it was mine. Deirdre was there, too. Your dad's buried in my grave, Lissa.'

'No! They wouldn't have. He couldn't have done that.'

But in my head I heard the anguished whisper of a dying man: *Tell Lissa I'm sorry.*

I sank into an armchair. 'You're not Grandad's son.'

'I am,' he said. 'And Angharad is my mother. She would have christened me Hywel, if the choice had been hers to make. But instead she gave me up for adoption—to John and Deirdre Threlfall, who named me Richard.'

It was too much to take in. Turning to Ian and Robyn I asked painfully, 'Have—have you known, all this time?'

Ian answered for them both. 'I'm sorry, Lissa. Dad got in touch a few years ago. Of course I told Robyn, but we didn't know anything else.'

'What else is there?'

'The truth,' Richard said. 'The whole truth, and nothing but.' He raised the glass to his lips, eyeing me over the rim as he sat down and laconically crossed his legs. I wasn't fooled. The brandy rippled with the tremors in his hand. 'Harry and my real mum, Angharad, met in McCavity's bookshop,' he said. 'Love at first sight. But he was engaged to Charlotte, your grandmother. She had money and the old house took a lot of upkeep. Harry went on seeing Mum, delaying the decision.' Richard drank deeply before adding, into his glass, 'Then Mum fell pregnant with me.'

Grandad had wanted to have his cake and eat it— marry Charlotte and have the use of her money, to keep Angharad and their baby in comfort. He had reckoned without Charlotte, who threatened to cancel the wedding unless he cut off all communication with Angharad.

'John and Deirdre Threlfall saved his bacon,' Richard said. 'They'd been trying for years to have kids. They offered to adopt me, so long as I'd be brought up as their own. Deirdre spent a few months in Wales with Mum, and came home with me. She and John let most people in Malvern think they'd separated for a while because of marital problems, but had patched things up after I was born.'

He held out his empty glass to Robyn, who moved to refill it. Ian watched, still clearly shell-shocked by whatever we had yet to hear.

'Harry had this obsession about passing down his inheritance, eldest son to eldest son,' Richard continued.

'As if it bloody matters. Well, I was his eldest son, and Simon was mine.'

Kit said dryly, 'Not in law.'

'No…but Harry got on well with Simon. They were close. So when Harry found the quarto—'

'The forgery?' I said. '*Love's Labour's Won?*'

'Well, bloody well. Read Edgar's journal, did you? Pity Harry didn't unearth it from the loft before he found the alleged Shakespeare. He so wanted the quarto to be genuine, I think he convinced himself it was. Before he called in expert advice, he dropped a few hints to the family, but he showed the bloody thing to Simon. Let the boy assume it was for real. Promised it'd be his one day, and…' Richard sighed deeply. 'He told Simon that he and Angharad were his real, biological grandparents. He wanted to give Simon a stake in the future, you see? The boy was stealing alcohol, playing truant…Maybe I'd been pushing him too hard.' He drew a long breath, and met my eyes. 'Then Simon overheard a phone call. His mum…Carol, my wife…was playing away with Joshua Nix.'

Kit perched on the arm of my chair to take my hand. 'Surprise, surprise,' he murmured.

'We all knew Josh couldn't keep his hands off pretty women,' Richard said. 'I just never dreamed that Carol…'

'So you caught them at it,' Kit said, 'and killed him.'

'I didn't catch them.' Richard clasped both hands around his glass. 'Simon did.'

This time the silence was one of held breath. It was I who finally stammered, 'Simon k–killed him?'

'He'd bunked off school again, and come home. Maybe he wanted to catch them. Anyway, he heard them upstairs.' Richard grimaced and set his glass down, rubbing a hand over his face. 'Carol called me at work. I was a sales manager, in Malvern. She was barely coherent. I rushed home, and found...' He swallowed, and went on with difficulty, 'He was only eleven, for Christ's sake! If he'd hit Josh with something...but to fetch a kitchen knife, and stab him in the back...' Richard's voice shuddered into silence and he bowed his head.

I glanced at Ian, barely able to imagine what he must be feeling. He made no attempt to comfort his father but held my eyes in helpless misery, his haunted expression warning of worse to come. I couldn't conceive how this could get any worse. *Simon*...

It was Robyn who rested a hand on Richard's shoulder; she who took up his story. 'Joshua was sitting on the floor,' she said. 'The knife was still in him. Carol was trying to cover him with a blanket.'

'Jesus Christ,' Kit muttered. 'So where was Simon?'

Richard lifted his head. 'Standing by the window, just looking out. In shock, I thought, like Carol and me.'

'And you just let Nix die?'

'If we'd called an ambulance, he'd still have died, and Simon would have ended up in some bloody detention centre.'

'Maybe that was the right place for him.'

'Kit, please!' Robyn said.

Kit looked both shamefaced and defiant, like a small boy being deservedly scolded. At any other time his expression would have made me laugh.

Richard patted Robyn's arm and sighed. 'I made Carol take Simon to a hotel, while I cleaned up. Josh kept trying to talk. Apologising, mostly. Then he said, "Your son's crazy. He enjoyed it, Rich. He'll do it again."'

'Should have listened, shouldn't you?' Kit said.

'I promised Josh I'd get him to a private doctor, if he'd keep his mouth shut and never come back to the

Malverns. I found his cheque book and told him to sign a cheque, to help with his medical bills...and he did. He was so desperate to believe I'd try to save him. Then he wrote a letter for Jodie.'

I recalled the wording of that misunderstood farewell note, *'I'm so sorry, I just can't stay any longer.'*

'He realised I'd lied to him,' Richard said. 'He was past talking by then, but he knew. After he was dead, I burned his clothes and shoes. Late that night I wrapped him in a blanket and took him to The Eyrie. I didn't know where else to go.'

Richard and Grandad hid the body behind the hall fireplace. It took them two nights to fetch sufficient debris from the woods and the stream bed, move Joshua to the dungeon under the tack room and seal him in the tunnel.

Some days later, they visited Elizabeth Nix. Grandad kept her talking while Richard stole a few documents; such as Joshua's driving licence, which hadn't been on him when he died. When Elizabeth eventually found the papers had gone, she assumed Joshua had taken them with him. It added weight to her assumption that he'd left her for another woman.

But the conspirators had more trouble deceiving close relatives. My dad and Deirdre Threlfall grew suspicious, and Grandad had to tell them the truth. Dad tried in vain to persuade him as well as Richard to go to the police. Deirdre was shocked enough to tell her friend, Angharad, who had started seeing Grandad again after he was widowed. No one confided in John Threlfall. They knew he would never help to conceal a murder.

'Harry and I agreed to see Josh's wife and daughter all right for money,' Richard said. 'But I was broke. I took some cash from my father's safe—John Threlfall's, I mean—but he went ballistic. Told me to pay it back or he'd get the law in. I was in a hell of a state. Carol wanted a divorce...' He drew a long breath. 'Anyway, your mum and dad, Lissa...they persuaded Carol and me to take a break with them. A sailing weekend. I thought it might help me fix things with Carol, and the boys would be away. I'd already come clean with your dad by then, about being adopted as well as everything else, and we chose Aberdyfi so I could visit Angharad. I wanted to tell her my side of...what had happened to Josh.'

'You all went to see her,' Kit said, 'on Easter Saturday.'

'Yes. But that night, Simon turned up at the boat. He'd hitched from Ross-on-Wye. Said the canoeing trip was crap, everyone hated him.' Richard sighed again. 'I let the school know. Next morning, he asked to visit his real grandmother, so I took him to the cottage.'

'Did Simon blow up the boat?' Kit said.

'I didn't believe it at the time. Mum—Angharad—thought he might have turned on the gas just for mischief, without realising what could happen. But later...Harry told him he'd had *Love's Labour's Won* analysed by an expert. It was a fake, and he'd burned it. Simon thought—wrongly, I promise you—that he was being conned out of his rightful inheritance. After Harry died, Simon said you must know where the play was, Lissa, and that if he could win you round...'

'He didn't love me at all,' I said.

'He did.' Richard hesitated, watching me. 'I asked Simon straight out if he'd attacked you the other day. He denied it, of course, but he said it might do you good, to be the one to suffer for a change.'

Kit drew in his breath with a hiss, and Richard flicked him a despairing look.

'That was when I knew,' he said, 'about the boat. He'd seen me pump the bilges on the Saturday night...and he knew it was done to expel any gas as well as the water. If he turned the gas on, he knew what he was doing. It'd be a longshot, someone might have noticed...'

'But they didn't. And Lissa's parents died as well.' Kit stopped on a catch of breath. 'Jesus. He planned it. He killed them because they knew what had happened to Nix. He's a fucking psychopath.'

Richard was silent. He didn't look up.

Kit went on savagely, 'When we met you in Hay, you kept asking how I'd been injured. You thought your bloody son had done it. You were afraid he was a loose bloody cannon and needed to be stopped.'

Richard raised his head at last. 'I thought I could talk to him. I thought he'd changed. He's a teacher, for God's sake!'

'Got it wrong, didn't you?'

Richard stared at the floor again, elbows on his knees, finger ends pressed lightly together, shielding his mouth. The mannerism I had seen in Hay; the mark of a keeper of secrets.

'When Carol and the others died,' he said, through the steepled fingers, 'it was a terrible shock...but it gave me the chance to start afresh. No one had seen Simon come aboard, and he and I had rowed the tender ashore early in the morning, to visit Angharad. As far as the harbourmaster knew, I'd died with the others. After dark, I went back and set the tender adrift, and I called Harry and asked him...begged him...to say Roland's body was mine.'

'Why would he do it?' I whispered. 'How could he?'

'Roland was beyond help, but he could give me the break I needed. And the boys would never go short. My adoptive father was loaded.' Richard smiled twistedly. 'Simon and Ian were expecting a good-sized inheritance when he died. It made Simon bitter, finding out he'd given most of it to charity long ago.'

'So that was the consequence of old Mr Threlfall's death,' Kit said. 'That's why you wrote to Grandad Byrne.'

'Partly. Plus, Ian had found his diary and hired Chubb to trace Josh.'

'I didn't know Nix was dead,' Ian said. 'Even when you said Dad was calling himself Joshua, I didn't believe it...' His voice broke. He sank down on to the sofa, and Robyn sat beside him, holding his hand.

Kit spoke into the lull, with deceptive calm, 'What are you planning to do about all this?'

'Richard's leaving,' Robyn said. 'Angharad is upstairs, asleep. She'll stay with us for a while.'

'And?' Kit said.

'Ian and I will talk to the police. We'll tell them Simon let something slip, about Joshua—and about attacking you, Lissa. We won't mention Richard or Angharad. And if Simon did blow up the boat, it'll be up to Hughes to get him to confess.'

'So why the urgency to get us here?' Kit said. 'And why go to the law tonight, on Christmas Eve, when they'll be up to their ears in pub fights and drunk drivers?'

'Because,' Robyn said, 'Simon talked to his dad this afternoon.'

Richard interrupted, 'He said everything would be different after tonight. He wouldn't tell me what he meant. Just said he had to meet a couple of old friends and make a fresh start.'

Kit breathed out slowly. He stood up, encouraging me to do the same, and I found myself steered towards the door.

'I'm taking Lissa right away from here,' he said over his shoulder. 'Now, before the weather closes in.'

Robyn half ran to catch us up in the hall doorway.
'Kit, wait!'

He stopped. 'How much did you really know,
Robbie?'

'That Richard was alive and calling himself Hywel
Price. Ian knew he'd taken money from the Threlfalls'
safe. That's all. Kit...' Her eyes were huge with fear.
'You're not going back to The Eyrie, are you?'

Relenting, he kissed her cheek. 'Just to pack a few
things. We'll be fine.'

'Take great care. And phone me, as soon as you're
safely away from the house.'

'Sure. If Simon turns up here, don't let him in.
Promise me?'

'I promise.'

It was some comfort to know that she would have
the strength of mind to keep her word.

*

'Are we really going home?' I asked uneasily, as Kit drove
us back the way we had come.

'I want the passports more than anything else. You
can wait in the car, if you don't mind locking yourself in.'

But, as he had once pointed out, I had seen too many
movies.

'No thanks,' I said.

A minute or two later he said, following his own grim
line of thought, 'Grandad talked to Old Southbrook
about a pre-emptive strike.'

I hadn't forgotten. 'He'd have killed Simon,' I said.
'His own grandson.'

'He didn't buy Richard's idea of talking Simon round,
that's for sure. I think he was scared there wasn't enough
evidence to get a conviction. That's why he didn't want
to involve the police. Maybe he did invite Simon to the
house, the day he died. He may have felt there was no

more time to waste.'

I looked out of the window, at the fleeing night. I felt punch-drunk. I couldn't even cry.

'I never saw it,' I said. 'What Simon is, underneath.'

'Don't beat yourself up, Liss. I didn't guess, and I loathe the bastard.'

'Do you think he loved me, or just saw me as a way to claim his inheritance?'

'Christ knows.' Kit swung the little car around the bends of Hereford Rise. At the house, he opened the gates and padlocked them again behind us. The security lights came on as we parked by the front door. 'Did you set the alarm?' he asked.

'No, I—I was thinking about Robbie. Did you?'

'Nope.'

I got out of the car, glancing wildly around me, but there was only the rising wind. It had even stopped snowing, for the moment. The forecast had warned there was more to come.

Kit locked the car, strode around the bonnet and took my fear-chilled hand. We let ourselves in and turned the lights on, and Kit locked the front door and headed for the stairs.

I realised what we had forgotten. 'The horses!' I said. 'We can't leave them out all night. It's going to be minus six.'

'They've got the field shelter.'

'Kit!'

'OK, we'll ring Charles once we're on our way.'

He went on upstairs. I followed, driving both hands into my coat pockets. The deep chill of the hall seemed to strike through into my bones.

I did my packing; or rather, I rammed the basics into my overnight bag and ran downstairs in Kit's wake. He only had his laptop bag. Maybe he wanted to keep a

271

hand free.

Two paces from the front door he stopped dead. 'Listen!' he said.

'What?'

'Ssh!'

We held our breath. All I could hear was a ticking clock, and the wind in the trees outside. After half a minute I whispered, 'What did you hear?'

'Could have been the wind rattling a window.'

'But?'

'Sounded more like someone trying to get in.'

We stared at one another.

'Call the police,' I whispered.

He was already tapping in the nines. To the switchboard's credit, they connected him fast.

'Yes, an intruder,' he said. 'The Eyrie, Hereford Rise, Little Malvern. Make it quick, we think he's armed.'

As he rang off, I said, 'They'll be busy tonight, won't they? They might be delayed, and if Simon's here...if he gets in...'

Kit nodded. 'I'll go out first. Stay behind me, keep moving, get in the passenger seat and shut your door. I'll lock us in. OK?'

'OK.'

He switched off the hall light, turned the key in the mortise lock and opened the front door. I was standing to one side of him; the opening door blocked my view of the drive.

It happened very fast. There was the briefest flurry of movement. Kit dropped the bag and keys and doubled over, staggering back into the hall. He fell to his knees. In the dimness I could see his hands held close to his chest, half-clenched and shaking, as if he didn't know what to do with them.

I slammed the front door and turned on the light. It

was only then that I screamed.

The leather jacket hung open as he bent forward, and the handle of a kitchen knife was sticking out of his chest.

CHAPTER TWENTY-NINE

I should have locked the door. Didn't think of it. The shock was so immense that it left no room for anything else. I dropped to my knees and held Kit sideways against me—and the night wind blew cold on my back.

I whipped round. Simon stood framed in the doorway. He was dressed all in black, including gloves. The porch light shone through his rippling auburn hair, giving him a wild, fallen-angel aura.

His brows creased as he flexed his empty right hand. Kit's fast recoil had caught him by surprise. He hadn't planned to lose the knife.

He needed it back. The instant before he moved, I saw the intention in his eyes and came up into a crouch, snarling, 'Keep away from him!'

Simon blinked, hesitating. Then without a word he strode past us to the kitchen.

Kit whispered to me, 'Go!'

But he knew I wouldn't. The despair in his eyes was not only for himself.

Simon was coming back. Walking purposefully, weighing in his hand a carving knife from my own knife block. He smiled at me; a sour twist of the lips. The brilliant blue eyes were cold, as deadly as cobalt.

'Simon,' I said, struggling to sound calm, 'this isn't what you want. It can't be.'

'Can't it?'

'You can't hate me this much.'

'No? After you've given me so much practice?' He began to circle us at a distance. 'The old man said you'd never want me. Told me straight. I should have believed him.'

Whether he meant Grandad or John Threlfall hardly

mattered. I had to keep him talking. In a few minutes the police would arrive.

'That's not true,' I said. 'I've always been v-very fond of you. I don't know why you're doing this, but I...I'd really like to understand.'

'Don't talk such crap! Do you think I'm an idiot, because I haven't got a Master's degree from Cambridge?' He stopped and held the knife at arm's length towards me, just out of reach. 'Where is it?'

'Where's what?'

'You know damn well! Your bloody inheritance that should be *mine!*'

The final word was a shout. The blue eyes burned into me. I ran my tongue over dry lips. I could tell him the truth. He'd either be convinced and kill us on the spot, or he'd think I was holding out and start hurting me...or Kit.

How long before we could expect the police? Five minutes? Ten? Too long. Even if I could make him believe the quarto was here in the house, we'd have no way out when he discovered I had tricked him...

There might be another way. A tiny, crazy chance.

'All right.' My voice shook. 'It's up at the field shelter.'

He didn't move, didn't lower the knife. 'If you're going to lie, at least make it credible.'

'I'm not lying! Why should I? The bloody thing's not worth dying for.'

He narrowed his eyes; I felt they were boring into my soul. After a pause that seemed endless he said, 'Harry wouldn't have left it in a field.'

'It's underneath the shelter. He dug a pit. Lined it. He was worried about it rotting, or something eating it. But he wouldn't leave it in the house or even the stables. He said, if anything happened, if someone came looking...I thought he meant a burglar. But he didn't, did he? He meant you.'

'What was wrong with a bank vault?'

'Oh, Simon! You knew him. He was old-fashioned and stubborn and he wouldn't listen to sense. I tried a hundred times to get him to use the bank.'

Another eternal silence.

He lowered his arm. 'Well, then, you can show me where it is.'

I felt sick with relief. He was a long way from believing me, but the doubt had been placed in his mind. He needed to check it out.

'I'm not going without Kit,' I said.

'I'm afraid you'll have to.' Simon regarded his old enemy with dispassionate appraisal. 'I did a neat job on him. Knife in the heart. I'm amazed he's lasted this long.'

Kit returned his stare with loathing. 'And fuck you, too,' he whispered.

Simon's face changed. He said with sharp urgency, 'Why do you look so much like him?'

It took my brain a moment to shift gear and realise what, and who, he was talking about. Kit didn't even acknowledge the question.

Simon was not about to let it rest. 'That night,' he said, 'when you walked into Ian's house, after five years…God, for a minute I thought I was seeing his ghost.'

'Feel haunted, do you?' Kit was speaking with obvious difficulty, but his voice held all the force of consuming hatred. 'About fucking time!'

I heard myself whimper in terror. The whimper became a shriek as Simon bounded forward. Again at arms' length, he held the point of the second knife to Kit's neck.

'Who—are—you?' he whispered, spacing each word like a curse.

Kit looked up into his eyes with, incredibly, a glint of spiteful humour. He mouthed almost silently, *'Guess!'*

I thought it was the end for both of us. The point of the knife jerked, nicking the skin.

'No!' I screamed. *'No!'*

Neither of them so much as glanced at me. A trickle of blood ran down Kit's neck, while he and Simon held each other's eyes in vivid, fierce communication; and it was Simon, in the end, who backed off, the knife still a threat but no longer imminently murderous.

'Your mother.' He had no trouble believing it. 'Your mother and Nix. Just like mine.'

Kit said nothing.

'Nix's son.' The knife in Simon's hand flickered with light as his hand started to tremble. 'You have had *everything* I wanted. The place at Cambridge...the career...Jesus Christ! Who the hell becomes a celebrity from reading *history*? And Lissa. Always Lissa. Even my wife, even Jodie...' He broke off, eyes wide as the implications occurred to him.

Kit raised a parody of a smile. 'Nix had a lot to answer for.'

'Oh, he answered. He answered for it all. You want to walk to the field? Do it. It's your funeral.' Simon chuckled, appreciating his own sick joke; then the smile dropped from his face. He said quietly, 'And by Christ, I'm going to enjoy watching. Let's go.'

Looking at Kit's face, I didn't think it could be done. But I picked up the dropped keys and took his arm. He closed his left fist around the wicked blade, pressing the hand to his chest.

I understood. Imperative to keep the knife still. It cut his hand as he struggled to his feet. Blood ran between his fingers but he held on. Stood nearly upright, swaying.

The chest wound wasn't bleeding much but the blade

had gone deep; only a few centimetres of serrated steel protruded from beneath his left breast. Like any layman—like Simon—I knew where the heart was, but not to the nearest centimetre. And Kit hadn't died instantly. Did that mean there was hope, if I could get him to a hospital fast enough?

I didn't know. Wasn't sure that it mattered either way. The chances of getting him anywhere looked non-existent.

As we went through the doorway, Simon latched the door and stayed a pace or two behind us. We walked slowly around the side of the house, and the security light flared into life. Having the car keys was not going to help; Simon's car was parked outside the gates, blocking our escape route even if we could have reached the Fiat.

Kit said something, too low for me to catch. I looked a question. His haggard eyes met mine, gleaming in the spotlight's glare. There was a sheen of sweat on his face. He glanced down at his jacket pocket, and mimed, 'Phone.'

Of course! All I had to do was quick-dial the emergency services, and they could surely trace the call. They might even hear us talking...hear Simon convict himself...if I could do it without attracting his attention...and if, under the spotlight, he failed to notice the phone light up.

I slid my hand into Kit's pocket.

Maybe I tweaked the jacket, or else Simon caught the end of our brief, silent communication. He swore and grabbed Kit's shoulder, spinning him round hard enough to jerk the hand clutching the knife blade.

I was the one who screamed. Kit dropped to his knees on the gravel and stayed there, hand clenched on the knife, head bowed in defeat and dreadful pain. Simon bent and delved in his pocket, rising with the phone held aloft. He drew back his arm and hurled it away, over the side fence into the trees beyond. I heard the dull thud as it landed.

He met my eyes. His own were alight in a way that made my flesh crawl.

'Where's yours?' he asked.

I had thought I was beyond tears. 'In the car.'

'Take your coat off. Give it to me.'

He must have feared that searching my pockets would distract him, leave him vulnerable. I didn't know what he thought Kit could do to him now. I took off my coat, and he snatched it with a satisfied smirk.

'Well done,' he said. 'Shall we go on?'

I put a hand under Kit's elbow and helped him up. His gasps for breath terrified me more than any amount of groaning would have done, but he set one foot in front of the other and kept going. All I could do was hold on to him and pray. The tears on my face were cold in the wind.

The back gate was locked as usual. I said to Simon, 'The key to the padlock's in my coat. On the ring with the house keys.'

He unlocked it himself, watching us out of the tail of his eye, the second knife glinting under the bright mockery of the security lights.

I don't know how long it took to reach the field. Every time Kit swayed against me my heart jumped. At any moment...any moment he might collapse, and that would be the end, and nothing would matter any more. Once, when we stopped, Simon drawled, 'Giving up already? You disappoint me.' But he made no attempt to hurry us. He had spoken the truth, back at the house. I had given him the opportunity to wreak a prolonged and sadistic revenge, and he was relishing every second.

When at last we came to the field, I opened the gate

with my free hand, feeling a twinge of protest from the healing ligaments. The horses were up in the shelter. I didn't shut the gate but kept walking, guiding Kit. Smoky ambled down the hill, snorting a friendly greeting.

Simon had stopped. Suddenly there was clear ground between us.

'Why are they here?' he snapped.

'I didn't have time to stable them.'

'You bitch. You little *bitch!*'

Smoky came right up to us and nudged me with her head, then shied a little, catching the scent of blood. I had to act fast, before Simon could think what to do, before he decided to risk grabbing Kit and putting the knife to his throat—or pulling the other knife out of his chest.

I tugged the mare's head round and slapped her as hard as I could on the flank, screeching in her ear, *'Yah!'*

Anxious as she already was, even Smoky was not going to put up with that. She neighed in alarm and galloped off, not aiming at Simon but heading in his direction.

With a yell he stumbled back, caught his heel in a tussock and sat down hard. The mare slowed to avoid treading on him, put her head down and blew enthusiastically in his face. He tried to scramble out of range, while her nuzzling head kept him pinned to the ground. At any other time it would have been funny.

I had given us a few seconds. Not more. Simon would evade the mare's friendly overtures soon enough, and this new humiliation would make him more dangerous than ever. Leaving Kit by the fence I raced to the shed adjoining the shelter, yanked the door open and snatched up the two lead ropes. Tempest was standing by the shelter, looking interested.

I gave him no time to rethink his attitude. I made a

grab for his head collar and clipped a rope to each side. He jerked his head, rolling his eyes indignantly. Muttering soothing words I dragged him to the fence and climbed it fast to mount with an ungainly scramble. Tempest stamped and snorted. A token protest. I had occasionally ridden him bareback.

Pulling the horse's head around I saw Simon scrambling back from the mare. He was shouting something, some dire threat.

I shouted to Kit, 'Get up in front of me!'

He lifted his head; I sensed his eyes on me in the dark. God knows I didn't blame him for hesitating, but I couldn't afford to sympathise now.

'Kit! *Do it!*'

He got a foot on the fence as I had done, seized the post and slowly, slowly pulled himself up on to the lowest slat, his whole body trembling with effort. I couldn't bear to watch and couldn't bear to look away. I bit my lip and tasted blood.

Smoky had lost interest in Simon, who was back on his feet but standing dead still. He wouldn't approach Tempest's restless, plunging hooves. Perhaps it was more than the simple fear of horses; perhaps he thought I would disregard the knife and ride him down.

Perhaps he was right.

He cried out, 'You little bitch, I *loved* you.'

He had left me injured and alone in the place of my nightmares, in the tomb of his first victim. He had murdered my parents, and maybe Grandad too. Because of him, the man I loved was dying in front of my eyes. If Simon Threlfall suffered in any way whatsoever, I would be the last person on earth to regret it.

Standing on the second fence slat, Kit let go of the post and clasped my hand. His eyes were on a level with mine. He only had to step aboard. Anyone could have done it. Even Simon…but not with a knife in his chest.

Ignoring the pain in my wrist I gripped both lead ropes in my left hand. With the other hand and Kit's desperate help I dragged him towards me. He straddled Tempest's withers and sat hunched forward, shuddering with each breath, eyes tightly shut. Tempest shied and whickered, trying to bite, assaulted now by the combined smells of fear and blood.

I had to believe I could control him; had to believe the horse trusted me enough. We were committed now. It would have been easier with Kit behind me, but I couldn't have checked his fall if he slid sideways.

With an improvised rein in each hand I steered Tempest to the gate at the top end of the field. I didn't dare urge him faster than a walk. I was too afraid of what it might do to Kit.

On the edge of vision I saw Simon jogging back towards the exit to the track. He wouldn't have given up just like that. He must have some plan.

We were at the top gate. I bent to open it, swung it wide and walked us through, latching it again behind us. Kit's breathing had slowed now that the worst exertion was over, but he was still audibly gasping. Whatever the internal damage, he was running out of oxygen.

I needed to find a phone. Couldn't go back to The Eyrie. Simon might be waiting, and I couldn't bargain on the police being there. Better to use the hill paths. It would take only minutes to reach civilisation.

Tempest whinnied and threw up his head. The horse was not just cantankerous, he was scared, hating the uncomfortable weight and the worrying smells. I should have picked Smoky instead, I thought wildly; but Simon might have found the courage to approach her. I had calculated the risks and seized the moment. No use regretting it.

Tempest was ready to bolt. I took both ropes in my right hand, struggling to control the shying horse. We were asking too much of him, but I couldn't leave Kit here and go for help. He'd die of hypothermia. And besides, Simon might come back.

'Darling,' I whispered in Kit's ear, aware of how sound might carry. 'We're going to slide down, OK? As slowly as we—'

Tempest bolted.

I let go of the ropes. A survival reflex; better to hit the ground now than in another minute, at forty miles an hour. The horse shot out from under us and I landed flat on my back, with Kit on top of me.

The ground under the thin snow was mostly leaf mould, but his weight crushed all the breath from my lungs. I couldn't move him, and couldn't drag in even a trickle of air. It was stupid to panic but he was killing me...

He gave a low moan and shifted position. Not much, but enough. I squirmed free and drew in a crowing breath. His eyes were closed, sunk in shadow. I might have thought him unconscious, if not for the hand clutching the knife.

I sat up, still trying painfully for breath. 'Kit?'

'Where's Tempest?'

The horse stood ten metres off, watching us; a tense, silent shadow in the dark. I called softly, 'Tempest!'

He was having none of it. With a whinny of outrage, he turned and galloped into the woods. I shut my eyes, concentrating on breathing, trying not to care, to tell myself it didn't matter...

Kit muttered, 'We'll have to...go back.'

'No...The police might not be there yet, but Simon could be.' I chewed at my lip. A wrong decision could prove fatal for Kit, and quite likely for me too. 'We'll

283

make for the hotel, where the path meets the road. We can manage on foot. It's not far.'

He sat still, head bowed. Summoning courage, I thought; and my heart twisted with love and pride and unbearable pity.

'OK,' he said.

'You need to be warm.' I pulled my sweater off, which roused him to some attempt at opposition.

'No. You can't.'

'Hush.'

I helped him to sit up, unzipped his jacket all the way and tied my sweater around his waist inside it, knotting the sleeves to secure the extra layer. With extreme care, terrified of brushing the knife handle, I zipped up his jacket half way, then ripped a sleeve out of my shirt and wrapped it around his gashed hand. I kept talking to him all the time, telling him to hold on, I'd get him to hospital and everything would be fine, just fine; but inside me the voice of reason whispered that it was hopeless and we'd never make it.

I said aloud, 'We'll make it, do you hear?'

'Sure.'

With his help, I got him somehow to his feet and took his arm across my shoulders, and we started along the path.

The woods closed in. The silence was disturbed only by the wind in the trees, and by our own breathing and the occasional soft *whoosh* of dislodged snow. Kit's arm was a yoke weighing me down.

He sagged suddenly against me, and we went down on our knees in the snow. I saw the luminous dial of his watch. Eleven-forty. We had travelled about two hundred metres in ten minutes.

'Come on, darling,' I said.

'Can't. Sorry, Liss. Just can't.'

'You must.'

'Yeah.' But he didn't move.

I gripped his arm. 'Don't be such a wimp! Get up!'

'Liss...'

'Do you *want* to die?'

He made a choked sound that defied interpretation, and muttered what sounded like, 'Mouse into Amazon.'

But he let me drag him up again. We staggered on through the dark and the freezing wind, and that treacherous inner voice kept saying over and over that he was dying, that we should have risked going back, and whatever I did couldn't possibly be enough.

The trees had gone. We were climbing a bare, windy slope. I thought about Simon. Was he lying in wait near The Eyrie? Or driving along the roads below us, searching, hunting...

'Is this...Swinyard Hill?' Kit said.

'Yes. We rode up here, remember?'

'Wasn't snowing, then.'

It was snowing now, a few large flakes drifting innocently down.

Oh God, don't let it snow, please don't let it snow...

The flakes went on falling, eerily silent in the dark. We kept moving southward, one agonising step at a time. Kit stopped trying to talk. The snow began to fall more thickly, in gusty, often-horizontal swirls as the wind rose and eddied across the hill. It was difficult to see the path. Difficult, finally, to be sure that we were still on the path at all.

We had travelled perhaps a quarter of a mile when I knew that Kit would never make it down to the road. It was not a matter of courage or resolution. He simply couldn't do it.

'Darling,' I said, 'you know the cave? Clutter's Cave? Where we made love once?'

The last time we were here, I thought he had forgotten that summer afternoon; but now his free hand reached for mine and squeezed gently.

I swallowed the lump in my throat. 'I'll take you there,' I said, 'and fetch help.'

A barely perceptible nod. He was saving whatever breath he had left.

I squinted through the disorientating snow flurries. If that darker shape ahead was a hill and not some illusory cloud mass, it could only be the Herefordshire Beacon. We should turn off near here.

Even knowing the hills as I did, I very nearly missed the cave. Just in time I recognised, through whirling snow, the small outcrop on the west-facing arm of the hill. I could have cried. For an instant I felt like Henry V at Agincourt; a victor against impossible odds.

The moment was short-lived. As we entered the cave, struggling over a drift that half-blocked the entrance, Kit slumped to the floor and lay still. I knelt beside him in the blackness and smoothed the damp hair back from his forehead. I was cold myself, but his skin struck like ice.

'I must go, darling,' I said. 'I'll be as quick as I can.'

He stroked my bare arm. 'I've got...all your clothes.'

'Not quite all. Anyway I'll be running, I won't feel the cold.'

Snow and ice could kill, but they were also insulating. Eskimos in their igloos survived the most severe conditions. The drift across the cave entrance would shield him from the wind. It was something...but not enough. Not enough.

I held his hand against my cheek and wept silently, torn by the sheer injustice of it, that such a monstrous thing should be allowed to happen.

'Liss,' he said. 'I did mean it.'

'What?' I dashed my hand across my eyes. 'Mean

what?'

'You didn't believe me.'

'I did, I believe everything. Everything you've ever told me.'

'I would have come back, this Christmas...without the old man's letter.'

'I know, my dear love. Don't try to talk any more.'

'Couldn't forget you. Tried. Just couldn't. My little Amphelisia.'

I was glad of the darkness. I didn't want him to see my face. If he knew he was dying, he might stop trying to live.

'You'd like...Saint Lucia,' he said.

'Oh, yes, I would. I will. We both will.'

'Please, Liss. Be quick.'

I kissed his cold lips, and they parted not in love but in pitiful hunger for air.

'God bless you, my darling,' I said.

His fingers brushed mine in farewell as I turned away.

*

Leaving that cave was the hardest thing I had ever done, but I didn't look back. I set my face to the weather and ran.

The snow underfoot was not deep but very fine. Eddies of wind drew it up in whorls like smoke or will'o'wisps, forming patterns so wild that often I lost all sense of direction and had to stop, peering into the swirling dark until things made sense again.

Eventually, running and stumbling downhill, I looked up at the grass ramparts rising on my left. British Camp, the ancient hill fort that crowned the Herefordshire Beacon.

Not far, Kit. Not far now.

Maybe he had a chance; if internal bleeding, or heart failure, or shock hadn't killed him already—and if he hadn't passed out. Even discounting the unthinkable possibility that he might roll on the knife, I had heard that the tongue could fall back into the throat of someone lying unconscious.

I wished I hadn't remembered.

There were bells ringing somewhere, far away, remote as the drowned echoes of Cantre'r Gwaelod…

No, that was the legend. The bells I could hear were sounding the end of the Midnight Mass, far below in the valley, their rhythm synchronised with the single word that kept repeating itself in my head like a prayer.

Please…please…please…

I hurtled down the last slope, skidding on patches of ice, knees buckling with weariness. The snow was falling less thickly now. Among the trees below I could see the roof of the hotel.

I had long since ceased to worry about the ice underfoot, but where the slope of the footpath met the level car park I slipped and went down hard, putting my hands out to save myself.

Searing pain flared through my injured wrist. For a couple of seconds I lay there, sobbing for breath, but the voice of panic in my head was goading me: *Get up, you silly bitch, you bloody coward!*

Groaning, I struggled to my feet and stumbled on, across the snowy car park. The hotel was right there, on the far side of the road, white walls glowing against the backcloth of trees.

A vehicle turned fast into the car park and stopped. In the blinding glare of headlamps I stopped too, throwing an arm up to shield my eyes; but I didn't need to see what I was facing. I had glimpsed the car's outline before it had turned. Enough to be certain.

Simon had found me.

CHAPTER THIRTY

I felt no terror. Only rage. It seemed so bloody unfair that, after all the struggle and the suffering, we were going to die anyway.

Well, Simon could go to hell and take me with him, but I'd be damned if I'd go without a fight. I ran, screaming to anyone within earshot, to the snow-filled night itself, 'Help! Help me!'

The driver's door swung open. His tall figure lunged at me; and he discovered, as I had, that the snow overlay a sheet of ice. He slipped and fell.

I tried to run faster, sliding and skidding. Knew he was coming but didn't look back.

His fingers closed around my injured wrist and he dragged me round to face him. My scream this time was completely involuntary. Simon clamped a hand over my mouth.

'Shut up!' he hissed, jerking at my arm again.

I closed my eyes, thinking vaguely that it would serve him right if I was sick in his hand.

'Any more noise and I'll kill you here and now,' he said, and took the hand away from my mouth. He propelled me towards the car, opened the passenger door and shoved me inside. Then he slammed the door and walked around the bonnet.

I opened the door and scrambled out, managed to run a few paces, fell and staggered up again. Heard him swear savagely behind me.

With what seemed deliberate sadism he gripped my wrist again, dragged me to the car and flung me inside. I didn't see his face. My eyes were shut. But I heard him hiss, 'Now fucking stay there!'

The door slammed for the second time. I was lying

half in the footwell, half across the centre console, the gear stick digging into my shoulder.

It seemed important that Simon shouldn't find me like that.

By the time he got into the car I had dragged myself up to sit in the seat, cradling my left arm. I didn't know how bad the damage was but it felt horrible. I could barely think straight, let alone plan a course of action. No guts, as Grandad would have said.

Simon shut his own door with a bang, started the engine and pulled out on to the road. 'Hurt you, did I?' he grated. 'Well, why not? You've hurt me often enough.'

He was driving much less smoothly than usual. The car was not his MG, but his gran's old hatchback. Deirdre had been right about the smell of petrol. It was making me feel distinctly nauseous, and the pain didn't help. I swallowed hard. Had to think.

'Where are we going?' I said.

'Somewhere nice and quiet.' He shot me a sour look. 'Not the field shelter. The play's not there, is it? It never was.'

'It was a forgery. Grandad destroyed it years ago.'

'Ah, yes. That tired old line. Well, it'll wait. First things first. Where's Kit?'

My heart jumped at the change of tack. Better to try a bluff, I thought, than face a battle of wills that would certainly involve pain for me and pleasure for him.

'We separated,' I said, 'in case you followed us. He took the horse.'

'You left him? Your *true love*?' He spat out the words as if they were poison. 'Left him alone on the Malverns with a knife in his chest? You'll have to do better than that.'

I drew an unsteady breath. He was right; I would have to do a lot better.

'He died,' I said.

'Stop playing games with me, Lissa.'

'Tempest bolted and we fell.' I spoke hardly above a whisper, looking down at my lap. 'I couldn't catch him afterwards. We tried to make it on foot, but Kit...Kit lay down in the snow...and didn't get up again.'

Simon stopped the car. His hand streaked out to grab my arm. 'Look at me! Look me in the eye, you sly bitch, and tell me the fucking truth!'

I raised my eyes to his, giving rein to fury that was all too real. 'Why do you think I'm dressed like this? Or do you think it's normal to be out in a blizzard with no sweater, and the sleeve ripped out of my shirt? I gave Kit everything I could spare. I tried to save his life but I couldn't, all right? I couldn't.'

I was genuinely crying now, with the bitter knowledge that Kit's life was slipping away, moment by moment, while I wasted time on this worthless, twisted creature.

'He died,' I sobbed. 'He just died. So what are you going to do, you sick bastard? Go up there and slash his body to bits, just to make sure?'

He slapped my face, hard enough to jerk my head sideways. The sting of it brought fresh tears into my eyes, but what were a few tears more or less? I lifted my chin and met his blazing stare, aware of a change within me; a hardening of purpose. Simply to escape from him no longer seemed enough.

'Well,' he said, matter-of-factly. 'I can't leave him where he is.'

My stomach dropped. 'W-what?'

'I need to move his body.'

Oh, dear God...

'It w-won't help you,' I said. 'Ian and Robbie know everything. They...they'll be at the police station by now.'

'Don't talk crap. They know sod all.'

'Your father told them.'

'My father's dead.'

'Is he?'

'They'll have nothing on me if they can't find a body. So you're going to take me to it.'

'Go to hell!'

The look he gave me was one of pure hatred. 'I should have finished you when I had the chance, shouldn't I?'

'In the dungeon? Why didn't you?'

'I'd only gone there to look for the play. I'd tried once before, the night Harry died, but your fucking boyfriend turned up. So I had to go back, to search the dungeon, as you so quaintly call it. Thought Harry might have been moving the thing around, trying to keep me guessing. I found bugger all, of course. Then that bloody horse got the wind up, and the rest, my sweet, is history. I was tempted. Thought it was time you suffered for the way you'd treated me.'

'Did you want me to die?'

'Didn't much care at first. Then I thought, yes, she's deserved to go, and slowly. Surprised myself—though if I'd known they'd buried that fucker Nix down there, I'd hardly have left you alive to dig him up.'

'You must have suffered a bit yourself, then, watching the local news afterwards. You must have been scared out of your inadequate mind.'

Another black glance. 'You're such a little charmer. How could I ever have deluded myself that you were the woman for me?'

'I thought Grandad told you I wasn't.'

Simon let out a breath of mirthless laughter. 'Would you believe, the old bugger tried to kill me? He invited me to the house, that Saturday afternoon. It must have been right after his row with your aunt. I thought he wanted to give me the play, at long last. But no, not Harry.'

'Did you kill him?'

'Of course I bloody didn't. He told me to go down to the cellar, and I'd find what I wanted. He was behind me. I saw his arm go up. He meant to clout me with the torch. To knock me down the steps. I dodged and he lost his balance. I just gave him a bit of a shove.'

'You killed him.'

'It was an accident.'

'Like the Aberdyfi Belle?'

He drew a sharp breath through his nostrils.

'And Daniel Chubb?' I said.

'Oh yes, Chubb!' His tone held nothing but contempt. 'The little prat was checking out my whole family. He even went to see my old headmaster. Sooner or later, he'd have found out I'd gone AWOL from the canoeing trip. And then, after Ian told me what he'd said at the inquest...What did Harry mean to do, chuck me in the cellar and then spin Chubb some yarn to put him off Dad's scent? For all I knew, Chubb could have seen me leaving the house.'

'And I'm supposed to believe you'll let me live, if I do what you want?'

'No.' He gave me a rueful smile. 'It's just a question of how you want to go. Hard or easy. Now, if I turn the car around and take us back to the car park, will you show me where Kit's body is?'

I averted my eyes, afraid of what he might read there. 'All right,' I said dully. 'What's the difference? You can't hurt him any more.'

Simon grunted with relief. He started the engine, manoeuvred the car through a three-point turn and headed back the way we had come. The blizzard of half an hour ago had eased; the flakes were small now, the road clearly visible.

'What will you do with him?' I said. 'With his body?'

'I'll think of something.'

'Why not under your gran's rose bushes? She won't tell. She'll be too scared. That's about your mark, isn't it? Attacking women and old men. For anyone else, you need a knife. What a hero.'

He ground the gears, and the car gathered speed. 'How you must have laughed to yourself,' he said through his teeth, 'when we used to call you Mouse.'

We were approaching a left-hand bend. There was no pavement along this stretch of road, and on the bend a steep, high bank rose beyond a shallow lay-by. Simon was watching the road, not looking at me.

Now or never. Now, before he slows down.

I yanked the handbrake up.

Simon yelled, fighting the wheel as a violent skid slewed the car to the right.

I opened the door and jumped.

The tarmac came up and hit me. I tumbled helplessly, hearing a noise like a long scream of terror going on and on…but that was the car…and then a rending crash and the sound of breaking glass.

I lay in the road, blinking dazedly. The car was on its side against the bank, headlamps arcing skyward. The driver's door started to open. I saw Simon's hand pushing at it.

I had to get up. Had to run.

I made it to a sitting position before my surroundings span dizzily. I put a hand to my head and felt a warm trickle of blood.

The car door swung wide. Simon's head and shoulders emerged. He started pulling himself out.

My vision doubled. I shut my eyes. There was a

curious sound, a great *whoomph*, and a gust of heat on my face.

I opened my eyes. The car was ablaze. The tall figure was still there, half out of the doorway, struggling to escape the inferno.

'Lissa!' he shrieked. 'Help me! *Help me!*'

I didn't move. He went on heaving and struggling and screaming, until finally a cocoon of flame wrapped itself around him, feeding on him, roaring like the predator it was. His scream now was a thin, terrible sound. The wind on my face brought with it the smell of petrol and grilled meat. I sat in the road, gagging and retching, while Simon Threlfall died in flames, and I made not the smallest effort to save him.

*

An elderly man from a nearby house dialled the emergency services. I told him who was in the car. His wife wanted to usher me indoors but I refused to go, so she trotted off muttering about shock and returned with a blanket and a flask of hot tea, telling me to sit next to her on the low garden wall. She was large and motherly and wore a cardigan randomly buttoned over her nightdress. The cold was making her teeth chatter.

Two younger couples and a tall man in a combat-style jacket appeared; there were a few houses further along the road. The newcomers asked questions, wanting to help, crowding me. My shivering guardian told them to give me room to breathe, and after a while they drifted off to stare at the car.

The ambulance was the first emergency vehicle to arrive. I pushed myself upright, just as two figures in fluorescent jackets leaped down from the cab and started towards the burning car. One was a woman of about my own age. As her colleague kept running, she stopped beside me, assessing my general condition with expert eyes.

'Were you in the car?' she said.

'Yes, but—'

'Was anyone with you, apart from—'

'No! Please listen!' I clutched her arm. 'My friend's on the hills, in Clutter's Cave. He's been stabbed in the chest. Please…please help us!'

'All right, it's OK.' Her arm came round me. 'Is there a road to this cave?'

'Not all the way. It stops…I don't know…half a mile lower down, by the reservoir.'

She called out to her colleague, who was talking to one of the bystanders, unable to get close to Simon's charred body because of the heat.

'Mack! Get over here!'

He ran back to us, skidding on the ice.

'We've got another male casualty,' she said. 'Knife wound to the chest. Up on the Malverns.'

The news didn't noticeably faze him. He had a blunt, kind face, beaded with sweat from the heat of the flames.

'Helicopter job?' he asked.

'They're grounded until the storm blows through. Andy told me. He said it could be an hour or more.'

Mack grimaced and spared a backward glance at the car, but it was plain that there was nothing a paramedic could do for Simon.

The young woman said, with decision, 'If we're using the sling we'll need two more people.'

Mack nodded. 'Rustle them up. Get someone with his own car.'

She ran to the assorted spectators, approaching the man in the combat jacket first.

Mack turned to me again. 'What's your name?…Right, Lissa, while Jasmine's recruiting, did you lose consciousness when you hit your head?'

'No.'

'Not even for a minute or two? No memory gap?'

'No, I—I felt a bit dizzy, that's all.'

He grunted, put a hand on my shoulder and turned me gently towards the light, staring into my eyes.

'Pupils still working to order,' he said. 'How about your arm?'

'Oh…that's not from tonight. It's strapped up already. I'm fine. I can show you the way.'

He began guiding me to the ambulance. 'In that case,' he said, 'you'd better ride up front, with me.'

*

Had I known the hills less well, I might not have recognised the lane leading up to the reservoir. It looked so different in the dark, with snow drifting against the verges. Mack turned sharply at my instruction and attacked the slope with confidence. The vehicle laboured but we got there, tyres gripping reluctantly one minute, then spinning on ice the next. A glance in the wing mirror showed the car behind us having similar problems.

Mack asked only necessary questions. What was the casualty's name? How long ago was he stabbed? What sort of knife? How much bleeding? Had he been conscious when I left him? He was less concerned about who had done it, but I told him that as well, shivering inside my borrowed blanket.

As soon as we stopped, he and Jasmine went into action, taking a shoulder bag and the portable stretcher, the 'sling' which they had mentioned earlier. The pair of them exuded efficiency; a slick, practised team, accustomed to crises. Jasmine handed one torch to her male recruits and the other to me.

'Can you take the lead, Lissa?' she said.

There was no discernible path, but it had stopped

snowing. I could orientate myself by the silhouette of the Herefordshire Beacon. It wasn't far. Half a mile had been a fair guess; and despite being hampered by equipment both Jasmine and Mack were sure-footed and fit, and the other men made no complaints. I was the one in trouble, adrenaline fighting a losing battle against stress and exhaustion.

It was far colder now. Not minus six. Not yet. But cold enough to kill someone already in shock. Maybe snow would have blocked the cave entrance, keeping out the wind...

If it had, I might not find the cave at all.

Jasmine caught me up. 'You OK, Lissa?'

I couldn't answer her. I sank to my knees, crying helplessly.

She knelt at my side. 'Do you want to wait here?' she said. 'We'll find it now.'

'You won't. It's tiny. You won't.'

She put her arm around me and pressed her head briefly against mine. 'You can do this,' she said. 'You can do it for Kit. Come on. We'll stick together, shall we?'

With her help I staggered to my feet and went on. The man in the combat jacket materialized at my other side and put a hand under my elbow. Mack and his companion followed, an occasional murmured comment passing between them. Jasmine's calm presence at my side allowed the disabling panic to ebb a little. I could study the shapes of the hills with clearer eyes. Even under snow, they were the same as ever. I knew where I was.

Twenty metres from the cave, we heard him breathing. The tearing gasps petrified me, but at least he was alive. I broke away from the others and ran to the entrance, treading down fresh snow, shining the torch ahead as I scrambled inside.

I lost all hope. He lay on the floor, head thrown back, body arching upward in a tortured struggle for air, blood running down his bandaged hand that still clutched the knife blade. Despite the cruel cold he was pouring sweat. The veins and tendons in his neck stood out like cords. He turned his face towards me, squinting into the torch beam.

Mack, tripping over my heels, said urgently, 'Lissa, give us some space.'

With a deft economy of movement he and Jasmine lifted Kit outside and on to the stretcher, offering him reassuring words and fast action.

Jasmine asked Mack quietly, 'Should we get a line up?'

He shook his head. 'Not here.'

She nodded as though relieved to have her own instincts confirmed. She drew the bottom of the sling up over her patient's lower body and secured an oxygen mask over his nose and mouth, while Mack directed the other men to their stations. The sling had eight handles, two at each corner, and I realised why the medics had brought volunteers. They couldn't have managed with only my feeble assistance.

'You'll be all right now, Kit,' Jasmine said. 'Just keep breathing. That's great, that's fine...'

It wasn't fine. He stared up at her, wide-eyed, comprehending the situation all too clearly.

'You're a tough cookie, aren't you?' she said. 'Lissa needs you to hold her hand.'

We held hands all the way down the hill.

By the time we reached the ambulance his breathing was better, though I wasn't sure how much that signified. The medics transferred him to the wheeled stretcher inside the vehicle. Our helpers returned to their car. Jasmine had said all the right words to them, but I don't know if I thanked them personally. I think I did.

Mack drove, as before, but this time I stayed in the back, helping Jasmine to undo Kit's jacket without disturbing the knife. As my eyes met his, I tried to arrange my face suitably.

'Don't worry, darling,' I said, 'you'll be all right now.'

Jasmine set up two drip lines and pressed her fingers to the side of his neck to find the pulse. She frowned, moving her fingers slightly.

'What's wrong?' I said.

'Sometimes it's hard to feel a pulse, that's all. It comes and goes, and what I can get is weak and rapid.' Abandoning the attempt she wound a cuff around Kit's arm to take his blood pressure. After a minute she compressed her lips and went through the process again, then undid the cuff, saying nothing.

I let out my breath on a sob of despair.

She patted my shoulder, saying brightly to Kit, 'I keep telling her you're tough. She doesn't believe me.'

He looked into my eyes and pressed my hand; but his own eyes were full of fear. He didn't believe her, either.

'Don't give up now,' I said. 'Don't you bloody dare!'

*

When we reached the hospital he was still alive, just. A team of medical staff surrounded the stretcher as Mack wheeled it in, and the medic rattled off a lot of technical information, which I didn't understand. Before I knew what was happening, someone else was asking me questions and Kit was whisked away into a cubicle, the curtains swiftly drawn. There hadn't even been time to kiss him goodbye.

I sat in the waiting area and cried. A nurse appeared with a kindly smile and handed me a form on a clipboard, but she was called away almost at once to give succour to someone else.

I didn't realise the others had arrived until Robyn sat

down next to me and gently took charge of the paperwork. Charles was with her, and Ian of course, with tears running down his freckled cheeks. I looked over his shoulder, fearful of seeing Inspector Hughes. Robyn understood.

'We were with Hughes when the Malvern police rang him,' she said. 'We went to the scene of the crash. He's still there. An old couple said you'd gone off in the ambulance. They said someone had been stabbed. Was it Kit?'

I told them what had happened, haltingly and as briefly as possible. Robyn put her hand to her mouth, and Ian went paler than ever.

Charles was staring at me blankly. 'You led them to the cave?' he said. 'You did all that, after...'

'I had to.'

'My God,' he said. 'My God.'

I gathered the courage to look Simon's brother in the eye. 'I'm so sorry, Ian.'

He nodded, taking it not as an apology but as a simple expression of sympathy for his loss. 'They're both gone,' he said. 'Simon and...Hywel.'

'Hywel Price?' Charles said. 'The man they thought could have attacked Lissa? What's he got to do with it?'

I don't think Ian even heard the question. 'I suppose...' he continued, 'I mean, he did promise...he'll get in touch again, one day.'

He had lost his father as well as his brother. Robyn stood up and held him close, and my own eyes stung with fresh tears, but there was nothing I could say. Charles shrugged, bewildered, but he had enough sensitivity not to mention Price again.

We all sat together, surrounded by the casualties of Christmas Eve. A youth with a cut head, who had been at the wrong end of a broken bottle. A woman who had scalded her arm while cooking something exotic for the festive season. I don't remember the rest. Different images filled my mind: Clutter's Cave, and the feel of Kit's icy hand in mine. The soul-chilling light in Simon's eyes as he took his revenge. The look on his face as I let him burn.

It was only a few minutes before the doctor came to see us; a tall olive-skinned man with tired, velvet-dark eyes. I went cold at the sight of him and stood up, as if it would make things any better to face bad news on my feet.

'Kit's dead, isn't he?' I said.

'No.' The doctor ran a weary hand through his hair. 'The knife only nicked the heart but the pericardial sac— the bag which contains the heart—was filling with blood, which had caused a cardiac tamponade.'

'A w-what?'

'I'm sorry.' He closed his eyes momentarily, pinching the bridge of his nose between thumb and forefinger. 'I mean there was a build-up of pressure around the heart. It was unable to expand sufficiently at each beat. Kit's blood pressure had fallen extremely low and his pulse was barely palpable. However, we were able to insert a needle to draw the blood from the pericardium, and his pulse and BP are now returning to normal. We've stabilised his condition for the moment.'

Charles cut in, 'Does that mean he's out of danger?'

'I'm afraid not. He's lucky, of course, to be alive at all, and we do need to act quickly. The weather has improved a bit, so we'll transfer him by helicopter to the cardiac unit at the Queen Elizabeth Hospital in Birmingham. They'll operate to remove the knife.'

'It's still in him?' I whispered.

'We can't carry out the necessary procedure here, but they'll expose the heart and deal with the knife, as well as

302

any clots and excess blood.'

'Expose…' I felt myself sway. 'You're talking about…open heart surgery?'

'A thoracotomy, yes. There are risks, but please don't assume the worst. This is an uncommon condition, but not unheard of. In such cases the patient can make a full recovery, provided he receives treatment in time. Kit is young and fit—'

'He was out on the hills,' I whispered. 'It was an hour and a half.'

'Nevertheless, if he comes through the operation…'

He must have said more, but I didn't hear it. I wasn't even aware of hitting the floor.

*

They let me see Kit, once I had convinced the medical staff that I was basically intact and not likely to pass out again. They had taken off his shirt, and the knife protruded grotesquely from the dressings keeping it immobile. He was still attached to a drip and a chest drain, and a nurse moved efficiently around me, checking the drain and adjusting the trolley, preparing to move him as soon as the helicopter landed.

'Hi,' I said.

He pulled his oxygen mask down to talk to me. At least his breathing sounded normal.

'Hi yourself.' He smiled, and reached for my hand. 'Gave you a bit of a fright, did I?'

'Not just me. Robbie and Ian are here. And Charles.'

'Really?' His eyes glittered and he blinked, embarrassed by the weakness. 'One of the nurses told me what you did. Showing the medics the way.'

'Well…' I smiled faintly. 'That's your Christmas present, then.'

'I nearly gave up on you. Guess the ambulance got delayed, because of Christmas Eve.'

'Sort of.' I squeezed his hand. 'Tell you later.'

'They're going to cart me off to Birmingham any minute.'

'Yes, I know.'

'A right bugger.'

'It's just a little op,' I said.

'Yeah. Piece of cake.' But his eyes slid involuntarily to his chest and flinched away. He looked up at me again. 'I love you, Liss. Always will. Till death us do part.'

My breath caught in my throat. I mustn't cry, mustn't let him see how afraid I was. I raised his fingers to my lips and kissed the knuckles.

'I love you, too,' I said, smiling again. 'Till death us do part. That's the next seventy-odd years taken care of.'

'Are you coming with me? In the helicopter?'

'Do you think I'd let them stop me?'

He rolled his eyes, and managed a grin somehow. 'Mouse, my arse,' he said.

EPILOGUE

There is no wind this evening. The cloud is flat and grey, its western rim lit by the setting sun. The beach is deserted.

I glance down at the spray of lilies in my hand. The dead are owed a little more than two minutes, now. Looking out across the estuary, it's easy to imagine the *Aberdyfi Belle* sailing downstream, cutting through calm water, its crew of three laughing as they head towards the open sea.

I've thought a lot about Dad, since Christmas Day. If I choose, I can still tell the police everything, and Dad's body will be exhumed and re-buried decently, under his own name. I long to set things right, to see him treated with dignity. I long to lay flowers on his grave.

The trouble is, Richard was his friend. Dad could have gone to the police after Joshua's murder, but he didn't. So I've brought my flowers here, to Ynyslas.

I walk down to the water's edge, picking my way carefully, mindful this time of the sand sucking at my shoes. Hard to believe that it's only six weeks since Kit and I were here. I can visualise the two of us standing together, but it's like watching a film of someone else's life. I hardly recognise the woman as myself.

I don't know how far I've really changed. I'm still scared of the dark. But a lot of things seem less intimidating than they used to.

I took a taxi to see Aunt Melody and Uncle James on Boxing Day. They didn't invite me in, but kept me standing on the doorstep. Uncle James looked wary. My aunt seemed lost for words rather than hostile. Her eyes were bloodshot, which may have been only the result of too much festive alcohol. Strange to think that I used to be afraid of her.

'I thought,' I said, 'you might want news of your youngest son.'

Aunt Melody blinked. It was Uncle James who ventured quietly, 'I phoned the hospital before he had the operation…and after.'

'I see.' I looked straight at my aunt. 'But you stayed here, enjoying your Christmas. You don't even feel guilty.'

'*Guilty?* If my father hadn't gone with that woman—'

'Angharad Price?'

'I wouldn't expect you to understand. When I think of how he let my oh-so-Christian mother lecture me about duty and fidelity—and all the time, he was seeing *her*. Oh yes, even after he was married. Mother never knew that. I didn't find out till I was married myself.'

'So you slept with Joshua.' I was shaking with futile anger. 'And every time you looked at Kit, you saw your dead lover. Is that your excuse? Is that why you didn't come to Birmingham?'

'We phoned the hospital, didn't we? How dare you turn up here, passing judgement!'

'You're right. Why did I waste my time?' I turned to her husband. 'I thought better of you, Uncle James. I don't know how you can live with yourself.'

For once, he didn't even glance at his wife for guidance. He said defensively, 'If I'd thought…if it would have made a difference—'

'It would have made a difference to Kit!'

I can still see the defeat in my uncle's face. The shame in the grey eyes as they avoided mine. Maybe I should have been kinder, to him at least, but I couldn't feel sympathy for either of them. I had to walk away. Maybe one day I'll go back.

My lilies are luminous in the falling dusk. I hesitate

only for a second, then fling them out across the water. They settle and float, bobbing gently, drifting towards the sea.

In the quiet even-time…

The bells are silent. The past is lost. Irretrievable. The future is mine to choose. I turn away from the sea, taking out my phone. The number I want is in the internal directory.

The ringing tone sounds once, then a familiar female voice, a little more subdued than usual, says, '*Age of Gold*, Nick Darwin's office.'

'Fran, it's Lissa.'

'Oh, hi. I meant to call this morning, but then everything kicked off.'

'Is Nick there?'

'Are you kidding? He's bouncing off the walls, saying we might lose the funding from Janssen because—'

'Can I talk to him? Please?'

'Oh…I suppose. If you dare.'

A two-second pause, then Nick's voice, gruff and ominous. 'Well, well. Lissa Byrne.'

I run my tongue over dry lips. 'It's about the researcher's job.'

'What about it?'

'When would you need me to start?'

'Monday week. How much longer is bloody Kester going to be off?'

'Another three weeks. If I could start work when he does—'

'*Three weeks?* He's had a month already, for Christ's sake!'

'He needs time to convalesce.'

'He can convalesce here! I've got sodding Janssen on my back. Tell Kester I need his input *now!*'

I have a sudden, heart-lifting vision of Kit, lounging

307

on the sofa at The Eyrie. He looks up from a perusal of properties for rent near the River Medway and rolls his eyes in mock despair, saying with a grin, 'He means it, too, the bastard.'

Alone on the beach, I feel myself smile. It will be late when I get home. He'll be in bed, listening for my car on the drive, waiting for me to creep shivering under the duvet beside him. My man, warm and alive, never to be taken for granted.

Janssen can wait.

Printed in Great Britain
by Amazon